"MINE EYES HAVE SEEN"

"MINE EYES HAVE SEEN"

Operation
Vanguard

A. M. MOULTON

"MINE EYES HAVE SEEN"
OPERATION VANGUARD

iUniverse books may be ordered through booksellers or by contacting:

iUniverse
1663 Liberty Drive
Bloomington, IN 47403
www.iuniverse.com
844-349-9409

ISBN: 978-1-5320-8817-9 (sc)
ISBN: 978-1-5320-8818-6 (e)

Library of Congress Control Number: 2021904551

Print information available on the last page.

iUniverse rev. date: 03/02/2021

For Erica, Mike, Endora, and Xander.

Thank you as well to everyone that helped me compose this book.

"Improvise, Adapt and Overcome"
-United States Marine Corp (Unofficial Mantra)

CONTENTS

INTRODUCTION

What is contained in this book is the interviewed documentation of Operation Vanguard. The events discussed relate to the human element of Operation Vanguard and the human aspect of what transpired. The intention of this manuscript is that you, the reader, understand what went through the minds of all individuals in what is also known as the Mathews Incident. This interview process that was used gives an in-depth look at the people involved both directly and indirectly with the incident and all events leading up to Operation Vanguard. Direct interviews allowed us to link emotions and perspective to people that were previously looked at as just names. The knowledge gained through the interviews may start the healing process in hopes of achieving forgiveness. We hope this document helps the victims in understanding why Operation Vanguard happened. It is hoped that the interviews also benefit later generations.

Because of the research provided in the interviews, we were able to solve many unanswered questions surrounding Operation Vanguard. Most of the questions were about Brigadier General Mathews and his character as a leader. The interviews provided in this manuscript were able to show the person Matthews was and his potential motives for his actions. The interviews gave us a look into the mind of Matthews that until this point have never been known.

We understand that not all opinions can be changed. We also understand that there will always be a certain bias to what had transpired. The intention of this document is to understand every side of the history of Operation Vanguard. By being able to see everyone's point of view, we can come to a mutual understanding of the events. The knowledge that is gained can hopefully bridge a gap between the myth and truth of why Vanguard happened.

This document contains all information provided by the direct witnesses and individuals involved in Operation Vanguard. Names have not been changed unless asked by that individual. All individuals that were question have given written consent. Consent was also given by family members and next of kin of the victims involved. All recordings were kept with original content, without changes. All information contained is in its original form. However, certain parts of this transcript were omitted. The omitted information was foul language, names, and companies that did not want their brands involved. Specific buildings or institutions that felt their involvement in the incident may hurt their character or reputation were also taken out. Any material transcripts given for this book were subject to the strict guidelines from the U.S. Department of Defense, Homeland Security and the Federal Bureau of Investigations and approved for this distribution.

Until case file 31008639-A (the Investigation of Operation Vanguard/ Matthews Incident), what was known of Brigadier General Matthews was only what the world had seen on national television and speculation. The information provided by Special Agent Sean Gordon and Agent William Chris was invaluable in piecing together the events that led to the Mathews Incident. Hours of research and interviews were conducted across the United States to compose this document.

-Brian Samuels, Director of the Federal Bureau of Investigations

SPECIAL INVESTIGATIONS UNIT (SIU)

Approximately a year after Operation Vanguard, the Federal Bureau of Investigations started a face-to-face investigational inquiry of individuals involved with Vanguard. The objective is to get a true understanding of Vanguard and what motivated Brigadier General Mathews. The gathered information will then be processed, studied, and recorded.

A team was established to personally interview individuals directly involved in the Matthews incident. A board of senior F.B.I. members agreed that the two individuals who were best suited to gather the information that was desired. The instruction given to these two agents would be to obtain as much information as possible and build working knowledge of what lea to Vanguard and document it.

First Chosen was Special Agent Sean Gordon. An eleven-year veteran in the bureau and is widely noted for his personal excellence and dedication. He has been dependable since his academy days and is trusted among his peers. His name was suggested because of previous involvements cross training with the U.S. Military. He was notably mentioned for his help capturing the Tacoma bomber and involvement in the Gatlin Kidnapping case. Gordon was promoted a few years later to Special Agent after the arrest of Arron Keppel in Gainesville Georgia

*see case files: 25199-212511 Louis LaVeau "The Tacoma Bomber"
18854-15662 Arron Keppel "The Gatlin Kidnaper"
020511-8535 Beau Remy "The Shadow box murderer"*

The second to be assigned is Agent William Chris, who is known for good work ethic and strong personality. Agent Chris spent the last five of his seven years working on codes and ciphers for the F.B.I., and local law enforcement agencies and state agencies. He is noted for his intelligent, friendly positive outlook, and hard work.

The Special Investigations unit set with manpower was now going to work. With a growing need for understand and information into the criminal mind and large investigations like Vanguard. The questions of why such tragedies happen looms constantly over criminal psychologist and law enforcement alike. Special Agent Gordon and Agent Chris begin their exploration and examination into Vanguard and possibly other case files.

HISTORICAL MEMORANDUM

On a bright and early Tuesday morning, cell phones went crazy, social media exploded and local news media erupted with the news of D.C. being under attack. The world became focused on the Capital like never before at the thought of this unlikely event that was unfolding. Emergency operators became quickly overwhelmed with calls of both panicked and terrified individuals. Most operators were unable to understand or comprehend what they were hearing from the incoming phone calls.

The first several calls reported gunfire and military vehicles. Later calls were screams of terror and the cries for help then a dead phone line. The initial report was a lone gunman to several gunmen. It was finally determent by police that it was in fact military weapons, military personnel, and military vehicles attacking the Capital Building, and White House. Later the calls were confirming military personnel on the lawn of the White House and on the steps of the Capital building. Washington D.C. was a scene of complete chaos. Within nine minutes of the first calls to 9-1-1, the operators were now overwhelmed, and the local police also could not keep up with their direct emergency line as well. Shortly after the critical ten-minute mark, the 9-1-1 dispatch system collapsed and failed due to the choking numbers of incoming calls. The system would not be restored for nearly sixty hours.

The First responding officers to arrive on scene consisted of six police cruisers and a total of ten officers that arrived eight minutes after the first report. Within seconds of arrival, the officers were thrust into a life-or-death struggle. Four minutes after arriving on the scene, nine officers would be dead, two would be wounded. The officers all reported that they were currently engaged in a shootout with what appeared to be U.S. military. Later reports would identify the military unit as the Second Marine Division led by Brigadier General Joshua Mathews. At the height of the incident, four thousand three hundred Police, eleven thousand Army National guardsmen and two thousand one hundred civilians would be engaging nearly forty-three thousand Marines in combat on U.S. Capital soil.

For nearly fifty hours, our government, our freedom, our democracy was held hostage by this Marine Unit. We as a nation were on the brink of total collapse.

In memory of: Senator Patrick Sharpe, Congressman Myra Clash, Congressmen Joseph Patterson, and all the Secret Service members and police officers whom their names had to be withheld for national security, may you Rest in Peace.

-Richard Lamont
U.S. Journal, New York, Editor

Eyewitness Accounts of Operation Vanguard

"I saw people shooting, and I was just in shock! It was military and police shooting at each other on Pennsylvania Ave. I was paralyzed and confused. I had no Idea what was happening. My boyfriend grabbed my arm to pull me away from the street. I feel so stupid now when I think about it. I just stood there staring off as bullets were flying all around. I could have been killed."

-Jen Dorson (U.S. Journal, Brent, 2026, p.1)

"You could hear the bullets bouncing off the road, sidewalk and the walls of the buildings. You see this stuff on television or the movies, not in person. I saw these trucks just unload all these soldiers, at least twenty of them at a time. They just started to shoot at the police. It was truck after trucks pouring the military out, the police were overwhelmed in minutes."

-Allen Rule (U.S. Journal, Brent, 2026, p.5)

"I just didn't know what to think, you know? The cops were just not enough. The military just had to much fire power. They rolled them over! It was the scariest thing I've ever seen"

-Joe Tallow (Todays News, Myers, 2026, p.1)

"COMING OF THE LORD"

DEATH OF PRIVATE FIRST-CLASS ALLEN ECKHART

Interview of Corporal Joseph Thomas Witlit

Monday, June 5th, 2028
United States Disciplinary Barracks (USDB)
Fort Leavenworth, Kansas

WANTED

BY F.B.I.
Status: Captured

F.B.I. No. 188731
WANTED FOR: MURDER/MANSLAUGHTER/TERRORISM/TREASON

Joseph Thomas Allen Witlit
ALIAS: THE EXECUTIONER, WHISKEY 4

Description

AGE:	25	SCARS OR MARKS:	FULL ARM TATTOOS
HEIGHT:	5'11"	EYES:	GREEN
WEIGHT:	170 LBS	COMPLEXION:	LIGHT
BUILD:	MEDIUM	RACE:	CAUCASIAN
HAIR:	BLOND	NATIONALITY:	AMERICAN
OCCUPATION:	MILITARY	FINGERPRINTS:	ON FILE
		CLASSIFICATION:	FELONY LEVEL 1

CAUTION

Status is captured and being held by the Department of Corrections.

IF YOU HAVE ANY INFORMATION CONCERNING THIS PERSON PLEASE CONTACT YOUR LOCAL F.B.I. OFFICE IMMEDIATELY

This recorded session is called to order by the head of the Federal Bureau of Investigations, Special Investigations Unit.

GORDON: Its 10:30 A.M. in the United States Disciplinary Barracks, Fort Leavenworth Kansas, Maximum Security Wing, Block 7. Sitting next to me is Agent William Chris and across from me is Corporal Joseph Thomas Allen Witlit: Case file 31008539-A, Operation Vanguard or "The Matthews Incident". Corporal Witlit is 25 years of age, is 5'11", weight is 170 Lbs. He is of medium build, blond hair, has full arm tattoos, has brown eyes, and a tan complexion. He is Caucasian and an American. His fingerprints are on file and classification code-1 for the following: several counts of first, second- and third-degree murder, manslaughter, and involuntary manslaughter. He is also accused of treason and conspiracy of treason, terrorism and is considered a traitor of the United States of America. He is currently awaiting Court Martial.

Key testimony involving the Death of Private First Class Allen Eckhart and the months leading up to his death. Corporal Witlit is at this time not at current liberty to speak about General Mathews or operation Vanguard by the Supreme Court and is placed under a gag order.

GORDON: Good Morning Corporal, we are here to talk about Operation Vanguard and Brigadier General Matthews. We specifically want to know about the incident involving Private First Class Eckhart. We hope that you are willing to cooperate and talk with us. Any information given will be extremely helpful in our inquiry and investigation as well as historical value. We are part of an in-depth look into the actions of yourself, others, and Matthews. Do you understand what we are asking and why we are here meeting with you?

WITLIT: First things first, I was advised by my lawyers to not speak about Vanguard or Matthews under the pretense that anything I say can damage my case or be used against me. I am sorry that you wasted your time here. I am not interested in doing more time in jail then I already have too. It is nothing personal, I already looking at probably of at least one life sentence without the possibility of parole. Why do I need a second one?

GORDON: I utterly understand that. We would like to talk to about Private First Class Eckhart, not Vanguard, if that is okay? We are aware of your inability to speak out about Brigadier General Matthews as well. We just ask that you stay, sit, and talk for a while.

CHRIS: This is for the history books and for knowledge, as corny as that may sound.

GORDON: Exactly.

CHRIS: We are here to learn from you and talk, not damage your case. In fact, the legal aspect of what happened is none of our business or concern. We represent the Bureau as a special investigation's unit designed to learn and build our knowledge base. We look primarily in the "why" and "How" something happens. We want to know what drives a situation, the cause. We already know the effect. The outcome was noticeably clear, the reason why is not.

WITLIT: So, learn what exactly? I will talk about Eckhart if that is all you want. I have no problem with that at all.

GORDON: We hope to really learn anything about Eckhart that we can. Whatever you can provide, the person he was, the things he liked and did not like. That kind of general information.

WITLIT: Is this a situation where my rights need to be read to me or to be under oath?

CHRIS: No, nothing like that. This is an opportunity to tell us your story. The part of what happened that may have never been told otherwise or ever known. We want to know what you saw and how it all came about. We know how this all connected with Vanguard. We know that Private First Class Eckhart was the first steppingstone of Matthews's plan for Vanguard. But that is all we know. At this point Eckhart is just a name to us in some notes that Matthews had in his personal log entries. Eckhart is just words to us now. We want the full picture of who Eckhart was.

GORDON: Exactly. Your story helps us build a better foundation for why Vanguard happened. I am sure no one has asked your side of this story. Honestly, until this point, I am guessing that you really did not expect to ever tell this story. People mostly like to point fingers and judge a person from what they read online. It is deeper than that, you are more than that.

WITLIT: So, just talk about Eckhart, that is it? I know I am repeating myself it is just that everyone asks about Vanguard. I am just surprised. I am also making sure I understand.

GORDON: Just Eckhart. If you chose to talk about General Matthews, that is fine if it does not violate your gag order. We are not interested in Operation Vanguard.

WITLIT: I get it, I understand what you are asking now. Where would you like me to start then?

GORDON: Well, I guess simply, what may have caused Private First Class Eckhart to take his own life and why his death was so important to General Matthews. Again, we understand what you can and cannot talk about. We do not want you to incriminate yourself.

Let it be known that prior consent was given by the Supreme Court that Corporal Witlit may speak about the character of Brigadier General Mathews but not details of

Operation Vanguard. Any information about the Character of Brigadier General Matthews is considered common knowledge. It is also understood that the information given by Corporal Witlit can be considered opinion based and therefore not damaging to the current trial and investigations that are being conducted by other peoples or agencies. It should also be noted that prior consent was granted by the family of Private First Class Eckhart as to any information leading to his death.

WITLIT: I feal that I can do this, I can talk about who Brigadier General Mathews was. I might as well start there because it will go there anyway. Starting there makes the most sense. Otherwise, this conversation will be confusing.

GORDON: That is fine, start however you like.

WITLIT: General Matthews was about six foot two inches; medium build and I would say late fifties. He always seemed to me to have no sense of humor, none! I never seen him crack a smile or even tell a joke at any formations. Thinking about it now, I do not really recall him ever laughing. He had a serious face to go along with the stern character. He mostly just stood before us while we were in formation and just barked at us. He was a true leader, however. That is hard to find, he was clearly born to lead. He would take us on these crazy training evolutions. The kind of training that you are up for days and its always raining. But we did it without complaint. He was there with us doing the same things we were. We all respected him whether he was talking or yelling at us.

CHRIS: Did he speak like he was scolding you guys for something you did wrong or just yelling?

WITLIT: I guess it was not really yelling but more of a speech or loud guidance. He just felt this need to tell us about our progress or our performances during the training.

CHRIS: What kind of things exactly?

WITLIT: The most unusual current events, that kind of stuff. General Mathews took those kinds of things very personally.

CHRIS: Why do you think that is?

WITLIT: I do not know exactly, he just did. He always got newspapers delivered every day from all over the United States. It was weird.

CHRIS: So, what happened usually after he read those papers?

WHITLIT: He would call these formations and just tell us what he thought about the current events he read. Keep in mind, General Mathews was a Brigadier General, not a Captain or Colonel. Getting formations like that together is not an easy task for a company. Let alone all the companies of an entire division. However, what a General wants, a General gets. And it happens as quickly as possible, no questions asked or lame excuses. You are at that formation and standing tall. I remember a few Marines called it "soap boxing". I never heard that term before and honestly did not care to ask what they meant at the time.

GORDON: Was the name Theodore Roosevelt mentioned at all?

WITLIT: He was mentioned, like I said, I did not really care for the reference. Anyway, so General Mathew's would just stand in front of us for this long amount of time. He would just go on and on about what ever got on his nerves that day or week. It is not unusual for an officer to talk a lot or be longwinded. As I said, it could have been anything that General Matthew's would go on about. Another shooting in a school or a kidnapping of somebody we never heard of. I am not downplaying this but at five in the morning, that is not what I really want to hear. He was also a mustang, are you familiar with that term? That means he was enlisted first.

GORDON: Why is that important?

WITLIT: It is about respect. He was one of us at one time. No special treatment like most officers expect. You must see it from our point of view. He ate the same dirt in boot camp as I did. He has literally been in my boots and walked that mile. And because of that, his orders were always followed, they were like biblical law. I do not expect you to really understand, but that's how Matthew's had the powers he did, it was respect.

GORDON: I have heard of such loyalty before. I think I get it.

WITLIT: It exists and has for a few hundred years in the Marines.

CHRIS: Respect and power are two different things. I get what you are saying about respect, what about the power aspect?

WITLIT: General Matthews was a Staff Sergeant before he became an officer. I also was told his degree was in military history. A history degree is better than a photographer or something silly like that. Do not get me wrong, there is nothing wrong with being an officer, hey it has its nice perks. But, if you are an Artist, it does not really give the warm and fuzzy feeling to the men when you try to lead them into a firefight. I guess a historian does not either, but the enlisted rank helps. He knows where we come from. He knows that the private gets nothing and works for what he has earned. The history degree just tells men like me that General Matthew's has the records of hard work in the military. The military runs on the backs of the Privates and Lance Corporals, that is a fact. A lot of officers overestimate their importance. Look, the officer may have your word deleted on paper. It is the Sergeants that you fear and run the show.

CHRIS: How did you find all this out? I mean General Matthews's background.

WITLIT: General Matthews would always say things like, "I know where you come from" or "I've been in your boots". He was interesting. As I said, Matthew's would have these huge formations. Understand that he is a General not a Captain. Seeing him as often as we did is unusual in most cases. Matthews was not like most officers, he wanted interaction with his men. He knew most of us by name. That is not a few Marines but thousands. It still amazes me that he could do that.

GORDON: That is impressive given the number of Marines under his command.

WITLIT: It really is. He would just show up in random places too. You could be out training, and his command vehicle would pull up and he would watch the training. He would come over and interact with us. Telling us what we were doing right or wrong. He did not mind getting dirty; he would just jump right in. We were filling sandbags once, I hated filling sandbags, but it had to be done. Halfway through the work I hear, "Lance Corporal Witlit, is that how filling sandbag this supposed to be done?" I just jumped to attention and tell him it was not; I was filling them halfway and I knew it. I just wanted to get it done. He made me redo the ones I half deleted. He stood there watching me until I was done. Most officers would walk away as I worked, and word deleted when I was done.

CHRIS: Was he watching over you all the time? Did it have to
            do with your unit?

WITLIT: Not exactly, it was like he felt that his presence would
            make me work harder. It is the idea of seeing the person
            you are working for and it motivates you. He did it for
            all the units.

GORDON: Did it work?

WITLIT: Yeah actually, it did. I worked harder because I knew
            he was there watching me. Then there was his uniform,
            which was something to see.

GORDON: What about it, I can only assume it was not messed up.

WITLIT: No, it was not. His uniform was always just... well,
            perfect. You know that new flawless press look? Like it
            was straight out of the store kind of ideal. It was over the
            top impeccable. Look, we always have a high standard
            in the Marines. We always look clean cut, but he was
            just, more. His hair was always perfectly cut, his belt
            the perfect length, his boots always shined. He was just
            crisp. I bet he had his hair cut three times a week. He
            always looked the same every day. It is the definition of
            uniformity, I guess. And man did he work! He practically
            lived in that battalion building when not visiting units.
            General Matthews could not have had a family, no way.
            If he did have a family, he was never home. He could
            always be seen at his office, the light was on Monday
            through Sunday, and all night. We would go out on
            the weekends and he would be in the battalion building
            doing something. Always at work he was known for
            walking around the barracks too. Matthews would
            inspect constantly, just poking around. He would check
            doors in the barracks, or just knock on a random door.
            You would open the door and there was Matthews

standing in the doorway. He would invite himself in and look around. Matthews would just talk to you to get a feel of you. Ask you for your General Orders. You never wanted to mess those up with him. You would be standing duty for a week. He wanted to know you, who you were. He always would find something to give you some crap about. Matthews demanded perfection.

CHRIS: Why do you think he was like that? Do you think there may have been an underlying point to how he was?

WITLIT: I honestly do not really know. I guess he really loved his job and the Marines. Maybe Matthews had nothing better to do. I just cannot say, I do not really know. There had to be a reason, there always is. That is why you are here now talking to me. You want the same things, the reason why.

GORDON: So, what do you think motivates someone like that? What drives someone to be that way? I know it sounds the same, but I am asking for a root to the problem. Not good work ethic, we both know that.

WITLIT: like I said before, I really cannot say. There is one thing I remembered if it helps.

GORDON: What is that?

WITLIT: It is not related to the working habit, just something unusual about General Matthew's.

CHRIS: Go ahead, we want to know.

WITLIT: It was this song; I cannot remember the name. The Chaplin played it all time in the Sunday church services. General Matthew's would either be humming it to himself or singing it quietly under his breath. I bet he whistled it in his sleep. He was obsessed with it. He had quotes of it all over his office and quoted from it constantly. General Matthews pretty much used it as an outline for his life, or so it seemed.

CHRIS: Do you remember the tune or the words?

WITLIT: Yeah, something like, "His truth is marching on" and "glory, glory, hallelujah".

GORDON: "The battle hymn of the republic"? Does that sound familiar?

WITLIT: Yeah, that is it!

CHRIS: It was written by a poet named Julia Howe.

WITLIT: You and General Matthew's would have gotten along if you are that familiar with the song.

CHRIS: I went to church a lot as a child.

WITLIT: Well General Matthews drove us crazy with that song. The quotes were strange from it too. Just all the time, it was annoying. I guess everyone has a quark or something strange and unique about themselves.

GORDON: We had talked about motivations and what drives a person, specifically someone who is like General Matthews. You said that you did not know what drove him. Did you ever make any theories personally as to why he was that way? Not just the idea that someone loves their job. I guess what I am asking is more of a "why" question. Why did he go to such extremes? It is one thing to love a job but another to push one's self to a breaking point. If I understand it right, that is what you are saying about General Matthews.

WITLIT: Yeah, just like that. Me personally, I think it is where a person comes from. I do not mean the state or the county, yes that can be an influence. But that is not what I mean in this case. Well look at me. I was a disappointment from the very beginning according to my dad. Not only did my mom die while giving birth to me but I am sure my Dad wanted a girl. I think he resented me because of those factors.

CHRIS: Why would you not being a girl be a factor?

WITLIT: He probably thought I would be just like him. My dad was a real mess and a word deleted up his whole life. He really offered nothing to society, and I guess he thought I would be the same.

CHRIS: Are you like him? Do you think your dad was right?

WITLIT: Yup. I am just like him; I could do nothing right and he was no better either. For a man that judged me so much, he had the same issues. You would think that he would use that judgment on himself from time to time. If he did, he probably would not have raised me in such a trashy town.

CHRIS: Where are you from exactly? Our files say a town called Bellefonte Ohio, is that right?

WITLIT: That's right, Bellefonte Ohio. That town had nothing going for it, nothing! Its unemployment rate was crazy high, like seventy-five percent. Well unless you count drug dealing, then there were plenty of people employed. Bellefonte always reminded me of the hole-in-the-wall town in a corny western movie. Like I said, it had nothing. No hotel, no mall, just nothing. I am sure I have overused the term nothing by now, but that town should have been named Nothing Ohio. To be honest with you and myself, I think I could have been something. I have always believed I was meant to do great things in my life. I do not think that Bellefonte got to me. Oh no, it was my dad that got to me. I think that town broke his spirit and then he broke mine. I always wanted that good job son, I never hear that one. Loser or dumb Word Deleted and the occasional moron, I hear those in plenty. Never I am proud of you son. It makes me wonder if things would have been different if my mom had not of passed. Which of course my dad gave me Word deleted for. I obviously never had my mom's death in my master plan when I was born. Like me causing her to die was number one on the things to do list. It is funny really when you think about it. Disappointment can really make people do some crazy things; you know what I mean?

GORDON: I know what you mean. People will go to great lengths for another's approval.

WITLIT: What always got me about General Mathews was that he had this presence about him. I know that is off topic, but it is true. I just felt it needed to be said to understand him. I never felt the need for approval from him because I felt that he knew I was giving him my best. I really cannot go into too much detail because of the gag order. I hope you understand that. I can say that he had strong trust for his Marines. If he knew he could trust you, he would utilize you. He would put responsibilities on you that he knew would play to your personal strengths.

GORDON: Did General Matthew's have that kind of trust in you?

WITLIT: He did, General Matthews always gave me jobs that he felt were important. He always called on me and I never let him down. I cannot give you any more details right now, but yeah. General Matthew's trusted me, and I always gave him one hundred percent.

CHRIS: Can you give any examples?

WITLIT: I do not think that I am at liberty to really say currently. Like I said, he trusted me, with his life.

CHRIS: We do understand, and it is fine. You are doing a great job so far.

GORDON: Right now, I would like to change our focus if that okay with you Chris? We should get to the topic at hand.

CHRIS: That is fine.

GORDON: At this time, I would like to ask about Private First Class Allen Desmond Eckhart. I know he was in your Battalion, were about exactly.

WITLIT: He was in my platoon, second platoon.

GORDON: He was in Corporal Meadows Squad correct?

WITLIT: Correct, Corporal Meadows squad. So, what exactly are you interested in? What do you really want to talk about with Eckhart?

CHRIS: We want to talk about the death of Private First Class Eckhart. Are you alright to talk about that? From what the report says, you were pretty involved with his death.

WITLIT: Involved?

CHRIS: What I mean to say is that we know that you were close to him. We understand if you are uncomfortable talking about it. We are hoping that you would still be willing to talk about it with us.

WITLIT: I do not like talking about it but given the circumstances, I will talk about it. I realize that it is important to talk about his death in this interview. It must be, you would not have traveled all this way otherwise.

GORDON: Your willingness to speak with us is appreciated. Just know that the information you give us will be invaluable and is important. We think that Eckhart's story is where Operation Vanguard started. We are truly trying to understand what got the ball rolling with General Matthews. We feel Eckhart's part of the story can shed light on a lot of unanswered questions.

CHRIS: Exactly, it is not just about Vanguard and we know that. It is about the people involved. It is about the lives of everyone involved. It is the beginning.

WITLIT: I understand that. So where do you want me to start?

GORDON: We just want you to talk. Whatever comes to mind? Just say it and start talking and go from there. We can guide you if necessary.

WITLIT: Ok, just talk...well. To begin, Eckhart was a strange dude to start with. Not that, I must watch him kind of strange, simply different. He did not fit in to the Platoon. That is why I liked him. He was different in a good way. Do you know what I mean?

CHRIS: So, he did not hang out, go bar hopping, that kind of thing?

WITLIT: No, He did all that. It is hard to explain. It is like a perfectly set up table that is set for dinner and a bowl is just sitting a little off from the rest. Everything else is where it belongs except that bowl. It was that kind of way.

GORDON: How exactly?

WITLIT: He was normal if you understand what I mean. Marines are by nature are strange and just a little different. So, in his normality he was the outcast. Look, I am not saying that all Marines are outcast or messed up dropouts, some are. But most of us are just a little broken. I joined to be less of a Word Deleted up in my old man's eyes. Eckhart was perfect. He had the perfect family, perfect education with perfect schools. He had everything that anyone would genuinely want, and then boom! He flushes it all and joins the United States Marine Corp or as we delightfully called it "Uncle Sam's Misguided Children". I guess thinking about it now, all Eckhart really wanted was to Word Deleted off his dad!

GORDON: So, you think he joined out of spite then.

WITLIT: Definitely! He had a college degree, and it was a good one. Eight years if I remember correctly. He went to an ivy league school on a scholarship for academics. Until I met him, I have only heard of the ivy league types but never actually met one before Eckhart. An ivy league Marine, that is a dream and a half. A general and a Captain maybe but not an enlisted, we do not get that kind of treatment in our lives. That is why we enlist in the first place. Eckhart told me he was a straight A student, 4.0 and made dean's list countless times. Eckhart said the school always said, "A 4.0 or you go"! Eckhart would laugh all the time at that. I never saw the humor in it myself.

CHRIS: Did you guys talk a lot?

WITLIT: A good bit. I really liked him. I had field watch a few times with him and we would talk when we went training. It was refreshing to hear someone talk about things other than cars and women all the time. He talked about different stuff, things that were deeper, I guess you would say. He knew these strange little facts like the distance to the moon or the sun. That would get us talking about other things.

GORDON: How did you two get acquainted? I can guess that it was through working.

WITLIT: Sort of, Eckhart got put on a lot of special duties because he was a Private First Class. It was always those jobs, picking up cigarette butts or Word Deleted like that. It is all just stupid work. You talk to kill time when doing such mind-numbing work like that. In the Marines they call jobs like that working parties, like it is going to be fun. Thinking about it now, it was fun with Eckhart. As I said before, he always brought up good conversational points. One-time Eckhart was talking about the golden ratio. I never heard that term before, and he was happy to explain.

CHRIS: How did you get on that topic?

WITLIT: He found a snail shell and asked if I ever heard of the golden Ratio before, and I said no. So, Eckhart goes on to tell me that most of life follows this number of 1.61. The tree limbs on a tree and the snail shell size, even people's arms to leg ratio. It was interesting. I have never heard anything like that before. But that is how Eckhart was, introducing me to new word deleted all the time. I respected that about him and thought it was awesome. As I said before, not normal guy talk.

GORDON: I am simply curious; do you know any more about his education outside of anything you already had said.

WITLIT: Well, like I said, it was an extremely expensive school. He did the work to get the degree and just walked away from it. He has a master's-degree from Word Deleted! If I remember correctly, it was a degree in some sort of science. Man, I would give my left deleted to bet most of our Captains do not have that kind of education. Eckhart tells me that he only had one argument with his father, just one. It changed everything, that is all it took to alter his mind on his education. It shocked me knowing that it only took one small argument to do all that. Not a fight, mind you. He said an argument. From what he described, it sounded more civil then even that. I think about the arguments I had with my dad and we almost went to blows several times. It did not sound anything like that when he described it.

CHRIS: Did he say what the argument was about, other than just the education? Do you remember?

WITLIT: The family business. His dad wanted to have his son by him to run the empire, as Eckhart would call it. Eckhart loved calling it that. He made his dads business sound very ominous and dark. All his dad really wanted was a father and son working duo. Then boom, the argument and then Parris Island Eckhart goes. Not a Marine Officer as you may expect but a regular ground pounding Marine. Eckhart had the brains to do any job in the Corps, any. He could have done them all, from officer or enlisted. He takes a standard trigger puller, an infantryman. That is why I think it was out of spite. He has a hundred thousand dollar a year education for almost a decade and here he is doing the same job as a high school dropout. You know what really gets me?

GORDON: What is that?

WITLIT: His dad did not even cut him off from the bank accounts. Eckhart still had an open wallet and a blank check to use freely. No questions asked by Eckhart's father. My dad, oh, I would have been excommunicated on the spot, no doubt about that. My dad would have made sure I was punished properly. Obviously, Eckhart's dad was different than mine.

CHRIS: You never said who his dad was. Who is he?

WITLIT: Ever heard of Thomas Eckhart, the pharmaceutical genius and multi-billionaire?

CHRIS: That was Private First Class Eckhart's father?

WITLIT: It sure was. That is why Eckhart was never strapped for cash. The family had more than enough.

GORDON: How did Eckhart's enlistment never make it to the newspapers? I never heard a single word about any of this.

WITLIT: You know, I asked the same question. Eckhart told me once that his dad spent some serious cash to keep things quiet. There was a lot of nonsense that happened in that family that never made any newspapers, good lawyers will do that. Eckhart said that his father believed he was going through a phase. His dad felt he would eventually grow out of it. His dad also wanted to move on and forget about the Marines. In the end, the lawyers did their jobs, you must give them that. Everything in that family was so hush hush, that only a few of the Marines knew that Eckhart had that kind of money. Eckhart had been with the company no more than three or four months before questions started coming up about him. Let us be honest, Eckhart was not trying to hide it, that he had money. He would not brag about either.

CHRIS: What do you mean? What kind of questions came up?

WITLIT: Like, how does a Private First Class afford the biggest flat screen television I have ever seen and have it in his barracks room? How can a Private First Class afford full leather couches, well, couches in general? How about, how does a Private First Class always have cash after all those things? Eckhart had it all. Every Word Deleted electronic thing you could imagine. He had stuff so expensive it blew my mind on more than one occasion. It was truly crazy the amount of stuff he had. One of the Staff Sergeants in the platoon took notice of all that Eckhart had. He had Eckhart drug tested. They brought drug sniffing dogs to all the rooms and obviously did not find anything. The command really thought he was selling drugs in the barracks. Eckhart had an amazing way of keeping the command very confused. It was a constant source of entertainment for him. Did you know that Eckhart was a lonely child?

GORDON: No, I did not know that.

WITLIT: Yup, a lonely child. Eckhart was milking his dad of all his money, well, as much as he could. Eckhart told me that he spent the money as fast as he could just to see if his dad would get Word Deleted off at him. Things like that make me think about my dad and how differently things were between Eckhart and me. My dad had a gas station and body repair shop. His old boss Tommy Umland sold it to him for cheap because he was dying or something. I thought that after my dad got the gas station that I could work there. I was dead wrong. My father called me everything but his son and told me that there was no way in word deleted that he would employ me. It was so bad that my dad told everyone he knew to not hire me. He really screwed me over. I had to do something, so, I joined the Marines. I went to the recruiting office and spoke to Staff Sergeant Snider and signed up. I went home to tell my dad. His reaction was less than inviting. All he said was good, now you can get off your Word Deleted lazy Word Deleted and get the Word Deleted out of my house. I can only imagine how Eckhart's dad took the news that his son was now going to be a Marine. The whole thing is just a big joke when you put it into perspective and just a bit ironic.

CHRIS: I get it. You spend all the time you can with your dad and all he wants is for you to leave. Here we have Private First Class Eckhart on the other hand, who could not wait to leave. Is that it?

WITLIT: Exactly! All I wanted was the normal family. I never got it. Eckhart had the chance for a normal family and never wanted it.

CHRIS: It is a real role reversal with a twist of irony. Your childhoods were total opposites. It makes sense why you two got along so well.

WITLIT: I never looked at it that way, but it is the truth. My dad was just a grease monkey, like I said. He was nothing important. I used to watch him fix cars on the weekend out on the front lawn. He would sell them for parts or get them working again. Whatever he could do to pay the bills, he did. He worked hard. There is no doubt about that. It made him a hard man too. I learned a lot from him and was really hoping to work with him. I had dreams of changing the name of the shop from "Tommy's" to "Harry and sons" or something like that. My dad clearly had other plans. I was obviously just a burden and a bad memory. I really wanted to work with him. That is all I really wanted in my life, plain and simple. It truly sucked when my dad did not want to share that idea. My dad in the end was just a major Word Deleted. All the while, Eckhart's dad never gave two thoughts to the money. Maybe that is why I always looked up to General Matthew's and never wanted to disappoint him, like a second dad.

GORDON: Why would you say a burden and bad memory?

WITLIT: My mother died in childbirth and I am sure that he did not want me to begin with. My mom dies and now I am his problem.

CHRIS: He never wanted you?

WITLIT: Nope, like I said, never. He wanted a little girl and got me.

CHRIS: So how far did Eckhart go with this spending spree?

WITLIT: Farther than I ever thought, much farther. There was this one Friday night, right before a holiday. I cannot remember which one. Anyway, we all go out drinking and Eckhart pulls the tab. He says, "Drinks on me, drink up boys!" I was like, you do not have to tell me twice, which was exactly what everyone who was in the bar thought too! And so, we all drank.

GORDON: The whole bar!

WITLIT: The whole Word Deleted bar! This went on for several rounds. Eckhart must have, well… he must have dropped ten thousand that night! It was just insane. The crazy part, this happened several times. He was not cheap about it obviously. Top shelf only, "only the best for the Corp" he said.

             You would not believe the money he could spend. There was this one Sunday morning. It was like six or something close to that. The sun was barely in the sky and Eckhart starts banging on my door. I hear him yelling "Joe, Joe, Hey Joe, are you up yet!?!" I am thinking that Yeah, I am now. I let him into the room, and he starts asking if I like football. I tell him that I do, and we briefly talk about teams and things like that, just small talk as I get dressed. I did not see a point to the conversation.

GORDON: You did not find that the least bit strange that he asked about sports first thing in the morning like that.

WITLIT: Actually no. As I said before, he was odd at times so it was not surprising that he would be a morning person. It also was not a surprise when he asked random questions like that. It was his norm. That also was not the first time he woke me up with odd questions on a weekend, it was typical of Eckhart.

CHRIS: That was normal morning conversation?

WITLIT: He was just like that. He was always up early and always in high spirits. Even after a night out of drinking, he was up early. That is just how he was, and it was always entertaining. Anyway, after I am dressed, we head downstairs and out to his Word Deleted.

GORDON: Wait, what? A Word Deleted!

WITLIT: Oh Yeah! Money has its privileges.

CHRIS: I am sorry gentleman, but I am not too familiar with that make of that vehicle.

WITLIT: They are exceedingly rare, like only three hundred made by Word Deleted Company. They were a concept car in 1963. Like I said, only three hundred rolled off the line. And the value is outrages. We are easily talking a quarter of a million or better. Eckhart's was in mint condition.

CHRIS: And he just went and bought it?

WITLIT: No, a birthday gift from his dad. It was a few weeks before he woke me up about football. His dad bought Eckhart things like that all the time. It was like his dad was reminding him where Eckhart came from. I think his dad did it to show off. So, this big shipping truck shows up at the barracks one day. The Duty Officer walks up to Eckhart's room, bangs on the door and yelling that he has a delivery. Everyone came down to see what was going on and what the noise was about.

GORDON: The Duty Officer was that loud?

WITLIT: No, news travels fast. It is very boring in the barracks, so anything new is a big deal. Anyway, this car rolls out of the truck, and the driver hands him a receipt and a letter addressed to Eckhart. He thanks the guy and tips him three hundred dollars for his time. The letter was from his dad wishing him a happy birthday, which was that very morning. The car was amazing! It was even signed by Word Deleted. He is the designer of the car, by the way Agent Chris. As I said, it was easily worth two hundred thousand. I have read about Word Deleted, but never actually seen one in person before.

CHRIS: That is amazing, just dropped it off like that.

WITLIT: Just like that, and of course he gave rides for the rest of the day to anyone who wanted to ride in it. I even took a picture of myself sitting in the driver's seat. I hung that picture in my locker. His father even went as far as to pay for the insurance ahead of time so Eckhart would not have to worry about it. I jokingly asked Eckhart if his dad was thinking of adopting anytime soon. Two weeks later, a second vehicle was delivered. This time with my name on it! Eckhart told his dad what I said and so he sent me a new truck, a Word Deleted! Just as rare and unique. It was astounding! Who does that? His old man set up a trust so I would not have to worry about insurance or taxes. The money paid for itself and the car. His dad even paid for the gas. It made my head spin. My dad has that truck in storage right now. What is even funnier is that his dad sends a card with the truck too. The letter said something to the effect of "Sorry I couldn't find a name deleted so I bought something just as impressive." It was a right off the line original! It is a special series made in 1966 and they only made a couple hundred. I got the fifth off the line! I loved driving that truck. I would be doing it now if I could.

GORDON: Just like that, purchased a truck for you?

WITLIT: Yeah, I never even met the guy. I guess Eckhart talked about me, so his dad felt it was worth doing. I do not know, but I sure was not complaining. What were we talking about again, oh yeah, I could talk about that truck all day and I know that is not why you are here?

GORDON: You started talking about a football game and that Sunday.

WITLIT: Oh yeah, so we drove two states over to watch a football game. Eckhart had decided to see the game last minute and got tickets. This wasn't nosebleed section but real box seats. I do not mean standard box either. We sat next to Word Deleted, you know that guy that produced and made the movie Word Deleted! How much did that movie make last year?

CHRIS: That movie grossed an easy hundred million.

GORDON: Corporal Witlit, please continue about the tickets and how he got them.

WITLIT: Yeah, I know. Anyway, it was crazy. So now I am sitting next to Name Deleted talking about dumb Word Deleted like I know him. Stupid stuff like what is for lunch and the weather, I had no idea what to say to him. I have never been around famous people. He had some chick on his arm, what was her name? Word Deleted Word Deleted Word Deleted, that is it. She was so coked up she had no idea where she was. I am sure her managers and publishers love seeing her act like that when she is not on T.V. It was nuts. The whole thing was so surreal, I have never seen anyone of any importance in my life and here these two are and others. Keep in mind… this was not just a normal run of the mill game. This was not pre-season; this was the play offs! I asked how Eckhart got the seats and he tells me that he just called up Word Deleted Word Deleted.

GORDON: You mean the owner of the Word Deleted Word Deleted!

WITLIT: The one and only, I guess because his team did not make it to the playoffs that year does not mean he cannot get seats for friends. Eckhart knew a lot of people.

CHRIS: That is just wild!

WITLIT: Right! That is exactly what I thought! We sat with to two-time MVP Word Deleted Word Deleted, the guy from that war movie a few years back… oh yeah Word Deleted Word Deleted too! I got their autographs on a jersey that night. We had it all that night, everything. It was full layout and drinks from one wall to the other! I even met the commentators for the game that night, the ones that were on T.V. for the game. Eckhart's dad had some serious pull, still does. Those seats must have cost more than the house I grew up in, well yours maybe. I have seen broken down cars worth more than my house, trust me.

So, we watch the whole game and meet most of the players on both teams after the game. After the game, we went to dinner and had drinks with two of the players on the losing team. That also happened to be Eckhart's favorite team. We must have gotten back at 4:30 A.M. That is just how things were, totally crazy and mostly spontaneous. All while trying to Word Deleted off his dad which never happened.

GORDON: This does not really sound too outrageous, just expensive.

WITLIT: That was only the beginning. That car I mentioned, well, wait to you hear this one.

GORDON: Okay?

WITLIT: A few months later, after the football game. Eckhart, me and two other Marines decide to go out for a drive. The two others were Word Deleted and Word Deleted by the way; they were from our platoon. We were going to some hole in the wall called Word Deleted. It is right off the bypass and every Marine knows about it. Anyway, it is Saturday afternoon, Eckhart just pulls up to some random dude's house after he suddenly turns the car around. This house was very average except for this beat up old car for sale in the front lawn. Eckhart gets out of the car and starts up a conversation with this guy in his front lawn. As I said, we were just driving along, and he makes a U-turn and pulls into this guy's driveway. I never saw this guy before and had no idea who this dude was. But there we were, sitting in the driveway of this guy's house while Eckhart talks to him.

CHRIS: Could you hear the conversation?

WITLIT: I could not make out a word of it. He just starts chatting to this guy and at the time, I had no idea what they were talking about. This conversation goes on for about ten minutes as we are freezing in the car. Eckhart finally looks back at us and waves for us while yelling for us to get out of the car. As were getting out, the guy Eckhart is talking to goes into his house. It is like ten minutes before he comes out again. We are all standing by the car as the two of them start talking again. I see Eckhart pull out his wallet and had the guy something. They talk again and the guy pulls out some keys from his pocket and starts playing with the ring to the keys.

GORDON: What kind of key, car keys?

WITLIT: Yup, car keys.

GORDON: For the name deleted?

WITLIT: yup, name deleted. Well, Eckhart pulls out his keys, takes them off the ring. Eckhart gives the guy a handful of cash, a business card, and the car keys. Eckhart then gets the set of keys from the guy and starts putting them on his key ring. I overhear the stranger say something like "Are you sure?" and Eckhart say, "yeah man, all good". Eckhart tells us to all pile into this old sedan.

CHRIS: I do not get it. I must be missing something.

WITLIT: He traded the Name Deleted and gave the dude, Insurance info and money for gas in hand.

CHRIS: Who was this guy, a friend or something?

WITLIT: That is the punchline, the real question. The answer is no, Eckhart never met this guy before. Eckhart did not even know his name. He just saw this dude's car and traded it. That crazy expensive Word Deleted for a beat-up Word Deleted, pink slip and all! That guy sure hit the lottery that day. Man did that junk car stink, it smelled like pure Word Deleted and baby Word Deleted.

            So, as were driving in that messed-up car and Eckhart calls his old man while on our way to the bar. Eckhart tells his dad about the selling of the car. His dad does not say a word, does not even raise his voice at him. Not a Word Deleted thing. I truly could not believe it. I thought his dad would hit the roof and fly all the way down here to beat his son's Word Deleted! Eckhart does not say a word when he gets off the phone. He just sat in the driver's seat for a few minutes after we parked. After a while he comes in. While there, he does not drink or eat, just sat silently. The only thing we eventually hear out of Eckhart was that he wanted to leave when we were done eating. Eckhart pays the check, and we bounce.

CHRIS: Not a thing? No food, nothing?

WITLIT: Nope, nothing. We eat and leave, that is it. Eckhart tells me he did not feel like getting hammered that night and so he does not. Eckhart says that what was on the menu was not good and the beer cost too much. He had not had a problem with the menu the five other times he was there with us, but that night, he did. In fact, I remember him being happy with the wings, he ordered them every time. I do not know about you but, if the food sucks and their beer is so expensive, why keep coming back like he did.

GORDON: What is your opinion of Eckhart selling the vehicle? Was it about attention? Do you think he wanted attention that bad from his dad, that even negative attention was good?

WITLIT: I am guessing attention. I could never see wanting that kind of attention. If Eckhart wanted negative attention, his dad did not care.

CHRIS: Do you think part of it was showing off to you and the others? Trying to impress you maybe?

WITLIT: I do not think it had to do with us at all. He just wanted us around, he liked us. We were his family. I really think that is all he wanted from his dad. I think he wanted his family to be a real family and act like one.

GORDON: Why do you think his dad was not around? His dad letting him do whatever he wanted does not necessarily mean he was not supportive or apart of his life.

WITLIT: I bet Eckhart had a nanny or something and was raised by them. I think by Word in off his dad, he was just trying to get a simple "look at me dad", that kind of thing. Why else would you do something like that? Trading a crazy expensive car for a junk one when you could just buy it, why would you do that? This was not the only time that Eckhart did strange stuff either. Hey, can I get some water or something?

S.A. Gordon calls prison official over for water, no need for conversation to be added to the record.

WITLIT: Thank you.

GORDON: Not a problem, you said there was more to his behavior?

WITLIT: Oh yeah. So, Eckhart goes one day and orders a maid service to come and clean the barracks rooms. That was great. You want to talk about class and funny at the same time. That is one of those moments that you just do not forget. It was truly funny.

CHRIS: I do not get it? Why is that funny? Maids are common. I am guessing not that common in the Marines.

WITLIT: They are not common in the Marine Corp, trust me. We cannot afford them. When I say we, I mean lower enlisted? I am sure officers have that kind of luxury, but our ground pounders do not get that kind of treatment. Cleaning is one of our more annoying but necessary jobs in the Corp. We call it Field day and it sucks!

GORDON: Field day? Like in school, games, and things like that? How does that relate to cleaning? It is obvious that it is not the same, but I do not get the reference difference.

WITLIT: Oh, I Word Deleted wish it was fun. Look, every Thursday after work, everyone goes to the barracks, I mean everyone. It did not matter if you were married or not, living there or not. You were there at the barracks. We clean that place from top to bottom, like ants in an ant hill. Everything gets pulled out of the rooms, and I mean everything. The next morning, Friday morning to paint the picture. Command Sergeant Major or the platoon Commander, or Staff Sergeant goes through every room and inspects it. If it passes, no big deal, but if it fails, you do it Friday night! On Saturday morning you get inspected again. It is just one of those ways the Marines Word Deleted with you. I never understood the reference of naming it field day. That is just what it was called.

GORDON: So obviously a maid means you do not clean, I get that. It is a guaranteed pass. So why is it funny?

WITLIT: It was awesome and funny. We just sat in fold up chairs in the courtyard and watch the barracks get cleaned. Watching and drinking, it was perfect. See, the command loves to find ways to mess with your head or your personal time. Eckhart had found a way to beat the system. We did not have to hear the First Sergeant yelling "this place is a Word Deleted pigsty". Like I said, it is just a game to them. If I remember correctly, it was five maids. They came every day, Monday through Friday. They were there at 5 P.M. sharp, 1700 for you military types. The rooms looked perfect, so clean you could eat off the floor. It was all paid by Eckhart! He was a hero!

GORDON: That sounds smart.

WITLIT: It was pure genius, that is why the platoon Sergeant flipped out. He finds out about the maids and puts us in a formation and just goes off about personal responsibility and acting like men. It was all laughable. The platoon Sergeant then takes Eckhart to the side and starts reaming him again all over about the same Word Deleted.

CHRIS: Is this Staff Sergeant Grey?

WITLIT: Yeah, Staff Sergeant Grey. Eckhart did not care at all what Grey had to say. Eckhart did not even get upset. Eckhart just blew the whole thing off. The key to money is, it can fix a lot of problems and make you care an awful lot less about small things. Do you want to hear my opinion on something?

GORDON: Sure, that is why we are here.

WITLIT: I think Staff Sergeant Gray was just jealous that Eckhart took his leverage over us. If the barracks is spotless, they cannot play games. Best part, Eckhart found a new play toy.

GORDON: You mean Staff Sargent Grey?

WITLIT: Correct.

CHRIS: That's staff Sergeant Kyle Thomas Grey, I want to make sure were talking about the same person.

WITLIT: Yup, that is him. I guess because Eckhart's dad did not care, he would get Staff Sergeant Grey to care. Boy did Eckhart make his job hard. So, after the Staff Sergeant gets on Eckhart about the maids, Eckhart only has them come to the rooms on Thursday nights. However, women still came to the barracks every night if you get what I am saying.

CHRIS: I do not get it, not maids?

WITLIT: No, they were not. They were dressed like maids. Eckhart gets in contact with one of the strip clubs right outside the base. There were two of them to be exact. One was this little doublewide trailer with the windows painted black. You only went there if you were strapped for cash. Five-dollar cover to get in, that is it; you got what you paid for. I mean hey, at least they were women, not first class, but women. Trust me when I say you saw your fair share of C-Section scars and stretch marks. That was the White Rhino, or as we called it the right grind and Word Deleted. The place closed six months later, which is typical for a place like that. They open and close constantly. Places like that have different names and managers every year. Then there was the Sapphire, as it was called then. I do not even know what it is called now. They had some amazing women there. They also had amateur nights on Tuesdays too, that was never a disappointment. Eckhart goes and gets with the owner of the Sapphire about renting the girls there that were off. Eckhart made sure of course that the owner got some cash on the side for his troubles. He offers the girls five hundred bucks a piece per night! The girls came all right, it was good money. Plus, they made tips. Sorry about the laughing but it is still funny.

GORDON: They made serious money plus tips, who would not go? I do not see why that is funny, I do not get it.

WITLIT: Tips was an inside joke. Some of the girls would get friendly or do certain favors for the right price. They were not shy telling the Marines they were interested in making a few extra bucks. Within a week, Medical sick call was full of STD cases. Like all good things, someone snitches, and the girls were not allowed on the base anymore. Eckhart just smirked that off and the Platoon Sergeant blew up again. This time they got him, unfortunately.

CHRIS: They?

WITLIT: The Command. They hit him for immorality or some stupid bull like that. It is a stupid thing to punish someone over. We are Word Deleted Marines for Word Deleted sake not quire boys. Screw Morality, I want to be laid! In the end, all Eckhart got was a sharp talking too. Thinking about it now, that's when Eckhart got weird.

GORDON: How did he get weird?

WITLIT: Well, Eckhart just stopped, you know? Weird, it is hard to really pinpoint, it was simply weird. He was not himself anymore.

CHRIS: Stopped what exactly.

WITLIT: Well, everything. He just stopped doing what he always did. Just pumped the breaks on life, you know.

GORDON: Can you be more specific and exact when you mean stopped. Like what, he stopped drinking and spending money? That kind of thing, like that?

WITLIT: Well, yeah. That kind of stuff, it was like he just gave up. He even stopped eating as often, lost a lot of weight too. Like everything, man. He just stopped caring about us, the Marines, and his dad. Eckhart just gave up. He was like a tire with no air. See, he got in trouble again, this time for real, Eckhart just stopped showing up to formation, so they punished him. We have a set routine, get up every day and run at 5:30 A.M. After the run, then we have a formation. He was not there. They found him in bed, crying. It was like 8:30 A.M. by that point. It was sad.

GORDON: What did the command do then?

WITLIT: Like I said, they punished him instead of talking to him or sending him to a Chaplin or head shrink. The command is always good for stuff like that. Do not fix the problem, just make it worse. I can give a thousand examples of that. Look at field training. It all goes smooth until the higher-ups get there and Word Deleted it up. They could not get Eckhart for the maid thing, so they got him for not showing to formations. They busted him down to private, that did not do a Word Deleted thing or make things better. So, it happened again, Eckhart did not show for another formation, this time he went on barracks restriction. Barracks restriction means he cannot leave the barracks for anything but work and food at the chow hall. They also took half his pay this time, that is a real joke. The command thought that would teach him a lesson. The command clearly knew nothing about him and his family. He carried a year's wages in his wallet every day. Well, not really but it seemed that way. So, he is on house arrest and cannot go out, he did not care. It was not a big deal to him. This was all about a month before what happened to him.

GORDON: Did anything else happen in between those times?

WITLIT: Besides not talking a lot, he just clammed up for a long while. Then just overnight, he was fine. I really thought it was strange but blew it off.

GORDON: Was it like a light switch just flipped over night?

WITLIT: Just back to his state of normal, I guess you could say. He was acting like himself again if that makes sense. I did not think anything of it after a while. None of us did. He started talking to his dad again too, that was good to hear.

CHRIS: He was not talking to his dad before that time?

WITLIT: Until he straightened up, no one. It was good seeing him happy. It is better than seeing him stare at the wall or sealing. He would totally dismiss you, like you were not there, then like magic, back to normal. We would always ask him if he needed anything, he would say nothing at all to us or just say no.

It was about a week after he snapped out of it that he did what he did. I had duty that night. Duty in the barracks is just a ton of walking in circles and looking around. It is babysitting adult men. Its frankly Word Deleted stupid. All the while making sure they do not break anything.

GORDON: Do you want to talk about it?

WITLIT: I really do not like too, or honestly want too. All I can say is that morning sucked. I just finished my walk around the building and just got back to the duty office, it was around 3 A.M. I just sat down when I heard something hit the ground outside. I found out shortly after that it was Eckhart. Sergeant Hillard would really be the one to ask at this point. I did not see much of anything. I just remember the sound Eckhart made when he hit the ground, it was just horrible. It was like a bag of potatoes hitting the ground. It was a horrible, crunching thump. I am not sure I can say much more than that. Like I said, I did not see Eckhart. And to be honest, I really do not want to talk about it anymore. I like to think about the good times with Eckhart, not that moment. I appreciate that you let me speak a little and hopefully I helped.

GORDON: We understand and thank you for your time.

GORDON: This is Special Agent Sean Gordon. The time is 11:41 A.M. at the United States Disciplinary Barracks, Fort Leavenworth Kansas, Maximum Security Wing, Block 7. We have just finished interviewing Corporal Joseph Thomas Allen Witlit. Case file: 31008539-A, Operation Vanguard or "The Matthews Incident".

This formally concludes the Interview with Corporal Witlit. No further entries were made on this date or for this part of the interview.

Interview of Sergeant Nelson Deckard Hillard

Wednesday, June 14th, 2028(Flag Day)
Lindstrom, Minnesota

This recorded session is called to order by the head of the Federal Bureau of Investigations, Special Investigations Unit.

GORDON: Its 11:30 A.M. in Lindstrom Minnesota. We are currently at the home of Sergeant Nelson Deckard Hillard. We are seated at his kitchen table. Sitting next to me is Agent William Chris and across from me is Sergeant Hillard: Case file 31008539-A, Operation Vanguard or "The Matthews Incident". Sergeant Hillard is 32 years of age, is 6'1", weight is 179 LBS. He is of slender build, brown hair, is currently employed as an apprentice blacksmith, has no discernible marks or scars, has brown eyes, and a tan complexion. He is Caucasian and an American, his fingerprints are on file and he has no classification code.

Key testimony involving the Death of Private First Class Allen Eckhart and his death. Sergeant Hillard is currently not under oath and has been willing to speak about the Eckhart incident.

GORDON: Good Morning Sergeant Hillard.

HILLARD: Good Morning, how yawl gentlemen today?

GORDON: Good thank you Sergeant.

HILLARD: You can call me Nelson; I've been out for a while now.

GORDON: Okay Nelson, Agent Chris and I are here to discuss Operation Vanguard and the suicide of Private First Class Eckhart. Everything is being documented. Anything you can tell us is a true privilege. This is for historical record and research.

HILLARD: I am more than willing to help and will definitely do my best. Sitting for an interview like this is a new thing for me and I'll do what I can. I didn't mean to repeat myself there, sorry.

CHRIS: No worries, this is just an informal interview. No pressure.

HILLARD: So, I talk to one of you …or both of you, how does this work?

GORDON: You just talk as were both listening, which we are. Or you can address one of us. It does not really matter. Think of this as a conversation and all we want to do is listen. Of course, from time to time we ask a question. It is just that easy.

HILLARD: Okay, that's sounds easy enough. Just so you know. I don't want to waste your time, but I don't actually know anything about the Matthews incident. Other then I served for him and saw what happened on the television after I left the Marines.

GORDON: Thank you for your honesty, we appreciate that. Like we said, it is mostly about Private First Class Eckhart so do not worry about General Matthews right now.

            Let It be known that prior consent was granted by the family of Private First Class Eckhart as to any information leading to his death may be used for this investigation.

HILLARD: I can do that, sure. That was such a shame what Eckhart did. Not a bad kid, I never saw any real problems with him. I didn't talk much to him, he was in a different platoon, but I saw him around. I knew him mostly because of that car he drove.

GORDON: We know truly little as to what happen to Eckhart. The files just say suicide. It gives no information as to the actual event itself.

HILLARD: I'm not really surprised that there was little detail in the reports. It wasn't pretty. So, I'm guessing you want the meat and potatoes of what really happened?

CHRIS: That is exactly what we need. We think that you would be able to fill us in as to why General Matthews took the death of PFC Eckhart so personally. We understand that every Commanding Officer takes it to heart when something like this happens. We just want to know why it was so different.

HILLARD: I guess it was the way Eckhart did it. It was very extreme, and it made it personal. The way Eckhart died brought a lot of questions with him. A person will jump off a building, I get that. I understand if someone poisons themselves. Word Deleted, I even understand if someone shoots themselves. What Eckhart did is beyond understanding.

GORDON: Before we dive into that, can we get some background of what happened. We're trying to paint the picture of what led up to the death.

HILLARD: You may want to use different wording, it's inappropriate.

GORDON: I'm sorry, I meant no disrespect. What I meant was get into Eckhart's death, we just wanted some information first.

HILLARD: It's okay, no big deal. I'm just trying to be respectful of the dead. You may have wanted to speak to Lance Corporal Witlit first. He was always around Eckhart. Those two were always clowning around and getting into trouble, two troublesome peas in a pod.

GORDON: Cpl. Witlit was our first interview last week. He did a rather good job at giving us a good solid background up until the night of Eckert's death. He was able to really give us an understanding of Eckhart's personal life.

HILLARD: Corporal? Hoo Boy, I guess they will promote anyone in the Marines now-a-days! First things first, I got out two months after Eckhart had died.

CHRIS: Got out?

HILLARD: I EAS-ed.

CHRIS: EAS? What does that mean?

HILLARD: EAS is an acronym, boy the Marines love those, anyway. EAS is end of active service. The time I owed Uncle Sam was up and I was free to do what I wanted, and I was definitely done with the Marines. I did eight years and found it just wasn't my thing. So, we broke the marriage up and I got the dog they kept the house.

GORDON: That's funny.

HILLARD: It is because I don't own a dog? I'm just kidding. A good laugh can fix a lot in this world. I'm honestly really glad that I left when I did. The crap my Battalion pulled was something I really didn't want to be part of. Second off, as far as Corporal Witlit ...that's hard to swallow. He is a real piece of Word Deleted! He always was and always will be. Where is he now? Let me guess, working for that no good Dad of his in the little crap town he came from.

GORDON: He's in Fort Leavenworth on trial for Murder, manslaughter, terrorism, and treason actually. He was a big part in Operation Vanguard.

HILLARD: I'm not surprised he's in jail...I just figured it would be for different reasons. That kid was disrespectful, sneaky, and just dumb. He played to many games, always up to something and it was never good. Did he mention the hookers in the Barracks that were dressed as maids? I'm sure he did, always gloating about that one. Witlit always said it was Eckhart's idea, but I think Witlit came up with it. No good, Witlit is no good. So, what did the dumb word deleted do anyway?

GORDON: Unfortunately, we can't discuss that.

HILLARD: That's probably a good thing because... second thought, I really don't want to know what he did to end up there. Boy, you got to screw up fairly good to end up there! Anyway, where do you actually want me to start, I'm getting sidetracked.

GORDON: Corporal Witlit left off at the night Eckhart had died, can you start there?

HILLARD: Yeah, I can do that. Where did he leave off? I can just start with that night.

GORDON: Whichever you like.

HILLARD: Let's see, I took over the duty watch that morning about zero eight. I did change over with Sergeant, ...crap! what was his name.... He's a tall fellow, black hair...that sounds like every Marine. I might have well said short hair, oh now I got it. It was Sergeant Dillan from third platoon. Good guy, always on time and never said a bad thing about anyone. He was a good Marine. So, I take over the post and Witlit is late, as always. Everything went smooth for the rest of the day, nothing to really write home about. General Matthews stopped by the barracks at one point around noon. Other than that, smooth sailing until the next morning. It was just after three in the morning when I sent Witlit to do a round. We switched off every half an hour or so. I could have made Witlit do them, but I was board and it got me walking around. Duty is very dull. Witlit comes into the guard shack and gives his report "Sergeant, Lance Corporal Witlit reports the barracks is all Secure". So, Witlit sits down and I start to write the report down in the log. I'm sure you are aware of the logs we keep while on duty.

GORDON: We are aware of them.

HILLARD: Good, then you know we write everything down with great detail. Every bit of the "who, what, where, why, when, and how's". I always took personal pride in my logs; I want them neat and detailed. Some guys handwriting looked like a chicken had a seizure when they wrote. How the word deleted am I supposed to read that, it looks like a doctor's signature. If there is important information, I want to know what it is. In turn, I want others to be able to read it too. It isn't that hard, but some people like to work harder and do things twice, I guess. Not me, keep it simple. That was LCpl. Willits issue most of the time, never took pride in what he did. Always half word deleted things, never right the first time. I hated having duty with him. It's nothing personal just couldn't stand him.

CHRIS: We saw the log; it was incredibly detailed. Here is the transcribed copy of the log entry. Can you make sure that this is the log?

HILLARD: Yup, that's it all right. You guys do your homework. I respect that. Good on you. It's good to have just in case I missed something important.

The official log entry was obtained properly through the Department of Defense. All rights and prior consent though the Supreme Court was given before its official use in the investigation.

0800	I, SGT. HILLARD, HAVE ASSUMED ALL DUTIES AND RESPONSIBILITIES OF THE DUTY NCO FOR BUILDING 2101. I HAVE IN MY POSSESSION: (1) NCO DUTY LOGBOOK, (2) DUTY BELTS, (1) NCO, (1) NON-NCO, (1) VISITORS LOGBOOK, (1) FLASHLIGHT, (2) DUTY BINDER, (1) LIBERTY LOGBOOK, (1) BARRACKS DISCIPLINARY LOGBOOK. ALL SPECIAL AND GENERAL ORDERS REMAIN THE SAME. I HAVE NOTHING TO REPORT AT THIS TIME--
0810	SGT. HILLARD ROVED THE BARRACKS, NOTHING TO REPORT AT THIS TIME--- SGT H
0844	LCPL. WITLIT ROVED THE BARRACKS, NOTHING TO REPORT AT THIS TIME--- SGT H
0903	SGT. HILLARD ROVED THE BARRACKS, NOTHING TO REPORT AT THIS TIME--- SGT H
0933	LCPL. WITLIT ROVED THE BARRACKS, NOTHING TO REPORT AT THIS TIME--- SGT H
1022	SGT. HILLARD ROVED THE BARRACKS, NOTHING TO REPORT AT THIS TIME--- SGT H
1033	OFFICER OF THE DAY, LT. HOLLINGSWORTH ON DECK. POSTED ALL REPORTS AND REPORTED ALL SECURE. NOTHING FURTHER TO REPORT--- SGT H
1051	LCPL. WITLIT ROVED THE BARRACKS, NOTHING TO REPORT AT THIS TIME--- SGT H
1119	SGT. HILLARD ROVED THE BARRACKS, NOTHING TO REPORT AT THIS TIME--- SGT H
1131	LCPL. WITLIT ROVED THE BARRACKS, NOTHING TO REPORT AT THIS TIME--- SGT H
1200	LCPL. WITLIT GOES TO CHOW-- SGT H
1205	BARRACKS MAINTENANCE ON DECK FOR BROKEN LIGHTS ON FIRST DECK: 101, 104, 109 AND 123. SECOND DECK ROOMS: 203, 207, 219, 220, AND 229. THIRD DECK ROOMS: 308, 311, 317, AND 319. FORTH DECK: 415 AND 422. -- SGT H
1207	SGT. HILLARD ROVED THE BARRACKS, NOTHING TO REPORT AT THIS TIME--- SGT H
1211	OFFICER OF THE DAY CALLS FOR INFORMATION ON LCPL. NAME DELETED--- SGT H
1230	LCPL. WITLIT RETURNS FROM CHOW. SGT HILLARD GOES TO CHOW-- SGT H
1239	LCPL. WITLIT ROVED THE BARRACKS, NOTHING TO REPORT AT THIS TIME--- SGT H
1300	SGT. HILLARD RETURNS FROM CHOW-- SGT H
1318	S-3 OPERATIONS CHIEF MASTER GUNNERY SERGEANT HALLS CHECKING BARRACKS ROOM AVAILABILITY ROSTER--- SGT H
1330	WEAPONS BATTALION FIRST SERGEANT, FIRST SERGEANT TALON ON DECK. POST REPORTED. ALL SECURE. NOTHING TO REPORT AT THIS TIME--- SGT H

1341	LCPL. WITLIT ROVED THE BARRACKS, NOTHING TO REPORT AT THIS TIME-- SGT H
1352	OFFICER OF THE DAY CALLS FOR INFORMATION ON LCPL. NAME DELETED ASKING WHEN HIS BARRACKS RESTRICTION ENDS-- SGT H
1405	SGT. HILLARD ROVED THE BARRACKS, NOTHING TO REPORT AT THIS TIME-- SGT H
1422	OFFICER OF THE DAY CALLS FOR INFORMATION ON PFC. NAME DELETED ASKING WHEN HIS BARRACKS RESTRICTION ENDS-- SGT H
1449	LCPL. WITLIT ROVED THE BARRACKS, NOTHING TO REPORT AT THIS TIME-- SGT H
1522	SGT. HILLARD ROVED THE BARRACKS, NOTHING TO REPORT AT THIS TIME-- SGT H
1528	BARRACKS MAINTENANCE OFF DECK-- SGT H
1531	LCPL. WITLIT ROVED THE BARRACKS, NOTHING TO REPORT AT THIS TIME-- SGT H
1625	SGT. HILLARD ROVED THE BARRACKS, NOTHING TO REPORT AT THIS TIME-- SGT H
1641	LCPL. WITLIT ROVED THE BARRACKS, NOTHING TO REPORT AT THIS TIME-- SGT H
1700	LCPL. WITLIT GOES TO CHOW-- SGT H
1705	SGT. HILLARD ROVED THE BARRACKS, NOTHING TO REPORT AT THIS TIME-- SGT H
1730	LCPL. WITLIT RETURNS FROM CHOW. SGT HILLARD GOES TO CHOW-- SGT H
1744	LCPL. WITLIT ROVED THE BARRACKS, NOTHING TO REPORT AT THIS TIME-- SGT H
1805	SGT. HILLARD RETURNS FROM CHOW-- SGT H
1820	SGT. HILLARD ROVED THE BARRACKS, NOTHING TO REPORT AT THIS TIME-- SGT H
1830	OFFICER OF THE DAY, LT. HOLLINGSWORTH ON DECK. POSTED ALL REPORTS AND REPORTED ALL SECURE. NOTHING FURTHER TO REPORT--- SGT H
1855	LCPL. WITLIT ROVED THE BARRACKS, NOTHING TO REPORT AT THIS TIME-- SGT H
1917	SGT. HILLARD ROVED THE BARRACKS, NOTHING TO REPORT AT THIS TIME-- SGT H
1946	LCPL. WITLIT ROVED THE BARRACKS, NOTHING TO REPORT AT THIS TIME-- SGT H
2007	SGT. HILLARD ROVED THE BARRACKS, NOTHING TO REPORT AT THIS TIME-- SGT H
2030	LCPL. WITLIT ROVED THE BARRACKS, NOTHING TO REPORT AT THIS TIME-- SGT H
2100	TAPS-- SGT H

2106	SGT. HILLARD ROVED THE BARRACKS, NOTHING TO REPORT AT THIS TIME--	SGT H
2141	LCPL. WITLIT ROVED THE BARRACKS, NOTHING TO REPORT AT THIS TIME--	SGT H
2219	SGT. HILLARD ROVED THE BARRACKS, NOTHING TO REPORT AT THIS TIME--	SGT H
2238	LCPL. WITLIT ROVED THE BARRACKS, NOTHING TO REPORT AT THIS TIME--	SGT H
2322	SGT. HILLARD ROVED THE BARRACKS, NOTHING TO REPORT AT THIS TIME--	SGT H
2340	LCPL. WITLIT ROVED THE BARRACKS, NOTHING TO REPORT AT THIS TIME--	SGT H
0005	SGT. HILLARD ROVED THE BARRACKS, NOTHING TO REPORT AT THIS TIME--	SGT H
0038	SGT. HILLARD ROVED THE BARRACKS, NOTHING TO REPORT AT THIS TIME--	SGT H
0126	LCPL. WITLIT ROVED THE BARRACKS, NOTHING TO REPORT AT THIS TIME--	SGT H
0148	LCPL. WITLIT ROVED THE BARRACKS, NOTHING TO REPORT AT THIS TIME--	SGT H
0215	SGT. HILLARD ROVED THE BARRACKS, NOTHING TO REPORT AT THIS TIME--	SGT H
0252	SGT. HILLARD ROVED THE BARRACKS, NOTHING TO REPORT AT THIS TIME--	SGT H
0317	(LATE ENTRY) TIME OF INCIDENT 0304. A SOUND WAS HEARD OUTSIDE THE BARRACKS DUTY OFFICE. I SGT. HILLARD AND LCPL. WITLIT INVESTIGATED. A MARINE WAS FOUND UNRESPONSIVE IN THE COURTYARD. THE OFFICER OF THE DAY WAS CONTACTED IMMEDIATELY AND 9-1-1 WAS CALLED. THE BARRACKS IS ON LOCKDOWN UNTIL FURTHER NOTICE PER THE OFFICER OF THE DAY. I HAVE NOTHING FURTHER TO REPORT AT THIS TIME-------------------------	SGT H
0321	9-1-1 ON DECK, OFFICER OF THE DAY ON DECK. UNRESPONSIVE MARINE HAS BEEN IDENTIFIED AS ALLEN D. ECKHART; PFC. ECKHART HAS BEEN TAKEN TO THE HOSPITAL. NOTHING FURTHER TO REPORT AT THIS TIME---	SGT H
0350	OFFICER OF THE DAY OFF DECK---	SGT H
0409	SGT. HILLARD ROVED THE BARRACKS, BARRACKS STILL ON LOCKDOWN. NOTHING TO REPORT AT THIS TIME--	SGT H
0423	OFFICER OF THE DAY CALLED TO REPORT WE ARE NO LONGER ON LOCKDOWN. I HAVE NOTHING MORE TO REPORT AT THIS TIME--	SGT H
0430	SGT. HILLARD ROVED THE BARRACKS, NOTHING TO REPORT AT THIS TIME--	SGT H
0445	LCPL. WITLIT ROVED THE BARRACKS, NOTHING TO REPORT AT THIS TIME--	SGT H

0500	CALL FROM STAFF SERGEANT ELIS FROM THE MAINTENANCE VEHICLE RAMP. SSGT. STATED THAT THE RAMP HAS BEEN BROKEN INTO. THE OFFICER OF THE DAY HAS BEEN NOTIFIED AND THE BARRACKS IS BACK ON LOCKDOWN PER THE OFFICER OF THE DAY PENDING INVESTIGATION. THE OFFICER OF THE DAY IS EN ROUTE TO THE MAINTENANCE RAMP. I HAVE NOTHING FURTHER TO REPORT AT THIS TIME. --- SGT H
0507	MP'S IS ON DECK AND SECURED THE MAINTENANCE RAMP-- SGT H
0512	LCPL. WITLIT ROVED THE BARRACKS, REPORTS THAT THE 4TH FLOOR ROOF HATCH IS UNSECURE. THE LOCK IS ALSO MISSING. THE OFFICER OF THE DAY WAS NOTIFIED VIA RADIO TRANSMISSION. I HAVE NOTHING FURTHER TO REPORT AT THIS TIME-- SGT H
0530	NCIS IS ON DECK WITH THE OFFICER OF THE DAY AND BRIGADIER GENERAL MATTHEWS. THE BARRACKS REMAINS ON LOCKDOWN. ALL MARINES ARE NOW CONFINED TO THEIR ROOMS UNTIL FURTHER NOTICE PENDING INVESTIGATION. ALL OFF BASE PERSONNEL HAVE BEEN RECALLED TO THE BARRACKS AND ARE TO MEET IN THE FIRST FLOOR COMMON AREA. --- SGT H
0530	REVEILLE-- SGT H
0533	BRIGADIER GENERAL MATTHEWS CANCELS PT FOR THE MORNING. ALL ARMORY PERSONNEL AND ARMORIES ARE TO REMAIN CLOSED UNTIL FURTHER NOTICE. ALL RANGES ARE CANCELLED UNTIL FURTHER NOTICE. SPECIAL ORDERS GIVEN PER BRIGADIER GENERAL MATTHEWS: NO VISITORS TO THE BARRACKS. NO ONE IS TO LEAVE THE BARRACKS EXCEPT FOR CHOW. ALL NON-NCO'S ARE TO MOVE IN FORMATIONS OF AT LEAST 4 MARINES AND ESCORTED TO CHOW AND BACK BY AN NCO. CHOW BREAK IS ONLY A HALF HOUR, NO LONGER. ALL MARINES LEAVING FOR CHOW MUST SIGN OUT WITH THE BARRACKS DUTY OUT OF THE LIBERTY LOG. THERE WILL BE NO MOVEMENT THROUGHOUT THE BARRACKS OR BASE-- SGT H
0544	SGT. HILLARD ROVED THE BARRACKS, NOTHING TO REPORT AT THIS TIME--- SGT H
0545	LCPL. WITLIT GOES TO CHOW-- SGT H
0604	SGT. HILLARD ROVED THE BARRACKS, ALL OFF BASE PERSONNEL ARE ACCOUNTED FOR AND IN THE BARRACKS-- SGT H
0605	LCPL. WITLIT RETURNS FROM CHOW-- SGT H
0625	FORMATION HAS BEEN CALLED PER BRIGADIER GENERAL MATTHEWS. ALL PERSONNEL ARE REQUIRED TO BE THERE AND ACCOUNTED FOR UNLESS STANDING DUTY-- SGT H

0709	SGT. HILLARD ROVED THE BARRACKS, NOTHING TO REPORT AT THIS TIME-- SGT H
0731	SGT. HILLARD ROVED THE BARRACKS, NOTHING TO REPORT AT THIS TIME-- SGT H
0745	I, SGT. HILLARD AND LCPL. WITLIT HAVE BEEN PROPERLY RELIEVED BY GUNNERY SERGEANT ZEPP'S FOR QUESTIONING BY NCIS. THIS COMPLETES MY LOG ENTRIES FOR THE DAY--- SGT H

HILLARD: So, I'm guessing you want to talk about what the log entries didn't say. What I actually saw and what the investigations turned up.

GORDON: Correct. My understanding is that Corporal Witlit didn't actually see Eckhart's body.

HILLARD: No, he didn't. I wouldn't let him. I knew they were friends and I felt it was something that he didn't need to see. I felt it was the right thing to do. Witlit seemed terribly upset when they figured out it was Eckhart.

CHRIS: How did Eckhart get Properly identified?

HILLARD: The duty officer checked his wallet. Eckert didn't have his Dog Tags on him, so he looked there. Duty Officer found his I.D. and it looked like Eckhart and determent it was in fact him. The investigators also confirmed it. I'm not sure how they did it, but we were right, it was in fact Eckhart.

GORDON: I understand you not letting Witlit see. What exactly did you see? We want the less…I'm looking for a word to describe this Chris.

CHRIS: Do you mean less uptight and professional Gordon?

HALLARD: That's two words Agent Chris…, I got what you mean. You want my words not Sgt. Hillard's words. What I felt when I saw him. I also understand why you want me to describe it. It had to be bad enough that Brigadier General Matthews took it personally.

GORDON: That's it to the point. Only if you are comfortable talking about it.

HILLARD: Its fine, I don't mind talking about it. It's something I personally dealt with a long time ago. Things like this, you just have to look at and deal with. It isn't as easy as it seems in the movies. Marines are close, he was a brother. It was simply hard on everyone. I know I'm stalling; I haven't talked about it in a long time and it isn't easy.

It was just after three in the morning. I had just finished doing my round in the Barracks. It was a slow quiet night. Not much really happened all day. The Officer of the Day was a Marine that I had Duty with a few times. Let me think of his name.

CHRIS: Lieutenant Hollingsworth

HILLARD: Yeah, that's Hollingsworth. Good Marine, probably a Major by now.

GORDON: I'm sorry to tell you this now but he was killed during Operation Vanguard.

HILLARD: Oh...That's a real shame, real shame. Like I said, good Marine, good man, I hope he died well. You probably don't know how it happened, do you? It's just a morbid curiosity, I guess.

GORDON: We don't have that information, I'm sorry. I only have the names of those alive and dead, not how. I'm sorry about that Nelson.

HILLARD: it's okay. Simply hard to wrap your mind around, I guess. I'll continue then.

GORDON: Thank you. We understand how hard it is.

HILLARD: Like I said, three in the morning. I just sat down with a cup of coffee when there was this loud crunch thud. That's the only way I can think to describing it. It was startling. I just about spilled my coffee on my lap. I look over at Witlit and he clearly had jumped too.

CHRIS: How close was the noise to where you were sitting?

HILLARD: There is one big window in the Duty Office. It sounded like it was right outside that window, and it was. It was about five or six feet from the office. We both jumped up and I asked Witlit what that sound was. Witlit said he saw something hit the ground outside the window. I told Witlit to stay in the office while I go and have a look. As soon as I stepped out of the door, there was Eckhart's body. It was bad, really bad. I couldn't tell who it was at first.

GORDON: How far did Eckhart fall?

HILLARD: At the time, I had no idea. Our barracks is four decks or floors high. The gangways are open like a California motel. He could have jumped from any of those levels.

GORDON What do you mean by California motel?

HILLARD: A walkway goes around every floor. The walkways are on the outside of the building. Not on the inside. Hotels have the rooms facing each other on the inside. These rooms face outward onto a landing or gangway, as we call them. We always called them California styles, not sure why. Do you get it anyway?

GORDON: I get it now. I see what you are saying. Please continue.

HILLARD: Thankfully, Eckhart had landed in the grass; he missed the concrete. I guess it really doesn't matter now that I think about it. It looked bad enough anyway, the concrete would have been much worse. So, Eckhart was lying on his back with his face in the grass in a massive pool of blood. His right arm was broken and under him. His left leg was at a strange angle from his body, which was a compound fracture. The bone was clearly sticking out of his thigh. He had a strange white rope wrapped around his neck with a strange metal buckle on the end.

The rope was surprisingly clean and new looking but clearly had been used before. I saw what seemed like a fizzy white substance coming from his mouth. That stuff was mixing with blood that was around him. His nose was flattened as well. There was a dent in his head. I can only guess that the buckle hit Eckhart when he landed.

GORDON: Wait. That doesn't make sense. You said Eckhart was lying on his back and then you said face down? Which is it?

HILLARD: You think I misworded myself. I didn't. He was on his back with his face in the grass. His face was facing down because his head was backwards. You know, the wrong way.

CHRIS: That's crazy. You mentioned the metal buckle. What was it?

HILLARD: At the time I didn't recognize the metal buckle. Later I saw it was a "Daisy release", I'll explain when I'm done if that's okay?

GORDON: That's fine. Tell us as you like.

HILLARD: I have to tell you about the foam in Eckhart's mouth. There was a strong odor coming from it and like I said before, it fizzed. I noticed it was now smoking as it touched the grass.

GORDON: What kind of smell?

HILLARD: Like this rotten egg smell, it was bad. I see burns all around Eckhart's mouth and lips and blistering. Whatever the foam touched; it was burning. The blistering was strange too. The Blisters were black. Not any burn that I've ever seen.

CHRIS: That's horrible.

HILLARD: You're telling me, I saw it. By the way, I later found out from the maintenance guys that a daisy release is a test release tool. There is a gauge on the female end. You turn that gauge to a certain weight and when the weight gets to that point. The daisy releases. It's for the boom on their wrecker vehicle. It's just a stupid name but an effective tool.

CHRIS: You said something about the rope looked different and really white? Like it was new maybe?

HILLARD: The maintenance guys told me about that too. It's some special rope called non-slip run rope, want to guess why?

GORDON: I'm guessing because it doesn't snag or bunch up.

HILLARD: Real college types come up with these names if you couldn't tell. It took me a minute to figure the whole thing out at first too. The rope was used to break Eckhart's neck, obviously. I remembered that his ankles were broken too. I wasn't too surprised. Even a fall from the second floor isn't a good fall. I guess there isn't any good fall, but I think you get my point.

GORDON: Do you think it was from the second floor?

HILLARD: I'm definitely not an expert in falls or forensics but his legs were bad. He lived on the third floor. At the time, that would have been my best guess. We found out later that it was from the roof top.

CHRIS: What about the foam and the smell.

HILLARD: I later found out from our NBC guys what that was all about.

GORDON: NBC? I'm assuming it's not television related.

HILLARD: It's an acronym for Nuclear, Biological and Chemical. They loved calling themselves the "chem' reapers". They knew right away what the foam was. They said Eckhart must have swallowed drain cleaner. It's basically, sulfuric acid. The smell is something added by the companies to help people stay safe from it. It makes you aware of it. It works too!

CHRIS: Drain cleaner!

HILLARD: Drain Cleaner. This suicide was not a cry for help or an "attempted". Eckhart meant to die and clearly didn't want to screw it up. It's sad to say that but it's the honest truth. No one likes to admit such things out loud or to themselves. But this boy wanted to die. This wasn't using a dull knife to make small marks on his arms or small razor cuts. As I said, Eckhart wanted to die! That's clear as water! I mean, think about it. You break several laws and if caught? The Brig is and expected thing. Eckhart first commits breaking and entering and theft at the maintenance ramp. Goes back to the barracks and breaks the lock to the roof. Then there is the act itself. Ties one end of the Daisy to a strong pipe, the investigators found his fingerprints on several different pipes and fixtures on that roof. Eckhart was clearly looking around for the right load bearing pipe. So, Eckhart attaches the rope to the Daisy and makes an eight loop hangman's noose. Eckhart must have roughly decided where to set the Daisy release to his own weight on the gauge. He set the length of the rope and Daisy for the second story. And by the way, making a noose with that kind of rope, it isn't easy. I tried myself just to see. It's hard to get the rope to want to stay long enough to get the knot. So anyway, Eckhart puts the noose around his neck, and then drinks a crap ton of drain cleaner. It was at least twelve ounce bottle.

We later found the bottle on the roof. Then Eckhart simply, walked off the roof. Eckhart didn't scream or yell. He just silently fell to his death. Eckhart made sure he wouldn't live. If the broken neck didn't get um' the fall would. If the fall didn't get um' the drain cleaner did. It was scary efficient, and he was clearly committed to his own death. It really gives you chills when you sit and think about it. Let me tell you, there were many nights I thought about it. I thought about the sound he made a lot in these past years; you don't forget it.

When we found him, I made sure no one touched him. I assumed it to be a crime scene. I also knew that we, the Battalion were going to pay for this. I knew Brigadier General Matthews would chew us out. I heard General Matthews chewing the platoon sergeant out later that morning. General Matthews later reamed all the Corporals and Sergeants out too. We got off easy compared to the platoon sergeant.

GORDON: That was Staff Sergeant Grey, right?

HILLARD: By sheer luck or bad chance, Grey was also the Officer of the Day that coming morning. He got screamed at for an hour! I often felt for Grey, he had such a crap job, and it wasn't even the job he signed up for.

GORDON: He didn't sign up for, what do you mean?

HILLARD: The command makes you a Platoon Sergeant. It's just a roll that has to be filled. You basically are in charge of the platoon. You hand out mail to the platoon. You make sure we get to dentist and doctor appointments. You are like a mother, it sucks! He has to work in the main building with all the paper pushers. He can't win. He handled it all, including the situation that morning. I'll give him that.

CHRIS: You said the Officer of the Day was Lieutenant Hollingsworth the night of the incident. How did he do that night?

HILLARD: He did a great job. He was pretty new to the Battalion. He had only been there a few months before all this happened. As soon as I told him what happened to Eckhart, he was all over it. He called 9-1-1 and told me to wait for further instruction. He gets to the barracks within a few minutes and already has surgical gloves in hand. Hollingsworth had two pairs of gloves to be exact, one for me and him. We pat down Eckhart and find his wallet and his I.D. in his pocket. Hollingsworth then goes straight back to work, getting things done. Hollingsworth bags up the stuff he found on Eckhart and gives me an order to not let anyone touch Eckhart which I already was doing. Hollingsworth runs back to the battalion building. He actually ran too. He gets everybody and their mothers to the barracks in a flash. He was organized! He made the call to lock the barracks down as well. He had me and Witlit do a head count too. We had Eckhart's I.D. but the head count confirmed it was him.

GORDON: How did you check that?

HILLARD: I woke everyone up that wasn't already awake and counted Marines. Eckhart's room was empty aside from his note. Eckhart also wasn't signed out of the liberty log. Either it was him lying out in the courtyard or he went AWOL. About that time, is when they took Eckhart's body to the hospital. I can't really figure out why. I mean, he was definitely dead. I really think that the ambulance crew was in a state of shock too. Eckhart was really hard to look at. What a joke, he didn't need an ambulance, he needed a priest! Word Deleted Word Deleted head was on backwards! He was definitely dead!

I know the human body can take a lot; I've seen my fair share of combat. But I've never seen anything like Eckhart. Witlit may have seen them take Eckhart away. I'm not sure. I don't think he saw any of it.

GORDON: I saw in the log that the Naval Criminal Investigations Services interviewed you both as well as the Provost Marshals office. How did that go?

HILLARD: It was the same twenty questions asked thirty different ways. They took Witlit and me to the battalion building and put us in two separate offices to get our statements. I was in the S-1 Chiefs office and Witlit in the Sergeant Majors office. We both finished up about the same time. This was the first of three interviews. When Witlit comes out of the office, Witlit just looks at me and throws up. I can't blame him, that's a crap night. A bad night of post and he lost a friend. That's a bad day in anyone's book. It seems stupid now, but I asked him if he was alright. Man, what a dumb thing to say. Of course, he's not okay. I just didn't know what else to say. What can you say? I felt like such an idiot for saying that. First Sergeant Talon takes the cake. He actually glares at Witlit and tells him to clean up his mess because Witlit has to get ready to be interviewed again. I couldn't stand Talon. After Witlit goes for the second interview I finally get the time to finish my logs and Talon rolls out to the main building. He later calls and says were off lock down. That night really sucked.

CHRIS: How did they find out about the vehicle ramp being broken into?

HILLARD: Staff Sergeant Elis's noticed something was wrong first at the ramp. Eckhart wasn't stupid. I found out later from Elis's that Eckhart disconnected the sound system connected to the alarm. The alarm was inside the building so it couldn't be disabled from outside. So, Eckhart had to have disabled it while at work. An alarm should have sounded at the Battalion Duty office too, Eckhart disconnected that as well. No way all that work could have been done that night. That siren is stupid loud; you can hear it for miles. So, it must have taken Eckhart a few days to do all of this work. But he did it.

GORDON: Then how did Elis's notice it.

HILLARD: Oh yeah, right. The barracks and the vehicle lot aren't really close. The sound to the alarm was cut but Eckhart couldn't disable the red light outside the maintenance building. When the alarm is tripped, that red light blinks. It's not very bright but Elis saw it. Elis told me that he was going to use the head.

CHRIS: Head?

HILLARD: Bathroom, sorry. Old Marine Corp habits are hard to break. Elis said he saw a blinking red light because he wanted to see what it looked like outside after going to the bathroom. Elis doesn't like running in the rain. Elis is one of the Maintenance Chiefs, so he got dressed and walked over to look. Elis had noticed the light flashing with no noise. That thing is loud enough to wake the dead, as I said.

GORDON: I'm guessing you couldn't see the lights from the office.

HILLARD: No, not at all. So, Elis uses the phone that's mounted outside the fence. It's used for emergencies. Elis calls the Barracks Duty which is me. When he hangs up with me, calls the Officer of the Day.

CHRIS: You said the Maintenance area was broken into?

HILLARD: Elis said the lock on the gate was broken or cut.

GORDON: Did he see anything inside.

HILLARD: Elis said he wasn't going inside until the MP's arrived. The armory is part of the ramp, it's on the backside. He clearly was worried about the armory being broken into. I would be. Eckhart didn't touch the armory, I'm grateful for that.

GORDON: How about the roof door?

HILLARD: It was just after five in the morning, Witlit was doing a round. Witlit said that he felt air on him as he walked up the stairwell to the fourth floor. The stairs are inside the building going up the center of the barracks. The stairs lead out to the gangways. Right in front of you is the common area. The stairs also divide the barracks into two pieces, a left wing, and a right. Witlit went to the common area to see if a window was left open. The common area door was wide open at the time, so he closed it. Witlit walks out of the common area and still feels the breeze. Next to the stairs is a steel ladder that heads to the roof. Witlit sees the hatch at the top of the ladder is open and that's where the air is coming from. Witlit also noticed the lock was missing. Witlit climbs the ladder to see what's going on. Witlit said he didn't see anything on the roof. Witlit didn't actually walk out on the roof. I wouldn't have either honestly.

CHRIS: Why wouldn't you have gone out on the roof?

HILLARD: No reason too. It's a flat roof with an AC unit on top. Nothing really to see, if someone were up there, you would clearly see someone. So Witlit secured the hatch and reported it to me. I felt it was pretty obvious that Eckhart had used the hatch. It never occurred to Witlit. I think he was still in shock.

GORDON: Is that door always open?

HILLARD: No, it should be locked as I said.

GORDON: Should be? Why wasn't it? I mean other than Eckhart of course.

HILLARD: I have a suspicion that the Marines knew that hatch was open because they probably smoked up there and most likely drank up there too. I think that's why Witlit never thought twice about Eckhart jumping from there. I believe it being open was common. It may have occurred to Witlit later felt that he should say something to cover his own butt. I call Hollingsworth, again and told him about the hatch, which at the time everyone thought was unrelated. Hollingsworth tells me that he's going to the vehicle lot and will update me when he returns. Hollingsworth confirms to me later that the locks had been cut to both the building and the fence. He said the maintenance shops were good, but the tool room was broken into. That's really all I know about that.

GORDON: I understand. You didn't see the ramp so you can't tell us what you didn't see for yourself. Like we said, we understand.

HILLARD: The whole thing bothered me for weeks. I was really glad I was getting out by this point. I had a plan when I got out and this whole situation just put it on hold. I thought about it a lot. Not how I really envisioned ending my time in the Marines. That's not a way to leave. I felt guilty for leaving, I still do. You never leave someone behind when they need help. I didn't like Witlit, but it doesn't mean I wouldn't fight beside him or do my best to help him. At the time, I thought I was doing what's best for me.

CHRIS: In my opinion, you did your best.

HILLARD: I appreciate that, it's just a hard pill to swallow. It was then and still is today, I felt selfish.

GORDON: If you don't mind me asking, what bothered you aside from the obvious of what you saw.

HILLARD: It was what I saw and how it hurt Witlit. At the same time how Witlit did just not seem to care either. It's hard to explain, I've done my time in combat, but a man's head turned around will chill you to the core. You could see the individual bones in the neck that were broke because the neck was pulled so long. The skin was tight and lose at the same time. I'm surprised his head didn't pop off like a dandelion. His neck had to easily be twice its normal length. His face was smashed pretty well too. I'm not sure if his face hit the ground first or not. The eyes were hard to look at. Eckhart was just staring down at the grass, wide eyed. His mouth was open with that crap coming out mixed with blood. Just blankly staring at the grass was unnerving. It looked like he was yelling in silence, not screaming like you would expect. He looked angry. It was really scary. His eyes were filled with such hatred yet blank. I've seen that look before. When you catch an enemy soldier, they give you that look. It's this look of blank distain and loathing, like your scum. You get this feeling like a lawyer or the taxman is more welcome than you. I realize I'm repeating myself but it's just that it's burned into me, it's part of me. I wish I could let it go. Eckhart had these bruises all over him too. They started turning purple and dark. That didn't help the effect at all.

CHRIS: That sounds just horrible. I keep repeating that, but I don't know what else to say.

HILLARD: It was that foam was coming out of his mouth, nose and even a little out of the eyes. His legs were mangled. Eckhart's legs were at a strange angle beside him. His foot was near his ear, that's the leg with the compound fracture. It was just bad, like a car wreck.

GORDON: You said Eckhart had a note?

HILLARD: He did, Eckhart taped it to the inside of his door.

GORDON: Do you remember anything that it said.

HILLARD: I remember more than a bit; I remember the whole thing. It was short and made its point. It said, "Today I leave a loveless world precisely where it belongs, behind me". That's all it said. It had nothing else but that. No reason or rhyme why. Eckhart didn't even sign it. That note was the reason Witlit and I had been interviewed so much. Not to sound dramatic but the MP's suspected foul play. Sounds like a bad novel, but it was true. NCIS went through every room and spoke to every Marine in that barracks. I was later told that NCIS thought it was a hostage or kidnapping thing gone wrong. What a stupid idea, why hang the guy you would kidnap. That never made any sense to me. I also understand that NCIS thought it might have been over money and gambling. Again, stupid theory, Eckhart didn't gamble, and he didn't owe anyone. Most of that investigation was a waste of time. Eckhart's fingerprints were everywhere. The note he left was definitely his handwriting.

CHRIS: Why do you think that?

HILLARD: His handwriting was just too neat. Everyone else in the barracks should have been doctors by the way they wrote. Well, doctors can spell... I hope. Maybe that's why medications have crazy names. Sorry, I got off subject.

CHRIS: Is there anything else you can think of?

HILLARD: Unfortunately, no. That's all I really know that could be useful for the information you want. There is one person you may want to talk to. Find Captain Bryant Tessle. He was Brigadier General Matthews scribe. Tessle followed Mathews around as a personal security. He may be able to get all of Matthews's formation notes. He might even have them from that morning. If you can find Tessle, you can hear everything Matthews had to say. That's about the best I can do for you guys.

GORDON: Thank you for your time Nelson.

HILLARD: Not a problem. I just hope you find what you're looking for. Tessle is your guy, he is the one to talk to, and I guarantee it. Good luck.

GORDON: This is Special Agent Sean Gordon. The time is 1:25 P.M.in Lindstrom Minnesota. We have just finished interviewing Sergeant Nelson Deckard Hillard. Case file: 31008539-A, Operation Vanguard or "The Matthews Incident".

This formally concludes the Interview with Sgt. Hillard. No further entries were made on this date or for this part of the interview.

*Clipping from the Minnesota Harrold.

Nelson D. Hillard

Nelson Deckard Hillard, 32, of Lindstrom, Minnesota chose to end his own life on Monday July 17th at his home.

He was born September 14th, 1996, in Lindstrom, Minnesota, Son of Jenna and Deckard Hillard; he was the older of two siblings. He was never married.

He graduated from Chisago Lakes Senior High school in 2014 and joined the United States Marine Corps in August of the following year.

He served honorably in the Marine Corp as an infantryman. After his discharge from the Marines, he worked for Ironsides Metalwork's as a Blacksmith's apprentice and horse farrier. He volunteered at PFC Floyd K. Lindstrom's Department of Veterans Affairs. He was a volunteer at the Marine Corp ROTC and enjoyed running with the kids and marching.

His personal passions were fishing and hunting. During fishing season, he could be seen out at Leap's Pond. The local kids called him "Big Bear" because of his strong voice and personality. He was always smiling and pleasant to be around. He always had jokes to raise your spirits.

A service will be held on Monday, July 24th at Barlow's funeral home on 3rd street, Lindstrom, Minnesota. It will be a closed casket ceremony; open to the community to attend. He will be buried with military honors at Fairview Cemetery.

"Find what gives you that fire in your soul and don't let anyone throw water on it. Spread that fire of life with everyone before you burn out"-Nelson Hillard

Interview of Captain Bryant Justin Tessle

Friday, July 21st, 2028
United States Disciplinary Barracks (USDB)
Fort Leavenworth, Kansas

WANTED
BY F.B.I.
Status: Captured

F.B.I. No. 188883
WANTED FOR: TERRORISM/TREASON

Bryant Justin Tessle
ALIAS: TANGO 3 ACTUAL

Description

AGE:	35	SCARS OR MARKS:	NONE
HEIGHT:	5'10"	EYES:	BROWN
WEIGHT:	149 LBS	COMPLEXION:	MEDIUM
BUILD:	MEDIUM	RACE:	CAUCCASION
HAIR:	BROWN	NATIONALITY:	AMERICAN
OCCUPATION:	MILITARY	FINGERPRINTS:	ON FILE
		CLASSIFICATION:	FELONY LEVEL 1

CAUTION

Current status is captured and beheld by
the Department of Correction.

**IF YOU HAVE ANY INFORMATION CONCERNING THIS PERSON
PLEASE CONTACT YOUR LOCAL F.B.I. OFFICE IMMEDIATELY**

*This recorded session is called to order by the head of the
Federal Bureau of Investigations, Special Investigations Unit.*

GORDON: Its 9:47 A.M. in the United States Disciplinary Barracks,
Fort Leavenworth Kansas, Maximum Security Wing,
Block 5. Seated next to me is Special Agent William
Chris. Across from us, at the interview table is Captain

Bryant Justin Tessle, Former Administrative clerk, Personal Assistant, and Records Officer to Brigadier General Matthew's: Case file 31008539-A, Operation Vanguard or "The Matthews Incident". Capt. Tessle is 35 years of age, is 5'10", weight is 149 Lbs. He is of slender build, brown hair, has no discernable marks or scars, has blue eyes, and a light complexion. He is Caucasian and an American. His fingerprints are on file and classification code 1 for the following: several counts of involuntary manslaughter. He is also accused of treason and conspiracy of treason, terrorism and is considered a traitor of the United States of America. He is currently awaiting Court Martial.

Key testimony involving the Death of Private First Class Allen Eckhart and the months leading up to his death. Captain Tessle is at this time at liberty to speak about Brigadier General Mathews and operation Vanguard by the Supreme Court and not under a gag order.

TESSLE: First off, I'm Court ordered to sit here. I didn't want to do this. I'm sick of the interviews and sick of the photos. I'm tired of being looked at like I'm a monster or and animal in a cage. I want to make this truly clear! Even though you have been provided with all my previous notes from the Battalion, it doesn't mean I want to cooperate with you. You have assumed way too much about me and my willingness to work with you. I don't have too! If I can't leave, we could easily just sit here and stare at each other for the next hour. I didn't kill anyone and yet here I sit, rotting away!

GORDON: It's true, you don't have to help. However, if you do, we will also help you. Remember that any help you provide us will encourage the judge to be lenient on your case and sentencing. We understand that your alleged crimes were not as severe, but you were still implicated and active in Vanguard. Be aware that this interview is a case study or historical fact, not a witness prosecution. That has no bearing on our motives for questioning. We just want to know what Matthews said to your division after Private First Class Eckhart took his own life. We also hope that we may speak to you further if necessary.

TESSLE: I understand what you're saying. Don't take this the wrong way, but I don't trust you. I'll help if you put what you just said about the judge in writing. I want it all. I'm not saying another word unless I have a JAG officer present.

CHRIS: Here you are Captain. This is a copy of the agreement already disclosed and prepared by Supreme Court judge Milton. As you see, it is signed by Judge Milton, Special Agent Gordons and myself, it is notarized. No lies, no small print. It's all in black and white.

TESSLE: This changes everything gentlemen. Why, it looks like we have a deal then? You will of course provide me with a copy in hand.

CHRIS: Already done and here.

TESSLE: Perfect, thank you.

GORDON: Can we begin?

TESSLE: Whenever you like.

GORDON: That's good to hear. I will start then.

TESSLE: Please do, ask away.

GORDON: What affiliation did you have to Brigadier General Matthews?

TESSLE: I was Gen. Matthew's Scribe.

CHRIS: What exactly is that a scribe?

TESSLE: It's an administrative assistant. It's a desk clerk of sorts. I kept files and information up to date and made appointments for Gen. Matthew's. I kept records, took notes, simply basic administrative things.

GORDON: We were under the impression that you kept all the records of the formations and all the briefings that Brigadier General Matthews gave too. Is that true?

TESSLE: That is true.

GORDON: How were these records taken and kept. Why were those kinds of records kept?

TESSLE: Approximately a year before all this started. The Marine Corp felt that it was a good idea to keep audio and physical copies of all special announcements, meetings, and briefings. My understanding was there was a need for more disseminated information. That information became a giant web called AMMID. AMMID stands for "All Mobile Military Information Directory". It helped to keep everyone on the same page. A commander has a certain question that pertains to their unit. They can look it up to see if others did too. They can access the master directory. Within the directory you can look up notes from other units and all sorts of unit information. It had a lot of useful functions. You could look any information up that any unit entered. The only downside is that someone has to take the notes and keep the records. That's where I came in. I became a records keeper. I and others like me followed unit commanders, battalion commanders and leaders around all the time, keeping notes of everything they did.

GORDON: That makes sense. How did you do it exactly?

TESSLE: It was easy actually. The Marine Corp made my position a fillable admin position, just like most officer positions. You get issued to a unit, when you are promoted, you hand the job off to someone else. It all started with the issuing of small digital recorder. All the formations and meetings are then recorded and every day. Then transferred into a file on our computer or HADA. HADA is the "Hard Admin Data Analysis". The file was already pre-typed from the recorder and transferred easily to the computer. We just had to go through the notes that were entered and check the accuracy of what was said. The recorder would mistranslate some words so we would go back and fix them. Cat may sound like hat, little things of that nature. The process wasn't too bad, but it could be long work if something were messed up.

GORDON: As you know, we brought the files with us. They were copied from the originals. We want you to check the authenticity of the transcripts and ensure they are right.

TESSLE: I can do that. You said that you wanted to start with the morning that Private First Class Eckhart died?

GORDON: We ask that you read and review the records and explain any questions that may arise as you read. The reason is that the Supreme Court has given permission for you to review the file, we are not allowed to read them. Agent Chris and I do not have the clearance from the Department of Defense to access such information. However, you can read the documents to us. You may begin when you're ready. We wanted to start with the Eckhart's briefing.

TESSLE: You can't look at them?

CHRIS: No, we cannot.

GORDON: Please continue with the briefing.

TESSLE: Briefing, oh it was a briefing alright. Well, Matthews calls the Division to the parade deck, our football field. He brings us to attention and makes us stand there for a few moments in silence as Matthew's gets his thoughts together. He finally begins to speak; it's with both verbal guns a blazing. He really dug into us.

"Ladies, Gentlemen…Marines. Today was an unacceptable day and it hasn't truly even started yet. One of our own took his life. One of our brothers in arms, a comrade to us all is gone. To me, he is truly absent without leave. His post stands abandoned, and someone had to know it was going to happen. Someone had to share his life. A Marine doesn't just snuff his life out. As I said, someone knew how he was doing and saw the warning signs of what he was going to do. We have a responsibility to the future of this nation and to each other. We do not let one and another down. You let him down, we let him down. We let his family down by not taking care of him and looking after the Marine. It is a failure, and this failure is unacceptable and will never happen again on my watch. We have tarnished our Honor and have shown that we lack courage and give no commitment to each other. A Marine doesn't simply quit his post when things are hard. The honorable thing would be to stick it out and push through the problem. Private First Class Eckhart lacked the courage. He had a fear that he simply couldn't stand up too; we are trained better than that. We are made in fire that forged us harder than his weakness. He simply took the easy way out of his commitments and left us behind.

It truly sickens me to see how we, Americans have fallen. So low have we gone that we will never see our way to the top again. We have no further to fall for we are truly grounded. The wings of the Eagle are broken. And why is it this way, why is this nation so weak? It starts within the family. The family is destroyed! Eckhart's family is just one of the broken types of family in this nation that I see on a daily basis in the news. But Eckhart isn't the average. Let's take a minute and talk about the average, shall we.

A common boy is brought into this world by a couple who didn't care for him or have the needed respect for life. Truthfully, it's amazing he was born to begin with and not aborted. We will call this child "little Joey". For a simple five hundred dollars, you can make sure Little Joey is just a bad memory. That's it, five hundred dollars. Just simply hit the delete button on a life and use your poor judgment and Little Joey never happened. Society screams that it's a "mother's body", but the mother isn't the one that dies for that small amount of money. But according to society, it's not the mother's fault that she makes poor decisions. It's somehow the rich or someone else that she can blame, never their own poor decision making. So Little Joey is now raised by the mother because the father is absent. Of course, providing the mother could afford the abortion. The mother is left to raise Little Joey because the father can't get his Word Deleted straight. It of course isn't the father's fault that he does drugs, it isn't the father's fault that he drinks, and it isn't the father's fault that he sees other women. Somehow society has said that this kind of lifestyle is now acceptable. Look at marriage. That has become a royal joke, hasn't it? You just haven't lived unless you have had three marriages under your belt these days. The average marriage last only six months, anyway, so why not make them disposable. The days of thirty or forty year anniversaries are gone. You're lucky to see a second anniversary. But again, society said this is okay and acceptable. Who needs structure anyway? Let those of chaotic, childish lifestyle raise an unwanted child. I can't imagine what's wrong with this, please excuse the sarcasm. It's hard to take things seriously when the problem is noticeably clear but being ignored. Now Little Joey isn't a baby anymore but a little kid. He is raised in a household that has multiple other siblings that all have separate fathers. The mother is always bringing a new boyfriend home every month or two, they are disposable. Of course, these disposable fathers treat Little Joey like trash. They beat him and just abuse him. It doesn't go much better for the mother. She is just as physically and emotionally abused as Little Joey. This continues for years. More children for the mother, more siblings for Little Joey and the daily abuse. After time passes, Little Joey is now a teen. If he hasn't been shot or over dosed on drugs first. Little Joey most likely sells drugs or will in the future. He then will also most likely shoot someone or be related in gang activity. This is the next generation, the youth of our nation. Remember it's not Little Joeys fault for Little Joeys poor decisions, this is our future. By this time Little Joey is fifteen and hasn't been to school in years. This of course isn't Little Joeys fault or his mothers. Joey and his mom believe that they are held back by individuals they have never met, a continued taught ideology almost as strong as a religion. Little Joey can't understand the idea that it's his fault he lives a street life. Not this fictitious millionaire. By now Little Joey gets a girl pregnant and the cycle starts anew. Which again isn't Little Joey's fault but someone else, nothing is his fault; so sayeth society. And society has convinced him that it will never be his fault.

And who is paying for all of this? We pay, we all do except those like Joey. They don't know what work is, so they suck off of us. They leach off us, bleeding us dry as we break our backs to survive. Work... they think selling drugs is work. Little Joey things steeling is work. He thinks home invasions are work. Little Joey thinks robbery is just a way of life. Society has set this standard. It is seen as the norm, and nothing is being done about it. It's just a loop that never ends, it's an ouroboros.

Little Joey is a discharge on the system, a permanent stain. The stain we turn a blind eye to and ignore. So are the women Joey is with and all of Joey's friends. Feeding off the backs of others that work hard. So, what's the next step, well, Joey will get a gun and will most likely get a gun charge or murder charge. It wouldn't be surprising if it were a robbery charge, as I previously stated. Now Joey goes to jail. Yes, jail, that place that normal people can't even imagine ending up in, but not this teen. Let's be honest with our selves, Little Joey is a young man now. Jail is a rite of passage and is "just part of life". That's the twisted mindset that the family has gotten too. For Little Joey it's just "time", he flitters it away. Joey sits and enjoys his free cable and eats his free meal while slurping off of us again. Little Joey never gives a second thought of why he's there. All the while, what really goes through Little Joeys head? He thinks that if his victim were only caring more money, Joey wouldn't have gotten mad and shot that a-hole. Of course, it's the victims' fault Joey's in jail. It's never Little Joeys fault because society has said that he is "a good boy and would never hurt anyone". The news spreads this lie to feed those fat, stupid minds that watch just for more ratings. The news never once considers the damage it causes by bending the truth. Society eats up the lies and believes the lies. A few sports figures that want attention get their faces on the news or internet and bring the people to a boiling point, meanwhile never telling the "whole story". We let nobody tell us what to think, we let sports stars tell us politics and actors tell us morality; like it's the new religion. Society eats the lies and is happy for it.

Of course, this young man is a constant problem in jail. That's something never said in the news. He feels that it's the cop's fault for arresting him and how the correctional staff has it out for him. It all has nothing to do with Little Joey's poor attitude, which isn't his fault of course. Joey will eventually strike one of the staff at the prison because Joey shouldn't have to listen to authority. Little Joey has also been told by society that he shouldn't have to be subjected to others telling him what to do. Little Joey will repeat the same old line of "he's a grown Word Deleted man", yet he makes childish decisions. Little Joey doesn't care that the staff member was doing their job properly or that the staff member has a family. It's not Joey's fault he's in jail. Now Joey is doing more time in jail because of assault on staff, yet society says he was never wrong, and the prison was "out of line" with him.

Why did things swing out of control like this? Its personal responsibility, Little Joey has failed to accept the faults that he has placed in front of himself. Joey will always blame someone else for his own shortcomings. He wants to blame a societal idea that one group of people has had it out for him his whole life, and he calls them racist or bigots. Little Joey blames the rich for his problems or blames people that got out of the bad situation because he can't. Little Joey calls the ones that get out of the vicious circle, sell outs because they live well now. Little Joey has no respect for himself or others because he doesn't know what respect really is. Joey thinks respect is at the end of a gun. Joey also thinks he can say what he likes, and no one cans speak to him that same way. The endless hypocrisy of his lifestyle…

People like Joey do nothing but leach and take. They use the welfare system as constant source of income, never attempting to find employment. Why do they live like this? Because again, they don't want to work and it's not their fault. Imagine if they were drug tested for government programs, more than half would be out; guaranteed. But somehow, expecting people who use government assistance to be clean is considered unfair. Society says *that the illegal use of drugs is okay when you want government help. It's just blatant acceptance by society to break laws.*

I know exactly what you are thinking. This is a racist rant or comments…it's not. The abuses cover every race. The abuses cover every gender. The abuses cover every creed. Truth is, I hate saying race, we are American's, and your race doesn't matter. It doesn't need to be used as a crutch because it does not define you. The person that you are defines you. Little Joey is only limited by the work he is willing to put in life. Our decisions determine the people we are, and the people we become. The people we surround ourselves with, is a mirror of who we really are.

And again, you think, Eckhart doesn't fit into all of this. Oh, but he does. His father didn't care about him. Eckhart's father cared about his fortune, his profit gain. Because Eckhart came from money doesn't mean all his problems simply drift away or just don't happen. The problems still do happen. Eckhart's father belongs to the new order of things. Money made hand over fist. His company makes a bottle of pills for twelve cent and turns around and sells that bottle for four dollars a pill! That's the new order, capitalism; the new god, capitalism. Again, there is no morality or moral fiber in the home. It's certainly not taught in the home by the family and practiced in adult life. But, because Eckhart's family was rich, it's all their fault. It's easy to blame the rich. Greed, wealth, power, gold, and stocks, that's what drives this country anymore, and we except it. Society accepts it.

So, what happens to the adult Little Joey? Now after a long time spent in prison, does Joey reform, or fall back to his old ways. Let's just assume for the moment that he tried to better himself and has learned the lesson that society wanted him to learn. Where will he work? He is a felon with a fifth grade education. He can try and find a way but most likely he will blame some fictitious figure that is holding him down. Joey can try to go back to his friends, but they now see him as a "sellout" for trying to do better. So, he ends up in the cycle again because others still believe the lie that Joey tried to walk away from.

The immoral cesspool of depravity festers simply in the minds of the lies this country tells itself. We have the best public schools, best teachers, best military, best colleges, and universities… again, all lies. Then you have the other side of the story that says we are nothing but filth, terrible public schools, terrible teachers, terrible military, and terrible colleges. So, which is it? It's neither! It's all terrible people! Eckhart was just an example. He was weak! He had a weak mind and a weak back! He was so weak that he took his own life because he couldn't find the attention that he wanted. Did I know him personally, no! But I've seen his type and know them. "Mine eyes have seen", I have seen that we need a cleansing, ratification, a revelation!

Lastly Marines, society does not owe you anything, you owe it to yourself. When you do wrong, it is your fault. You just can't blame someone you think you know. You can't expect others to pull your weight. I also will not pay for the transgressions of my forefathers and their short comings."

Matthews then right faced us and then ran us for six miles. That was his way. That's how he was.

GORDON: That is intense! He really had a lot to say.

TESSLE: Very intense. But like you said, that is how he was. He led like that. Worst part of it was, he lived by example. He was never a hypocrite. This happened every time he read something or saw something on the television. He had strong convictions. He felt that the world was sick, and it needed a cure. Somehow, I guess Matthews felt he was helping by vocalizing his opinions. I agreed with some of the things he said, not all. We are all entitled to our own opinions. They are neither right nor wrong. We are all allowed to have them.

CHRIS: How often did this happen?

TESSLE: At least once a week, sometimes more. He would run the crap out of us afterwards. Like Matthew's was going to run the problems of the world away. I have never cared for running, but it was too much sometimes.

GORDON: How did the Marines feel about all of what Matthews said?

TESSLE: The Marines ate it up! They loved his lessons. That's what Matthews called them, lessons. He commonly referred to the time of the formations as "Educational Training", like a priest and the flock. The truth is, the higher in the ranks you go, the more time you get to speak your opinions.

GORDON: How did you personally feel about his talks?

TESSLE: Matthews was an amazing speaker; he was full of life and commanded authority. Matthews would grab your attention and hold it.

CHRIS: Were all his talks about current affairs?

TESSLE: No, sometimes Matthews would call out a Marine that may not have been pulling his own weight or was not functioning correctly in the social hierarchy of the Marines. There the Marine would stand in front of thousands of Marines and get verbally decimated. Matthews didn't do it to every crappy Marine, just a few here and there. But when Matthews gave it to you, you got it. He would break you down shotgun style. He could see your weakness and throw it verbally in your own face. Matthews just had this way of looking into the person you were. He could just read people. We had this one Marine, Witlit that got a DUI. Matthews had us in formation as he called this Marine worthless, irresponsible, and barely fit to be called a Marine. This is a few weeks before Eckhart had died. Later Mathew's had that Marine call his dad and tell his dad how he failed his fellow Marines. The Marine was actually made to verbally prostrate himself to his own father. That's embarrassment, that's punishment. Matthews then had the Marines tell his father how much he failed him and his family. Matthews went so far that he made the Marine say to his dad that he dishonored his own family name. After the phone conversation, Matthews had the Marines cover his name tape with black electrical tape so no one could read the Marines dishonored name. I was told later but wasn't sure if it was true. There was a rumor that Matthews made that same Marine cover up his name on his Dog Tags and I.D. card too. I can't confirm that, but I do believe it happened. There were several times this happened. The amazing part, Matthews always gave these Marines a chance to prove themselves. I remember that Marine working hard to gain back Matthews respect. That's how Matthews led his Marines and they respected him for it. Matthews would break you down and then build you up. Crazy part, that kid is now synonymous with the Matthew's incident. What did they call Witlit?

CHRIS: The newspapers called him "the executioner".

TESSLE: That's right, the executioner. There was this one other situation that you might find interesting. General Matthews had gotten word that one of the Marines in the division wouldn't shower after the runs or any physical training. The Marine would go back to bed after his exercise with his sweaty clothes still on, then thirty minutes later jump up, put on his uniform, and roll to work.

GORDON: That isn't exceptionally clean and pretty gross.

TESSLE: That's not the worst of it. While this Marine slept, he would actually suck his thumb! The word was that he would suck it while watching movies on his computer too. The Marine had subsequently named his computer by the way. Some chick name, it was creepy. Plus, the Marine was just dirty all around. Matthews blew his top over this kid; I mean lost it. He puts this kid in the back of a formation like the kid is getting a special award. He calls him out and then reams him out in front of all of us. When he's done, orders the Division to an about face and tells the kids, "Get the Word Deleted out of my face, you make me sick!" Matthews disgraced the Marine. Like I said, made all the Marines turn their backs to show he was no longer part of the team until he straightens up, which the Marine did. His tactics worked.

CHRIS: That seems harsh to me.

TESSLE: Harsh, no, not at all. Look at the other armed forces branches. They have their own demands but when it comes to the Marines, we expect a lot. That's just how it is, just like you. You're not local cops, you are the elite! That's just what you do. This one lesson sticks to mind, let me see if I can find it... I found it. Do you remember that guy in Nashville, he was a wannabe terrorist? He's that guy that barricaded himself in and a whole bunch of others in ta restaurant that he just shot up.

CHRIS: Jason Tallston or Taltson, something like that. He called himself "New Mecca". Refresh my memory.

TESSLE: That's the guy, Jason Tallston. So, Tallston walks into a local downtown restaurant singing some religious songs from the Karan, pulls out a rifle and just goes to town. Obviously Tallston is a religious extremist and truth be told, not the most stable. Let's be frank, sane people don't just go off and one day decide to kill people. I wish all the pro-gun guys would talk about that and the Anti-gun people would see it. Anyway, it happens that an off duty cop was there at the time and tried to put Tallston down. Right as the cop starts to act. One of the hostages inside speaks up and tells Tallston that the cop is going to shoot him. So Tallston starts to act and goes to shoot the cop. Now the cop has to draw his weapon and they both shot at each other. The cop did get shot and killed Tallston. Matthews goes insane over this! The first part that Mathews went off was, we know the criminals name but not the cops! Then the civilian cop is trying to save people's lives and almost gets killed himself. Why? Because the cops got such a bad name that the criminal is now some kind of martyred hero. The city had a candlelight vigil for Tallston, treated him as the victim. Mathews brings us to formation, as I see him coming out, he's humming that religious tune. There was irony in that. He has just seen the Nashville shooter and felt that we needed a lesson. Here is that transcript.

"Ladies, Gentleman… Marines, "Mine eyes have seen the coming" for you see "I have read a fiery gospel writ in burnished rows of steel". That is the warning, hard days are upon us Marines. With school shootings, mass shootings, suicide bombers, it is all Hell on earth! Shakespeare is quoted as saying in the Tempest, "Hell is empty, and the devils are here". It rings true. No one has done anything about the chaos, violence, and disorder except throw fuel on the fire. A Police officer that's simply doing his job, to serve and protect…is now almost brutally gun down. Not only was put in danger by the crazed gunman but a civilian helped the gunman. She claimed she felt it was her "civic duty" to protect a killer… her civic duty. We vivify the villain and scorn the hero. It's easiest to blame the authority instead of taken the blame for ourselves, and accepting one's actions.

We live in days when we call riots "peaceful protest" because it's too hard to accept that maybe we are wrong for a change. We blame the violence on the tool and not the one using the tool. If you hit your thumb with a hammer, do you sue the hammer maker? Of course not. Both sides of gun control never want to acknowledge the truth, a mad man killed people, a sane person never murders. So anti-gun activist will make more gun laws and do nothing to the criminal. The law makers forget that a criminal doesn't obey laws to begin with, that's why they are criminals. Law makers rather punish those who obey the laws. Law makers never help those with serious mental disorders all because they don't want to offend them. Maybe if the lawmakers were more on their game, Private First Class Eckhart wouldn't have taken his own life weeks ago. They probably didn't want to offend Eckhart by asking if he needed any help.

And now we stand to be attacked! Lawmakers feeling that if we the people simply put our weapons down, the world will follow. This is the mindless thinking of the day. These same people call us killers for fighting their wars! These same people call us animals for doing the dirty work. Oh, but when the wolf is prowling around the door, those people scream for help and justice. Once the job of saving the people is done, what happens next? We get thrown in the kennel when the job is done and scolded for being "to mean". The law makers tell society that we kill children in war without proof, but at home those lawmakers kill thousands of children. It's all a double standard. It's all do as I say and not as I do.

Matthews doesn't say any more about Eckhart. That's the last that we hear his name. I would have thought he would have brought Eckhart up more as angry as Matthews was.

GORDON: Did he actually say specifically why he was angry? I get the fact that Matthews said he was weak. That's not really a reason.

TESSLE: I think it was the way his father took the suicide.

CHRIS: He didn't take it well I assume.

TESSLE: He didn't take it at all. The Division had a funeral for Eckhart. Have you seen a Military funeral on base before Special Agent Gordon?

GORDON: No, I haven't. I've seen funerals of Veterans with a few military members to present the flag to the family. I've never seen an active duty funeral or viewing.

TESSLE: Agent Chris, You?

CHRIS: No, I haven't.

TESSLE: It's an Informal formation held in the Chapel and the family is invited. The family is flown down to view the body as it's prepared for flight back to the home of residence. Then the family is invited to the formation to honor their loved one. It's incredibly sad, Eckhart's was even sadder given the fact that his father never came.

GORDON: Why?

TESSLE: I honestly don't know. I was in the office when the call was made about the death of Eckhart. My understanding is that Eckhart's father didn't even seemed bothered by his death. I thought that couldn't be true until he never came down. In fact, he never even contacted the battalion or division asking for directions or information for the services. We never heard a single word from Eckhart's father. Mathew's called Eckhart's father after the funeral, his father simply said, "was that today?" Matthews just hung the phone up, Matthews looked disgusted and angry.

CHRIS: Horrible.

TESSLE: It was. We packed up all of Eckhart's things and sent a detail inventory with Eckhart's body. We didn't think his father would show up to receive Eckhart.

CHRIS: Did he show?

TESSLE: No, he never showed. In the end of it all, a butler showed up to receive the body and made all the arrangements for burial. The butler was over two hours late, only being told of Eckhart's death moments before he was sent to get the body.

GORDON: Where was the father?

TESSLE: I was told that he was at work. I doubt his father even showed for Eckhart being put in the ground. The only thing his father did was keep it out of the news, that's it. I was later told that Eckhart's father only kept it out of the news to keep his stocks up. That honestly shocked me.

The man was more worried about profit then the loss of a son. This is why the Marines listened to Matthews. He took an interest in them.

That's really all that I have. I hope it was enough.

GORDON: We genuinely appreciate your cooperation in this matter and will come to see you again with any further information as needed. Thank you for your time.

TESSLE: Your welcome, I hope that my interview helped. I understand that Matthews says a lot of harsh things, but he said them for the betterment, the hard truth. Right or wrong, he meant only the best. Sometimes truth hurts.

GORDON: This is Special Agent Sean Gordon. Its 11:07 A.M. in United States Disciplinary Barracks, Fort Leavenworth Kansas, Maximum Security Wing, Block 5. We have just finished Interviewing Captain Bryant Justin Tessle. Case file: 31008539-A, Operation Vanguard or "The Matthews Incident".

This formally concludes the interview with Captain Bryant Tessle. No further entries were made on this date or for this part of the interview.

Memorandum from Special Agent Sean Gordon

TO: **Brian Samuels, Director of the Federal Bureau of Investigations**

FROM: **Sean Gordon, Special Agent**

DATE: **Friday, July 21st, 2028**

RE: **Death of Private First Class Eckhart**

Good Evening,

As per protocol, I am giving my informal opinion of the investigation of Private First Class Eckhart and my personal opinion to what I witnessed.

No one can deny that the loss of a life is a terrible thing. I feel that is important and must be said first. After I Interviewed Cpl. Witlit, Sgt. Hillard and Capt. Tessle, the story of Private First Class Eckhart's life has become truly clear. It is also just as clear that Gen. Matthews took it very personally. The true question is why he took it so personally.

Cpl. Witlit had and unusual attitude towards the investigation. Witlit showed a lack of emotion while sharing his story. The focus of Witlit was to not accept that he had a large role in the death of Eckhart. Witlit couldn't admit to himself that he failed to see the signs that Eckhart was going to hurt himself. Witlit never shared his feelings at the death of Eckhart other than saying he really doesn't like talking about it. No emotional breakdown, no moments needed for composure, Witlit was just acting like a story was just being re-told.

Sgt. Hillard on the other hand, had compassion for Eckhart. The happy, well collected Hillard was clearly bothered about reliving the night Eckhart died. We could see that Hillard had little liking towards Witlit. Hillard had a definite look of loathing when speaking about Witlit and seem genuinely entertained by the idea of Witlit's promotion. All the kindness Hillard showed Witlit after Eckhart's death was pure professionalism. Hillard showed a look of guilt when speaking of Eckhart's death; However, Hillard blamed Witlit for the death of Eckhart without actually saying it in my opinion. Sadly, two days after our interview, Hillard took his own life. A suicide note was recovered and stated that he regretted the night Eckhart died, feeling responsible for his death.

Capt. Tessle was hard to work with and didn't want to help. Clearly Tessle was only willing to cooperate unless he got something for his help. Tessle however did give a good insight to how Gen. Matthews was and how the General spoke. It was unknown that Witlit had been punished by Matthews before the incident with Eckhart. It did explain the distain that Hillard had for Witlit. I believe that Hillard was just as wrapped up in Matthews as all the other Marines. I also believe that Hillard would have had a part in Vanguard provided that he had of gotten out of the Marines when he did. Tessle showed little regard for Eckhart. He remembered the Marine but was very indifferent about what happened. Tessle said the normal reactions of "it's a shame" and "it's sad", but no real emotion behind the words. Tessle also showed no remorse in his part of Operation Vanguard, going as far as a full denial that he had done anything wrong. Tessle mentioned that he had not killed anyone personally, so he is not responsible. Tessle however did not say "He was just following orders". Tessle has not come to terms with his actions in Vanguard.

I believe Gen. Matthews took Eckhart as a personal failure and a failure of Eckhart's family and friends. Matthews clearly felt that family is fractured and there is no responsibility in society. Matthews had a magnetic personality and drew others into his world. Matthews pushed his personal ideologies on others and made demands that were very unreadable. After reviewing the material, we realized that Matthews called a formation just two hours after the death of Eckhart. That's a truly short amount of time to try to collect so many people together. That short time seeming nearly impossible, The Marines obeyed Matthews and made it happen. Matthews ruled as king over his domain and the subjects loved him. I wonder if Matthews had been writing the family speech in his head before he made it or was it simply improvised on the spot. Tessle never mentioned that Matthews had notes or cards that he followed. This leads me to believe that all his talks were impromptu. I find that Matthews also repeats himself, often. So often in fact, saying the same things maybe seven or maybe eight times within one speech, almost to the point of being annoying. I thought this was for emphasis but later through research found that Marines are taught to say things like that in secession to ensure it's remembered. Matthews clearly disagrees with how society has become, so he constantly reinforces his disappointment.

This was the first steppingstone that Matthews took to start planning Vanguard in his notes (see Matthews, Gen. Notebook 4 pg. 23). Matthews is quoting as saying "the road before me is clear. Something needs to be done. The death of this young Private First Class was unacceptable. I lay down the first piece of my puzzle in hopes to find a way to keep order in the world of chaos".

It's unclear how Matthews views himself at this time. I haven't determined if he has a God complex or just a zealot. All we can really tell about him is from his personal memoirs. To date, we have been unable to find a war journal. Aside from Matthews Memoirs, he kept notebooks, very closely resembling a journal. The information in the notebooks is just pieces of Matthews's thoughts or ideas. It is clear that little things mattered to Matthews. Matthews was particular in his actions. "The small things will work out the larger, just as the Chaos theory explains. The small river will one day become an ocean." (See Matthews, Gen. Notebook 5 pg. 110).

Sincerely,
S.A. Sean Gordon.

Eyewitness accounts of Operation Vanguard

"I remember this sharp feeling in my chest, I just went blank and hit the ground. I could feel something, like, sliding into me…or crawling, I guess. It was hot! All I felt was it slowly moving in me. I had this cold sensation rush through me. It was a cold wet sensation. I just realized, "Oh my God, I've been shot!" I didn't see or hear the shot, I just felt it. I was told later at the hospital; I was hit by a sniper on the Capital Building. The nurses saw me get shot on T.V.! It's unreal. I was told it was from a thousand yards. The whole world saw me get shot."

-Officer Jim Toms (D.C. Morning News, Blacken, 2026, p.1)

"I just laughed, my Sergeant handed me an AR-15, not an M-16. They had Word Deleted machine guns and he gave me a civilian model of a military weapon. I knew I was screwed."

-Officer Brian Archer (Eagle News, Allen, 2026, p.5)

"I saw about forty of the white house security dead on the white house lawn. They were just lying there. I thought to myself "how did this happen?""

-Michael Luke (The weekly Journal, Malcom, 2026, p. 3)

DEATH OF OFFICER
JOEL BENJAMIN NELSON

Interview of Dr. Blake Samuel Walton

Friday, August 11th, 2028
Ackley, Iowa
County Coroner's Office

GORDON: Its 4:37 P.M. at the Franklin and Hardin county
Coroner's office. Next to me is Special Agent William
Chris. Across from us, in the conference office is County
Coroner, Dr. Blake Samuel Walton. Dr. Walton is 56
years of age, he is 5'8", 150 LBS., He is slender, grey hair,
and occupation is County Coroner. No scars or marks,
eyes are light brown, medium skin tone. He is African
American and is an American. He has fingerprints on
file and has no classification.

*Key testimony involving the Death of Officer Joel Benjamin
Nelson and the months leading up to his death. Dr. Walton
is at this time at liberty to speak about Brigadier General
Mathews, Operation Vanguard, and Officer Nelson by the
Supreme Court and is not under a gag order.*

GORDON: Good afternoon Doctor Walton

WALTON: Good afternoon gentlemen, it's not often I get the F.B.I.
down here. I honestly don't know when I last saw an
Agent to tell the truth.

GORDON: We are actually here to speak to you about an accident
that had happened a few years ago. Do you remember
the Nelson family and the accident that happened?

WALTON: I do remember the Nelsons. They were traveling through
our county when they were killed.

GORDON: That is correct, that's exactly to what we are referring to.
We were hoping to do an interview on that accident if
you are okay with that?

WALTON: I don't really mind talking about it, but I really don't
see why this case is important enough for the F.B.I., let
alone send two agents. Quantico should know that the

file and case study is closed. I can provide copies of the Corners report if necessary and my license is up to date.

CHRIS: You did nothing wrong and we don't need to see your license. I know the report was complete.

WALTON: I still don't see how all of this is important now.

CHRIS: Well, as a matter of fact, it has a great deal of importance, more than you may even realize. The accident was mentioned in memoirs from Brigadier General Matthews.

WALTON: Brigadier General Matthews, Operation Vanguard Matthews? I find that hard to believe that such a small car accident would have ever gotten to someone like him. I don't think he was even from the state of Iowa, let alone been here or lived. Why would he care about this little town?

GORDON: Matthews was not from Iowa and yes, he knew of the accident and it did actually play a part in the Operation.

WALTON: I find this really hard to believe.

CHRIS: It's true. What we need from you is the why it was important to Matthews.

WALTON: I'm not sure why you think I would know; I didn't know Brigadier General Matthews. I've never met the man or even heard of him until Vanguard.

GORDON: That's not what we mean. We know that you never met Matthews. We want to talk about the death of Officer Nelson and his family. Matthews knew of the family's death; it grabbed his attention. We could have easily read the old newspaper files, but we wanted to hear the facts from you. We know it's a small town. We want to feel the incident and not just read it. Not from someone else that is guessing what you would have said or what the papers say you think might have happened. You were there, you would know. That's why we wanted to talk to you. You were one of the first people on the scene of Officer Nelsons family, is that correct.

WALTON: Matthews knew of the Nelsons?

GORDON: He in fact did.

WALTON: Did Matthews know the Family personally?

GORDON: He did not. Matthews mentioned the Nelson family in his personal notes.

WALTON: That's very strange.

GORDON: It is, and that's why we are here. As I asked, you were one of the first people on scene for the death of the Nelson family. Is that correct?

WALTON: I was one of the first, yes. It was me and Sheriff Word Deleted.

GORDON: Would you mind running us all the way through what actually happened.

WALTON: I don't mind, where do you want me to start?

CHRIS: Whatever you think is a good place.

WALTON: I guess I'll start with Tara Nelson and her two kids, Kyle, and Mary. Kyle was twelve and Marry was nine. Tara was driving her car through Iowa, to visit Tara's sister in Pierre South Dakota. Tara was heading home to Saint Louis Missouri when the accident happened. It's about a twelve hour drive and Tara was stopping every few hours to take a rest. She was stopping for things like breakfast and such. It was a casual drive. Tara was not trying to go in one hard drive. Or at least I and the sheriff suspected.

Having young kids like that would be tough to drive twelve hours. We also found wrappers and store receipts all the way from South Dakota.

CHRIS: All that from wrappers?

WALTON: We also found an Itinerary sheet with the places Tara was going to stop at. We found that in the wreckage. I forgot about that, sorry. It was pretty detailed. It looked like Tara would stop every hour or so. That bit of paperwork told us, or at least suggested that Tara wasn't too tired. We thought all the driving and being tired might have played a part in the accident until we saw the itinerary.

CHRIS: That makes sense, please continue.

WALTON: Tara was planning to stop at a hotel in Iowa Falls. Give me a few minutes if you could. I have the information in my cabinet.

15 minutes passed

WALTON: Here it is. Tara was going to the Kennings House Inn. She had a reservation already set up.

CHRIS: How did you know about the reservation?

WALTON: Sherriff name deleted called and asked if they heard of Tera and the Sherriff was told that they never checked in, obviously.

GORDON: What time was Tara planning on being at the Hotel?

WALTON: Tara was planning on being to the Kennings House around 11 P.M. or 11:30 P.M. Tara was driving through Ackley at about 10:30 P.M. Tara was about fifteen minutes from Kennings. She was ahead of schedule. Before I go any further, I have to ask. James Healy, do you know who he is?

CHRIS: Mr. Healy was the gentleman driving the other vehicle, correct?

WALTON: That's him. James was forty-five at the time of the accident. It's a true miracle that he made it that far. James would often go to his Brother Todd's house and drink till he passed out. That particular night James had left his brother's house to go home to sleep. I can only assume that James didn't want to sleep at Todd's place that night. Todd and his current girlfriend fought constantly, during questioning the sheriff was told that. Todd said James and he had been drinking all day so and it really made Todd's girlfriend mad. James thought he could drive home which he was way too drunk to do. Of course, Todd was too drunk and busy with his girlfriend to argue with James, so they let him drive. This wasn't the first time James drove home in this condition. James and his brother only lived about ten minutes apart so driving home drunk was pretty normal and something done without a second thought. To make matters worse, it was raining surprisingly good that night too.

Both vehicles, James Healy and Tara Nelson were in U.S. Highway 65. The vehicles were on the overpass over Lindy Road which is also called County road 65-130 when the two vehicles collided. From the tire marks left by Tara's vehicle, it was concluded that James vehicle had swerved over the yellow lines and into Tara's lane. Tara tried to swerve, but James's vehicle broad-sided Tara on the driver's side. The impact sent the Nelsons vehicle skidding into the guardrail and over it. Tara's car fell approximately twenty-five feet onto Lindy road. It was also determined that she was doing the speed limit of fifty-five miles per hour. James on the other hand was doing an excess of seventy-five miles per hour. From the lack of breaks, it was clear that James didn't try to stop and most likely passed out behind the wheel. Sadly, James survived without any major injury, like most drunk drivers. James is currently at the Iowa State Penitentiary. He is serving twenty-five years and is eligible for parole in 2051. I hear that his brother goes to the prison weekly to talk to him. Subsequently, Todd and his girl broke up, she was three girlfriends ago. The word around town was that Todd was going to try and sue Officer Nelson for some stupid idea of wrongful imprisonment. Todd believes to this day that James never hit Tara's car. Todd also states that if anything, Tara hit James. I guess it never crossed Todd's mind that James truck had obvious evidence of a collision and paint from Tara's car on the truck. I'm sure Todd has a logical explanation for that, UFO's, or something. Todd and James are two drunken hillbilly's that finally ended up in jail. Well James at least. Sorry for being so syndical.

CHRIS: What happened to Tara and the kids?

WALTON: To be honest with you, it was a bad fall. Even with the seatbelts working, it wasn't good. Tara was ejected from the car. When the car landed, it landed grill first, halted upright for a moment and then fell on its roof. Unfortunately, where it fell, Tara was lying. She was killed almost instantly. There really wasn't much that could have been done for her under those circumstances, as you can imagine. Like I said, she was killed almost instantly. Kyle was ejected from his seat in the back and flew into the passenger's. He was also crushed when the car tilted to its rest. I realize that a really nice way of putting it. It's hard to sometimes remember.

Tera and Kyle suffered severe and deep lacerations, broken bones, and contusions. Tara had a shattered Pelvis and several vertebrae shattered as well as a skull fracture. Kyle had a shattered spinal column and a crushed skull. The car did most of the damage.

GORDON: What happened to Mary?

WALTON: Marry was in bad shape. Her spine was in a bad way, she most likely wouldn't be able to walk again. The expectation was she would be a quadriplegic. She had her left arm amputated at the elbow. It was crushed horribly. When we arrived, she was actually conscious.

GORDON: Were there any witnesses to the accident?

WALTON: There was a vehicle that was behind Tara, he saw it happen. He wasn't close enough to see everything. Mr. Name Deleted wasn't close enough to see James hit Tara. Mr. Name deleted said he saw the lights from Tara's car spin and then goes off the overpass. Mr. Name Deleted drove down the embankment and tried to help all he could with Tara's car. Mr. Name deleted was with Marry when I arrived on scene. I was on call that evening; it's a small town so we arrived relatively fast. I'd say less than ten minutes.

GORDON: That's actually pretty fast, how did you manage that.

WALTON: We were fairly prepared and standing by, we always get ready for the drunk driving accidents. We get them occasionally. It happens usually between 1am and 3 A.M. That's the only reason we arrived so quickly. Unfortunately, it was exactly why we were ready.

CHRIS: Is it normal for the coroner to be first on scene. I would expect a coroner to be an afterthought.

WALTON: I had a private practice for a long time before I became the County Coroner. I volunteer a lot as a first responder. It cuts a lot of corners in some ways. You don't need to call me if I'm already there.

GORDON: That makes sense.

WALTON: The fire company was alerted to the accident pretty fast, the Sherriff asked them to bring something to cut the family out of the vehicle and lift the vehicle. I ran to the fire truck and explained the situation when they arrived. Aside from the obvious car upside-down, the fire company needed to know if anyone was trapped. I assumed they would need to know the urgency of the situation. I was surprised when the firemen had a second vehicle show up to the scene. That ambulance pulled in right behind the fire trucks.

CHRIS: Was there concerns of fire at all from the vehicle?

WALTON: I was surprised how well the car actually held up. It was messed up, don't get me wrong. It was a standard Sudan, a word deleted, or word deleted. That car took the punishment, I was shocked. The gas tank didn't rupture, and no gas was spilling out. Nothing had caught fire. The obvious oil and antifreeze were everywhere. There was glass everywhere as well. I guess that goes without saying.

GORDON: You said the fire department rolled the vehicle?

WALTON: Yeah, they used a strap attached to the biggest truck and pulled Tara's vehicle. They also used a hydraulic jack to help lift and support. The firemen lifted the vehicle enough to get Tara out from underneath the car. The firemen then started to work and cut Marry out of the vehicle too. The firemen got Marry on a stretcher then to the ambulance. The fireman got Marry out of the vehicle quick, it was surprising. Also Mr. Name Deleted helped a lot with the vehicle. We really couldn't have done it without him. Mr. Name Deleted kept Marry from bleeding out. We got Marry to Franklin General as fast as we possibly could. We could see that Tara and Kyle were dead at the scene.

The firemen continued to lift the vehicle to try and get Kyle out. That's about when the police arrived and helped us. That took a lot longer than expected to get Kyle out. I'd say almost an hour.

CHRIS: Why so long?

WALTON: The car took a lot of punishment, lifting it like that just added stress to the already damaged frame. I know I didn't explain it well enough, but that car was a mess! It started to buckle under its own weight and the firefighters were afraid that it would just give out. The second fire truck was hooked up to help. We eventually got Kyle out. It was a true shame.

GORDON: How hard was it to identify Tara and the kids?

WALTON: It's sad to say but it was easy. Tara had an allergy to aspirin, so she had a medical tag on her wrist. The tag had a contact number for her next of kin. We got ahold of Mr. Nelson; he was obviously beside himself. Mr. Nelson said he would get to the hospital as soon as possible.

After hanging up with Mr. Nelson, I continued with the accident scene. The officers allowed for the removal of Tara and Kyle. I had called my assistant Name deleted shortly after talking to Mr. Nelson. Name deleted arrived shortly after with the coroner's vehicle. We loaded Tera and Kyle on it and my assistant headed to the office. As far as James goes, he was arrested and sent to Franklin General to be checked for internal injuries. I assumed they would do a blood test too. He was formally charged and arrested after the Doctors there cleared him for prison. I figured I would head to the hospital myself to see how Marry was doing. Mr. Nelson arrived a few hours after I did. I gave him the rundown of what had happened. I updated him on his daughter's current condition in surgery and informed him she was in surgery for the past few hours. I also told him that his daughter had lost consciousness sometime on the ride to the hospital but was in critical but stable condition when she arrived at the hospital.

GORDON: When did Mary get out of surgery?

WALTON: It was about noon. Nearly eight hours.

GORDON: Did her condition change?

WALTON: No, still critical but stable.

CHRIS: I understand Marry had in fact later passed away.

WALTON: Marry held on for a total of four days. She never woke up. It seemed like the whole Hospital reeled from her death. It was just a true tragedy. We all really were hoping she would wake up. I know for a fact her quality of life was going to be extremely limited. There is only so much the human body can take. Marry was at that limit.

GORDON: Where did they have the funeral and the burial? I would guess in St. Louis Missouri.

WALTON: That's a yes and no answer, Tara, Kyle, and Mary had two funerals actually. The town asked that they could hold one for Mr. Nelson. I guess we all felt like we had a part in the deaths because James was one of us. Mr. Nelson didn't say no to the request. That was strange too, as I think about it.

GORDON: Why is that?

WALTON: Well, flowers.

CHRIS: Flowers?

WALTON: There were a lot of flowers. Mary's room was filled with them and at the funeral as well. I never found out who they were from.

GORDON: You didn't see a card attached to the flowers?

WALTON: I didn't see one. It's possible that Mr. Nelson had it. I'm not sure, I really don't know.

GORDON: They were hand delivered to the funeral home the morning of the funeral, all roses. They were red to be exact.

WALSON: Yeah, actually. How did you know that?

CHRIS: There was a card, and we have it. It was addressed to Officer Nelson. It was obtained at Mr. Nelsons home.

Card Addressed to Officer Nelson

Officer Nelson,

With my deepest sympathy and humblest regrets, I'm terribly sorry for your loss. I understand how you must feel. Not many can say that. I know the pain you feel today, I have felt it too. I myself lost my wife and child to a drunk driver some years ago. I truly hope you don't mind the flowers, I felt it was the least I can do. I was passing through Missouri when I saw the news report of what had happed to your family. I felt I needed to do something but truly didn't know what I could do. Enclosed is a donation of $25,000.00 to help with any outside arrangement or needs that may come up. Funeral arrangements are paid for already and I'm currently in the process of paying for the burials in your family's plot in Missouri; If that's acceptable of course. I have provided transportation for you and your family home; I took care of as much as I possibly can for you and them.

Don't concern yourself with any payback and please take the money to help. Do something with that money to make your family proud. It will not be easy to pick the pieces up from your shattered life. Your family is irreplaceable, I know that. Your life will never be normal again; we both know that as well. I will not sugar coat the world by saying it will all be alright, it never is. The pain never goes away. You will take the pain wherever you go, it will be a part of you. You will have to learn to accept that.

I again give my deepest sympathy to you in this time of grief.

BGen J. Matthews USMC
(Evidence file: 04052954 Nelson J.)

WALTON: That can't be Brigadier General Matthews? That's impossible? How would he know or even care about an accident like this? We don't make headlines here in our state. I know for a fact that it never made the big news stations, or so I thought.

GORDON: Yes, that's General Matthews. He had his ways of getting information like that. He had sources and was always up to date on any current events, no matter how small.

WALTON: I'm honestly shocked! I don't know what to say to that.

GORDON: Matthews was traveling from North Carolina to California on business. While on a layover in Des Moines, he saw it on the news. As the card said, Matthews's wife, Ashly and his son James were killed. It was also by a drunk driver. We know that Matthews always watched the news and red newspapers, plus, after the death of his family. Matthews showed a lot of interests in drunken driving incidents.

WALTON: So, he sees this on the news and just arranges all this while in an airport?

GORDON: That's what we believe. That's also the reason that we came to talk to you. We came to see what drew Matthews to the accident. It must have been the family of Mr. Nelson.

WALTON: This is all just a lot to take in.

GORDON: We understand that.

WALTON: I just wouldn't have thought that monster would do something like this. Matthews went to a lot of trouble for a family he didn't know.

GORDON: Why would you say, a lot of trouble.

WALTON: Well, the limos, and the fact that his wife and kids were flown home and Mr. Nelson flew first class. I just assumed our town, or the insurance somehow paid for it.

CHRIS: Nope, probably Matthews. I'm sure he paid for it all.

WALTON: I understand him having an interest in DUI cases, but that seems a little much.

GORDON: As you know Matthews was an intense person, that just the kind of things he did. Matthews was all or nothing.

WALTON: Can I ask why?

GORDON: We can't truly pinpoint what goes through someone's mind, you know. From his notes and journal, we found. Matthews would just find something like this interesting or important and do something. Like we said, his family was killed too. The situations were remarkably similar actually. His wife was driving home, it was raining, and a drunk driver hit the vehicle. The drunk driver was simply fine, Matthews family wasn't.

WALTON: Isn't that how it always is. It isn't right. Until today, I never knew that about Matthews or any of this.

GORDON: Is there anything further you can add to the accident?

WALTON: I don't think so. I hope I was helpful. That's really all I know about the accident. I wish there were more.

GORDON: We thank you for your time. You did fine.

GORDON: This is Special Agent Sean Gordon. Its 6:00 P.M.at the Franklin and Hardin county Coroner's office. We have just finished interviewing Dr. Blake Samuel Walton. Case file: 31008539-A, Operation Vanguard or "The Matthews Incident".

This formally concludes the Interview with Dr. Blake Samuel Walton. No further entries were made on this date or for this part of the interview.

Interview of Officer Andrew Allen York

Wednesday, August 16th, 2028
Saint Louis, Missouri
Saint Louis Police Department

GORDON: Its 9:30 A.M. at the Saint Louis Police Department. Next to me is Special Agent William Chris. Across from us, in the rollcall room is Officer Andrew Allen York. Officer York is 35 years of age, he is 6'1", 210 LBS., He is medium build, no hair, his occupation is Police Officer, no scars or marks, eyes are Blue, medium skin tone, he is Caucasian, and is an American, He has fingerprints on file and has no classification.

Key testimony involving the Death of Officer Joel Benjamin Nelson and the months leading up to his death. Officer York is currently at liberty to speak about Brigadier General Mathews, operation Vanguard, and Officer Nelson by the Supreme Court and is not under a Gag order.

GORDON: Good Morning Officer York.

YORK: I was told you're here to speak with me about Joel?

GORDON: That is correct. We just wanted to ask about the death of Mr. Nelson and what actually transpired. We are also here to do a research study to the death of Mr. Nelson and its connection to Operation Vanguard.

YORK: I don't understand, I mean I get talking about Joel, but I don't understand about General Matthews. I wasn't involved in Vanguard or any of that and I would have known if Joel was involved too. I personally have never met Matthews and I'm quite sure that Joel never did either.

GORDON: Mr. Nelson wasn't involved directly with Operation Vanguard, but Mr. Nelson played a part in vanguards planning. I'm not saying he helped Matthews, please don't miss understand me. What I mean to say is that Mr. Nelson's death had an impact on General Matthews and was a catalyst that would eventually be Vanguard.

YORK: I'm sorry gentlemen; I'm not seeing the connection. I
            don't understand how one and the other relate.

CHRIS: We don't expect you to know the connection. Matthews
            was the gentlemen that paid for the funeral of Mr.
            Nelsons Family as well as their transportation back to
            Saint Louis…

YORK: You mean to tell me that Matthews is the "flower guy?"

CHRIS: The flower guy?

YORK: Joel talked time to time about a person that he called
            the flower guy. I can't believe it was General Matthews.

CHRIS: Correct, Matthews was the one that did all that. We have
            the original card written to Mr. Nelson from General
            Matthews; it was left with the flowers. Here is the letter,
            take a look.

            * 4 minute pause as Officer York reads.

            *Card Addressed to Officer Nelson

Officer Nelson,

*With my deepest sympathy and humblest regrets, I'm terribly sorry for
your loss. I understand how you must feel. Not many can say that. I know
the pain you feel today, I have felt it too. I myself lost my wife and child to
a drunk driver some years ago. I truly hope you don't mind the flowers, I
felt it was the least I can do. I was passing through Missouri when I saw
the news report of what had happed to your family. I felt I needed to do
something but truly didn't know what I could do. Enclosed is a donation of
$25,000.00 to help with any outside arrangement or needs that may come
up. Funeral arrangements are paid for already and I'm currently in the
process of paying for the burials in your family's plot in Missouri; If that's
acceptable of course. I have provided transportation for you and your family
home; I took care of as much as I possibly can for you and them.*

Don't concern yourself with any payback and please take the money to help. Do something with that money to make your family proud. It will not be easy to pick the pieces up from your shattered life. Your family is irreplaceable, I know that. Your life will never be normal again; we both know that as well. I will not sugar coat the world by saying it will all be alright, it never is. The pain never goes away. You will take the pain wherever you go, it will be a part of you. You will have to learn to accept that.

I again give my deepest sympathy to you in this time of grief.

BGen J. Matthews USMC
(Evidence file: 04052954 Nelson J.)

YORK: I had no idea. Joel had never mentioned Matthews name or this card. I never would have even imagined. Where did this come from?

GORDON: It was with Mr. Nelson's personal belongings. It was labeled as "BGEN".

CHRIS: Matthews had left notes and personal memoirs as well as bank statements. That's how we were able to obtain the connection. We have this as well; it's the mention of Mr. Nelson.

*Quotations in journal entry

> *"I find that life is so fragile and every day we waste away just a little more. I came across a news segment that mention the death of a woman and two kids: The Nelson family. I will have to ask Capt. Name deleted to look into this for me."*

(See Matthews, Gen. Notebook 2 pg. 14)

> *"Yesterday I received the information I asked for from Capt. Name deleted, I'm going to reach out to an Officer Nelson of Saint Louis, Missouri. It was his family that was killed by a drunk driver. I cannot let this go."*

(See Matthews, Gen. Notebook 2 pg. 16)

YORK: I'm sure I saw the evidence bag the note was in, I remember the BGEN. We didn't look through everything Joel left. So how does that all relate though?

CHRIS: Is this the evidence bag?

YORK: That is the bag, yes. The one with "BGEN"

CHRIS: I know you are not a graphologist; does the handwriting look like Mr. Nelsons?

YORK: That is Joel's handwriting, yes.

CHRIS: Thank you for confirming that. So, you said you do remember the bag, correct.

YORK: Correct.

CHRIS: How many bags did you see that day? Can you give an estimation to the number? I don't expect you to remember them all.

YORK: There were hundreds. There were all different sizes, just a lot of them.

GORDON: So why remember this one bag?

YORK: It was the "BGEN"; I didn't know what it meant. I've never seen or heard that term, it just caught my attention. Given that I had more time, I probably would have looked into it further. I don't think it would have mattered anyway. It would be a while until I heard the name Matthews, years in fact. So how can I help you exactly? You just popped all this information on me, and I can't even imagine how I could be helpful.

GORDON: We want to know the months that lead up to Mr. Nelson's death. Like we said, Mr. Nelson was mentioned in the notes from Matthews. We just want a clearer picture of why it was important to Matthews after the death of Mr.,

Nelsons family. We understand why he was interested in the DUI but why afterword's, its puzzling. Any and all information you can provide would be helpful. Just start from the beginning.

YORK: How far back are we talking, I knew Joel for nearly fifteen years.

GORDON: Wherever you like.

YORK: Well, Joel and I started in the same class at the academy together and completed the academy at the top twenty percent.

CHRIS: That's impressive.

YORK: Is it really that impressive?

GORDON: Sure, it is. it's something to be proud of.

YORK: Not if you're a class of seven. It was a joke that I and Joel had. I still laugh to myself from time to time about it. We started off in the Academy as roommates and then partners in our district, like I said we were partners for a better part of fifteen years; word deleted, Joel was my best man at my wedding. So, to say we were close was an understatement. We were best friends. We had cookouts at each other's houses on Memorial Day weekends, family beach trips; that kind of stuff. My wife said he was my work wife. Joel was a great guy, life just happens, I guess.

GORDON: That's great that you had a good working and professional friendship. You need that kind of trust in law enforcement.

YORK: What about you two, you don't have that?

CHRIS: Gordon and I have only worked less than a year together. We are on the road a lot, so we have a good working relationship. Trust is just part of the job.

YORK: Our jobs make tight bonds for sure.

GORDON: Yes, they do.

YORK: Well anyway, I'm sure you didn't come all this way to talk about our jobs. Joel and I had some tough times together and we had seen our fair share of good too. Off the top of my head, I can think of a few. There was a major drug bust our third or fourth year, stopped a kidnapping our sixth year. That one was crazy. A simple traffic stop turned into our pictures in the papers. We had to do a few surveillance jobs on this old mobster, nothing from that but fun bragging rights. Sitting there night after night for five weeks, the moments sucked, but the years were great. Little things like that make the job worth doing. I'm glad I got a good partner. You can end up with some real jerks. Or worse, a cop that isn't a stand up kind of guy. Now and then a few of them get busted by internal affairs; were always glad to see those kinds go. They give good officers a bad name. The job is hard enough. It doesn't need to be made worse by crappie cops.

GORDON: You mentioned a kidnapping. That caught my attention. Would you care to share about that? You said you got your pictures in the papers?

YORK: It was funny. Joel and I stopped a vehicle for not using their turn signal. The Driver was calling us fake cops; he felt that only highway patrolmen are real cops, I guess. So, the guy we pulled over goes on and on about how we had to make a quota, like that is a real thing. Just on and on, Joel kept his cool and cited him. As we were getting ready to walk away and finalize the citation, Joel thought he heard something come from the trunk of the car. Joel said he looked at the trunk and sees a piece of shirt stuck in the latch. Joel turns around and asks the guy what's in the trunk of the car. He tells Joel "none of your word deleted business.", so Joel asks him to get out of the vehicle. The guy just starts screaming about police brutality and how we are profiling him. Joel keeps his cool until he hears a little girl yell for help from that trunk. We draw our weapons and call for backup, sure enough; there is a kid in the trunk. Turns out, this guy took the girl from a playground and the amber alert came over the air as we put the cuffs on him. We looked like heroes, but it was all Joel. What does Joel do, throws a party for our shift. That was just how he was; he was a hero but could never admit to himself that he was; just an all-around good guy.

GORDON: That's awesome! It truly is.

YORK: That's an impressive thing, that's why we laughed about the twenty percent. We earned that twenty percent years later. We showed over time that we were good cops. Things were good, work was good. Things change however, nothing stays the same.

GORDON: You are referring to the death of Mr. Nelson's family.

YORK: I am. It changed him, obviously. I mean, who wouldn't change? When your life is just turned upside down like that, things are bound to be different. It must play at you emotionally and mentally. There is no way to take it easy when your whole family is taken out by a drunk driver. It had to eat at Joel. The drunk driver that killed Joel's family only had bruises. That's it, jut word deleted bruises. That guy should have died not Joel's family. That guy, that's all I can call him, I can't even remember his name.

CHRIS: It was...

YORK: I don't want to know! I shouldn't have to remember that piece of word deleted name. That's it! In some way, if I forget his name, he no longer exists. He took everything from Joel and then took Joel from me. That guy's name should be forgotten.

CHRIS: I'm sorry, I wish I could understand how you feel. It can't be easy.

YORK: It isn't easy, it's just something I must live and deal with. You know what I mean?

CHRIS: I understand.

YORK: Did you know, in that guy's trial, he never even said he was sorry! Joel drives all the way back to Iowa and stays for nearly a month for the trial. A word deleted Month! That word deleted head doesn't even say he's sorry. The judge gives him a chance to speak to Joel and the guy says nothing. I understand if he didn't know what to say; sorry would have been a start. But to stand there and say "nothing your honor" to the judge is just unspeakable. Deep down, that guy is the worst form of humanity, the kind that can't even say sorry to the man that he destroyed. How do you live with yourself? If I were that guy, I wouldn't have made it to trial. I would have hung myself in that cell. That would be the considerate thing to do, eye for an eye. But no, he decides to say nothing. The way I see it, he didn't even feel bad. I bet he was more upset that he got caught then having to say sorry.

GORDON: Did you go with Mr. Nelson to Iowa?

YORK: Of course, I did. He was my friend and my partner. Like I said, the guy says "no your honor". The judge just got this unhappy look on his face, and says "are you sure?" The guy mumbles "No your Honor". You could tell the courtroom was shocked, no one said a word. I was beyond word deleted off. Joel didn't say a word. Joel just watched the guy. It messed Joel up, bad. Joel at this time was given several weeks off from work. We drove most of the way in silence, I couldn't take it. I finally speak up to Joel and start voicing my opinion of the court situation. Joel just looks at me and says to let it go. All this and Joel just wants peace. I was wondering if Joel was going to kill that guy.

GORDON: Why do you think that?

YORK: I would! I would be plotting a plan to kill that creep. He deserved it. Joel felt that system would work itself out. Work gave Joel another week off after the trial. I was wondering the condition Joel would be in when he came back to full duty. The night Joel was due back he called off and called off for the next few nights as well. I felt bad for Joel but had no idea what I could do for him. That's when the changes really started with Joel. Joel never called out sick. I understand under the circumstances why he did, it was simply different. It was that scumbag driver that caused all this damage. It was just slowly eating at Joel. I truly blame that guy for Joel's death.

CHRIS: What kind of Changes took place with Mr. Nelson?

YORK: Well, Joel wouldn't drive.

GORDON: Mr. Nelson drove before all this happened, correct?

YORK: Yeah, Joel did. But he wouldn't after the family passed.

CHRIS: He wouldn't drive while off work?

YORK: Joel wouldn't drive anything. Joel wanted nothing to do with cars as far as driving was concerned. He took the bus or walked. He would ride along with you, but Joel would not drive.

CHRIS: Did Mr. Nelson ever say why he didn't drive anymore?

YORK: I asked him, he said he just couldn't. I guess it became a phobia or fear. Joel just wouldn't do it. His car just sat at his house collecting dust.

GORDON: How did he get around then, at work?

YORK: Joel started taking a taxi to work. I guess the bus got too much for him with all the people. Eventually the Captain found out about the taxis and told me to go pick Joel up at home in the morning and drop him off at night. So, I did. He would be ready to go. No problems. He would do everything that was demanded of him as a cop, just not driving. It really wasn't that big of a deal anyway; I drove most of the time when we patrolled. As far as home went, he ordered his food to be delivered and his grocery's too. He didn't go out much after the accident.

CHRIS: Did he still come to your house for cook outs and holidays?

YORK: No, Joel stopped coming to everything all together. He just stopped going places. He wouldn't go to stores, the park. Just anywhere people were. I asked him what was wrong, and he simply just told me he didn't want to be around crowds. He had no real reason, just couldn't. I could see it too. He would start to sweat, and his eyes would become panicky; constantly moving. It reminded me of a mouse looking for a cat that he knew should be around.

GORDON: How long did this go on for?

YORK: A few months, the driving thing too. It went on for about six months.

GORDON: About how long after the trial did all this start?

YORK: A week or two. Now that I think about it, it was two weeks. It was that week that he had off and the extra that he took. The driving thing was almost instant after the trial.

GORDON: Was there anything else unusual that Mr. Nelson was doing?

YORK: Well, yeah…It was about that point that Joel really started having a hard time with just functioning.

GORDON: What was happening?

YORK: I want to first say that I don't agree with what Joel did before I explain, it was wrong.

CHRIS: Okay, please elaborate.

YORK: Joel had an episode during a routine traffic stop.

GORDON: What kind of episode? He had a break down or something like that?

YORK: Kind of. It was our turn for night patrol. We do a swing shift. A few weeks of day shift, a few of night and a few of the graveyard. It's typical. Anyway, we were out late on Handover Street when we get radioed by dispatch. Dispatch said a person called in stating they saw a red car swerving all over the road. It's about 2am, so it would most likely be a drunk driver, which it was. We located the car and pulled into traffic behind it, and sure enough, the car was all over the road. We observe it for about two miles and then turn on our flashers and pull the vehicle over. Joel and I get out, but Joel crosses the front of our vehicle, going from passenger side to driver's side and approaches the car. Following his lead, I take the passenger's side. Joel knocks on the window and asked the driver to shut his vehicle off, the driver does so. Joel starts to go through the normal questions, "where are you heading?", "do you know why we pulled you over?" and finally "Have you been drinking?" I could smell the alcohol from the vehicle, this guy was clearly drunk, but we must go through the test and questions.

We must be one hundred percent sure he's drunk. The guy tells Joel in a clearly slurred speech, no, he's not been drinking. Joel's face just curls up in this grimmest look, and Joel punches this guy right in the face! Joel starts yelling over and over, "Don't lie to me" every time Joel yells it, he strikes the driver! I was just stunned, I couldn't move. Joel had never done anything like that. Joel never lost his cool. Joel gets five or six good ones before I can stop him. He had tears running down his face and starts sobbing. Joel just sinks to the ground repeating "he killed my babies, and he killed my girl." I was wondering if they brought him back to work to early, I knew then that they did.

Mr. Name deleted had a broken orbital, two broken teeth, a broken jaw, and fractured cheekbone. He spends the next four nights in the county hospital. He thankfully didn't press charges. Joel never formally gave him his Maranda rights, so the charges were dropped.

GORDON: What happened to Mr. Nelson, did he say why he did it?

YORK: He didn't have a reason, other than the obvious. Joel took his frustrations out on this guy. The Command put him on immediate administrative leave. Surprisingly, it never made the papers. I was sure that name deleted would have said something. He never did. I'm sure he never drove drunk after that beating either.

CHRIS: We know why it was never in the papers. Brigadier General Matthews was keeping correspondence with Mr. Nelson. We can only assume that Mr. Nelson was writing back but we have no proof of that. Again, it's only speculation that Mr. Nelson did.

YORK: I have a hard time believing that. I understand about the card with the roses but pen pals, really?

CHRIS: Here have a look.

Letter addressed directly to Officer Joel Nelson

Good Morning Officer Nelson,

I hope this day finds you as well as can be. Through my sources, I have heard about your incident and hope that I can help. I have already taken it upon myself to speak with the individual that you had the situation with and found a very profitable understanding with him. He will not be pressing charges and will keep his mouth closed about what had happened. A few of the local news media sources were also paid very well for their cooperation in this matter, so please don't worry about it. Everything has been taken care of.

I understand that the times you have experienced have been troubling ones, as it is said "the truth will march on". I understand your troubles and understand what you are going through. The world is a broken place, be patient my friend, one day it will be right again. People like you and I will have our day and the wicked will be punished.

May you find Peace and keep marching on.

Sincerely,
BGen J. Matthews USMC

CHRIS: Have you seen this before Officer York?

YORK: No, this is the first time I've seen this. I recognize the writing on the evidence bag, its Joel's, but I've never seen any letters like this. Were there more?

GORDON: There were several letters like this, seventeen letters total.

YORK: Wow, seventeen! What did Matthews mean by "His Sources"?

CHRIS: Brigadier General Matthews had several Captains in his battalions keeping an eye on the News. We also know that he had a few Colonels contacting individuals or places for information on both people and events. It's likely that he had someone keeping a tab on Mr. Nelson. We suspect that this letter was written only days after Nelsons incident, that's confirmed with Mr. Name Deleted. He said a man came to him in military uniform and offered him money for silence. To which he took happily. Mr. Name deleted didn't disclose the amount, but we can only assume that it was a great deal.

YORK: Was it Matthews that spoke to Mr. name deleted?

CHRIS: No, the gentlemen in question didn't fit the description of Matthews. We were eventually able to find out who it was. Mr. Name Deleted described the man as being about six foot brown hair and brown eyes and about one hundred and eighty pounds. And of course, the individual was wearing a military uniform. From Mr. Name Deleted description, it was almost any Marine, so the information was useless.

YORK: Where did Matthews get the money for all of this?

GORDON: Were still trying to piece that part together. Our best guess is that he invested his family's insurance policies. We can't confirm that because his bank records are sealed due to his clearance level.

YORK: Is that a "you know, and you aren't telling me", kind of thing?

GORDON: No, we honestly don't know yet. Like I said, the best bet it was insurance money.

CHRIS: What happened when Mr. Nelsons leave started?

YORK: He stayed mostly to himself at first with nothing unusual that I had seen. He just stayed home. I saw him twice, after his incident. Once when Joel came down to headquarters, and the second was when Mr. Name

Deleted went before the judge. Joel was outraged when he was freed because of the Maranda Rights. He was almost held in contempt of court. He stormed outside and punched through a window across the street. The people in that coffee shop where scared, at best. Our Captain asked him to come in almost two weeks later. I found out that later that the command said that Joel had to see a Doctor, or he would be forced to retire.

GORDON: We have information that he saw a Dr. Name deleted, she specialized in Post-traumatic stress. From the documentation from the Police Headquarters, he attended twice a week for four months before he stopped going.

YORK: The report didn't say why Joel stopped going?

GORDON: No, it didn't say. When we contacted the Doctors office, she wasn't allowed to release the information.

YORK: Joel mentioned that he started having night terrors. He started having horrible dreams about his family. He was also becoming edgy around loud, sudden noises. Joel felt that the Doctor didn't understand and didn't care, so he stopped going. That's about the time he stopped talking.

CHRIS: Did anyone try to get Mr. Nelson to go back to the Doctor?

YORK: The Captain got word he stopped going so he called me into his office. Capt. Name Deleted asked that I go with him to talk to Joel at Joel's house.

GORDON: Did you talk to Mr. Nelson?

YORK: We knocked for nearly twenty minutes before Joel answered the door. He looked awful. Joel clearly wasn't taking care of himself and hadn't shaved in months. Joel's clothes looked dirty and just unkempt, I can only assume he been living in them and sleeping in them. The smell was dreadful, his house just had this odor of rotting food. He and his wife never kept the house in a perfect state, but it was always good. But this was worse than I've ever seen it. It took us a while to convince Joel to have a seat so we could talk, but he finally cooperated with us and did so. That's when I found out that Joel was only sleeping about three hours a day. When he did sleep, he said he would wake up in the middle of the street.

CHRIS: In the dream?

YORK: No, sleep walking. Joel mentioned one occasion that he woke to find himself staring at a car. Joel never mentioned sleep walking before. The Captain and I suggested that Joel might want to see the Doctor again and that we would be happy to take him. He protested a bit but agreed. The next Tuesday, I picked Joel up for the doctors.

GORDON: And Mr. Nelson stuck with it?

YORK: Maybe a month or so.

GORDON: Why did Mr. Nelson stop going again?

YORK: Joel started going to church, which I thought was good. Joel also told me that he had someone that would take him to church and to the appointments.

GORDON: Do you have a name for this person?

YORK: No, I don't remember the name.

CHRIS: I don't want to seem disrespectful but are you sure this person was even real?

YORK: Joel was always honest with me, so I was confident he wasn't lying.

CHRIS: So how did he meet this person?

YORK: My understanding was the Doctor set it up. She had a person in mind that needed a friend and had them meet at the office. They worked out the driving schedule and they invited Joel to church. My understanding was that he had gone to church for a while. I guess he even started getting involved too.

I had stopped by to see him at one point and he looked better, but Joel was talking about his family more. He never talked about them after the accident. He kept saying that he felt that he should have been there when the accident happened. Somehow, he got it in his head that he could have somehow stopped all of this from happening if he were there. I told him that was nonsense and that he couldn't have went to begin with anyway. I reminded him that we had both been working that week on a special assignment and he couldn't have taken any time off to go. I also mentioned that he didn't want to go to see his sister-in-law anyway. He became incredibly angry at me for saying that. I made it clear that it was the truth and nothing Joel could do now could change what happened. But Joel continued to try to convince me that he should have been there. It would have been three months until we would talk again.

CHRIS: Why so long?

YORK: I don't know. He just stopped talking to everyone. We called several times and stopped by but no answer. Then just out of nowhere he calls me asking if he could come over.

CHRIS: Just called unexpectedly?

YORK: Yeah, just out of nowhere.

CHRIS: How did Mr. Nelson look?

YORK: Joel looked great. He just seemed well, in fact good enough to start talking to the Captain again about maybe reinstating him. The Command decided to not reinstate him, but they helped him with his disability. Eventually the command got Joel on permanent disability with a chance down the road of maybe coming back to work, maybe not on the streets but office stuff.

GORDON: How much time has passed since the incident with Mr. Name Deleted?

YORK: It was about a year. There was one thing strange. When he started to feel better, I stopped by and the house was clean, exceptionally clean. It was good to see the house clean again. It had been a long while since it looked that good. It made me feel that Joel was doing better. The only strange thing is that he didn't let me in the house. I could see from the front door it was clean.

GORDON: He didn't want you to come in?

YORK: No, he wouldn't let anyone in the house.

CHRIS: Was Mr. Nelson getting out of the house during this time period?

YORK: Yeah actually. The last time I saw him was a week before his death. He stopped by the Headquarters. No real reason to be there just talking to everyone. It was good to see him there.

GORDON: Was there anything notable in between the time at your headquarters and his death?

YORK: No, nothing. It was like normal by that point to go weeks without talking to Joel.

CHRIS: Do you mind speaking about Officer Nelson's death with us. Would that be a problem?

YORK: I don't mind, it needs to be said. It's sad of course. I don't talk about it often.

GORDON: Why would you feel it needs to be said?

YORK: Frankly, Joel's death was startling and shocking. I understand that all deaths are like that. Even when you know it's coming. It's never easy.

CHRIS: Do you remember where you were when Mr. Nelson died?

YORK: I do. I was about ten minutes from Joel's home when the call comes over the radio. The call was a *10-52* or an ambulance needed. The dispatch officer said there was a possible shooting or active shooter, and officers were needed to respond. Dispatch then gave the address to respond. I immediately got over the radio and announced that it was Joel's house, and all officers need to respond immediately. My new partner and I were the first on the scene. That's Officer Name Deleted, he's a good guy. He would come to the cookouts at my place on holidays. He was just as freaked out as I was when I recognized the address. Dispatch came back on the radio as we pulled up and advised us again that there may be an active shooter at the location.

GORDON: What did you see when you arrived, anything out of the norm.

YORK: A lot of things were out of place.

CHRIS: Like what exactly?

YORK: To start, we pull up and there is no one around on the street.

GORDON: Wouldn't that be normal for a shooting?

YORK: No actually, it's usually pure panic and chaos. Also, you usually see people milling around or a body.

CHRIS: You didn't see any of that?

YORK: No, nothing like that. It was business as usual on the street, other than us arriving in a hurry. Traffic and normal movement of day-to-day people.

CHRIS: That's very strange.

YORK: It is strange. It really raised the little hairs on the back of my neck. It just sent a real chill through your body. It was definitely awkward.

GORDON: Did you notice anything else.

YORK: The only thing was that Joel's front door, it was open. Officer Name Deleted and I got out of our squad car and approached the house very carefully.

CHRIS: You didn't wait for back-up?

YORK: We should have, it was the smartest thing. I admit that, but I was concerned about Joel. I realize that us just walking up to the house could have gotten me and Name Deleted shot. I just couldn't handle the idea that Joel may have needed me. Joel had been through so much that he didn't need any more crap laid on him.

GORDON: I can only assume everything was quiet as you approached the doorway.

YORK: We tactically maneuvered towards the door, my service weapon drawn, I took the right side with Name Deleted behind me. I took a moment to listen for noise; I didn't hear movement but could smell the cordite.

CHRIS: Cordite?

YORK: Smokeless gun powder. Name Deleted tapped my shoulder to tell me he was ready to move. So, I announced that we were police and heard nothing. So, I called Joel's name, still nothing. I decided to turkey peek around the corner. As I looked everything seemed normal until I looked at the center of the room about twenty feet from me. I didn't notice it at first glance but then I saw it, it was a black body bag in the room. The same kind the coroners use. I turned the corner of the doorway and just stood there in the door, shocked.

GORDON: What did you see?

YORK: The house as I mentioned before was spotless, except everything was either bagged up or wrapped up. Everything had a yellow tag on it. To my left were two tables set up. One table had lunch foods all set out and the other breakfast. Both had drinks ready to go on them. As I looked around, I noticed a piece of paper taped to the body bag. As I said, you could smell the cordite in the air; it was extraordinarily strong in the house. About that time is when the other units were starting to arrive.

CHRIS: You mentioned small yellow tags on everything in the house?

YORK: Yes, and everything was bagged up, everything! From books to shoes, all bagged. The tags, they were evidence tags, and they were numbered. As we started to look around and clear the house, we noticed on the coffee table a series of notebooks that were labeled for every floor of the house that corresponded numerically with the tags.

CHRIS: The house was cleared?

YORK: It was, there was no one in the house, and it was empty. No one but us and the body bag. As I looked around, I noticed all the tags had Joel's handwriting on them. Joel had put the description of the item, its location and what he wanted done with it. Things like "please sell" to "liquidate to estate" or "donate".

GORDON: I can only assume that the body bag had Officer Nelson in it?

YORK: Yeah, it was Joel. It was a self-inflicted gunshot to the head?

CHRIS: Self-inflicted?

YORK: What we later concluded was that Joel had gotten into the bag and called 9-1-1. When he got the operator, he said shots had been fired and he gave the operator his address and he just hung up. He took a .22 Magnum revolver, put it in his mouth and pulled the trigger. He obviously didn't want the round to come out the top of his head so it wouldn't make more of a mess. That's why the .22 mag, so we guess. I was the one that opened the bag and found Joel.

CHRIS: That's very macabre.

YORK: Very macabre, but that was just the beginning, we had nothing to do.

CHRIS: What do you mean by nothing to do?

YORK: Joel had done all the work. The way he stated the emergency on the phone, the coroner will show up. We didn't have to do anything. It was like being at a wake instead of a crime scene. Have you seen the suicide note?

GORDON: No, we haven't.

YORK: We have it. Give me a minute and I'll go get it.

14 Minutes pass

YORK: Here it is Special Agent.

GORDON: Thank you

To whom this may concern,

It may be hard to believe but I do this with sound mind and good judgment. I have willingly committed to the job of ending my own life in the hopes that I will find some true peace. I died the day my wife and beautiful children were taken from me by the carelessness of another. I was a walking husk of a man, a Ronin, doomed to walk the earth without purpose or meaning. There was nothing in my life that gave me pleasure; I felt only the sorrow of my loss. I could not escape the inevitable fact that I was forever alone. I had friends and I had family, just not the family that brought me the light of my life.

I will never see my son grow into a man. I will never see my daughter become a woman and someday a mother. I would never see their graduations, there first loves and their wedding days. I would never see my retirement with my best friend and partner, Tara. My life has no flavor.

I realize that my death will be a violent one, but a clean one as well. I felt that I could not put burden on those that did care for me, in both life and death. I did the best I could to. I will not need to be cut down or pulled from a river. Nor will I be needed to be cleaned off a street or taken from a bloody tome. I will also not take any life but my own. I went to the best efforts to ensure that my departure was as efficient as possible with minimal hassle.

I know that God will not forgive me. I know my family will not forgive me. I simply cannot continue to go on like this. This is not a life or a "life" worth living. I could see no light at the end of this tunnel. My heart is empty, it was full and overflowing. I have lost my smile and the reason for happiness. I could have asked for help; I just didn't want it.

Even though I breathe and my heart beats, I have been dead for years inside. I hope that I have at least made the burden of my death easy on my fellow Officers. I just hope that James Healy, the Murderer who killed my family, eventually finds he's as empty as I. May he never be forgiven! May he never find peace! May he never find happiness! May he never find rest!

I only ask of our God and Father that he understands Healy's wrongs and that he knows what he took from me.

May God find mercy on his soul as well as mine.

Sincerely,
Officer Joel Nelson

(Evidence file: 04052954 Nelson J.)

GORDON: That's terribly sad.

YORK: It is sad. We in fact determined that he had inventoried everything in his home. We think it must have taken a better part of a year to do so. He was meticulous in doing it too. Nothing was missed and all properly done. No one could have imagined him doing it. Joel's body just needed to be taken away. The state buried him with honors so that was paid for. The time it took to process the home was extraordinarily little. His next of Kin was contacted; I had the number to his sister. I don't really think there is to much more that needs to be said unless you need to see tags. Do you need to know the make and model of weapon Joel used? We have the weapon in the evidence locker if you need to see it.

GORDON: I really don't think that would be necessary. Those small things really aren't needed.

YORK: I can have a file sent to your office in the morning with the full reports if you like?

CHRIS: We appreciate it. We will keep the file in case something comes up. Thank you.

YORK: I hope that I was helpful in your research.

GORDON: That should be it

YORK: One last thing, if you don't mind me asking a question?

GORDON: Please do, ask away.

YORK: You had mentioned that Matthews had notes about Joel?

GORDON: General Matthews did. He had a series of speeches; Joel was mentioned once or twice.

YORK: Did Matthews mention how Joel's died?

GORDON: Yes, he did. Matthews called Mr. Nelson a hero. We believe that Matthews had a great deal of respect for Mr. Nelson.

Brigadier General Matthews Memoirs.

"...One of the few in this world that I utterly understand. Everyone should strive to be so compassionate and decent a person. Officer Nelson was the highest form of Hero. He sacrificed everything he had for his community..."

(See Matthews, Gen. Notebook 9 pg. 325).

"...when our backs are broken and our hearts are empty, push on, push on. Officer Nelson has pushed on, never looking back..."

(See Matthews, Gen. Notebook 9 pg. 391).

GORDON: These quotes are before Mr. Nelson took his own life. He wasn't mentioned again after his death.

YORK: Good, Joel deserves to be remembered as the hero he was.

CHRIS: You were also mentioned.

YORK: I was mentioned?

GORDON: According to our files, General Matthews mentioned you by name.

YORK: It's kind of scary that a man like Matthews knows about you and you don't know him. It explains a lot or maybe it doesn't: I don't know?

CHRIS: What does it explain?

YORK: About three days after Joel's death, I received a letter in the mail. It had no return address and was signed by no one. It's not unheard of to get stuff in the mail from people you arrested; most of it of course is mean and nasty.

GORDON: What did it say?

YORK: It simply said, "Officer York, you are a failure and a disgrace. Sincerely, the human race." I threw the letter away, it made me sick. I obviously never found out who it was from.

GORDON: I speak for both of us when I say that we don't blame you for the death of Officer Nelson.

YORK: Thank you. If there's anything else I can do to help, please let me know. I think I've answered as much as I possibly can.

GORDON: I think that is about it, we appreciate your time in these matters.

YORK: Your welcome gentlemen. Have a good day.

GORDON: This is Special Agent Sean Gordon. Its 11:01 A.M. at the Saint Louis Police Department. We have just finished interviewing Officer Andrew Allen York. Case file: 31008539-A, Operation Vanguard or "The Matthews Incident".

This formally concludes the Interview with Officer Andrew York. No further entries were made on this date or for this part of the interview.

Interview of Captain Bryant Justin Tessle

Monday, August 28th, 2028
United States Disciplinary Barracks (USDB)
Fort Leavenworth, Kansas

GORDON: Its 11:30 A.M. in United States Disciplinary Barracks, Fort Leavenworth Kansas, Maximum Security Wing, Block 5. Seated next to me is Special Agent William Chris. Across from us, at the interview table is Captain Bryant Justin Tessle, Former Administrative clerk, Personal Assistant, and Records Officer to Brigadier General Matthew's: Case file 31008539-A, Operation Vanguard or "The Matthews Incident". Capt. Tessle is 35 years of age, is 5'10", weight is 149 Lbs. He is of slender build, brown hair, has no discernable marks or scars, has blue eyes, and a light complexion. He is Caucasian and an American. His fingerprints are on file and classification code 1 for the following: several counts of involuntary manslaughter. He is also accused of treason and conspiracy of treason, terrorism and is considered a traitor of the United States of America. He is currently awaiting Court Martial.

Key testimony involving the Death of Officer Joel Nelson and the months leading up to his death. Captain Tessle is at this time at liberty to speak about Brigadier General Mathews and operation Vanguard by the Supreme Court and not under a Gag order.

TESSLE: Good Morning Gentlemen, what brings you back today?

GORDON: We are here to see if you have in your possession the log entries regarding an Officer Nelson and his death. Our records show that Officer Nelson was in correspondence with Brigadier General Matthews. We are pretty convinced that Matthews May have mentioned Officer Nelson in one of his speeches.

TESSLE: You will have to refresh my memory. Brigadier General Matthews wrote and spoke to a lot of people.

CHRIS: Officer Nelson's family was killed by a drunk driver in Ackley, Iowa. Nelsons Wife and two children were driving to Saint Louis Missouri. Does this sound familiar at all to you?

TESSLE: Is this incident regarding the apparent suicide in the home where the gentlemen had inventoried everything?

GORDON: That's the file that we are looking for.

TESSLE: I'm fairly sure I have the file. I will need a moment to recover them...If you don't mind waiting of course? It will only take a few minutes.

14 minutes pass

TESSLE: I found the file you are looking for. Officer Nelson was mentioned a few times, but this particular day was relevant to him. I believe it was the day of Officer Nelson's death.

GORDON: That's exactly what we are looking for. We wanted the immediate reaction of General Matthews.

TESSLE: General Matthews took this pretty personally. I could visibly see General Matthews was hurt by the loss of Officer Nelson. General Matthews just stood in front of us, looking at us. It felt like he was looking into us, through us. He had this way of making you feel vulnerable and almost naked. When Matthews would lock eyes with you, it felt like he was looking right into your soul. When Matthews did that, he could just read a person. He could tell when you were lying or tell when you were holding something back. He just always knew. I'm not suggesting he was psychic or something crazy like that, he just knew how people worked. Do you know what I mean?

GORDON: I think I know what you mean.

CHRIS: Like a mother or father would know? Do you mean like that?

TESSLE: Yes! Just like that. Matthews could read you like a book. It made him very affective. That's what he was doing that morning. Every Marine in the division was standing in formation in front of him, Matthews just paced in front of us at first, and he was gravely quiet. He was like a lion in a zoo, just back and forth. At first, he was looking at the ground singing to himself quietly. General Matthews then paused for a moment like he had collected his thoughts and turned to look at us. Matthews started pacing again, this time, as I said looking at us. One by one, he passed a Marine in the front line, looking dead into their eyes. Once Matthews was done with the first row, Matthews went to the front of the formation and called for the commanders to "open ranks". The order was obeyed, and the marines did as instructed.

CHRIS: Open ranks?

TESSLE: It's an order used to open a platoon or any unit size for that matter, up.

CHRIS: What is it used for.

TESSLE: Mostly for inspection or when you have been on a march with gear. We give open ranks to drop packs or allow in inspecting officer to move around easily. Get it?

CHRIS: I do, thank you.

TESSLE: That's fine, anyway. The units open there ranks and General Matthews then starts to move slowly through the ranks. He's looking at everyone one-on-one, and I mean everyone. Not a word is uttered. No words of encouragement or reprimand, just silently stalking up and down the files of marines.

CHRIS: How long were you standing there?

TESSLE: We stood in the position of attention for a better part of two hours before General Matthews actually spoke.

GORDON: Was this behavior normal for General Matthews?

TESSLE: No, this was out of the norm. The formations were obviously, but not him looking us over like that.

GORDON: What do you think General Matthews was looking for? Was he inspecting your uniforms?

TESSLE: No, nothing like that. This was different?

CHRIS: How was it different?

TESSLE: Well, with an inspection, you measure the uniforms for correctness. Name tape placement and things like that. Also, a commander or First Sergeant would accompany the inspector with paperwork to determine pass or fail. Also, the Marine would be required to present themselves to the inspector. In other words, formally address the inspector. That's like name rank and job.

GORDON: None of that?

TESSLE: No, none of that. Just silently looking into our faces.

CHRIS: You never said what General Matthews was looking for?

TESSLE: That's because I honestly don't know. All I can tell you is what Matthews said. If you like I can continue?

GORDON: Please continue.

"Marines, Ladies, Gentlemen, my children,

"Let the Hero, born of woman, crush the serpent with his heel", today is a sad day for me and the city of Saint Louis. One of their own, one of their finest took their lives today. The worst part of that his passing will not make a single headline other than the city he grew up in, but I remember, and thus you Marines will remember Officer Joel Nelson. Good and great people every day are overlooked and certainly not appreciated for their value to the human race.

This very day, there are a few people that are responsible for Officer Nelsons death, even though it was suicide. Nelson was pushed to do what he did. Nelson was pushed by the drunk driver that killed his beloved family, pushed by a society that doesn't care, and pushed by his friends. Well, one friend… friend…that's laughable, what kind of friend does nothing but stand by and watch his best friend fall apart? Today we all have " friends", sometimes thousands of friends.

* Ten Second Pause

On social media! Let me lay it out, those thousand are not " friends", at best acquaintances. People just don't know the difference. A friend is someone you admire or have a strong affection too, you both care equally for one and another. The disconnect is the acquaintances and that people don't know the difference. They know little of you and care less; you are a name or number to these friends. The family is broken and so is the fiber of personal relationships. We don't go and spent time with one and another, we just simply "Chat online". What a joke!

We have children growing up thinking that this kind of unipersonal relationship is healthy, it's not. Officer Nelsons "Friend" didn't have the wherewithal to identify his brother in arms was having serious problems, his friend was hurting inside. I'm just going to say it; Officer York killed Officer Nelson with his lack of empathy and caring. This happens every day!

So how do I make this judgment? It's actually amazingly simple. For a man to inventory an entire house, two thousand six hundred square feet, it doesn't happen overnight. His friend had not noticed that Officer Nelson had been planning this for over a year. It's easy for me to judge Officer York. I don't need to justify my actions. We were not friends, Nelson, and me. However, I paid for his Doctor's, I paid for his transportation, I paid for the Grocery's that Officer Nelson had eaten and I wrote him monthly. I did all this after his precinct stopped paying him. Mind you, he never wrote me back, but the checks were always cashed, I did as much as I could. Did York? No, Officer York did not. A man that Nelson never met did more than his so called best friend.

I washed my hands of this, York cannot. If you care about someone, you show it, you say it, you display it. Officer York's lack of empathy is apparent, he saw nothing wrong with a man who lost everything and pretends to be ok. A man that has lost everything is broken! A real friend would be able to see that. But Officer Nelson's friend goes about his life today as they bury Nelson tomorrow. At least Nelson is buried beside his family. I wonder if York cares enough to attend. Nelson's friends should be there. Just like his friend should have been there to prevent the death.

We as people have a responsibility to each other, we need to take care of one and another, we need to watch out for the others next to you. There is clearly a huge disconnects between Nelson and York and it was York. The sings were there, and Yok was too blind to see them. Officer Nelson became a recluse, he lost his job out of a random act of violence, he wasn't sleeping, and he was having nightmares. The list goes on and on...

*Ten Second pause

Officer York did nothing. I personally feel that he should be held accountable for the death of his partner, but that will never happen.

"You, Captain, Scribe. Make sure a letter gets sent to Officer York on my behalf about his failure as a human being."

*Distant voice
"Yes Sir".
He should know his failure and be aware of his personal worth.

I still am astonished how people want to make another person's suicide about themselves. They greave but do nothing to help. They shed tears but did nothing for that individual. We always speak kindly of the dead. Imagine how refreshing it would be to say the truth. Imagine giving the eulogy of truth. For Officer Nelson, he was a hero.

We as Marines understand the value of friendship, the civilian world does not. We watch out for one and another, they just stab each other in the back. They have no loyalty to anyone but themselves. Civilians have no honor, no courage, and no commitment. That is the Serpent, that is the evil... they just don't care. Civilians take no responsibility for their actions but cry at the end of their failures or short comings.

This house that we call home, our country, it needs to be fixed. It is not damaged beyond repair. It still has a chance. Our system of government, though young, has the chance to still survive and grow. It starts with personal responsibility and the willingness to act. We can fix it; we will fix it. We are more than mindless drones, we are Marines!"

TESSLE: Of course, General Matthews, then orders us to close ranks and runs us for many miles. I guess to wash away our sins if you will.

CHRIS: He sounded very mad, obviously.

TESSLE: Oh, General Matthews was. As we ran, he made us say "Officer Nelson, where you at?" in the formation as a cadence. We said that for at least three miles. It was just over and over again. I swear I heard in in my dreams for days. If General Matthews wanted us to never forget Nelsons name, he did a good job.

GORDON: Matthews asked the scribe, which I assume is you, to write a letter?

TESSLE: Yes, that was me. I was the scribe he was referring. I wrote a short letter to Officer York as I was ordered.

GORDON: Officer York had told us of the letter. He said it had no return address or no signature.

TESSLE: I didn't want Matthews to get in trouble for basically threatening a civilian. So, I didn't sign it. I followed Matthews's orders, I just tweaked them. Made them fit the situation and tread the proper lines.

GORDON: Was there anything else that Brigadier General Matthews said about Officers York or Nelson

TESSLE: No, that was his only entry that day and the only one relevant to Officer Nelson or York.

GORDON: We appreciate your time and thank you for the entry.

TESSLE: My pleasure, it's nice to get out of the cell from time to time.

GORDON: Try and have a good day Captain.

TESSLE: I will try, all I have is time. I have nothing better to do than have a good day.

GORDON: This is Special Agent Sean Gordon. Its 1:40 P.M.in United States Disciplinary Barracks, Fort Leavenworth Kansas, Maximum Security Wing, Block 5. We have just finished interviewing Captain Bryant Justin Tessle. Case file: 31008539-A, Operation Vanguard or "The Matthews Incident".

This formally concludes the Interview with Captain Bryant Tessle. No further entries were made on this date or for this part of the interview.

Memorandum from Special Agent Sean Gordon

TO: **Brian Samuels, Director of the Federal Bureau of Investigations**

FROM: **Sean Gordon, Special Agent**

DATE: **Monday, August 28th, 2028**

RE: **Death of Officer Joel Nelson**

Good Evening,

As per protocol, I am giving my informal opinion of the investigation of the death of Officer Joel Nelson and my personal opinion to what I witnessed.

Dr. Walton gave good insight to the death of Officer Nelson's family. I found him extremely helpful and knowledgeable. The interview established a clear connection between Officer Nelson and Brigadier General Matthews.

Officer York gave great detail into who Officer Nelson was, and what inevitably led to his death. Officer York showed no signs of feeling responsible for the death of his friend. What amazed me the most is how Officer York did not know that Officer Nelson was inventorying a three story house. A great deal of time and effort would be needed to accomplish such a task. I feel that Officer York should have taken more of an interest in Officer Nelson's life. York should have really tried harder. I only say that because there were times that Officer York didn't speak to Officer Nelson for weeks at a time. My feeling is that the signs for Officer Nelson wanting to commit suicide were very obvious. Either Officer York ignored the signs or was ignorant of them. York being ignorant to the situation is hard to personally believe due to all Officers taking suicide awareness courses annually.

Captain Tessle has proven to be a helpful tool in the information gathering of what led up to Vanguard. I have personally concluded that General Matthews comes up with his speeches in and impromptu manor. Taking the time at the moment to decide what he will say and then addressing everyone. We see the Mathews speech style of making every Marine personal to him. Looking everyone in the command personally in the eyes, I think this gives a personal feeling to what is said thus the Marines will retain it. I'm not completely sure this is taught or just something General Matthews does personally. I believe it's the latter of the two. I believe this is just the person that General Matthews was, but again, it's just an educated guess and I will follow this question up with more information at a later time.

From the information I was provided, it seems to me that General Matthews places the most blame on Officer York for the death of Officer Nelson. In fact, the Drunk driver that killed Nelsons family is rarely mentioned; I think only once by name. General Matthews shows a great deal of dislike towards social media. I could not find any reason why other than that it creates distance between people. General Matthews never mentioned about cell phone use for contacting friends as good or bad. General Matthews also has shown a high regard for traditional friendship and its importance. I can only conclude that the friend relationship somehow corresponded directly with the battlefield environment. I make this conclusion based solely on the idea of living with one and another in harsh environments. Going through such hardship would bring people closer together. Obviously, social media cannot come close to making lifelong friends like that.

General Matthews took the death of Officer Nelson's family very personally. This impart has to do with the death of General Matthews family. They were killed in a similar fashion. No information was really given as to what happen to the drunk driver that killed Matthews's family. It was so personal that General Matthews had Captain Tessle write a handwritten letter to Officer York.

Within regards to what General Matthews said to his Marines after Officer Nelson's death, Matthews never flounders in his intensity. General Matthews shows that he wants to make an impression on his command. General Matthews doesn't throw his power around, but laser focuses it on one thing at a time. He drives a point home with a simple message that is straight and forward.

Sincerely,
S.A. Sean Gordon.

Eyewitness accounts of Operation Vanguard

"You always just think to yourself, "Nothing like this happens anymore in our country." Our country can't end like this".

-Ashley Cook (New Mexico Times, Smith-Harris p.2)

"The Police were calling for anyone that had shooting experience, that could hunt, or anyone that was prior service. The police were just begging for help, asking if anyone had guns. There are no guns in this town. Gun free zones really screwed this pooch. It was almost sad and laughable. I told a cop that asked me "not in this city brother, no Guns!" I just thought to myself, Aren't you the guys with the guns. I used to go to all these rallies to make changes and make the world safer. Here we are, defenseless. We pay them to keep us safe, right!?! I saw them call in the National Guard, that's ironic...the military to kill the military. The Guard shows up and "BAM!!!" they were just gone! They were wiped out, clean! I saw the fight for the senate building, those guys that took the senate just cut down those National Guardsmen like grass. The police didn't do any better. This cop hands me some Assault rifle thing and says, "I need you to help me", I did the right thing. I threw that weapon of death right on the ground and said, "No Word Deleted way man, I hate those things". That cop had the nerve to threaten me because I wouldn't help. It was right after that the cop got shot! I just ran. I saw another cop; I ran to him. He was covered in blood. He was surrounded by dead or hurt National Guardsmen. He was pulling them out of the street, he yelled for me to help. I told him that real men don't kill and started to run the other direction. I guess the sniper on the capital building thought I was right because I saw later on the news, he shot that cop.

-Andrew Clark (Liberal Socialist Movement, Clark p.1)

"I saw the medic guys bring that congressman out of the capital building. I heard that he was executed inside earlier because he refused to cooperate."

-Corry Hennery (The weekly Journal, Malcom, 2026, p. 4)

TRANSATLANTIC FLIGHT LA-2100

Interview of Ashley Trisha Blackfoot

Friday, September 1st, 2028
Broken arrow, Oklahoma

GORDON: Its 8:30 A.M. in Broken arrow, Oklahoma. We are currently at the home of Ashley Trisha Blackfoot and Dr. Thomas Wyatt Moore. We are currently seated in the living room. Sitting next to me is Special Agent William Chris and across from us Mrs. Blackfoot: case file 31008539-A, Operation Vanguard or "The Matthews Incident". Mrs. Blackfoot is 39 years of age, is 5'6", weight is 121 LBS., she is of slender build, brown hair, is currently employed as a dental assistant, has no discernable marks or scars, has brown eyes, and a tan complexion. She is Native American (Seminole Nation) and an American. Has no fingerprints on file and has no classification code.

Key testimony involving the flight LA-2100 and the incident aboard the flight. Mrs. Blackfoot is at this time currently at liberty to speak about Brigadier General Mathews, Operation Vanguard, and Flight LA-2100 by the Supreme Court and is not placed under a gag order. It should also be known that all families involved in flight LA-2100 have given prior consent for this interview.

GORDON: Good morning. I wanted to let you both know something before we start. Both Agent Chris and I decided that we would interview you separately. We have vastly different questions for both of you and feel that for organization sake, it would be easier to do you independently. We will start with you Mrs. Blackfoot.

BLKFOOT: Good morning to both of you. That sounds perfectly fine.

GORDON: We came to speak to you about what had happened on flight LA-2100, are you still willing to talk to us about that?

BLKFOOT: I am still willing, yes. It will be hard, talking about it is never easy but I will do it. I feel it's important. People need to know what happened and how it happened. There has been way too much speculation or guessing. I need to tell what really happened.

GORDON: I'm glad you feel that way, it is particularly important. We are currently trying to piece together links between Mrs. McCarter and Brigadier General Matthews. That's why we came to speak to you.

BLKFOOT: General Matthews, the General Matthews? Like, Vanguard Matthews?

CHRIS: Yes, Ma'am, That General Matthews.

BLKFOOT: A link between them? They knew each other? Did he help her plan everything that happened?

CHRIS: No Ma'am, nothing like that. We know that they had correspondence while she was in jail after the flight. But only at that point, not before Mrs. McCarter was awaiting trial.

BLKFOOT: I'm not quite sure I understand what you mean.

GORDON: Brigadier General Matthews mention Mrs. McCarter in notes we found in Matthews's Office. That's all we know of the connection as of now. We hope to learn more. Like we said, we are sure it was after the flight, not before. As I understand, this is your first interview since the incident, correct?

BLKFOOT: Yes, this is my first interview since. I was asked a lot of questions the few weeks after the incident, but I figured I would grant the F.B.I. this interview. I figured that if the F.B.I. is sending agents, it must be important. It's a long way from Quantico.

GORDON: We appreciate the time you are giving us. This is just what we do, we travel and talk to people.

BLKFOOT: That doesn't sound too bad.

CHRIS: It had its moments.

BLKFOOT: It has to be more exciting than that.

GORDON: We have a quiet job; we like it that way.

BLKFOOT: There is nothing wrong with that.

GORDON: Your husband is Thomas Moore, it's that right?

BLKFOOT: Yes, that's my husband. It's the last name that's throwing you off, correct?

GORDON: Actually, yes.

BLKFOOT: We kept my maiden name, for family sake. It keeps my family and the old traditions alive.

CHRIS: That's truly awesome.

BLKFOOT: Thank you.

CHRIS: You are very welcome.

BLKFOOT: I'm sure you didn't come all this way to talk about last names, so where do you want me to start?

GORDON: Whatever makes you comfortable. You can start where you like.

BLKFOOT: I can tell you a little about myself if you like?

GORDON: Please do. That's a good place to start.

BLKFOOT: I have known my husband practically forever. I mean my whole life. We lived next door to each other, neighbors. Both our parents still live in those same houses today. It doesn't seem like it but we have been married for eighteen years now. My life, by my own standard is perfect. I work in the same dentist office that my husband does, we carpool. He is a dentist and I'm a dental assistant to one of the other Doctors. We live a good and happy life. I'm a proud member of the Seminole Nation. My mother was Native American, and I am proud. My mother and father met years ago by chance; I love telling this story. My father had a business trip out here and saw a woman on the side of the road with a flat tire. My father pulls over to help her and it was all magic from there. They are still together, and both are happy. I'm glad I found that special someone like my parents did. We are all so very blessed. Nothing in our lives is out of the ordinary. We were just the average family, aside from having no kids. We just love life, it's just that simple. It's strange how things can change without notice. The world can flip on its head without the smallest warning. However, at that moment, you have the choice to let it get you down or build you up. I always have been positive but when the world fell apart, I chose to look life in the eye and tell myself that it is all just temporary.

CHRIS: Things just happen sometimes, that's just the way of the world.

BLKFOOT: That is truly how it is, things happen. Anyway, my husband and I had been planning a trip for a better part of a year. This was our first real vacation to this point; it was always the stay at home vacation or someplace we could drive to easily that we have seen a thousand times before. Don't get me wrong, there is nothing wrong with staying at home, it's just nice to do something new for a change. So, we decided to do the European experience. We had plans to fly into the United Kingdom and spend a few days in London and then head to Scotland and then Ireland. We had all kinds of stops along the way, just beautiful places we have never seen before. It would end up being a month and a half total. I won't bore you with all the places and details. Trust me when I say it was a lot. As I said, we had planned it for nearly a year and saved longer. We were excited. We flew out of Tulsa and landed in New York. This was the farthest that we had ever been in the United States. I've never been to the East coast before and it as awesome. We had no problems on the flight, we actually rather enjoyed the long flight and looked forward to the even longer one. My husband and I actually enjoy our time together.

CHRIS: How long were you in New York?

BLKFOOT: We took a long layover. We were there all day and had to catch the plane the next morning for London. The day went well and so did the morning. We did a lot of sightseeing and just enjoyed the city. I have never seen anything like it before and genuinely enjoyed every minute. We got to JFK international around 6 A.M. the next morning only after staying at our hotel for a few hours. We wanted to get the most out of our time in New York. We weren't due to depart until 9 A.M. so we thought it better to get there early and get through all of the security. I'm always early and I hate rushing. I'd rather wait two hours then stress myself trying to run everywhere. The first hour we walked around, and the rest was spent sitting at the terminal until the flight. We didn't mind in the least.

GORDON: Did you notice anything unusual while in the airport?

BLKFOOT: That is a surprisingly common question. The one I hear the most. There was nothing out of the ordinary, just people walking around. We were just sitting at the terminal and waiting. People always assume that I saw

Bethany get on the plane or I saw her waiting to get on board. I didn't. If I did, I didn't notice her. Like I said before, nothing out of the ordinary.

GORDON: Is there any point that you remember Mrs. McCarter?

BLKFOOT: I was told after the fact that she was the greeting flight attendant as we boarded the plane. I kind of remember her.

GORDON: Not trying to repeat myself, but you don't remember her at all until on board?

BLKFOOT: You want to know if she had the bottle on her. Or as the news calls it "the vile"?

GORDON: That's basically what I'm asking? We only are asking because we just want to understand the whole story.

BLKFOOT: I don't know if she had the bottle on her? I never saw it if she did. Well, that's not totally true. I saw it after the fact a few months later. I never saw it at the time. But that's not what you're asking. You are asking at the time.

GORDON: How did Mrs. McCarter act at boarding?

BLKFOOT: No different than any attendant. She asked for our ticket and directed us to our seats. We put our stuff away in the overhead department and took our seats. Normal stuff, buckle seatbelts and get comfortable and wait for departure.

CHRIS: Where were you seated on the plane?

BLKFOOT: We were in business class, towards the middle of the plane. I don't remember the seat numbers off hand. I had the window, and my husband was seated in the middle. We had a gentleman seated next to my husband. He was a quiet gentleman; I don't remember his name. He didn't stay seated there for too long. He got moved a few seats back, they had a few seats open on the plane and wanted to make everyone as comfortable as possible. You know, let people stretch out and not feel like canned fish.

*Paper Shuffle

CHRIS: You were seated in 14-L. Your husband was in14-K. The gentleman next to your husband was Name Deleted in 14-J.

BLKFOOT: That's right, I couldn't remember his name, thank you.

CHRIS: Not a problem.

BLKFOOT: So, one of the attendants goes through the safety speech about buckling up, moving through the plane and the oxygen mask stuff. Like I said earlier, it was nothing out of the normal. Just a normal flight like any other, nothing special, everything was smooth.

GORDON: Did Mrs. McCarter give the Safety brief?

BLKFOOT: No, it was another attendant, an older gentleman.

GORDON: Did you happen to see where Mrs. McCarter had gone too?

BLKFOOT: No, she must have passed by at some point, I'm sure. I didn't notice. I only saw her next when she walked down the aisle to take her seat.

CHRIS: Where was that located, on the facing wall or the galley?

BLKFOOT: She was at the wall facing us. She just sat there as the plane started to taxi down the runway. She stayed there until the plane was in the air.

GORDON: So, you do remember her at this point?

BLKFOOT: Yes, I do. She was the only flight attendant that was in one of those little seats that's attached to the divider between class seating. She stood out, sitting there facing us.

GORDON: How long is the flight?

BLKFOOT: The flight was scheduled to take seven hours and a couple of minutes. We had no delays in take-off and didn't sit on the tarmac for awfully long.

GORDON: We know that there was a meal served on the flight at some point. Is that when the incident happened? It makes the most sense. Could you clarify the finer details?

BLKFOOT: I can. We were in the air approximately five hours when they announced that dinner was to be served soon. I remember that because on the back of the seat in front of me there was a screen with a map being shown on it. I remember that there was a distinct red line on the map.

CHRIS: That's called the "Point of no return".

BLKFOOT: That's right, I asked my husband that and he told me that too. I couldn't remember.

GORDON: That makes sense why the plane didn't fly back to New York when everything happened. The plane would have run out of fuel. The pilot had no choice but to land as soon as possible.

BLKFOOT: Yeah, that's why. So, one of the attendants announced that food was going to be served soon. I saw Bethany walking around asking what people wanted for dinner. She was caring a digital pad and nothing that was out of the ordinary. She finally approached us and asked if we wanted the Lasagna or chicken breast. We both had the Lasagna. The whole thing took about twenty minutes for her to ask everyone in our section.

GORDON: Did she do the whole plane or just your section? We know that the plane was short staffed on that flight.

BLKFOOT: She was doing our whole section. There were probably about ten rows in our section. So, it took about a half hour until the food started to show up. She went calmly down the aisle, row by row, seat by seat. She was just handing out the food to everyone. She was fast actually. I remember her being very efficient.

GORDON: Did you notice anything unusual while she served. Did the food look funny or smell strange?

BLKFOOT: I did notice one thing that I thought was out of place. Bethany didn't take the food cart to the galley when she was done.

CHRIS: She didn't take it back?

BLKFOOT: No, she started to serve us from behind, but she left the cart upfront and then just sat down and started looking around. I've never seen an attendant just sit down after service. I personally only saw them sit unless we were landing or taking off. Never in the middle of a flight, it was just really strange.

CHRIS: Was Mrs. McCarter doing anything while she was sitting there?

BLKFOOT: No, just sitting there with this wide eyed grin. She just looked overly satisfied with herself or something. I obviously know why that is now, but I didn't then of course. I remember that look. It was like a cat that knew the mouse was coming and it new it would have the drop on that unsuspecting mouse.

GORDON: Mrs. McCarter just sat there watching everyone eat?

BLKFOOT: Yeah, just sitting there. As I said, I thought it was a little strange.

GORDON: When exactly did you notice something wasn't right with the meal?

BLKFOOT: It didn't take long, not long at all, maybe five minutes or less if I were to guess. It was almost about the time that she sat down is when I heard the coughing start. I noticed right away that I had started to get a runny nose, shortly after my throat was starting to get scratchy. I also started to notice the skin on my neck was starting to itch and swell up. It was about then my husband has asked if I was okay? I told him I didn't know, and that I felt kind of funny. It was soon after that people started to scream and get hysterical.

GORDON: So, you didn't taste anything out of the ordinary with the food?

BLKFOOT: No, the food was fine. I didn't notice anything.

GORDON: What was Mrs. McCarter doing when the passengers started to scream?

BLKFOOT: She did nothing, just sat there. I saw all the flight attendants except her run to passengers to help them. She just sat there. I remember because I thought she should be doing something like contacting the captain or just someone. I started to cough really hard by this point and I started to have trouble breathing. I remember my husband talking to me, but I was getting tunnel vision. That's really all I remember from the flight.

CHRIS: When did you find out what happened?

BLKFOOT: I actually woke up in an ambulance. I had an oxygen mask on and was very confused. I must have been passed out for two maybe three hours. I was quite disoriented. It was the accents of the medical staff that threw me off the most. I know I was heading to England but to wake up to a man speaking proper English and asking if I was feeling better was a shock. I had no idea how much time had passed and really had no idea what had happened.

GORDON: Your husband was made to stay back at the plane, correct?

BLKFOOT: Yeah, the London Police made him stay. They wanted to ask him questions about the flight. He obviously wanted to stay with me. They wouldn't let him but assured him that I was stable and would be okay. As soon as I was put into a room, he had called and told me he would be there shortly to be with me.

CHRIS: How long did Scotland Yard Keep your husband?

BLKFOOT: It was hours, He told me that they had an idea of what had happened, and they needed him to run through his story over and over again. He finally got to the hospital and talked to the doctors about what had happened. The hospital wouldn't tell me anything. I guess they didn't want to scare me. They wouldn't even let me watch the television.

GORDON: I can only guess that the hospital did that because the flight was all over the news.

BLKFOOT: That's what they kept telling me. They didn't want me to worry about what had happened. They wanted me to just rest. Just rest, that didn't happen. I wanted to know what was done to me.

GORDON: Did the doctors tell you what happened?

BLKFOOT: They finally did, but only after my husband arrived. It took a lot of questioning before the doctor told us what had happened. What the doctors didn't realize was, by not telling me right away made me worry. I thought I had Ebola or something. I'm lying in bad wondering if they were lying to me, saying my husband hadn't arrived. I'm wondering if he had and I was just quarantined. Thinking back, I realize how silly that was. I clearly was not quarantined. But it scared me none the less.

CHRIS: So, were the news reports true?

BLKFOOT: They were true, it was peanut oil. Sounds silly, I know. But it is a serious allergy. Do you know that McCarter's lawyer tried to say we were not poisoned because peanut oil isn't a poison? Can you believe that? That argument clearly didn't hold water. I just wish the doctors would have been more honest or at least open with me. I understand why they did what they did but come on. It was really scary. Don't get me wrong, I'm incredibly lucky to be alive and for that I'm grateful.

CHRIS: Aside from the trial, is there anything else you remember about the flight?

BLKFOOT: No, nothing else. I just remember the ambulance, hospital, and the trial months later.

GORDON: We appreciate your time and thank you. I know you don't talk about what happened and we thank you for taking the time to sit with us. You were a big help.

BLKFOOT: I'm glad, thank you for your time as well.

GORDON: This is Special Agent Sean Gordon. Its 9:45 A.M. in Broken arrow, Oklahoma. We have just finished interviewing Ashley Trisha Blackfoot. Case file: 31008539-A, Operation Vanguard or "The Matthews Incident".

This formally concludes the interview with Ashley Blackfoot. No further entries were made on this date or for this part of the interview.

Interview of Dr. Thomas Wyatt Moore

Monday, September 4th, 2028
Broken Arrow, Oklahoma

GORDON: Its 10:45 A.M. in Broken arrow, Oklahoma. We are currently at the home of Dr. Thomas Wyatt Moore and Ashley Trisha Blackfoot; we are currently seated in the dining room. Sitting next to me is Special Agent William Chris and across from us, Dr. Moore: case file 31008539-A, Operation Vanguard or "The Matthews Incident". Dr. Moore is 38 years of age, is 5'11", weight is 167 LBS., he is of medium build, red hair, is currently employed as an Orthodontist, he has Heterochromia, has blue/brown eyes, and a tan complexion. He is Caucasian and an American. Has no fingerprints on file and he has no classification code.

*Key testimony involving the aboard flight LA-2100 and the incident of the flight. Dr. Moore is at this time currently at liberty to speak about Brigadier General Mathews, Operation Vanguard, and Flight LA-2100 by the Supreme Court and is not placed under a gag order. It should also be known that all families involved in flight LA-2100 have given prior consent for this interview.

GORDON: Good Morning Doctor Moore.

MOORE: Good Morning Agents.

GORDON: I'm glad you were able to make time in your schedule to meet with us about what had happened to your wife abord flight LA-2100. It's a tremendous help.

MOORE: I always appreciate the ability to help anyone, especially the F.B.I. It's not often you get to meet gentlemen like yourselves. I believe that homeland security did my interviews when all this craziness happened. I'm not really sure, if that's who I spoke too now that I think about it. If you don't mind me asking, why I'm being interviewed again? It has been an awful long time since all of this happened. Is there another indictment or something like that?

CHRIS: We deeply appreciate the kind words, thank you. The reason we are here is because we knew there was a connection between Brigadier General Matthews and Bethany McCarter. Please understand that Brigadier General Matthews did not plan what happened on the plane, he merely corresponded with Mrs. McCarter about it. We understand that the incident had caused such a news sensation that Matthews felt compelled to write to Mrs. McCarter. There had to be something that Brigadier General Matthews found interesting, that's why we are here to interview you. We want the details of that flight from your perspective. We obviously spoke to your wife. We just want to hear what you have to say about what happened.

MOORE: I would have never guessed a link between those two, ever. I will do my best to help you out. Where do I start?

GORDON: Your wife gave us a basic rundown of the events that led up to the flight and to the point where she had lost consciousness. We were hoping that you could shed some more light on Bethany McCarter and the flight itself after your wife passed out.

MOORE: Well, the flight was going great until it was dinner time. I saw nothing that raised any alarms or made me think anything was out of the ordinary. Our flight attendant was Bethany McCarter and she started to serve dinner about three quarters of the way through the flight. That's when people got sick and my wife got sick.

CHRIS: Your wife had stated that…

Papers Shuffle

Mrs. McCarter had "just sat down and started looking around" after she had served the food and sat down in her seat. Is that correct?

MOORE: That's correct. She went up and down the aisles serving the dinner, quite quickly if I remember right. My wife pointed out to me that she didn't take the cart back to the attendant area like I've seen other flight attendants do in the past. McCarter just pushed it into the next curtained area behind her seat and sat down watching the passengers eat.

GORDON: Why did that stand out to your wife.

MOORE: It only stood out to my wife because the attendant in the first class had said something to Bethany McCarter about putting the carrier away. Bethany had told him to mind his own business and that's when she sat down. Bethany wasn't quiet about it, she yelled at the other attendant. That's what grabbed my wife's attention. Bethany just sat there staring at everyone. I remember that people started to cough about the time she sat down. It started to get pretty loud and crazy fast. And there she sat, watching.

CHRIS: That's what your wife had said as well.

MOORE: Did my wife tell you that Bethany didn't get up at all to help.

CHRIS: She did say that, yes. Your wife didn't really go into too much detail after that.

GORDON: We weren't expecting too much detail. She did say she blacked out.

MOORE: I'm not surprised, by that point she was red as an apple and sweating. Her nose had started to run, and she was starting to wheeze and cough too. I could tell something

GORDON: When everyone started getting sick, what did you think was happening?

was obviously wrong. She wasn't the only one that this was happening too. There were a lot of passengers that were affected.

GORDON: When everyone started getting sick, what did you think was happening?

MOORE: At first, I didn't really know what to think. My mind had immediately gone to the idea of a gas attack or something to that effect. Like someone put something in the ventilation system or hid something in the overhead storage compartment. I then started to try and see if I was feeling sick like my wife was. I wasn't which surprised me. I then noticed we were eating the same thing and I had consumed the same amount; so, it wasn't poisoned. so, I thought. We were also drinking the same soft drink too. I looked around at those that were coughing and noticed it was people eating both meals and different drinks. It seemed so random. People started to scream by that point. I saw a guy two or three seats up from us just fall into the aisle. He was blue and swelled up. The people seated around him were trying to help him, he looked awful. My wife wasn't doing to much better either. She was really coughing by this point. I had some antihistamine pills with us and started giving them out to my wife and others. It seemed to help some but not everyone.

CHRIS: What made you think of doing that?

MOORE: I don't really know to be honest. I had nothing else with me and it was all I could think to do. I figured it couldn't hurt.

CHRIS: You were right, it helped a few people, and it was a good call. A lot more people would have died if you hadn't of done that.

MOORE: I was lucky. I panicked just like everyone else. I'm only glad it helped.

GORDON: What was Mrs. McCarter doing while all this was happening, still sitting there?

MOORE: She wasn't doing anything except grinning and watching people die. She had this almost demonic grin on her face. Totally pleased with herself. That really scared me. I knew then that something wasn't right.

CHRIS: I know I'm beating a dead horse but, she just did nothing? I find that hard to believe.

MOORE: That's all she did.

CHRIS: How was Mrs. Blackfoot at this time?

MOORE: My wife had started to get dizzy and I started to recognize what might be going on. That was just about the time the other attendants started rushing over to our section and started helping the passengers.

GORDON: And it was peanuts, correct?

MOORE: That's correct, peanuts. Everyone on the plane that was sick had a peanut allergy. It seems like such a small thing but it's extremely dangerous. At the time I thought it had to be a mistake in the food preparation. It's the only thing that my wife is allergic too.

GORDON: We realize that the investigators speculated peanuts and then later confirmed it. We wanted to hear it from the people that were there. So, you can confirm that?

MOORE: I'm not a medical doctor, I'm a specialized dentist. However, I know my wife and as I said, she is only allergic to one thing and that's peanuts. Thankfully, it's not a severe allergic reaction or she could have been number seventeen that day that died. By the time I figured out what it was she had already passed out.

CHRIS: Did you tell anyone?

MOORE: I actually didn't have time to say anything. A guy three rows back from me had figured it out when I did. He had just yelled for everyone with a peanut allergy to stop eating. I specifically remember that when we booked the flight on the web site, it had asked if anyone had any unusual allergies. In big red letters is stated that there were no peanuts allowed on the planes. I know it's been a while since peanuts have been on a plane. At least twenty years but we always check, and places are really good at letting patrons know.

GORDON: I know that most people carry auto-injecting syringes in case of a severe allergic reaction, didn't anyone have any? Did you carry one or your wife?

MOORE: She actually does have one and she normally has it on her at all times. However, it is against the security regulations to have them on the plane. I can't imagine someone trying to use an auto-injector to take over a plane, but that's not my business. It's silly and it cost a lot of people there lives that day. Almost my wife's. I know for a fact that Bethany McCarter knew that.

CHRIS: Why do you say that?

MOORE: McCarter fly's all the time as a flight attendant. She knows what can and can't go through security. It had to be the reason she used peanuts in the first place. Well to be more exact, peanut oil.

GORDON: What happened after the man yelled about the peanuts?

MOORE: There was complete panic on that plane. As I said before, no auto injectors so there was no way to help anyone. People were watching their loved ones and friends die and there was nothing anyone could do. And they're sat Bethany McCarter, with that word deleted eating grin on her face. She had such a judgmental look. Within minutes, sixteen people were dead. In the end, all because of her! I realize that she's not a serial killer, but she should be labeled as one.

GORDON: What did everyone do with the dead?

MOORE: A few people were going around and asking that same question. One of the older male attendants said he was going to speak with the captain. He walked behind the curtain and you could hear the receiver pick up. I can only assume it was the captain. A few minutes later, the attendant comes back out and tells us that the captain had advised him that we carefully move the individuals to the back of the seating area and drape a blanket over them. The attendant also said he would look to see how the food may have gotten peanuts in it. So, I made my wife as comfortable as possible and waited it out. There wasn't much I could do at that point.

GORDON: How was everyone acting?

MOORE: Everyone was obviously beside themselves but working together the best they could. Lots of people crying of course and for the most part, the plane was quiet. It was really hard to watch. A lot of people showed some true inner strength in dealing with the dead.

CHRIS: What was Mrs. McCarter doing?

MOORE: She never moved; she was still just sitting there. I was surprised that no one said anything to her. I guess people just thought she was in shock.

GORDON: You still thought that this was strange?

MOORE: Of course, because it was. I said something to a few people quietly, as to not bring attention to myself. They thought that it was strange that she was sitting there now that they noticed. I saw that the older flight attendant was about to pass me when I stopped him. He asks if my wife was okay and if I needed anything. I said she was doing good but mentioned that the attendant was just sitting there grinning. He didn't even notice her sitting there until it was mentioned. Keep in mind, all the other attendants were running around that plane like crazy. He said that it was strange, and he would go and talk to her. He walks over to her and starts to talk; I see them converse back and forth as I wait. He comes back a few moments later with a concerned look on his face. He tells me something isn't right, he said that he wasn't really sure what was bothering him about McCarter. Which I obviously agreed, then I had this thought and asked him a question. I asked, "who made the meals?" He looks at me for a long moment and says with a strange tone, "…she did". A long pause went between us. I said to the old attendant, we might have a problem here. He then tells me he will be right back.

GORDON: Where did he go?

MOORE: He starts walking around and continued doing as he was before. Just talking to the other people, he acted very casual and professional like nothing was wrong. He finally makes it back to me twenty-five minutes later. I ask what he was doing. He tells me that there are several off duty police officers on board and a few active and inactive military on board as well. He told me that he had brought up that she made the food and there weren't any peanuts on board. They all came to the same conclusion I did. That conclusion was that McCarter must have done something to the food. I know it sounds simple to think that now. But with all the chaos on that plane, it was hard to think.

CHRIS: You think she tried poisoning everyone on board?

MOORE: Exactly! Only our section got sick. The other areas, only the areas were fine. She prepped the food for us, and we got sick. The problem was that we were going to start our descent in about twenty minutes so if we are going to grab her, now is the time. We couldn't hesitate, we had to act now. The older attendant tells me that he is going to talk to the Captain and let him know what we are going to do. If the captain approves it, he will make an announcement that the smoking light is on. He would then make a count down from five. I said to him that there hasn't been smoking on a plane for a long time. He agreed and said that was best thing he could think of at the moment. I told him that I understood, and he winked at me. The older attendant then walked away to talk to the other passengers. I watched him go all around then he disappeared behind the curtain. I could hear babble behind the curtain, I looked over at Bethany. She was actually waiving to people that looked at her. It reminded me of a prom queen, it really creeped me out. I was wondering what she was doing, it seemed insane.

GORDON: Did he make the announcement?

MOORE: He finally did, it seemed like forever. I wasn't sure if he was trying to stall or talk to the Captain. I was wondering if the Captain was going along with the plan, either way the time finally came. He said in a typical announcer voice "attention everyone aboard flight 2100, the smoking light is on, repeat, the smoking light is on in five. He starts to count down and I could feel the tension in the air. Bethany McCarter didn't even notice. As soon as the Captain said one, the older attendant then yells "now". We all jump out of our seats and go running down the aisles at McCarter, eleven maybe twelve of us. She stands up holding a piece of plastic or something like that in her hand and starts waving it around. I found out later that it was a knife made from carbon fiber. She ready's herself and the older attendant fly's out of the curtain behind her and tackles her to the floor.

CHRIS: What about the knife, did anyone get hurt?

MOORE: Thankfully no, it got knocked out of her hand and one of the other passengers grabs it. I never found out why it was carbon fiber.

CHRIS: You can get the object through a metal detector. The flight attendants aren't required to go through the full-body scan, just the metal detector.

MOORE: I didn't know that thank you.

CHRIS: Not a problem.

GORDON: So, what happened after she was taken to the ground?

MOORE: We dog piled on her. Other passengers started to come to help too. This one lady starts grabbing lap belt extensions from the seats and suggests that we use them as rope to hold McCarter. It worked better than I could have ever imagined. She was buckled in so tight that she could barely wiggle.

CHRIS: Did Mrs. McCarter struggle or just give up when everyone jumped on her?

MOORE: She was like a fish. She was wiggling and writhing around trying to get free. All the time yelling at us, she was hysterical.

GORDON: What was she yelling exactly?

MOORE: She was yelling, "I'll kill you all for this" and calling us traitors. I was only glad to be alive. At one point, McCarter mentions that she did what she did to make us stronger. I found out after the fact that she had that intention all along. She wanted us to change and feel different. Again, this was explained after the fact.

CHRIS: Do you think it worked?

MOORE: That's tough to say, what she did was crazy. At first, I'd say no, it didn't change anything, but that wouldn't be true.

GORDON: What do you mean?

MOORE: Things had changed. Look, I went to good schools and a great university. I have never been in a fight in my entire life. So, I guess she did change things, I would have never tackled someone until that day. I look at people differently now, I guess.

CHRIS: Interesting.

MOORE: Anyway, we gagged McCarter with one of her own socks and propped her into a seat while the older attendant called the captain to give an update. As we buckled her in, I discovered she was holding a small vile or bottle with a cork. On it read "*Arachis Hypogea oil*", I had no idea what it was, but I turned it over to the police when we landed. I was told later that the vile was concentrated peanut oil. There is one thing now that I think about now and then.

GORDON: What's that?

MOORE: I never knew the older flight attendant's name. I never got the chance to ask him or thank him.

Papers shuffle

CHRIS: His name is Paul Hofstede.

MOORE: Paul, he looked like a Paul. A real good man, a brave man. Anyway, Paul comes out and tells us that the captain is ready to descend and we will be in London in twenty minutes, which was great news. We all buckled in and we landed without a problem.

GORDON: What happened when you landed?

MOORE: The police were waiting for us on the ground, as we pull up, they swarm the plane. They come on to the plane and take custody of her. As there taking her away, she starts screaming again. The sock unfortunately fell out of her mouth. This time she's screaming about how she just wanted us to see how she was making us stronger and that all the people that died did so for the betterment of the human race. She said that we would thank her someday for her sacrifice, saying that we will live happier lives now. She sounded crazy. She was kicking and screaming all the way to the Police car. As soon as she was off the other officer's and paramedics help take my wife and the other three off the plane that were sick. A special team came in to take all of us off and then the dead. I will say that it was amazing how efficient they were. The plane was far enough from the airport that the news people couldn't bother us or even get pictures. They put us in cars and drove us to a far off hanger. That's where the ambulance was waiting. My wife was still unconscious, but medics told me what hospital she was going and asked the officers to help with calling. I then spent hours talking to the police. When I finally was able to leave, I was questioned again by police at the hospital. I appreciated that they let me go to be with my wife, but they really should have given us a little more personal space instead of the constant questions. I was obviously upset at the time that they wouldn't let me ride with her, but I understood why they did that. They needed to know what happened so they could keep people safe.

CHRIS: Did you see Mrs. McCarter at all after they put her in the car?

MOORE: No, just at the trial. She pleaded guilty which surprised me.

GORDON: Why so?

MOORE: I thought for sure she was going with an insanity plea. She claimed to be the sanest in the courtroom. The trial was only a few days long and the judgment came fast. What took the longest was the waiting for three months for extradition which was annoying. Then waiting for the trial to start seemed like it took forever. It was a long and short process if that makes sense. That's about it really. There isn't really more to tell other than that. I hope it helped.

GORDON: It was a great help. We really appreciate your time and thank you.

MOORE: It was good to talk about all of this. It needed to be said. That woman is a monster, a true abomination. The world does not need someone like her in it. We all would be better without her in it.

CHRIS: I understand your anger.

MOORE: No, you really don't. That woman almost killed my wife and killed innocent people. Kids, mothers, fathers, sisters, brothers, husbands, and wives, she killed them all. She is a cancer and needs to be cut out!

GORDON: This is Special Agent Sean Gordon. Its 11:00 A.M. in Broken Arrow, Oklahoma. We have just finished interviewing Dr. Thomas Wyatt Moore. Case file: 31008539-A, Operation Vanguard or "The Matthews Incident".

This formally concludes the interview with Dr. Thomas Wyatt Moore. No further entries were made on this date or for this part of the interview.

Interview of Bethany Susan McCarter

Thursday, September 7th, 2028
Bedford Hills Correctional Facility for Woman
Bedford Hills, New York

WANTED
BY F.B.I.
Status: Captured

F.B.I No. 188731
WANTED FOR: MURDER

Bethany Susan McCarter
ALIAS: NONE

Description

AGE:	31	SCARS OR MARKS:	NONE
HEIGHT:	5'9"	EYES:	BLUE
WEIGHT:	130 LBS	COMPLEXION:	LIGHT
BUILD:	THIN	RACE:	CAUCASIAN
HAIR:	BLOND	NATIONALITY:	AMERICAN
OCCUPATION:	FLIGHT	FINGERPRINTS:	ON FILE
	ATTENDANT	CLASSIFICATION:	FELONY LEVEL 1

CAUTION

Current status is captured and beheld by
the Department of Correction.

**IF YOU HAVE ANY INFORMATION CONCERNING THIS PERSON
PLEASE CONTACT YOUR LOCAL F.B.I. OFFICE IMMEDIATELY**

> *This recorded session is called to order by the head of the
> Federal Bureau of Investigations, Special Investigations
> Unit.*

GORDON: Its 2:25 P.M. in the Bedford Hills Correctional Facility
for Woman, Bedford Hills New York, Maximum
Security Wing, Block F. Sitting next to me is Special
Agent William Chris and across from us Bethany

McCarter: case file 31008539-A, Operation Vanguard or "The Matthews Incident". Mrs. McCarter is 31 years of age, is 5'9", weight is 130 LBS., she is of slim build, blond hair, was a former flight Attendant for London/ American Airline Corporation, she has blue eyes, has no discernable marks or scars, and a tan complexion with blond hair. She is Caucasian and an American. Has fingerprints on file and she has a classification code level 1 for the following: murder 1 with sixteen counts, domestic terrorism and foreign terrorism and attempted murder. Her trial has concluded and is currently serving eleven life sentences.

Key testimony involving flight LA-2100 and the incident aboard the flight. Bethany McCarter is at this time currently at liberty to speak about Brigadier General Mathews, Operation Vanguard, and Flight LA-2100 by the Supreme Court and is not placed under a gag order. It should also be known that all families involved in flight LA-2100 have given prior consent for this interview.

GORDON: Good afternoon Mrs. McCarter.

MCCARTER: Good afternoon, I would first like to get this into the open, since I get to speak my mind freely. Word deleted General Matthews, word deleted him, and word deleted him, thank you!

GORDON: I guess we are starting then, as stated we are here to talk about the months that led up to the flight of LA-2100. I can only assume that you have just confirmed a connection between you and Brigadier General Matthews. I guess my first question is why the harsh start to the interview?

MCCARTER: You already knew that he wrote me?

GORDON: Yes, we do. Your name came up from notes retrieved from General Matthews's office and personal possessions. We actually had no idea about the note, but we had speculated. How did this note come about?

MCCARTER: After I was extradited back to the United States, General Matthews sent me a letter. That word deleted said some overly judgmental things and honestly, he knew nothing of my cause. That Word Deleted had not problems judging me. Then look at the crap he pulls …hypocrite. He had some nerve contacting me the way he did with such awful and fowl things to say!

CHRIS: What did Brigadier General Matthews write?

MCCARTER: I just want to ask, am I doing this interview correctly? Do I talk to one of you or both? Where do I start exactly with this?

GORDON: You can talk to either of us. It doesn't matter.

MCCARTER: I don't mind the interview, I've had hundreds, and I could care less about another. I've never been interviewed by the F.B.I. however, that's all new. And until that day, I never heard of General Matthew's. I don't know Matthews and never met him. Is that what you want to know?

GORDON: We just want to talk and listen. We will listen to whatever you want to talk about. We will guide you through the questionings. Sound good?

MCCARTER: Yes, sounds good.

GORDON: We know that Matthews took an interest in you. We believe that it wasn't just what got you placed in jail. We just want to know your thoughts and how you got to this point in life, not just the jail portion. As you were saying, Brigadier General Matthews wrote you.

MCCARTER: It was just about the time that my trial began that I got a letter from General Matthews. I got a lot of mail. Most of it was hate, I expected that. The uneducated took a dislike to me, word deleted them. I could care less what some backwoods hippie thinks of me.

CHRIS: What caught your attention with General Matthews's note?

MCCARTER: It was the military seal on the envelope that was different. At first, I thought it was a mistake or junk mail. That still surprises me.

GORDON: What does?

MCCARTER: That I get junk mail in prison. I never thought that would happen, but it does. So, I open the letter. Inside is a handwritten note, very elegantly written, good handwriting. That perked my interest. This letter says there is a right way and there is a wrong way to get a message across to people. Well, no word deleted! Matthews goes on by saying that I wasted my time with my misunderstood message, and it will be lost to most if not all people. How did he put it, oh yeah "good initiative, bad judgment"! Like I need his critique, what a piece of word deleted, why even take the time to write me. I have done fine without his stupid insight and I don't need it now or then. I expect hate mail, it is what it is, but his letter was unnecessary. Matthews must have had better things to do with his time.

CHRIS: Do you still have the letter?

MCCARTER: Nope, I threw it away, no loss in my opinion. Trash with trash!

GORDON: If you don't mind, I'd like to change direction.

MCCARTER: Okay?

GORDON: I'd like to ask about your personal history if that's ok? We have truly little information on your background, and we were hoping you wouldn't mind telling us how you grew up and things like that.

MCCARTER: That's fine, I have all day.

GORDON: Tell us about your past, what got you to, let's say to this point. All the way till you got put in jail.

MCCARTER: Ok, well I was born in Avondale Arizona. That's about twenty minutes outside of Phoenix Arizona. It's not a great place, it's just...decent, definitely wasn't making headlines across America. It was just an average place. I was born in West Valley Hospital. I can say without a doubt in my mind that I hated Arizona and couldn't leave fast enough. I hate the heat, never liked it. It's also just so barren and bleak. Just way too dry. I mean hey, its Arizona. My parents, Jamie and Allen McCarter lived in Avondale their whole lives. They loved it; they were happy. Good for them.

GORDON: Avondale was just that bad?

MCCARTER: Besides just hot?

GORDON: Yeah, besides the heat?

MCCARTER: Let's just say this, Avondale is not going to win any beauty pageants and it will never be a number one vacation spot. I'm sure people love it there; I know many do. It just wasn't for me. But my Parents loved it, like I said, my mom and dad lived their whole lives there.

CHRIS: What were your parents like?

MCCARTER: My parents were never going to win any awards, to say the least of them, at best they fed me. They were both drunks. Spend way too much on alcohol, way too much. I'm sitting at the dinner table eating a peanut butter and jelly sandwich for dinner and they are drunk. I mean plastered drunk, can't even stand tanked-up. The rent barely gets paid, but they are smashed! And the fighting was unreal. How two people that clearly hated each other stayed together is just mind blowing. Every Friday was fight night, the paycheck would come, and they would hit the liquor store, within four hours, they are pulling kitchen knives on one and another. And of course, my dad would beat the word deleted out of my mom. Right after getting home from school, I'm thinking "ding, ding, round one, fight". Like I said, a few hours later, beating the crap out of mom or us, well me. My sister name deleted could do no wrong. My dad had this belt that he called his "lesson strap", he loved to lace into me with that. I don't mean one hit on the word deleted. Oh no, that just wouldn't do. The face, my back, and his personal favorite, he would hit my breasts. My dad loved whipping that belt across my chest. The bruising was unbelievable. While beating me, calling me a word deleted, word deleted, and a word deleted. Really just any vile thing he could think of. One night he called me a fish!

CHRIS: Wait what, a fish?

MCCARTER: that's right, a fish!

GORDON: I'm sorry but I don't get that one? I don't understand the reference.

MCCARTER: It wasn't till a year ago that I understood it myself. That's why I remember it. I heard it one day and the light just came on. "I remember that", I thought to myself, which is a terrible thing to remember by the way. A fish is a prison term for the "new guy".

CHRIS: So, your dad spent time in jail then?

MCCARTER: Bingo! I come from high class breeding stock. Yup, robbery, armed robbery, extortion, selling drugs and rape, all but murder. The real kind of guy you bring home to mom. I don't mean to laugh but it's funny now. Yeah, he would just beat me and yell things like that. It became the norm, which is sad.

GORDON: So, what did you do that made him so upset that he felt the need to hit you, let alone with a belt?

MCCARTER: Upset, that's funny. As far as what I did, that's simple. I was alive, you know, born. I never had any issues with authority. I did my schoolwork and never caused problems at school. I was a model student and worked hard. I never started or got in fights. I never skipped classes or anything like that. I didn't even date. You can check my school record on that. I was a good kid and honestly, till recently, a model citizen. The abuse escalated as I got older too. It started as beating and just went on from there.

CHRIS: How so?

MCCARTER: Well, I was about fourteen years old. I don't remember the day or what time it was. It was a school night, I remember that. I guess my dad had to work late or something. Anyway, he gets home, and he is yelling as he walks in. He just walks up to me and punches me, like I was a grown adult man. I don't remember hitting the floor. When I came to, my underwear was around my ankles, and he was pulling his pants up. I remember feeling this aching pain…you know where. Word deleted it; I'm done talking about this part! You get the point and now you know what kind of piece of word deleted my dad was! Let's just leave it as…he was a real piece of word deleted. I'm not giving him anymore power over my life. The past just like him is dead and gone. Cheers to the worms that dine well tonight on the sorry sack of word deleted!

GORDON: I don't want to push the subject, but your mom just let this happen?

MCCARTER: She was no better, not at all. Like I said, she was a drunk too. She would just get wasted on a Sunday night and call out for work on Monday. They would blow all their sick time early in the year and get word deleted at me because they had to go to work later in the year when they were sick. Good parenting 101 there. I remember this one time, there was this boy who lived up the street from us, name deleted. A good kid, I hope he is doing well now. Got a nice home and a nice family, which could have been me. He liked me and I really liked him. He was the right kind of guy you want and should have. My mom however felt otherwise. Name deleted and I started dating, this is fifth or sixth grade. So, we are just holding hands at that point. My mom finds out, I think from my sister. My mom just goes completely off, yelling at me in front of name deleted and calling me a word deleted and a word deleted, real embarrassing. No reason for it, none whatsoever. He wouldn't even look me in the eye after that. I was so angry at my mom for what she had done. I never went behind her back. I'm not that kind of person. I wish I were now, maybe my life could have been more than it is now.

CHRIS: She didn't want you dating at all?

MCCARTER: No, she did, just not him. Anytime I brought anyone home, they were unacceptable. But the guys she introduced me too were no better than my dad or would grow up to be my dad. Thinking about it, many of them ended up just like him. She had no talent for picking men.

GORDON: How was your mom about the physical abuse? Did she try to stop it?

MCCARTER: She did her fair share too. She loved hitting me with yellow toy bats. It was one of those cheap plastic ones that you pick up in the discounted stores in the early spring. She would hit me in the back of the thighs with it. She was also fond of the broom handle. She would get it in her mind or dad would think that I did something wrong. That's when they would pull out this broom handle. That broom broke years before, but they kept it just for this special occasion. After hitting me with it, they made me kneel in it. It hurt so bad that my knees swelled like a grapefruit. It was hard to walk after that. I was messed up for a while after kneeling on it. My mom would tell me I was faking when I was limping, or I wanted attention. I could barely walk, and I wanted attention...they make me sick when I think about them now.

CHRIS: That is just truly terrible!

MCCARTER: To be frank, that's really not the worst of it. Remember when I said my dad came home and hit me, where do you think my mom was?

GORDON: I would guess not home.

MCCARTER: Oh, she was home all right, she watched him do it. Then told me it was my fault for making him mad! My fault, I was fourteen! I didn't deserve it! No one does. How could anyone deserve to be defiled like that? How do you simply not say anything? How can anyone honestly feel this is okay?

*3 Minutes pass silently

CHRIS: I'm so sorry.

GORDON: I just don't know what to say. I'm terribly sorry you went through that.

MCCARTER: Don't be, you weren't there, and you didn't do it. No one cares anyway, I'm just the monster from flight 2100, I have no feelings. Maybe I want attention. It doesn't matter.

GORDON: Do you want to continue? We can do this at another time.

MCCARTER: Now is fine. It wouldn't change things, talk now or later. It really doesn't matter.

           2 Minutes pass

MCCARTER: Please continue. I'm okay now.

CHRIS: Are you sure, we can reschedule. It's no inconvenience to us.

MCCARTER: Please ask your next question.

GORDON: What about your sister name deleted?

MCCARTER: She was the princess that could do no wrong.

CHRIS: Why is that?

MCCARTER: I have no idea but that was how it was. No matter what she did, it was my fault. She broke a mirror, I got beat. She talked back; I must have taught her to do it. She practically walked on water and there was nothing I could do about it. She started dating when she was in fifth grade, my parents said nothing.

CHRIS: They didn't say anything? Not a word?

MCCARTER: Nope, nothing. Not a single thing. I asked my mom why that was. Can you guess what the word deleted said? You know what she tells me? Go ahead guess?

CHRIS: I really don't know what?

MCCARTER: "name deleted can date whomever she wants, she's not a little word deleted like you!"

GORDON: Wow, that's crazy and very extreme if you don't mind me saying.

MCCARTER: Very crazy, and the ironic part is. My sister was actually sleeping around! Wouldn't that make her the word deleted? I never did that, ever! But here she was just giving it away! And I'm the word deleted!

CHRIS: Makes no sense. I can't understand the double standard.

MCCARTER: No, it doesn't make sense and don't try to make sense of it, there is none. What's worse is that I had to be home by dinner, which was at six every night. Name deleted had no curfew. She would stay out all night. I mean that too, all night. She would just get a ride to school with whoever she slept with that night. Provided that she even went to school that day at all. And if she didn't go to school that day, I get beat for teaching her. Nothing she ever did had a consequence, nothing. She was allowed to roam free and I was an inmate in "McCarter Penitentiary". But things change sometimes, for good or bad. Nothing stays the same, I guess. Nothing in life stagnates. Everything changes.

GORDON: Why do you say that? What changed exactly?

MCCARTER: Everything changes. The family changed a lot after my mother died. That was the first big change. My mom just got home for work and looked around to get herself something to eat. There was nothing in the house. I mean the cabinets were bare, the house was empty. In the rarest of occasions, my mother decides to be an adult and go to the store. As she's driving, she swerved off the road and hit a telephone pole, she was killed instantly.

CHRIS: That's terrible.

MCCARTER: Is it? She did it to herself.

CHRIS: She was still a person, a human being.

MCCARTER: You clearly had a better childhood than I had Agent Chris. I didn't force her to drink that day and I'm glad she didn't kill anyone else.

GORDON: She was drinking? That's why she went off the road?

MCCARTER: That's what I think happened. We were told that the brakes had failed. Supposedly the vehicle had not been inspected annually as it should have been and so my parents didn't know the brakes were bad. I personally don't care one way or the other. I heard the brakes grinding when I was in the car. In the end, it's all the same, dead is dead. That doesn't change.

CHRIS: How were things in the household after your mom's death?

MCCARTER: Things got worse because now my father blamed me directly for the death of my mom. Like I was the one that made her drink or get behind that wheel. That was her poor decision, not mine. My father didn't share that thought, however. The beatings became worse and I just lived with it. What else could I do?

GORDON: You could have told someone, the police, or the school.

MCCARTER: That's laughable.

GORDON: Why is that funny?

MCCARTER: It's funny because my father had friends. No one would listen when I spoke up. My father had everyone convinced that I was a liar. My mom's family didn't talk to us because of my dad. My dad's side didn't care. I had no one to turn too. And so, the beatings and abuse just went on and on.

GORDON: How long did this go on for?

MCCARTER: The silver lining question! Not long actually. My father ends up dropping dead from a heart attack a few years after my mom's death. Ironically, he was caught that morning drinking on the job and was fired. I guess the excitement of him coming home to beating the word deleted out of me finally killed him.

CHRIS: How old where you then?

MCCARTER: I was seventeen.

GORDON: Where did you go when all this happen, after your dad's death?

MCCARTER: My sister and I were sent to live at my grandmother's house in Ithaca New York. My grandmother moved there when my mother was twenty-five. It really annoyed my mom that she moved so far away.

GORDON: Why so far away?

MCCARTER: I guess my grandmother couldn't stand my dad either. From what I was told, my father threatened to kill my grandmother. So, she moved away.

GORDON: How was Ithaca, any better?

MCCARTER: I absolutely loved it! I thought it was everything that I always wanted and deserved out of life. When I was nineteen, I rented an apartment ten minutes from my grandmothers. It was wonderful in the fall, nice people.

Just a great place to live and to be happy, it was amazing. It was the best thing that had ever happened to me. I wish I had been able to move there sooner than later. I can't say enough good things about Ithaca.

CHRIS: How did your sister take everything?

MCCARTER: "Oh how the mighty had fallen", she went to pieces. My grandma laid the hammer down. My sister was finally treated like an equal and she hated every second. My sister went as far as to try and run away. My grandma had none of that. She called the cops, which is funny because the cops actually did something, and returned name deleted. My sister was boiling over, and my grandmother was going to keep control.

GORDON: Why is that funny?

MCCARTER: As many times as, I talked to counselors and talked to my teachers, as many times as I called the cops. Nothing was ever done for me when dealing with my dad. No one believed me, not one single person. When grandmother called the cops on my sister, things happen. My sister never understood the idea of "different town, different rules. It was a hard pill to swallow for my sister.

GORDON: I can't speak for those officers or officials, but something should have been done a long time ago.

MCCARTER: Something should have but didn't. Such is life.

GORDON: You said things were going hard for your sister but good for you. You said you moved out of your Grandmothers?

MCCARTER: When I turned nineteen, I was living on my own. My grandmother was so supportive. She thought it was good for me. She said I deserved it. My sister was beside herself. Because of the problems I had, I had to go to school a few years longer. I had to make up my junior and senior year. I wanted my diploma, not a G.E.D. I got through school and had no problems. Late in my senior year, I started working for name deleted, you know the chain store that everyone sings their stupid ditty to. I then graduated and started their full time.

GORDON: I know where you mean. It went well for you?

MCCARTER: At first it went really well. Within a few months, I was one of the assistant shift managers. Not the greatest money, but I got by without having to ask for help. Did you ever notice Special Agent that the world can fall apart around you and you are totally oblivious to it?

GORDON: I can't say that I have, no.

MCCARTER: I don't either, we share that in common. How about you Agent?

CHRIS: I have once or twice.

MCCARTER: You are lucky Agent Chris. You can read the signs that something is wrong. The special Agent and I unfortunately have been left behind in the evolutionary progress. That's of course if you believe in evolution. I'm not asking, just saying. Anyway, things start to fall apart. I don't even see it coming. My supervisor tells me that three employees have quit on the late shift and they need help to make the numbers. I'm okay with doing my part and say I'll help. This is basically what I missed. Name deleted, my supervisor, wasn't paying for the overtime I was working. Plus, the three people that quit all of a sudden were all young girls like me. And guess what?

GORDON: What?

MCCARTER: They got screwed out of there over time too, by the same jerk! This was his norm. He did this crap all the time and got away with it. All because his boss turned a blind eye to it and didn't care.

GORDON: You said that he did this all the time? How did you find that out?

MCCARTER: I asked around. Several employees said to stay clear of name deleted. I was told he was a scumbag.

CHRIS: Did you ask about the money that he owed you?

MCCARTER: I did, he tells me "Bethany, if you want to get anywhere in life, you have to give a little". I told him that I didn't understand what he meant. Long and short of it, he said the overtime was off the clock training. For whatever reason, I went with it and didn't question. So, week after week, he shorted me. Two more girls quit and I'm working nearly fifteen hours a day six days a week for forty hours a week pay.

GORDON: That's crazy. How long did this go on for?

MCCARTER: So, this goes on for about three months and I finally had enough and said that I'm not doing the overtime unless he starts to pay me properly. Name deleted calls me and ungrateful word deleted and if I want to make it anywhere in this business, he was the only way. He also said he could ruin me for getting a new job. I honestly thought I was stuck. He was convincing and I didn't know any better. From that point on, all he called me was a lazy word deleted. He never used my name, just called me that. And I took it for three more months.

CHRIS: You said this went on for about three months? You quit then?

MCCARTER: No, it just increased from there actually.

GORDON: How did it escalate?

MCCARTER: I was sent to the stock room to help clear it out. It was jammed packed with stuff that needed to get out on the sales floor. I find out that the logistical supervisor had quit, that's why it was so bad in there. I start moving boxes around and start freighting things to the carts to be taken out when name deleted walks in. He starts to ask how it's going, in a not so nice manor. I'm making it sound nicer than it was. In the process of him walking around, he starts to rub up against me.

CHRIS: You mean he was groping you?

MCCARTER: Putting his hands all over me, yes, he was. He stood behind me and grabbed my left breast and my groin with his right hand. I told him to get off me. I had to shove him away from me. He told me that I liked it and was playing hard to get. I told him to get out of the stock room immediately. He told me no so I left instead. He slapped my word deleted as I walked past him.

GORDON: Did you tell anyone?

MCCARTER: Tell who, I had no idea what Human resources was then, and he was my boss. I thought about telling the general manager but didn't because I knew name deleted would just lie and get me fired. I felt powerless and weak. For the next few weeks all was quiet, he left me alone. He then takes it to a whole new level again. I was grateful for the two weeks of rest from him, but it was getting out of control. I go into the lady's room to do my business, as I'm sitting there, I hear the door open to the bathroom. Since there are several stalls, I didn't think anything of it. I thought it was strange when no one went into any of the stalls and the sinks weren't running. I finished up and stepped out of the stall, there was name deleted. He was just standing there with his word deleted in his hand and stroking it while staring at me. I still remember that slimy grin he had on his face.

CHRIS: What did you do?

MCCARTER: I just walked out. I left the job with no intention of returning. I didn't know what else to do. The next day, I came back. I needed the money. I hated myself for going back but I had no other choice.

GORDON: That's just not right at all.

MCCARTER: It actually got worse; it wasn't over yet. At the time I thought it would be, but I was wrong. That's when it hit its peak. It was two or three in the morning when my phone rang at home. I looked to see who it was, the number came up unknown. The callers tried to contact me five more times, I then thought it might be my grandmother or sister, so I answered. It was name deleted telling me that he wanted to word deleted me and he was coming over. I couldn't think of anything to say. So, I told him the only thing that came to mind grossing him out, so I told him I was having my period and it wasn't a good time. He told me to plug it up and then hung up. He continued to call for weeks. He would leave messages just saying the most awful things and it was at all times of the day and night.

CHRIS: Couldn't you just block him?

MCCARTER: I blocked every number that came up that I didn't know.

CHRIS: Every number? He had more than one?

MCCARTER: The store we worked for sells throw away cell phones. I guess he was just taking them off the shelves. Either way, it was always a different number. It got so bad I thought about actually hurting myself. Even worse, I thought about scarring my face, just cutting it up with a razor, truly mangling my looks. They say that beauty is only skin deep, I wanted to put that to the test.

GORDON: That is truly awful.

MCCARTER: I started to call out because I couldn't take it at work. As I was leaving work one day, I saw an advertisement for a scholarship to the local college. It said to submit a paper on anything that you want, it will be judged by a board. If the paper is good, you will get a scholarship. The advertisement also said there were several scholarships to give out. I thought, what the hell, it would change my life at that point. I was tired of being the victim, and quit that word deleted hole. I told name deleted if he calls me again, I'm not calling the cops, I'm cutting his balls off instead. He starts to laugh, and I looked dead into his eyes and asked him if he thought I was kidding. I looked him hard in the face and told him that he had taken so much from me that I had nothing left to lose…but he had plenty to lose. He never called me again after that. I wonder how many other women he put through all that crap after I left. He was trash.

CHRIS: You just quit? Did you have the money to support yourself or a plan of any sort?

MCCARTER: Nope, nothing like that, I went all or nothing. I wrote a piece on sexual harassment and submitted it. For the time while waiting to hear back from the school, I worked at a local laundry mat sweeping the floors. Two weeks later, I get a phone call. The School loved the piece. I got the scholarship and was enrolled that same year for school. I ended up getting a job at the school and started my degree. Funny thing is I went for criminal justice, oh the hand of irony.

GORDON: How did things go from there?

MCCARTER: It went well, I loved school. My grandmother was so proud. I worked hard; I mean really hard. I took a lot of notes and wanted to be the head of my class. By my first six months, I was second in my class. I fell in love with learning and wanted more. I thought about halfway through my degree of changing my major.

CHRIS: What were you thinking?

MCCARTER: Psychology, I was so interested in how the mind works. However, history loves to repeat itself. It will loop and loop again until you finally do something about it. What do they call it, the snake eating its tail?

CHRIS: An ouroboros.

MCCARTER: Yes, that's it. It's the fact that things tend to happen again and again. It seems to me that no matter how much education we have in this world, we all forget our history. We always forget. Be it within years or a generation, history is compelled to live itself again over and over again.

GORDON: Are you referring to what happened at your last job?

MCCARTER: I am, the whole stupid harassment cycle started again. I don't know if it's just that I have bad luck or men are just disgusting. Please take no offence to that. I understand how I look but I have never flaunted it or showed it off. I do go to the gym; well, I use too. And I always ate well, I took care of myself. I have gotten use to men staring at me, that's just how things are. It doesn't mean I should be treated like meat. Anyway, it's my final year, four years without incident to be exact. I would be graduating that fall and maybe going on to get my master's in criminal justice and psychology. I had two classes to pass, that's it. It was American literature and basic anatomy. Those were the last two things on my plate and anatomy was a slam dunk, I had that one without a problem. American literature wasn't hard, but the professor seemed extremely hard on me. He would nitpick at the littlest things. I just assumed that it was me and I needed to work harder. I took it upon myself to go ask him what I could do to help my grade. I wasn't failing but I definitely didn't want to be average. Mr. Name deleted said we could discuss it over dinner. I honestly thought he was just being nice and felt it was okay. We are both adults and maybe he would offer me a job or something. I had no idea what he had in mind, but I felt comfortable that it was strictly school related. Just to put it out there, I wasn't wearing a low cut shirt and leaning over the desk. I dressed very conservatively and like looking nice, not Word Deleted. I want to earn what I have, not be given it because I'm pretty. I was actually happy to meet with him, I thought I could learn something from him, I was hoping he would maybe give me a recommendation for when I went for my Masters.

GORDON: Did he seem like that kind of guy that would take advantage of people?

MCCARTER: No, not at all. He seemed like a really nice guy, so I didn't think anything of it. It's not high school, we are all adults. We all should be able to act like one. He gave me the address to a pretty nice place, not what I was expecting. I expected a pizza place, not a restaurant. I certainly didn't have the money for that kind of meal. After we sat for a while we started to talk about the grades. Twenty minutes in, I see the problem arise. He wouldn't stay on topic; I was all business. He wasn't interested in business. He eventually slides the question to me, "if you do something nice for me, I'll do something nice for you".

CHRIS: He really said that?

MCCARTER: He really did, I was beyond mad. I told him he was acting like a complete word deleted! I was about to leave when he apologized and said he misunderstood our original conversation. I was confused how he could have gotten mixed signals but gave him the benefit of the doubt. He asked me to try and clear my head, take a moment and we can work it out. I told him that's fine and I was going to use the rest room. I excused myself and went to the lady's room. I was gone for about ten minutes and I came back to the table. I sat down and we started to talk again, everything seemed fine until I went to take a drink of my water, it was fizzing.

GORDON: Fizzing, he tried to drug you?

MCCARTER: Yes, he did, I was beside myself. He was actually trying to drug me; I couldn't believe it. What a piece of word deleted! What is wrong with people? I worked hard! I got scholarship after scholarship to stay in school. I made the Dean's list every quarter. I worked too hard for this scum bag to treat me like this.

CHRIS: Please tell me you didn't let that go.

MCCARTER: I didn't let it go. I called the police on the spot.

GORDON: Good!

MCCARTER: The cops came, and Mr. Name deleted was arrested. I was honestly hoping it would make this whole thing go away. Of course, it didn't. He of course made bail and was out within hours of his arrest. He had made up a story that I was coming on to him and he was the victim. The next morning, he told the school faculty and anyone that would listen his BS story. I finished his class in silence knowing that just showing up would pass me. I got by with a C, but I passed, that's all I cared about. I was hoping it wouldn't screw things up. Thankfully, it didn't. I spoke to a counselor at the school who talked to the Dean and the Administrative Board. They determined that his actions were a conflict of interest and passed me unbiasedly.

CHRIS: How did they do that?

MCCARTER: They went back through all of my work and seen that the grades were harsh or sometimes fabricated. So, they graded me appropriately. It was determined that he would give some girls bad grades so they would come and talk to him, like I did. When they asked about helping their grades, he would sleep with them and then fix their grades appropriately. He was trash. Unfortunately, there was nothing that could be done about what people said and believed behind my back. He had destroyed my reputation. However, school was done soon so I didn't care.

GORDON: That's good, it's better than nothing. What happened to him?

MCCARTER: He tried to pull the same stunt with another girl a few months later. That girl didn't take it as well as I did. She slashed his tires. The cops got involved and he got jail time for what he did to me and her. Some people never learn. I moved on with my life and graduated soon after what happened. I just wanted to get on with my life. I earned my degree in criminal justice and was happy with myself. I felt I would take a year off and see what I could do with my new degree.

CHRIS: That's good, you went above the hardships.

MCCARTER: I was good, but I had a hard time finding a job. I found a small job working as an office assistant and it paid the bills. I never actually had a plan for my degree, I just wanted one. It made me feel like I made something of myself. While at name deleted, that's the office I worked at, I met a really nice guy, a good guy. I felt that I deserved him. I tried not to be paranoid about men, I wanted to trust them, and I felt I could really trust him.

GORDON: That was name deleted, correct?

MCCARTER: That's him.

GORDON: How serious was it?

MCCARTER: It was very serious. We dated for several months and then moved in together. We were engaged a few months later. Things were looking up and I was happy. I even re enrolled in school for my master's and would be going back in the spring.

CHRIS: How did Name Deleted feel about you going back to school?

MCCARTER: He was great about it. I even enjoyed taking him to my Grandmother's house for dinner and everyone seemed to like him. But of course, the wheels of fate always need to turn. Nothing stays the same and everything has to fall apart, such is the way of the universe.

CHRIS: What happened?

MCCARTER: I find out one night as me and my sister got into an argument that name deleted had been sleeping with her. That was the final straw, which was just too much. I just couldn't take it. It truly ripped me apart. No loyalty among family, no loyalty among partners. I was just in shock. You know, in moments like this, it makes you wonder what you have done so wrong to deserve things like this happening.

CHRIS: She was sleeping with him, after all this? It didn't bother her? She didn't feel bad? Did she give a reason?

MCCARTER: She gave me a reason all right. She said it was revenge.

GORDON: Revenge for what?

MCCARTER: According to her, I was the reason that my parents drank, and I deserved to be beaten, and being raped was my fault too. She said I ruined her life and mine.

CHRIS: How did she come to this conclusion?

MCCARTER: My mother told her years ago. My mom said all of these lies to name deleted in a drunken fit. All my parents' problems were because of me? She never even talked to me; I was considered guilty without a trial in her eyes. To name deleted, all of what my mom said and what she did was totally rational. She now made the coherent decision that both of our parent's deaths were my fault as well. Where that idea came from, who knows. Only name deleted could answer that. But she bought the whole lie and now was spitting it at me.

GORDON: You know she wasn't right?

MCCARTER: I do, but I wondered how many times she repeated the lies and made others believe it.

GORDON: How did you handle all of this with her?

MCCARTER: I was done, done with being the one that people lied about, the one people abused, and I was done being pushed around. I did something that no one expected, I changed. My first order of change was breaking my sisters' nose and jaw for what she said and done to me. I broke her nose for putting it where it didn't belong, and I broke her jaw for the lies she told. I then drove home and pulled all of name deleted stuff out. All of it, his clothes, his movies, anything he own was thrown onto the lawn. I just stood there for a minute and wondered what to do next. So, I went to the garage and got some gasoline and burn his word deleted. Name deleted pulls in the driveway as his life is on fire. He was just getting home from work. He was just stunned at what I did, his mouth was hanging open and he just couldn't say anything. I asked him how my sister was doing. He looked confused and responded with "what "or something like that so I repeated the question. I told him to check his phone, which might help. When he looked down to pull his phone from his pocket, I kicked him as hard as I could in the balls. Served the son of a word deleted right. I didn't deserve to be treated like that. So, while he was on the ground, I stomped his head until I was tired, or when the cops pulled me off... which ever came first.

CHRIS: Did they press charges?

MCCARTER: No, they should have, if they were smart. They weren't that smart. I didn't do anything, but it was the simple idea that I could whenever I wanted to. Turns out both my sister and name deleted got together after all of that. They started doing drugs together. That's when my sister over dosed with him. A perfect Romeo and Juliet love story, it couldn't have been said better by Shakespeare himself.

GORDON: I'm really sorry.

MCCARTER: For what? It was her decision to put that junk in her arm. I guess she never saw the advertisements for "don't do drugs". I was tired of feeling sorry for others, and it started with her. When she died, I went a new direction with my job and my life. I saw that London/American airline was hiring so I thought that seeing the world would be better than what I was doing now. I got the job and my passport together, I was good. Got a new apartment and just moved on with my life. Left all that behind me in ashes.

GORDON: That's good. How was the change?

MCCARTER: It was good and good money too. I loved seeing Ireland, Germany, France, and Spain. I loved places like Bismarck and London. Life was complete, but life wasn't done with me. I found myself in the same situation but refused to be the victim this time. I had grown, I had changed. The pretty little girl was now a dangerous woman. Men must see a pretty blond and think I'm stupid. I'm smart and well educated. Did you know that I've had my IQ tested?

CHRIS: No, I did not.

MCCARTER: They tested me to determine if I was crazy or competent enough to stand trial. I scored a 135.

GORDON: Wow, that's really high.

MCCARTER: I'm no Einstein, but not far from it. I'm easily the smartest woman in this jail, as far as "guest" numbers go. I couldn't say about staff.

GORDON: You said that something happened? What happened?

MCCARTER: I got off my train of thought, sorry. One day, this son of a word deleted that I worked with actually touched me. I don't mean by accident but grabbed my word deleted. We were both attendants and I worked with him on my flight path for months. All of a sudden then he pulls this crap. I realized that something about me looks weak or people feel that they can prey on me, no more, no longer. I decided that I was no longer the weak one. First thing was first, I grabbed name deleted hand and broke his word deleted thumb.

GORDON: You broke his thumb.

MCCARTER: In one fast motion I bent it to his wrist. I told him that if he touches me again that I would take his member and drop it out of the plane somewhere over the Atlantic... maybe with him still attached if he's lucky.

CHRIS: Do you feel that this kind of change was healthy?

MCCARTER: It was perfectly healthy for me, not healthy for those that crossed me. People change, times change. Maybe it was time to be the person my sister thought I was. I got home a week later after that flight with name deleted. He quit by the way. I was fed up with the evil in this world. I was tired of good people being taken advantage of. Then I realized what was happening, they were teaching me a lesson.

GORDON: You said a lesson, what was that lesson?

MCCARTER: The lesson was simple. I needed to personally weed out the weakness, both in myself and others. I had to do something about the easily preyed upon, it was my responsibility. The weak needed to be pushed into action, or at least shown that they are stronger than they know. They had to understand like I did. Their eyes had to be open to the reality that only the strong survive and if the average person doesn't smarten up and go into action, they will be left behind. That's how I ended up here, I did what I had too. I did what had to be done because no one else would.

GORDON: You said it's your responsibility, why do you have to do that. Can't they figure it out for themselves like you did?

MCCARTER: The sheep of the world are blind, I was blind. It's not easy opening one's eyes.

GORDON: I understand what you mean, but why you?

MCCARTER: I had too, no one else that has seen the world for what it is, would do anything. I wanted to share the world like I saw it.

GORDON: And how do you see the world?

MCCARTER: I see freedom! I see the bonds the world has put upon me fallen away and I can do anything as I please. I don't need permission to think anymore, I don't need to ask to just exist.

CHRIS: Do you still feel free being in jail?

MCCARTER: When my mind was opened, and my thoughts expanded. No prison or society could control that. I choose to be me and no one else. I'm in this place because I did what I needed too for everyone. The close minded put me here.

GORDON: You mentioned about what you did. Do you have a problem talking about that?

MCCARTER: I do not have a problem with it at all. What specifically do you want to know?

CHRIS: How about what happened aboard flight 2100? Could you tell us approximately what happened?

MCCARTER: I don't mind, I pleaded guilty for a reason. I accepted the responsibility of being the martyr. Like I said, I want people to see and understand. I looked at the world and thought that I could make change. I just had to put my mind to it. So, one day I got online and figured out what most people are allergic too. I found out quickly that its peanuts. So, I simply figured out the easiest way to order some peanut oil and picked my time.

CHRIS: Why Peanut oil? Why not just peanuts that are chopped up?

MCCARTER: Those that are allergic to peanuts will undoubtedly look for it in anything they eat. So, I couldn't just go to the store and grind them up. I had to think of a way of getting the people to ingest it without knowing. That's when it hit me, peanut oil. It has no smell or taste, so it's easy to mix in anything.

CHRIS: So why not store bought oil then? You shouldn't have to order that?

MCCARTER: I used extracted oil, the kind that's solvent extracted.

GORDON: So, when you got the oil, how long was it until you used it?

MCCARTER: I waited nearly five months. I decided that I wanted to use the oil as close to my parent's anniversary as possible. So, scheduled myself to work on aboard a flight that very same day, which was flight LA-2100. I took that five months to plan out what I was going to do and so I went through with my plan.

CHRIS: How did you get the oil through customs and the metal detectors?

MCCARTER: I used a plastic applicator bottle that I put in my uniform where I knew it wouldn't be seen.

CHRIS: Where was that?

MCCARTER: You couldn't guess? I put it in my bra. I hid the bottle in plain sight. I intently wore a low cut shirt so when I went through the security check. They wouldn't be looking for anything out of the ordinary, it worked. The bottle also didn't set off the metal detector, obviously. So, I went to the employee lounge and change into my uniform, bottle in my pocket. At that point, I simply went about my job. Boarding people and getting them to their seats. It was all business as usual. Just before it was time to serve dinner, I put a little peanut oil in every tray main course. I heated everything and then served the food. When I was done, I just sat back and watch the magic happen. It took no time at all, five minutes tops which actually surprised me.

GORDON: You only did your section, correct?

MCCARTER: That's right, only my section.

GORDON: Why not the whole plane? Why just that section?

MCCARTER: I figured that the easiest way to start was to start small. Clean out a few people until I can get bigger and better plans. This was just the trial run and for the most part went well. I watched as people got sick and waited till, they died. I wanted to see how long the whole thing took, which wasn't long. I planned it out that we would be landing shortly after dinner was served. It was no more than a few hours. I was arrested promptly after we landed. It didn't take long for people to figure out what happened. It's not surprising; people's spouses recognized the symptoms of the peanuts. I was the only one that prepared the food. Unlike the horrible people in my life, I owned what I did.

CHRIS: Do you understand that it was more than just a few people that got sick. Most died of the people that were allergic died.

MCCARTER: twenty one got sick and sixteen died but everyone on that plane that lived was reborn. I converted three hundred and ninety people to my thinking.

GORDON: You mean everyone on that plane, three hundred and ninety.

MCCARTER; Yes, and they are strong now. The food taste better, the wine is sweater then it ever was before. I gave them meaning. I gave them purpose.

GORDON: Do you understand that they saw you as a monster, a horrible person that deserves death herself. The world in general felt the same way.

MCCARTER: Well, it's a shame that people just don't learn and still could see what I did. Since they wanted me to die, it's also a shame that New York State no longer executes prisons anymore. That's not my problem that the law makers were weak too to understand my meaning. Just remember, the people of early America said Abraham Lincoln was not fit to be president and was hated. Look at all he did and notice how they see him today. He's the great emancipator, the ender of slavery and war. A man held in reverence!

CHRIS: Do you feel that you stand beside President Lincoln and did something just as amazing?

MCCARTER: I have done great things. Look at how many I already started to free, just to start with three hundred and ninety. People will not forget what I have done. They will remember.

GORDON: It was brought up that you put up quite a struggle when you were detained on the flight, is that true?

MCCARTER: Its overly exaggerated. There was a little struggle but nothing life or death.

GORDON: What about the knife you had? Wouldn't that make the situation life or death?

CHRIS: Wouldn't already say that after what you did to the passengers was already life and death too?

4 minute pause

MCCARTER: I don't recall a knife. How would I have gotten a knife on the plane anyway?

GORDON: From our notes, it indicated that you did in fact have a knife, carbon fiber.

MCCARTER: People say things to blow a situation out of proportion, since you said they hate me, I'm not surprised that they are embellishing the story.

CHRIS: So, you deny have a knife with you?

MCCARTER: Yes, I do, I did not own a knife.

CHRIS: According to these police photos that were taken, you had a carbon fiber knife in your possession. Here is the photo.

5 Minutes pass

MCCARTER: One of the passengers that attracted me must have had it.

GORDON: We have copies from Scotland Yard stating that your fingerprints were all over that knife. There was only one other set on it, that was the individual that handed it over after landing.

MCCARTER: Then it must have been that passenger's knife.

CHRIS: How did your fingerprints end up on that knife then?

MCCARTER: Just like I said in my trial, I must have grabbed it during the struggle then.

CHRIS: We also have evidence from the trial that you looked up about knifes that wouldn't set off metal detectors on your home computer several months earlier. You also research how to conceal it so it can't be found during a routine search, do you recall that?

MCCARTER: Is there anything wrong with knowing how people could hurt me. I worry about those kinds of things when on a plane. Hijackings were a common place occurrence that happened quite frequently a long time ago. You don't think it could happen again?

GORDON: I'd like to ask then how you can explain the evidence that was used against you, specifically a receipt from an online military story. The receipt shows a carbon fiber knife that fits the exact manufacturer and model that was taken from the plane.

MCCARTER: My trial is over and has been for a while. I told the court that it was all lies, just like I'm telling you now. Is there anything else you want to know about? I can tell you about prison food and prison life. Neither is really great.

GORDON: I don't have any more questions unless Agent Chris has something else.

CHRIS: No, I don't have anything else to add. Thank you for your time Mrs. McCarter.

MCCARTER: Thank you both.

GORDON: This is Special Agent Sean Gordon. Its 4:10 P.M. in the Bedford Hills Correctional Facility for Woman, Bedford Hills New York, Maximum Security Wing, Block F. We have just finished interviewing of Bethany McCarter. Case file: 31008539-A, Operation Vanguard or "The Matthews Incident".

This formally concludes the interview with Bethany McCarter. No further entries were made on this date or for this part of the interview.

Clipping from the New York Reporter

Early this morning in Bedford Hill Correction Facility, Bethany S McCarter, age 34 was put to death by lethal injection. McCarter who has been sitting on death row for more than a year was looking at a life in prison until this latest decision. It came as a surprise to the country and state that Governor Hallow of New York overturned the execution bill. "The State now allowing for the taking the life of serial murders and mass murders is a change of our beliefs" says Collin Ballios of 21st street. It has been nearly seventeen years since executions in New York have been outlawed.

Governor Ellen Hallow had this to say "Everyone has a right to live free. Bethany took that right from 16 brave souls. It's the lease we could do for them and our moral responsibility". The Governor is under hot protest of her decision to overturn this bill without the consent of New York's people. Many citizens are outraged that Governor Hallow took it upon herself to make a monumental decision open the state for capital punishment.

(New York Reporter, Ben Harken p.1)

Interview of Captain Bryant Justin Tessle

Friday, September 22nd, 2028
United States Disciplinary Barracks (USDB)
Fort Leavenworth, Kansas

This recorded session is called to order by the head of the Federal Bureau of Investigations, Special Investigations Unit.

GORDON: Its 11:30 A.M. in United States Disciplinary Barracks, Fort Leavenworth Kansas, Maximum Security Wing, Block 5. Seated next to me is Special Agent William Chris. Across from us, at the interview table is Captain Bryant Justin Tessle, Former Administrative clerk, Personal Assistant, and Records Officer to Brigadier General Matthew's: Case file 31008539-A, Operation Vanguard or "The Matthews Incident". Capt. Tessle is 35 years of age, is 5'10", weight is 149 Lbs. He is of slender build, brown hair, has no discernable marks or scars, has blue eyes, and a light completion. He is Caucasian and an American. His fingerprints are on file and classification code 1 for the flowing: several counts of involuntary manslaughter. He is also accused of treason and conspiracy of treason, terrorism and is considered a traitor of the United States of America. He is currently awaiting Court Martial. We have returned to speak with Captain Tessle for a dialog of Brigadier General Matthew's regarding Mrs. McCarter.

Key testimony involving the aboard flight LA-2100 and the incident aboard the flight. Captain Tessle is at this time currently at liberty to speak about Brigadier General Mathews, Operation Vanguard, and Flight LA-2100 by the Supreme Court and is not placed under a gag order. It should also be known that all families involved in flight LA-2100 have given prior consent for this interview.

GORDON: Good Morning Captain Tessle.

TESSLE: I see that I can be of service again. So, what will it be today? On the by-and-by, I did check up on the paperwork you gave me, it's all correct. Thank you.

GORDON: Actually yes, we understand that Brigadier General Mathews spoke about flight LA-2100 and Mrs. Bethany McCarter, is that true?

TESSLE: It is true. You do understand that it may take some time to find that information. Do you mind waiting? I will have to go through the files, and it will take some time. I also think General Matthews only mention McCarter once if I'm correct.

GORDON: No, please take your time. We understand that we just drop this information on your lap. We appreciate the cooperation that you give us and the help you provided.

TESSLE: You honestly have no other choice then to deal with me, my understanding is that you still are not allowed to access the files that contain Mathew's formations. I also don't mind helping. You scratched my back, it's the least I can do. Besides, until my appeal goes through, I have nothing but time. I understand that you gave the judge the letter you spoke of stating that I was helping you, Thank you. It is much appreciated. I can only hope that it helps my situation.

GORDON: Not a problem.

            1 hour and 20 minutes pass

TESSLE: Sorry for the wait gentleman, I have found the information that you were asking for. It took some time but here it is. I also cross-referenced to ensure that it was the only time Matthews mentioned McCarter, which it was.

GORDON: Feel free to begin whenever you are ready.

TESSLE: Very well. According to the file, and as I read it, I do remember. General Matthews happened to have a formation scheduled that morning. It was to be a motivational run.

CHRIS: A motivational run?

TESSLE: The idea is that we all get motivated by each other while we run.

CHRIS: I don't find running fun personally, does it work?

TESSLE: It can, depended on who is calling the cadence and how good it is. The run itself is done at a relatively slow pace and it should be enjoyed.

CHRIS: I understand. Thank you.

TESSLE: Not a problem. So, we all were in formation by five that morning and waiting for General Matthews. He steps out before us and calls for the Sergeant Major to worm us up. She we do our stretches and some pushups, and we are ready to go. As were doing these warmups, General Matthews is pacing. Finally, General Matthews takes over and he starts to run. We go for a solid three miles and all is going well. At the end, General Matthews leads us to the parade grounds and tell us all to have a seat. We are all sitting around him in a giant circle. It was thousands of Marines listening to him as he speaks.

"Brother, sister, my Marines,

"Glory, glory, glory", I stand before you to speak about right and wrong and what is fair. The world is a harsh place that is truly unforgiving, we all know this. We don't get to choose the people that bring us into this world but here we are. We make the path we fallow, however. No one else can make that decision but us. We can't spend our entire lives blaming others for what we do. We are the writers of our destiny, and those words are bound in blood. The actions you take in life are yours alone to live with. When you stand before your maker, given you believe in such things. It is you that answers for your life, and no excuses will be accepted. The simple of idea of "he made me do it" will simply not work.

At times we individuals actually take responsibility for our own actions, an example is Bethany McCarter. She is the truest meaning of good initiative but terribly bad judgment. What can we honestly say about her, what can be said about her message? She wants to make the world stronger by weeding out the weak. I guess to easily put it; we are only as strong as our weakest link. But who then is the weakest link, the ones she killed or her herself? That is in fact a bold but true question. We are molded by pain, developed by it. The good times don't shape us like the hard, isn't that a "weeding out process" in itself? Because were told not to touch fire, doesn't mean it is a lifelong lesion. We have to physically touch it to understand why we shouldn't touch it. We all experience hardships; we all have that moment where our metal is tested. She didn't break! I will give her that, but she did bend... but never broke. She may not realize that she bent, but she did. Her metal wasn't as strong as she assumed. The problem is that she felt the change in here but failed to see how that change can affect others. It's the kind of change that makes the world look and feel different. It's a second birth. Most of us here in this formation had it in combat. I call it a "near life experience". That's really what it is, you now understand that you have changed, and you are born anew. You can't push that kind of change from one person to another. They have to want it or personally and go through it individually. You cannot force people to change, not like that. You can change physical things, but ideas are much harder. Ideas are built on strong foundations of principals and purpose.

Scribe!

Yes Sir!

Take this down and send it to Mrs. McCarter!

Yes sir!

It will read as follows. You want change, you ask for change, and you need change. Not everyone does. The world will never change by the methods you have used. Your message was lost, and your idea sunken. You cannot force the hands of fate. Good initiative, bad judgment Mrs. McCarter. That is all scribes.

Yes Sir!

Mrs. McCarter feels wronged by society and now feels that she should wrong it. She justified her actions by saying it was to make the people stronger. She is lying to herself. She wants to simply watch people fall apart like her life did. In her testimony, she openly admitted to sitting there and watching those people die, it takes a hard person to watch someone die like that. Mrs. McCarter belongs in jail but sees herself as a martyr. No, far from it, she is a spoiled child. But how can she be spoiled with such a sad upbringing? Simple, she had so much hardship in her life that when she found something good, she felt that life should have always been that good. She forgot the simplest of lessons in life. It's simply that life is not fair. Life will never be fair, it shouldn't be. We wouldn't learn anything from it.

Let's simply talk of her crime. It was murder, plain and simple murder. It wasn't for the higher cause as she likes to tell anyone who will listen. She wanted to kill others because part of her was killed by her parents. Killing is and under statement for her actions. We as Marines and service men take lives to protect the union and our way of life. We do it for freedom. It's our job and our calling. We take no pleasure in the act of taking lives but take pride in the service of our nation. We take pride in being good at what we do, yes, killing falls in that category. We do not enjoy it. We are surgeons in our own right. We cut deep and quick and resolve the issue as fast as possible without lingering effects. She savored the moment, drinking it in and enjoying the intoxication of the kill. She enjoyed the moment, every second. She is a black widow creeping around waiting for the perfect moment to strike and watching her prey die. Though at times we ourselves hid in the shadows and are as quiet as the night. We strike professionally and fast. We never look back at out kill and revel over it. We remember the faces in our dreams, we remember the feel of taking that life and we relive it every night as we close our eyes. She counts them as notches on a belt, a tally of numbers to brag about and enjoy. She smiled as she killed those people. Remember that. It made her happy.

The question now is what she could have done, besides blaming others for her problems. She could have spoken out agent's abuse and agents those things that held her back. She could have found a way to be spokesmen agents such problems in this country, instead of feeding the problem. In this country, you always have a choice, no one can dictate how you feel or react. If you think I'm wrong, you are part of the problem too. You bought a lie, you let others tell you how to think and you are obviously okay with *that. No one will tell me how I can think. No one will tell me how to act. I am my own person, and I don't let anyone control my life. In the end, McCarter is just telling people what to do, in her own way. That's one of the places that she screwed up, that's why she is broken.*

This country is founded on simple principles. It's all about freedom. She like many others misunderstands what freedom really is. People like her think that freedom is the ability to do what you want when you want. That is a lie! The belief is a Jonestown ideology, it's false and misleading. Freedom is the ability to live your life without other infringing on your pursuit of happiness and you not infringing on there's. That's the misunderstanding. That's the part she missed. She thought she was right.

"He is sitting out the hearts of men before His judgment-seat". Oh, brothers and sisters, the times we live in. I heard yesterday that it is now punishable up to two hundred and fifty thousand dollars to say the name of Bethany McCarter in some states. You can be jailed by simply trying to follow her belief of purity. In case you don't know this, a movement has started that anyone that feels she was right is now called "The sons and daughters of Arachis". The name Arachis or Arachis hypogea is the Latin term for peanut. These followers believe that her terrorist act was for a higher purpose. I understand how we as a people don't want violence in our streets. I understand how we don't want others to follow in her footsteps. However, what happened to our freedom of speech, what happened to our right to believe what we desire in our hearts? Are we so weak that words now can hurt us, are we so pitiful that we ban words because others are offended? My rights, my beliefs and my way of life don't get to be changed simply because someone else doesn't like it. The ironic part is that I'm expected to except their beliefs and ideas even if I don't agree with them. I belief that all are equal, I belief that everyone is worth the same amount, no one is better than the next. When did the Constitution just become a piece of paper? We have given our rights a way to these corrupted politicians. We have given over our rights to a government that isn't afraid of its people anymore. We have a king as we did hundreds of years ago, history has repeated itself. This time the tea party will be with blood when it comes for change. Americans will die. No one has the right to tell what I can think, and no one had the right to tell me what I believe, no one!

But I know how this change has happened, I've seen it evolve. It happened very quietly. It happened with tolerance. Through our tolerance, we became less tolerant, it's very ironic. If you have a point of view that someone doesn't agree with, it's now not uncommon for someone to spit out an insult and call you a Nazi or a Racist. Even though you said nothing like that, they simply don't agree with you. Regardless of how normal or standard your feelings are. Feeling... that's another laughable idea. Somehow feelings are now considered common sense, like how you feel is logical. You don't like the flavor ice cream I do so you're a racist, because I feel offended.

This is the world we inherited this is the way we live. Oh, how we have fallen "Glory, glory, and hallelujah!" there will come a day that the government, the lawmaker will pay for their sins."

Tessle: At that point it was business as usual. General Matthews took us for typical run. And everything seemed normal.

GORDON: Was this the point that General Matthews made the decision to try to change things? Did he start planning Vanguard?

TESSLE: Actually no, I think it really started with Marcus Dana.

CHRIS: I'm not familiar with him. You said Marcus Dana.?

TESSLE: That's correct. I suggest that you go and speak to him. I would tell you what it has to do with him, but I don't think I could tell his story better then he could. I would do it no justice. No pun intended. Just understand one thing. You may look at the world a little differently after talking to him.

GORDON: We appreciate the suggestion and will look into it.

TESSLE: I'm serious about this. He should be the one to talk to. That's the direction you need to go. You want to know what Matthews thought and why he went the way he did, this is the man you need to speak to. He is the next piece to the puzzle. You go and talk to him and I'll get the documents ready for you to comeback and review. What Marcus did really got Matthews worked up, that's why I'm saying and suggesting it. I'll be waiting for you.

GORDON: Thank you, we will find him and look into it.

GORDON: This is Special Agent Sean Gordon. Its 1:52 P.M. in United States Disciplinary Barracks, Fort Leavenworth Kansas, Maximum Security Wing, Block 5. We have just finished interviewing Captain Bryant Justin Tessle. Case file: 31008539-A, Operation Vanguard or "The Matthews Incident".

This formally concludes the interview with Captain Bryant Tessle. No further entries were made on this date or for this part of the interview.

Memorandum from Special Agent Sean Gordon

To: **Brian Samuels, Director of the Federal Bureau of Investigations**

From: **Sean Gordon, Special Agent**

Good Moring,

   As per protocol, I am giving my informal opinion of the investigation of Transatlantic Flight-2100 and my person opinion to what I witnessed.

   After Speaking with Mrs. Blackfoot, got a clear idea of how the entire flight went. To sum things up quickly, everything was normal until the food service. The plane was flying from New York to London. Nothing strange or unusual happened on the flight until about three quarters of the flight when the food was served. That's when Mrs. Blackfoot stated that she started feeling ill and people started to panic. Her last memory of the situation was being in the hospital.

   Doctor Moore was the second interview for this case. Doctor Moore is Mrs. Blackfoot's husband and was on the flight when everything happened. He gave more of in-depth perspective of what happened after the poisoning. From his side of when he experienced, Mrs. McCarter showed little to no compassion while people were dying in front of her. This was the first recorded record that stated that fact. All other accounts on file did not state who Mrs. McCarter was acting. One thing confirmed and calibrated was that she put up a struggle in the end. It was also stated that she was yelling a lot of "nonsense" as many put it. A lot of this was already stated in the report. I just wanted to sum them up for posterity sake.

   Mrs. McCarter was an interesting interview. On the surface she seems very normal, but while talking to her, you can see bits of her other side. Her life story is fairly consistent, but there are key questions that were brought silently to my attention. For example, she mentions her grandmother, but only when speaking about college. What happened to her grandmother? That remained unanswered. I came to this conclusion while talking to her but felt I shouldn't say anything just to see how she would tell her side. Her grandmother was never mentioned again. Her sister was also fairly consistent with the grandmother. I seemed that she would use her sister as an excuse for bad times and situations. Mrs. McCarter had saver mood swings and bouts of rage like anger while speaking to her. One of these fits was towards General Matthews. She started the interview very hostilely towards Matthews and then just became sociable. Mrs. McCarter could go from laughing to hysterical crying within moments. What really shocked me was when we questioned her motives on the plane. She changed, like a mask was reviled, an instant difference. That other face was ugly and cold as well as uncaring. I personally feel that she wanted revenge on the world. This was her revenge, provided that her story was straight. But in her mind, she could justify what she did quite easily. Before the trial, Mrs. McCarter was diagnosed as a true psychopath, meaning that she has no guilt or any remorse for her actions. She is also unempathetic of her actions as well. We also found that she was in denial of having a weapon on board the flight. While questioning, she would divert the questions asked and try to change subject. At this point, I am unable to confirm or deny Mrs. McCarter's past. I cannot trust the facts that she has given us. In my personal opinion, and the opinion of others, she is a black widow. She used her beauty to make people comfortable around her and then manipulates the situation. I really feel that Mrs. McCarter thought she would get away with what she had done.

We later got to hear whet General Matthews felt about Mrs. McCarter's actions. He was severely opposed to what she did. No approving of her, at all. General had strong opposition to the idea that all people are weak. General Matthews had a dislike for how society was changing and the direction it was going, which is very apparent. I wonder what General Matthews's overall opinion was of people. General Matthews loved his Marines but could not stand the outside world. I wonder if General Matthews ever made the connection with Mrs. McCarter's exploits and what he had done. They are remarkably similar in the end.

Sincerely,
S.A. Sean Gordon.

Eyewitness accounts of Operation Vanguard

"I just stared at the patch-work army fighting back agent the guys that took The White House. I just couldn't believe it; local cops, gang members, average citizens...side by side, working together. I just couldn't believe it, I still can't. You had regular people taking care of the wounded and hurt. Criminals helping the police! It was the most inspiring and horrible sight I will ever see again."

-Marry Bridling (Connecticut receiver, Gillian pg.1)

They just can't do it! I refused to let them destroy our way of life!"

-David Ford [wounded in fighting]
(Washington 26 News.com, Mallard)

"We just weren't ready; they were clearly better shots and better trained. They were war hardened already; we weren't. They lived the full military lifestyle, we don't. We just practiced war games. I actually thought at one point that I got one. My weapon was still on safe, he shot me twice. I'm a veterinarian for word deleted sake."

-Specialist Clinton Folks [Deceits] (Washington
26 News.com, Mallard)

DEATH OF ELIJAH PHILLIP JOHNSON

Interview of Marcus Eric Dana

Monday, October 2nd, 2028
Washington State Penitentiary
Walla Walla, WA

WANTED
BY F.B.I.
Status: Captured

F.B.I. No. 189142
WANTED FOR: MURDER, TORTURE

Marcus Eric Dana
ALIAS: Bone Yard

Description

AGE:	38	SCARS OR MARKS:	SCARE OVER R. EYE
HEIGHT:	6'1"	EYES:	BLUE
WEIGHT:	165 LBS	COMPLEXION:	LIGHT
BUILD:	MEDIUM	RACE:	CAUCASAIN
HAIR:	BLOND	NATIONALITY:	AMERICAN
OCCUPATION:	MAINT. TEC	FINGERPRINTS:	ON FILE
		CLASSIFICATION:	FELONY LEVEL 1

CAUTION

Current status is captured and beheld by
the Department of Correction.

**IF YOU HAVE ANY INFORMATION CONCERNING THIS PERSON
PLEASE CONTACT YOUR LOCAL F.B.I. OFFICE IMMEDIATELY**

*This recorded session is called to order by the head of the
Federal Bureau of Investigations, Special Investigations Unit.*

GORDON: its 10:30a, in Washington state penitentiary, Walla Walla, Maximum detention Block, Pod 2, Interview room. Seated next to me is Special Agent William Chris. Across from us, at the interview table is Marcus Eric Dana, Former Maintenance technician. Case file: 31008539-A,

Operation Vanguard or "The Matthews Incident". Mr. Dana is 39 years of age, is 5'11", weight is 179 lbs. He is of Medium build, Blond hair, has no discernable marks or scars, has blue eyes, and a light completion. He is Caucasian and an American. His fingerprints are on file and classification code 1 for the flowing: involuntary manslaughter.

Key testimony involving the death of Elijah Phillips Johnson and the months leading up to the incident. Mr. Dana is at this time currently at liberty to speak about General Matthews and Operation Vanguard. By the Supreme Court and is not placed under a Gag order. It should also be known that the family of MR. Johnson has given prior consent for this interview.

GORDON: Good Morning Mr. Dana.

DANA: Good morning to both of you. I hope you are both well.

GORDON: We are Mr. Dana, thank you for asking. I just wanted to say that we thank you for taking this time to sit and talk with us. I understand that you don't normal give interviews and we thank you for letting us sit with you.

DANA: I don't mind. I also don't think the F.B.I. would twist my words like most newspapers would. I'm sure it's a good reason you came to talk to me.

GORDON: It is actually, we would like to talk to you about few things. First being the event that got you arrested if that's okay for you to talk about. We would also like to talk to you about Brigadier general Matthews.

DANA: You know about me talking to General Matthews? How?

CHRIS: We have been in close contact to one of Brigadier General Matthews's staff, his scribe to be exact. Your name came up and it was recommended that we speak with you.

DANA: I got a letter from Matthews shortly after I was incarcerated. Now, just so you know, I got letters from people I've never heard of. It was just the most random people, lawyers, television host and even a few magazines. There was some guy that offered me money to write my story. I refused. I didn't like how most of them spoke to me. Some calling me a terrible person, others saying I did the right thing. I remember his because he scolded me like a child. That was the only letter like that. It stands out, trust me on that.

CHRIS: Do you still have that letter?

DANA: No, I don't. Sorry.

CHRIS: Do you remember what it said, specifically?

DANA: No, not exactly. It was mostly just him saying that what I did changed things, but I should be aware that it wasn't for the better. I never really understood what he meant by that. I really paid it no mind, to be totally honest. I felt no need to keep the letter. I threw it away with all the other hate mail. I don't need that kind of negativity anymore.

GORDON: Would you be interested in telling us your story? Brigadier General Matthews thought it was interesting. We defiantly want to hear it as well. We only want you to tell us if you are comfortable repeating it to us. If not, we understand.

DANA: I don't mind, I have no problem telling people what I did.

CHRIS: We actually want to hear more than just the reason you are here. We would like the whole story, what lead up to the incarceration.

DANA: I can do that. I guess I can start with my parents, is that okay?

GORDON: Wherever you would like to start, that's a perfectly good place.

DANA: well, I guess I'll start by stating a few facts. First, I will not state the name of the organization. I refuse to give that kind of power to the members, they have too much already. Second, don't think that my parents were bad people, because they weren't. They raised me well and loved me. My parents were good people, misguided by their parents, but good people at heart. My Dad did some bad things, I will not deny that. Because a person does a few bad things, doesn't make them a bad person. But Dad was a real product of his upbringing just like I was. No one is perfect, I'm not and neither were my parents. And lastly, I don't believe any of that crap that organization jammed down my throat, none of it. I kept my hatful tattoos to remind me to never forget my past. I have changed. I don't feed into that racist crap anymore. Are we ok with that?

GORDON: I see no problems with that. We can just call them the *"organization"*. We are also not here to make judgment calls. We just want to talk and listed. This interview is about learning something from you and about you. You tell us what you want us to know.

CHRIS: Exactly, we are here to lean not make judgments about what you did, that's now out place. You are being punished for your crimes, no reason to rub it in. We just want your side of the story.

DANA: That seems fair enough and I'm glad we agree. That's good. I guess I'll continue with where I grew up.

GORDON: That's fine, please continue.

DANA: it's a small town called Oak Harken and it's in Washington State. When I say small, I mean small. It has about 8,000 people. Everyone knows everyone and they all talk. It has its advantages and disadvantages when you live in a small community. In the end, makes the community and people awfully close. I saw the Mayor all the time at the grocery store and the two of the city councilors lived on my street.

GORDON: So how did the organization fit into all of this? Did they have a lot of influence there?

DANA: They did and sadly still do. They are everywhere! It's the guy that bags your groceries to the lady at the register. Word deleted, even the owner of the store. It's just deeply rooted. So much influence in fact that a lot of street names are named after former members and founders. It is just everywhere. And they advertise publicly too.

CHRIS: How did that happen? How can a town get so rooted into something like that?

DANA: Well, the town was founded around 1880 and it was all because *the Organization* moved west. This is right after the civil war, the confederate soldiers had nowhere to go. So, a lot just moved west. I know this because *the Organization* are very into history and making sure their members know it. History is a priority with them. They know history will repeat itself. Just so you know. There is a difference between the organization and the skinheads. The skinheads like that Neo-Nazi crap. It really would annoy me when I would get lumped into that group. We are not the same, at all. In fact, the two groups are not on speaking terms, if you get what I mean.

CHRIS: You will have to forgive my ignorance on this, but I don't understand.

DANA: That is very well put agent. Let me try and sum this up, *they* have quite different guidelines, rules, and beliefs then skin heads do. Skinheads think Hitler was a messiah. *They* believe in family and keeping things, well frankly, white. *The Organization* use to be very violent, not as much that I have seen. I'm not saying *they* aren't, there is just less violence. If you provoke the organization, they will act violently, but in most cases, you have no idea that they are even in a town. The main point, *they* feel that whites need to be in power. The skinheads, that's a whole other' problem and a whole lot of hatred towards a lot of people, they don't like anyone. *The Organization* gets along with skinheads just like everyone. Frankly speaking; it's hard to find a skinhead anymore. But most people lump the two together. I never understood why when I was with them, I get it now. Hate is hate!

CHRIS: Thank you.

DANA: Not a problem. It's important to grow as person, to do that you have to learn. Which was my problem, to be totally honest, I didn't grow up. It took me years until I really grew up.

GORDON: Do you think that was primarily because of you or your parents you didn't grow up? You said they were good people; I don't question that. I'm simply curious if they sheltered you in some way. Because of that, you feel you didn't grow as a person.

DANA: That's a really good speculation but really, I think it was just me. My parents were good people, worked hard. They really had a good work ethic and felt hard work is just part of life. My dad would say, "Sweat is its own reward". All he really meant was that through work you find peace. I only know that because I asked him why he always said that. My dad was a good man.

GORDON: Would you mind talking a little your parents. I think it would say a lot about who you are and where you come from. Is that ok with you?

DANA: No, not at all. I don't mind. Let me see, well, my dad's name was Eric Marcus Dana, and my mom was Tammi-Lynn Dana. Good people, highly active in the organization as well as school and home. My dad grew up in Oak Harken, my mom was from Newland, and they are neighboring towns, five minutes apart. They were both active in *the organization* when they were young and that's where they met.

As I said, my father was regularly active both in his professional life and family life. He was a member of *the Organization* for over sixty years. He had numerous awards and various things named after him. He was cornerstone of the community as well. My dad was the chairmen of the memorial parade and the homecoming parade float judge for a better part of thirty years. Everyone knew my dad and he knew everyone. *The Organization* named there meeting hall after my dad. The best part, I was never treated special. Sometimes kids get put in the shadow of their fathers, I didn't and I'm grateful for that. He died about ten years ago, he went in his sleep. Not bad way to go if you ask me. I'm glad he never saw me in jail. Mom found him in his chair with a smile on his face on a Sunday afternoon. He went to take a nap and went quietly in his sleep. That's the way he deserved it. The chapter was heartbroken and gave him a glorious funeral. My father was a chapter leader for twenty-five years, and no one could do better. He did as much for the community as he possibly could. If your house burned down, he would raise money for you or give you what he had, shirt right off his back. Food drives, clothing drives, volunteered for as much as he could. When he was younger, before he retired, he would put in his forty to fifty hours a week at his job as a furniture builder then go help fix somebody's house the whole weekend. Never missed church and never missed a meeting. That man was reliable, and we loved him, so did the community, obviously.

But my father had a dark side too. He never talked about it. I guess we all have our demons. No one is perfect and we all have a part of us that we don't want others to see. We all do. The Organization sometimes had to show its ugly side, and my dad was the face of the chapter. So, he had to be ugly too.

GORDON: Do you think he did such good to balance out the bad.

DANA: I don't think so. I think that he felt his darker side was just part of his duty to the Organization and in a way to his family. It was his idea of keeping us safe.

GORDON: Do you feel that your father may have regretted?

DANA: No, I don't believe so. It was all business not personal. He brought nothing home with him unless it was good things.

CHRIS: Do you have any instances or of his bad side? Did you personally ever see it??

DANA: I've seen a few things. He never talked about the things that I didn't see. He kept those things hidden away, like they weren't appropriate for his family.

CHRIS: I mean no disrespect but, I think it's odd to hold things inside so deeply and not feel bad. Do you think that may have been a front or coping mechanism?

DANA: I never really looked at it that way. When I asked him about it one time, he told me "What's done is done. You need to understand that boy. You do something, own it, you did it, and it's yours. "Alea iacta est. the die is cast son; the die is cast."

CHRIS: That's Julius Cesar, correct?

DANA: It is. Julius Cesar said those words when he crossed the Rubicon on January 10th 49 B.C. Knowing my dad, it was very fitting of him. He could have been a history professor if he wanted to be. He had some crazy knowledge. Like I said, he was a good man, just not perfect. It was said throughout *The Organization* that my dad had two or three bodies under his belt. I heard the sheriff say once that it may be as much as nine.

CHRIS: Really, nine? And the sheriff said this? Where did he get that number?

DANA: Not too sure, that's just town legend.

GORDON: You said that the Sheriff said this, correct?

DANA: Yup, Sheriff Name deleted, he was also a chapter member. He said he personally seen it. I guess it never got proven, or the law turned a blind eye to it. I can only speculate that they turned a blind eye, because the sheriff wouldn't brag like that if he were trying to arrest my father. If my dad did those things, he never showed it. My father flew an American flag, and the organizations flag every day. He seemed prouder then guilty.

GORDON: Your dad was a member for sixty years? That's a long time.

DANA: Well, sixty-two to be exact. My granddad got dad in when he was young and did the same for me. That was the way of the family. I know I was expected to do the same if I had a son.

CHRIS: How old were you?

DANA: I was six when I started becoming involved, just like my dad and granddad.

CHRIS: The seams really young to me. Is that normal?

DANA: It's actually a pretty common age. I had a lot of kids around when I would go with my dad to meetings.

GORDON: How involved where you at that age?

DANA. Not very, we would sit there and listen to them talk at the meetings. That's really about it. The only big thing that stands out to me happened when I was nine. There was a town lynching once.

CHRIS: Nine, you saw that at nine?

DANA: that's right, nine. I did my first march when I was eleven and a full member by sixteen. I was totally committed to the *Organization*.

GORDON: It just seems too hard to believe. You said you saw a lynching, what happened?

DANA: All I remember is the *Organization* was talking about this family that just moved into the area. That was a major discussion topic for weeks. It really became a concern to the Organization when the family tried to ally for a loan to start a business. That was too much for the *Organization* and they rallied in front of the people's home. Some nasty things were yelled at the people and then some members broke the door down, I remember seeing the people bring forced into their car and leaving. I never saw them again. I don't even remember what they looked like or what their car looked like either. I just remember the yelling and the cross in the front yard. I remember my dad was with me and my mom didn't want me to go. She felt I was too young for that.

GORDON: What is your Mother like?

DANA: She was awesome. She passed a year after my father, the same way too. She also deserved that too. She was a trooper after my dad passed. I knew she was hurting but she carried on. She was an extraordinarily strong woman and a great example.

GORDON: How active was she in the *Organization*?

DANA: Not as much as my dad, but she was royalty in the organization. Her father was a state leader for Washington chapter, a real big name. You might have heard of him name deleted name deleted.

GORDON: No, never have.

CHRIS: No, I haven't either, sorry.

DANA: That's okay, he was a big deal, just know that. People from all over knew my mom because of him. She lived in his shadow unfortunately, but she didn't care. She would throw her maiden name around to just shut people up sometimes. You got mouthy with her over something and you would hear her say, "You clearly don't know who my father is". She would drop his name and the argument was over, just like that. They knew my dad, that would have been enough, but hearing her dad, that stopped everything. It was kind of funny. She was a member of the women's *organization*, but just a member. She would attend a meeting here or there. My mom always made the meetings in the beginning of the month. That's the important one where the news for the month is talked about. The other meetings are just a hangout. She was a full member by fourteen and active for only a few years. She would talk about the things she saw from time to time, but nothing too big. She told me when she was seventeen or so, this black guy was walking down the street in Newland, that's where she was from. Newland was huge, and the population was much more intermixed. So, seeing a black guy wasn't uncommon.

However, it was still an *Organization* community, not as big as Oak Harken. It was big enough to control a lot of public and political affairs. So, she tells me that this poor guy is just walking down the street and not really paying attention. He walks right by my mom, that's all, just walked by. No rude comment, no obscene gesture. He just walked by. A few guys my mom knew that were also in the *Organization* saw what had just happened and stopped the guy and asked why he got so close to my mom. The black guy apologized and said he wasn't bothering anyone. My mom said those guys beat that black man mercilessly. She said he lay in the street for a while until someone finally took him home.

CHRIS: What exactly did he do wrong?

DANA: You really don't know? You don't get it?

CHRIS: No, I'm sorry, I don't understand.

DANA: He was walking down the same side of the street as my mom walked on. The worst part was he was rude and didn't speak to her.

CHRIS: All that seems so trivial to assault someone over?

DANA: It's not trivial to the *Organization*. That man knew the rules, I guarantee it. He broke the rules and had to pay. That's just how things are. It's an unspoken understanding in the community. "You never make waves", it just that simple. He broke the rules, and something had to be done. Good order and discipline must be maintained and kept or the whole house of cards will fall...So says the Organization.

CHRIS: That's really crazy and really unnecessary. I find it almost impossible that the law never got involved.

DANA: Why would the police get involved, they were the *Organization*, All of them. It was everywhere and it was deeply rooted in the towns and the culture.

GORDON: That just seems out of control.

DANA: It is, and it happens. It was worse than that at times, trust me. That guy got off easy. My mom was involved in one of the worst fires in Dublin County. People were seriously hurt, and it was said that it was all because of the *Organization* and supposedly, as the story goes. My mom had the honor of lighting the apartment on fire. If you can call that honor, I probably thought that then, I don't anymore. She was so honored that the *Organization* offered her a chapter to run. She politely refused. She said she wasn't interested in that kind of role and felt it wasn't her calling.

GORDON: Do you think your upbringing was different than other children not involved in the *Organization*. I mean in general, your family life.

DANA: I do actually, I think it was different.

CHRIS: How so, why do you think that?

DANA: I think a lot of families go to church on Sundays. I see that as a normal thing. But our family went to meetings twice. We had our local chapter meetings Thursdays and the county chapters on Wednesdays. I got a child's handbook from the *Organization* to study and learn when I was really young. My mom and dad reviewed with me and read it to me often. It had all kinds of historical stuff in it and prays from the bible. It has all the rules and bylaws plus big names that a member should know. All this information had to be memorized before you can become an official member. You also spend a lot of time together. You have your meetings, church, you have Sunday night dinners. The kid's always play together, everyone knew everyone else, and it's a family. You are just constantly surrounded by the Organization. Thinking back now, I guess it wasn't all that normal.

CHRIS: It sounds kind of like a mod movie.

DANA: That really kind of what it's like. You get involved with everyone and everyone is involved with you. When new people move into the town, and if they are white, then they are welcomed with open arms. If they reject the invitation, life becomes exceedingly difficult for them. The *Organization* has its fingers in everything in those counties, it's kept incredibly quiet. You are taught to keep it quiet from the very start. And the things you see, you wouldn't' believe.

GORDON: So, I said that your dad took you to your first lynching when you were nine. That means you have seen other lynching's.

DANA: I have, yes.

GORDON: Would you care to share one.

DANA: It was my second and last thankfully.

GORDON: So, what happened?

DANA: I don't want to speak badly of the dead, and thankfully no one died that day. I want to get that out of the way. The people that got lynched were Desmond and Shirley Sharp, they just moved into a house on Tilton Road.

Prior consent was given by the family and individuals involved.

They seemed like a really nice couple, unfortunately they were black. That right there made them a target for the *Organization* and the trouble was just starting. The small things started almost immediately, that's the rocks through the windows and the constant yelling of foul language like racial slurs and such. It's just to see how the people will react to it, to see if the family will say anything to the local cops.

GORDON: Did they contact the police?

DANA: They did, it didn't go so well. As I said before, Sheriff Name deleted was a full time member and so was most of his staff. The Sharps didn't know this of course, it's like telling the enemy your current position. So of course, it's mentioned that Wednesday at the meeting and it is now its being spoken about how the *Organization* can get the Sharps out of town. Within a week of the conversation with the sheriff, people started painting words on their house, scratching the paint on their cars. This goes on for a few days, a week at most. Sharp goes to the police again, that gets him nowhere and by Thursday morning, Sharps tires are slashed, and his windshield is broken out. As always, things go from bad to worse. Turns out that Sharp owns a nice lever action rifle, and he knows how to use it. So, he stays up and waits for the next person to mess with his new tires. Sure, enough just after midnight, he spots somebody messing with his car. He gives out a warning shot. Keep in mind, sharps place is on Tilton Road, its way out of the main part of the town. His warning shot isn't going to hurt anyone. However, the next morning the Sheriff Name deleted is there to talk about him shooting his rifle. His nearest neighbor is a mile away, he is outside the city ordinance for shooting, but there is the sheriff anyway. Sharp gets fined for discharging a firearm within city limits, $1500.00, but nothing is said about the individual that slashed Sharps tire. Of course, Sharp brings it up and the Sheriff tells him that not the point and blows it off. Sharp takes it on the chin and doesn't complain. See, the *Organization* wants you to complain. It gives them a reason to act and it justifies whatever they do to you. No one messed with Sharps car for a while, but things were starting to boil anyway. It doesn't take long for things to get out of hand. So, the guy that Sharp shot at, well he sees Sharp at the store and makes a comment like "how are those tires doing?" Sharp recognizes the guy and Sharp confronts the man. A fight starts, and the police are called, now Sharps being charged with harassment and arrested. Sharps bail is made hours later by his wife and he is released. This was the point things got out of control, in my opinion. At the time, I honestly didn't feel that way, I do now.

My dad comes home the evening that Sharp makes bail. Dad goes into our den closet and pulls out his and my mom's robes. Dad tells me that he has a set of robes for me too. I never had robes until now, they looked brand new. We put them on and head out to Tilton Road, the crowd is already gathering. Then this big name deleted truck pulls up, and this man dressed in red gets out. That was the rank of name deleted. It was impressive, a sea of white and this red spot. Everyone mills around him, he's like a rock star.

GORDON: And who was that?

DANA: It was Elijah Johnson.

GORDON: Please go on.

DANA.   Well, a few minutes pass as everyone is talking' and this black car pulls up. It looked like Mosses parting the waters. My dad told me before about this car, so I knew it was name deleted. He was the states name deleted, the state leader. He had these amazing emerald green robes. He stands next to Elijah and starts to talk, speaking about the wrongs of our people and how we need to fix them. About that time, Sharp comes out of his house and starts yelling that we all needed to leave. The crowd starts yelling at Sharp, I thought it was starting then when Elijah told the crowd to silence. I was amazed at how the crowd got so quiet. Elijah had some key words to say to Sharp. I will not repeat them, they just aren't appropriate to repeat.

CHRIS: We understand about the language. We get that it was probably very racially loaded. It isn't worth repeating, please continue.

DANA: It was bad. So, everyone gathers around Elijah's truck and starts pulling lumber from the truck and the crowd start constructing a giant cross. One the cross is together the crowd stands it up in the front yard of Sharps house. The crowd then starts to grab some gas cans from the back of Elijah's truck and handing them out. I look back it now and think about it, one thing stands out.

CHRIS: What is that?

DANA: It's Sharp, what do you think he was doing Agents?

CHRIS: I don't know, probably yelling, that's my guess.

DANA: And you?

GORDON: I don't know, probably freaking out or getting his wife from inside the house.

DANA: Noting, he was just standing there watching in silence.

GORDON: Did he look surprised at all?

DANA: Nope, just stood there quietly, watching as the cross was being set up. I have no idea what was going on in his head, Sharp just looked so calm about everything. But he just watched and did nothing. I think about it now and it really makes me question a lot of things in my life. The biggest being bravery, Sharp was brave. I probably didn't think so, I know he is now. I wouldn't have said that then. If I could tell Sharp one thing today, I'd apologies to him. Anyway, they had the cross up and the crowd started throwing gas on it and Elijah starts it burning. The cross goes up in this giant puff sound! I could feel the heat on my face and skin. It was the hottest thing I ever felt or seen in my life. I was so shocked. But there was Sharp, still just standing there, staring that horrible fire down.

CHRIS: Why wasn't your dad in charge? Wasn't he a chapter leader?

DANA: He was for a long time. He stopped about the time I was 5. He wanted to be home more for me and mom. He was chapter leader on and off for years.

CHRIS: I get it, I was confused.

DANA: I'm sorry about that. I guess I didn't explain that well enough. Where was I?

GORDON: You said that Mr. Johnson just started the fire on the cross.

DANA: Yes, that's right. So as the cross is burning the Name Deleted, the guy in green calls over the crowed "who here is the youngest of us?" My father speaks up and says, "right here my brother" and picks me up so name deleted can see me. Name Deleted tell my dad to bring me to him, and so my dad walks me through the crowed. When I get their name deleted hands me a torch and says that I get the honor of lighting the first torch. This is the torch that all the torches will be lit from. It's a great honor to the *Organization*. So, I light it off the cross and hold it the torch over my head and all the members start to crowd in with their wood. I remember seeing the lit torches above me. It looked like a giant mouth full of teeth that were in blazing in the night. Just this perfect circle of fire above me and it was powerful and scary. I don't know when Sharp went into the house but when all the torches were lit, he was no longer on the porch. I was led to the front and the second honor was given; I was told to throw the first torch on the house. And so, I did as I was told and threw the torch. As soon as my torch hit the front door, all these other torches filled the air. The torches were landing on or around the house. They started to throw the gas cans after that. The house went up fast, real fast.

CHRIS: Did firemen or police show?

DANA: No, they couldn't show.

GORDON: Why?

DANA: Because they were part of the crowed. As I said, everyone was involved. That house was going to burn to its foundation, I could see that. It was an enormous inferno, a pyre of destruction. I know that sounds dramatic, but that's how I felt then, still do. We stayed for the hour until the fire was totally out.

CHRIS: Did you hear screams from inside?

DANA: No, the Sheriff noticed that too. He went back the next morning to the remains of the house. I mean my father and a few members and the Sheriff. The house was built well so a good portion was still there, that surprised me. I thought for sure the way the fire was going that the only thing left would be a basement hole. But no, it was there, it was bad though. It would have to be demolished and then rebuilt, no one could fix that. So, like I said, the Sheriff goes back to see if he can find the bodies of the Sharps, there wasn't. He thought they must have gotten out through a back window.

CHRIS: Was everyone in the front yard or around the house, because wouldn't you see someone get out?

DANA: They were around the house and yes, they were seen. The Sharps had to be. A few people must have turned a blind eye to them getting away. Thank God.

GORDON: Did anyone see the Sharps again?

DANA: They were seen by a few people the following morning. It was said that Sharps wife had taken a bus somewhere, probably back where they came from.

CHRIS: Only Mrs. Sharp?

DANA: The Sharps probably didn't have enough money to both go. They probably only had the cash on hand. The house went up fast.

CHRIS: Where did Mr. Sharp end up?

DANA: He was picked up by the sheriff a week later and charged for being homeless vagrant, Insurance Fraud, and Arsine. It was claimed that he started the fire for the insurance money.

GORDON: So, Mr. Sharp ended up in jail then.

DANA: Not exactly. Two days after Sharps arrest, Sharp somehow escapes custody and went back to his house. No one saw him escape and no one saw him return to his house. Sharp was found the next morning hanging from a tree in his found yard. The Sheriff said it was an apparent suicide of guilt. No suicide was found. Also, no excuses as to how Sharp escaped was ever mentioned. The local paper and the official police statement were ruled suicide by hanging.

CHRIS: I doubt that it was suicide.

DANA: Me too, but that what I was told. Sharps wife never came back and never asked about her husband. He was buried in an unmarked grave in the town's cemetery. It was all a real shame. But life went on like nothing happened after they burred Sharp. The remains of the house just and were forgotten or ignored.

GORDON: Were they the only black family in town?

DANA: No, just the newest. Being a new family to the town really brought a lot of attention to the Sharps, bad attention. There were older black families in the town. They kept to themselves and defiantly didn't want the *Organization* to notice them.

CHRIS: How did they do that; you have to work.

DANA: The families had small, quiet jobs that were seen and not heard. All just little odd jobs here or there, never drawing too much attention.

GORDON: Where you involved in a lot of things like this? You said this was your second and only lynching. Is there anything else that comes to mind?

DANA: Not too many things come to mind right away. We did a march once in Mount Devlin a few years after the Sharps were forced out of town. I was fifteen at the time on this march to Mount Devlin.

CHRIS: Any reason that came to mind first?

DANA: That's where I got the nickname "Bone yard". We scheduled the permits a year in advance and notified the township that the *Organization* was doing a peaceful march. The *Organization* also notifies the township three months prior and a month prior, so everyone knew we were coming. That way if the town wants law enforcement there, they can schedule it ahead of time.

CHRIS: That seems like a lot of work?

DANA: It is but the *Organization* enjoys it. The *Organization* knows people will come out to protest, and they like the buzz that they cause. They feel it's worth it and it makes there point. We get ready about three hours ahead of time, to make sure we are in rank and file and ready to go. We usually have horses too, that can take some time. The crowd is usually not friendly and that is to be expected. I had the privilege, according to them to finally have a hood and cloak but was not a member. I was at this time an Honorable Member.

GORDON: What is an Honorable Member?

CHRIS: Is that the same as an Honorary Member, basically made a member but not.

DANA: Sort of, I haven't taken my vows but am called brother. I'm privileged to almost all the normal activities but get no rank involvement.

GORDON: Okay, I get that. Please go on.

DANA: So, I had the privilege of walking next to my father who was on horseback. We were scheduled to march for approximately two hours, but it wouldn't take nearly that long. The whole route would take us down the center of the town and would be about a forty minute walk. So about ten minutes in, this kid to my right on the sidewalk, throws a stone and hits me on the left side of my face. I happen to turn and look to see him throw the rock but not enough time to move out of the way. My vision went blurry for a second and when my sight cleared, I lost my temper. Before my father could say a word, I broke rank and charged through the crowed to get to that kid, which I did. I pounced on him as he tried to run. We tumbled to the sidewalk in front of a store and it was on. I just started feeding him punches, one after another, blow after blow. I wanted to show no mercy, I wanted to prove a point.

CHRIS: What point was that?

DANA: That I was no joke, that we were no joke. I didn't want to make a name for myself, but I wanted the respect that I deserved.

GORDON: Do you think that point was made?

DANA: I did.

CHRIS: Why?

DANA: Because no one stopped me! No one raised a hand to me. For all the yelling the people were doing, running in the crowed like that should have been a death sentence. It wasn't. The police finally started to come over, but I was already done. As the cops approached the *Organization* had gotten to me first and the made a circle all around me, the cops couldn't tell us apart. What could they do?

CHRIS: They couldn't do a thing.

DANA: Exactly, they couldn't do a thing. That's what, and the *Organization* knew it. As were walking back to the formation, Elijah says "nice going kid, you sent that kid to the bone yard", the name stuck. That was my name from then on.

GORDON: How old was Mr. Johnson?

DANA: He was about thirty then.

CHRIS: How did your dad handle what just happened.

DANA: My dad was happy that I handled my business, but he told me it was unprofessional. I found out later that he was going to recommend me for membership but pulled it because of that incident. He made me wait till I was sixteen. That night they did hold a huge dinner in my honor and treated me like a king.

GORDON: Were there any repercussions from what happened.

DANA: There were. The next day, my dad gets a call from the Sheriff. He tells my dad that he received a complaint a guy named James Litton.

Prior consent was given by the family and individuals involved.

Sheriff says that this Litton guy wants an investigation on who hit his son. My father did not take well this new and was not happy. I'm sure the whole chapter would know in about an hour and wouldn't be happy either.

CHRIS: How did they take it?

DANA: As I expected, they were not happy to say the least.

GORDON: How did handle being told all of this.

DANA: I was nervous but was told that it would be handled.

CHRIS: And was it handled?

DANA: Legally, yes it was. Personally, it was not. I don't know who talked to Litton, but he found out it was me that hit his son and Litton came to our house.

CHRIS: Someone told on you?

DANA: Yeah, it turned out that we had a mole. The mole was feeding the news media information about us for money. Litton got lucky and asked the right guys for information. And the mole was happy to tell.

CHRIS: DID *the Organization* ever figure out who the mole was?

DANA: Nope, never did. He was lucky too. Bad things happen to people who talk too much.

GORDON: So, what happened?

DANA.   Like I said, this Litton guy came to our house yelling and screaming calling us all kinds of nasty names.

CHRIS: You didn't say where Mr. Litton was from. I'm guessing not Oak Harken.

DANA: No, he was from Mount Devlin.

GORDON: You said that Oak Harken was incredibly involved in *the Organization*, correct?

DANA: Involved, if I were to guess a percent, easily seventy percent or more. That's just as much as our town, and now he's at our door.

GORDON: So, Litton is in the wrong place with the wrong attitude I'm guessing.

DANA: Correct, and he was knocking on the wrong door. My dad took no crap off anyone. He didn't have time for rude or impolite people. My father was a perfect gentleman until you got on his bad side. Messing with his family was a one way ticket to his darker half.

GORDON: Did your father answer the door when Mr. Litton was knocking on it and yelling?

DANA: My dad answered and was ready for Litton. See the problem was Litton was black, and he is now insulting my dad. My dad was a prominent figure in *the Organization* and the community.

GORDON: This couldn't end well, why would Mr. Litton do this? He clearly knew that you were members. What could he possibly been thinking, it couldn't end well?

CHRIS: Was he drunk?

DANA: No, not drunk. Just angry and not thinking, I guess. It was all around a poor decision.

GORDON: So, what happened?

DANA: My dad answers the door and as soon as the door is completely open, Litton shoves my dad and starts yelling again. My dad instantly reacts by returned the favor and shoved Litton clean back through the doorway and onto the porch, where Litton landed on his deleted. Dad tells my mom to call the Sheriff and tells Litton to get off his property. Litton stands back up and starts threating my dad.

CHRIS: This isn't going to end well.

DANA: No, it isn't, Litton starts yelling that he will kill my dad and me, crap like that. My dad reaches behind the door where he keeps an old double barrel that his dad gave him. It's always loaded and ready to work. My dad keeps himself half behind the door so to keep the weapon out of sight, Litton starts yelling again, "You're a dead man" and starts to get up. My father stern and cold says "not today son" and gave him both barrels in the middle of his chest, Litton's back was blown out by the blast. He was only three maybe four feet away from my dad. Do you want to know the part that scared me the most?

CHRIS: Go ahead.

DANA: My father didn't even flinch. He didn't react at all, just cold as stone.

CHRIS: Man, wow. I can only guess that Litton was dead.

DANA: Yes, he was very dead. The Sheriff arrived shortly the shooting. He starts asking what happened and took my mom and dad's statements. It was handled without a problem, no trial, no questions. It all just disappeared.

GORDON: No inquiry?

DANA.   Nothing, that's just how things are with the *Organization*.

CHRIS: That's just messed up. I'm not saying your dad did anything wrong, but it needs to have proper channels. It sounds too quick, plus a trial should have been convened to show he was standing his ground.

DANA: The dead don't talk. It doesn't matter now anyway.

CHRIS: True, I guess it doesn't.

GORDON: Please continue.

DANA: Well, there isn't much really after that until I was sixteen, when I became a member. I attended every meeting until I was twenty-one and always volunteered everything. My dad was elected for a while then gave it back to Elijah who then turned it over to me when I was twenty-five.

CHRIS: Twenty-five, that seems really young

DANA: It was, but keep in mind, I was practically royalty and highly respected. Elijah was voted in as my second and things were normal for a long while. I went to the bi-weekly meetings for the county every month. It wasn't until I was almost thirty that things changed for me.

GORDON: What happened?

DANA. I went to a bi-weekly meeting, they had a huge attendance. I mean the place was packed. We all sit down and wait to hear the county rep talk. *He* comes out to a huge applause and the hall goes silent as *he* begins to speak. *He* said he had some big news. Keep in mind this is a festival auditorium we are sitting in. There are thousands of people in attendance. *He* starts to talk about Mount Delvin. Do you remember me talking about Mount Delvin?

GORDON: Yes.

DANA: One more thing, I'll just call the county leader "*he* or *him*". I have a great deal of respect for him. He left the *Organization* after I was arrested.

CHRIS: Why did he leave?

DANA: I opened his eyes. *He* didn't want to be part of the *Organization* anymore either. Well, the big announcement was that the last black family was removed from the town of Mount Delvin. They declared it white only town and community.

CHRIS: Wow! How many people live there, in Mount Devlin?

DANA: About twenty-five thousand people.

GORDON: That's a lot of people.

DANA Tt is a lot, and it is now the third largest town in the county that is totally white. Meaning most of the county is now white. It was a big deal because it was the biggest town too. Everyone starts to cheer and clap and in general just celebrate. It was a victory to the *Organization*. As things start to die down, a question comes out of the crowed. The question was yelled really loud so everyone could hear. The guy yelling says, "what do we do now that all the deleted are gone?" So, the county lodge leader says without a pause, "I guess we will start with eye color next!"

GORDON: What! Is he kidding?

DANA: No unfortunately *he* wasn't. Everyone one but me laughed, I didn't think it was funny.

CHRIS: That's just, well...

DANA: To be totally truthful, I was horrified. I was in total shock. It rattled me to my core. My world was left upside-down. I had nothing left to believe in and no one to turn to. It was all a lie. The only thing that I felt that had anything left in it was the bible. Everything else just let me down, my parents, my mentors, and my friends, all of it a letdown. I felt empty and for the first time truly alone.

CHRIS: You said *he*, county lodge leader evenly changed his mind about the Organization, after *he* says something like that?

DANA: *He* did. Look, we all believed the lie, even *him*. Sometimes it just takes longer for others to see the truth about hate.

CHRIS: What went through your mind when *he* said that?

DANA: look, I understood the hate part of what I was. I get the fact that what we did wasn't always the right thing. But this was a level of hate that I didn't understand or see coming. It was a hate that was focused on something totally new and different and one that I just couldn't wrap my mind around.

GORDON: That's interesting, why is that?

DANA: I just realized that my beliefs weren't about the duty of cleaning our country. It wasn't about saving my way of life and protecting my family. The *Organization* just said all of that to protect the lie and feed others into it. In the end, it had nothing to do about right and wrong, good, or bad. It was just about pointing a finger at someone and blaming all the problems on the world on. I knew then that we were no better than the skinheads that we hatted. We were the problem, not other people. I was so confused, angry, and just sickened.

GORDON: And what was that lie, Mr. Dana?

DANA: Special Agent, the lie was indiscriminate hate. We weren't hating for good or God, like I said. The lie was we hated to just hate. It didn't matter who, we would always find someone to target and blame. It took my foundation and rocked it. I honestly felt dizzy. I had to leave and did. I drove straight home and sat there in my living room, in the dark, all night. I also called work the next morning to say I wouldn't be in. Everything I was taught as a kid was a lie, all of it. I spent my whole life looking up to these people and it was just empty. I called Elijah and told him I wouldn't be at the meeting next week and he would run it until further notice. I don't know what to do.

GORDON: What did you end up deciding to do?

DANA: Well, it was about two weeks since I went to the county meeting. I went over to Elijah's house to talk to him personally. I told him that I was stepping down and he was now in charge. I also told him that I was leaving the chapter and leaving the *Organization* as well. I gave him my resignation of office and my resignation as a member, all in writing and official.

CHRIS: How did that go over?

DANA: Not so well, it went very poorly in fact. Elijah said that
            leaving isn't how things work. He tells me that we don't
            just leave, and that I can't. He wasn't pleading but was
            talking to me like I was a child. He didn't want to know
            why or what had happened. Then he says my father
            and mother would have been disappointed. I could have
            cared less at that point, the fed me the lie. I cared about
            my parents, but I didn't need their approval, even if they
            were still alive. I left Elijah's house hoping to be left alone
            from that point on. As I walk away, I hear Elijah yell
            "when you dance with the devil boy, it's like tap-dancing
            on a landmine". I look over my shoulder. He makes this
            child like sign with his hand like he's holding a gun and
            then pulled the trigger. I see him make puff face for the
            sound as his finger barrel was pointed at me then the
            mooch weapon recoiled. He winked and went into his
            house. It was a quiet walk home, a lot on my mind.

GORDON: Where you left alone?

DANA: No, and that's how I got here. This is where my story
            becomes something that people will write about. I leave
            the *Organization* and Elijah's home with the idea of
            just moving on with my life, I have no children and
            no wife so whatever I decide is my own business. I also
            wanted too just be something more then I was. I thought
            about trying to remove my tattoos or covering them.
            Like I said before, the tattoos remind me not to forget
            what I learned, so I kept them. The troubles started the
            very next day. I walk out to my car to go for a ride, to
            clear my head or maybe find a new place to go. I find
            my car pretty messed up; it was bad. I noticed first
            that the passenger window was busted out. I looked
            inside, to find the interior just ripped apart by a knife or
            something. The radio was gone and anything valuable

was gone. As I walk around the vehicle I start seeing more and more. My tires were slashed, and my trunk was broken into as well. Inside the trunk they took the tire iron and put it through my spare tire. My back window had also been broken out too. Someone was also kind enough to delete on the driver's seat and leave a dead animal in the back seat. It might have been a squirrel. The gas tank was messed with too, the car was trashed. I know they did it, but I felt that in a small way they deserved to let out some steam.

CHRIS: Do you know it was the *Organization*. Someone could have broken into the vehicle and gone a little overboard. I know it's unlikely. I'm just giving a theory.

DANA: I respect that Agent, but who would break into a vehicle like that. Plus, there hasn't been an incident of car theft or vandalism in years. So, it's obvious what had happened. It would be expensive, but I was willing to let them have that one. I hurt their feelings, so they are upset with me, it's like breaking up. I moved on with the day and set up transportation for myself and had a car by the afternoon. It wasn't too much of concern because of my work van too. I could still get around and get to work. The next morning seemed better the previous day, no problems with the replacement car.

CHRIS: That's always good.

DANA: The van, yeah, not so much. I got up for work on Monday morning and headed out, I go around the back of the apartment and my van, and the tires had been slashed too. I noticed that the van was broken into as well. This time they took all my tools. I had a few thousand dollars of equipment. It was all gone. I have insurance and they would cover it, but it really was starting to get to me. So, I call into work and tell them what was happening.

They understood I liked working for name deleted, they weren't part of the *organization*. So, they weren't giving me a hard time.

GORDON: How long did this go on for?

DANA: After my van was broken into, not much for a little while. I actually hopped that it was over. Work was steady. I worked on AC units and ventilation units. The work is pretty consistent. I recognize a lot of people because I do work around town. Elijah was buying time to find new ways to make me miserable. He figured it out about a month later. I did this one job in an office downtown; I knew the guy from the meetings. No small talk just told me where the job was, so I just went to it. I get done and my cell rings, it's my boss. He tells me he wants to see me. So, I drive back to the shop and sit in with the boss and he tells me that there are about fifteen complaints about me and my work. My boss said that they were called in with in the past few days. Saying how rude I was and how I did terrible work. I explained what I thought was going. He listened and didn't believe me. I was suspended for three days without pay. I sat the bench until Monday and try to make the best of my day. As I'm driving to work that Monday, the Sheriff pulls me over. I already know there are going to be problems. He tells me that I have been drinking and I was arrested!

GORDON: I can only assume that you hadn't, corrected?

DANA: Nope, I haven't drunk for years at that point. I'm held for three days until I was finally let go. I had to prove to my boss where I was and that they could charge me. At this point I wonder how far my boss will let this go. Well, I was pulled over three more times and my boss had enough, I was terminated. I was beyond angry.

CHRIS: That is truly awful. Was there anything you could do?

DANA: No, the cops were all in on it. I didn't have the money to really go anywhere and my newly purchased car was also violated. I just sat at home for the next week planning on where I was going, and where to move too. I had no other family and nowhere to travel too. I was stuck.

CHRIS: It seems that way.

DANA: I was but I accepted it and tried to go along with it. A week had passed like this. I stayed indoors day and night. My cell rings at two in the morning, it was an unknown caller. All night my phone is ringing non-stopped until about eight that morning. I was so angry that it got me out of the apartment. I walk out the door and noticed all the cars at the building were gone. That was just strange.

GORDON: How many people lived at the apartment?

DANA: It was four family's total. It was an exceptionally large house divided into smaller living spaces.

GORDON: The families owned vehicles?

DANA: They did.

GORDON   And there were no cars at all?

DANA: Nope. Not one, no one was even going down the street around my block. It was all empty.

GORDON: But why?

DANA: I had no idea. I found out the next morning actually. The families were told to move and relocated or else. Later that same day, moving trucks showed up and the families were gone by that very same night. I found a job earlier in the previous week. It was a small gas station job just outside of town, overnight job. It was something and paid the bills. I would leave for work and come back to an empty apartment building, it honestly creeped me out. I found out from one of the families that came back for something that they were told to leave by Elijah.

CHRIS: Why did he do that?

GORDON: I'm guessing to minimize collateral damage. Mr. Phillips probably wanted to make sure that if they did something to a vehicle or property it would actually be Mr. Dana's vehicle or property. Is that right?

DANA: That's exactly why Elijah had the local *Organization* do it. I'm impressed.

CHRIS: That's clever. How did you know, Gordon?

GORDON: That's what I would have done. Mr. Dana has been changing vehicles from the sound of it. It just makes sense to make the target easer to spot and find. Plus Mr. Dana could be easier to follow if Mr. Phillips wanted too.

DANA: They have been doing stuff like this for a while. There is good at it.

GORDON: Please continue.

DANA: I worked all week without a problem. I just stayed home. I watched movies a lot to pass time and eventually went to sleep. I wake up, probably three maybe four hours later. The house was dark, I mean pitch black. I found that the power was off. I reach for my phone to see the time, no service. That was shut off too.

GORDON: They are really pushing at this point.

DANA: Oh, it gets better. The *Organization* drained my bank accounts and closed out the account too. Who knows where the money went, I never got it back, and it's just gone? All I know is, I don't have my money to this day. Now I'm determined to leave that very next morning,

I'm done. I start to pack what little I have when I notice the sound of a car drive by, really slowly. The windows explode in with gunfire. I dive under the coffee table and what seemed like forever, the shooting stopped, and they pulled away. I wasn't seriously hurt but done playing.

CHRIS: Did you see the car? Was there more than one?

DANA: No, I didn't see the car unfortunately. I wasn't in the right position to see it. I'm sure there was only one car.

GORDON: Did you leave at that point?

DANA: I started too. I got up and headed for the door and headed down starts. I saw the *Organization* members from my old chapter pulling up to my yard. My whole lodge was there in their hoods and they started building a cross. Not a regular cross but a St. Peter's cross.

CHRIS: Why that cross, why not a traditional Cristian cross?

GORDON: St. Peter was seen a traitor by the romans, that is the best symbol for a traitor. It's the idea of "If Mr. Dana wanted to be the martyred, and then Mr. Dana will be".

DANA: That's exactly why. So, the chapter, they have the cross erected and now started calling me a white deleted a traitor and pretty much any crap they can think of. Then they light the cross on fire and their torches. I have nowhere to run at this point so I run back into my apartment to see what I can find to protect myself. I try the water at the sink, nothing, no power. I go and grab my blanket off my bed. I can hear the torches hitting the apartment building now. I know I only have a few minutes to do something or I'm dying in this building. I go down stars and try the lower first apartment, the door is locked. The hall is filling with smoke at this point and there is a reddish glow from under the front door. The house is going up and I'm running out of time. I try the second apartment door and of course, the door is locked. Down the hall is the last bottom floor apartment and I assumed it's locked too. It's towards the back of the house and figure that I should try anyway. I run to that door and sure enough locked. I start to kick and kick at the knob and the door, the door starts to give as I start to get tired. I stand back and grab the last bit of inner strength that I have and charge the door, it gives way and the door buckles in. I hit the ground with a hard thud. My eyes and lungs are burning from the smoke, which is filling the bottom floor. I get to my feet and run to the back bathroom, throwing the blanket in the toilet. I rip the porcelain lid off the toilet and throw it through the window. The fire is now at the door of the apartment, I can see flames for the first time. I grab the wet blanket and try to start to climb through the broken window. I assumed that the walls outside the apartment are on fire too, but I had to take the chance.

CHRIS: What about the lodge? Wouldn't they be out there too? There probably everywhere.

M. Dana: I wasn't even thinking about that problem at the moment. I was just hoping I didn't cut my hands to bad. I started to climb through when I was forced through the window and thrown outside. I hit hard and was dizzy, I had no idea what happened. I roll over and look up to see the top floor of the building fell in on itself. The rush of air pushed me though and knocked most of the lodge on their backs outside as well. It put most of the touches out and debris was everywhere, I got to my feet and ran. I was just hoping no one seen me getting away. I knew if I were caught, there would be Hell to pay.

CHRIS: Did they see you?

DANA: Thankfully no, they never expected me to be in a different apartment, my apartment. They were all gathered out front and as I ran, I heard them cheering as the building completely fell in on itself. They thought I was in the top floor, well what was left of the top floor.

GORDON: Where did you go? I assume you had no money on you.

DANA: I had nothing on me except what I was wearing. I panicked and ran to the first place I could think of. I ran to the old Sharps house.

CHRIS: You said it was burned down, right?

DANA: It was, but the basement was in decent condition. I hopped the fence that the township put around it to keep the homeless out. Obviously, that didn't work. There are no homeless in the town anyway. I kick the storm cellar door in and go down inside. There were enough leaves in the basement to lie on for the night, and so I hid. I knew it wouldn't be long until they realized I wasn't dead. I found out later that they didn't look for a body, too much work. I was presumed and declared dead on the scene of the fire.

GORDON: How long did you hide in the Sharps house?

DANA: Two days maybe three days, I don't know. I lost track of time. When I woke up, the first night, it was dark. I realized that I had slept nearly 20 hours. But I had this dream, it stuck with me, do you know those dreams? You wake up and you can't shake them, that kind. It just sits in your mind like a song that you get out of your head. Do you know what I mean?

CHRIS: I know what you mean. As a kid I had this dream that a clown was waiting on the school bus. It was a Friday and all I thought about until that Monday morning was that clown.

DANA: Just like that, stuck in my mind.

GORDON: What was the dream?

DANA: I dreamed that I had Elijah tied to a rock. I touched him Elijah and he filled with a bright beautiful light. Then that light just ate him up, wilted him away like a dried leaf into nothingness. For days I wondered about the dream and what it meant. I dwelled over the dream and what I was going to do next. At night I went out, rooting through garbage for food until I walked by Johnsons Insurance, Elijah's business. The poster out front is Elijah sitting on a bolder while holding a cactus in one hand and in the background was hospital. The sign reads "Take a trip before business kills you". Man, what an omen. Do either of you believe in God? I know that seems out of nowhere, but I have a reason to ask. I don't mean to be too personal. I realize that you have to be professional, but it's just a simple question. So, do you?

GORDON: I never really decided, to be frank. What about you, Agent Chris?

CHRIS: Well, Yeah, I guess I do. I mean I never really totally decided either. I think there is something bigger than us, I just don't know what. Why?

M. Dana: I do, I believe in God and I think sometimes he talks to people. I'm not cray and I don't mean that I have lunch with the almighty. Just hear me out. Look, I know the things I've done but that doesn't mean I'm evil or insane. Church was a big part of the *Organization*. I always felt you have to believe in something. You have to have something in life that gives you meaning.

GORDON: So, you thought that God was talking to you?

DANA: No, I think God led me there to that place at that moment. What I do is all up to me, I made the choice when God gave me the option to walk past there.

GORDON: That sign could mean anything. Take a trip, run to the desert, it could have been anything.

DANA: I agree.

GORDON: You do?

DANA: Sure, I do, sure, why not. Things like this are widely open to interpretation. It very well could mean anything to anyone. But to me I knew what I had to do. It was simple really, just watch and wait. That's why Elijah was on the bolder in the picture. It had to all be connected.

GORDON: Watch who, Elijah?

DANA: yes, Elijah, that's who I had to watch. And so, I did. I just moved through the city quietly, watching Elijah and waiting.

CHRIS: How long did you do this for?

DANA: A few weeks. I saw that Elijah had a pattern to his life. Elijah would leave his house every morning at 7:15 A.M. to 7:17 A.M. He drove straight to work, never deviated, the same route every day. He would arrive at work at 7:30am and would stay there until lunch at 11:30am. He would leave his officer and goes three doors down in to name deleted restaurant. He remained there until 12:30 P.M. and back to work until 6 P.M. and straight home. I felt that at his home would be the hardest to get him.

GORDON: Get him?

DANA: Like I said before. He was tied to a rock in my dream, so I had to tie him up somehow. I knew that the restaurant wasn't run by members of the lodge and I never ate there before. I knew that was the place I had to get him from because the owner didn't know me. So, I got a job there watching dishes, and with the money I made I put it towards things I needed in the Sharp house to survive.

The meals came with the job, plus, I could catch Elijah in the restaurant without anyone knowing it. Elijah's diversion from the day was his meal, but at 12:20 P.M., after eating. Elijah always used the bathroom. The bathroom was a small three-man bathroom with two stalls and a urinal. I stored what I needed in a cleaning bucket in the bathroom corner. It was about four months after the fire that I picked my moment. He left his house on time that day, at 7:15 A.M. Elijah's wife left shortly after he did. She was picked up by a friend that morning. I broke into the house and stole her car keys and her car.

CHRIS: How did you get into the house?

DANA: That was easy, I knew Elijah for years. He had a fake rock out in the garden with a key in it.

CHRIS: I see, please go on.

DANA: I drove over to the restraint and parked the car out back. I went into the restaurant and went about my job as usual until 11:25 A.M. I waited in one of the stalls until Elijah showed. And like clockwork, 12:20 P.M. Elijah walks in. As he is using the urinal, I crept up behind him, silent as a whisper. I hit Elijah in the head with a roll of quarter that was wrapped in a sock. I quickly lock the door to the bathroom and begin by bagging him up and binding him in packing tape. There is a small window in the bathroom that I fit him through and slid though myself. And throw him in the trunk of the car. I slide back through the window and go talk to my boss. He noticed I was gone for an hour and I told him I was sick. My boss promptly let me go home. I get in Elijah's wife's car and I take him to the Sharp house. Once there, I tie Elijah to one of the remaining support beams. I tied him so he was on his feet. I take the car back to Elijah's house and replace the key. I left everything like it was when they left that morning. I knew that I had at least six hours till questions were asked where Elijah was. I used Elijah's cell phone to text his workers to tell them he had to leave on sudden notice and would be gone for the week or so. I then texted his wife telling her that he had an emergency state meeting and wouldn't be home for thee maybe four weeks.

GORDON: How common was it for him to leave for a month?

DANA: Sometimes it was necessary for me to have to do that. It happened and his wife and co-workers would be used to it, nothing out of the ordinary. Now I had a plan. I had all that I needed by this point to start to do what I felt I had too.

GORDON: And what exactly was that? Was it revenge?

DANA: please try and understand, I did what I did because I wanted to teach him and the *Organization* a final lesson. I was tired of people like him. I was tired of people messing my life up. He destroyed my life.

CHRIS: Do you know if Mr. Phillips actually did all those things. I mean to your car and such.

DANA: I don't know if he did them personally, but he ordered it. Following orders or not, what he did to me was wrong.

CHRIS: Was it any different than the other families, like the Sharps?

DANA: Yes, defiantly. I never did anything to the *Organization*.

CHRIS: Did the Sharps do anything to the *Organization*?

DANA: No, they didn't, and that's my whole point. They needed to be taught that lesson. I wanted to be the first that fought back at them. I also admit that the things of the past were wrong. I didn't understand that when I was part of them. I understood then and now, I can't change the past.

GORDON: What did you do next?

DANA: I stripped Elijah down keeping his hands above his head. I had a bucket and some smelling salts to wake him. He wakes and starts too screaming his head off for help. I tell him it's a waste of time, I sound proofed the walls. He starts to laugh at me and in a mocking tone asking what I'm going to do. He insists that I'm too weak to do anything that would get my hands dirty. He tells me that my father was a real man, and I wasn't my father. I grab his face, we are nose to nose. I look him dead in the eyes and tell him "Sometimes the Devil cries for what he has done, Elijah". The smile that was on his face fades away, he starts telling me that it was just business and we both knew that. He says that everything they did to me had to be done. I look at him and I can feel that I'm smirking at him and say, "the darkest monsters can be made in the brightest places Elijah", your fire made me something new and different. He starts to cry uncontrollably; he also pees himself. I left him in the basement sobbing for mercy. I couldn't stand to look at him anymore that night. I slept outside.

CHRIS: Excuse me Mr. Dana. You said Mr. Phillips made you something else?

DANA: I say that, yes. Elijah had made me different.

CHRIS: How exactly?

DANA: It's hard to explain. I just didn't care as much about how I made him feel or if I hurt him. I didn't care about my life or his. I didn't care about anything. The things that would normally bother me didn't. I was changed.

GORDON: Do you feel that God would be okay with what you are doing to Mr. Johnson?

DANA: Special Agent, I believe in God, I don't think God believes in me. God didn't then and he doesn't now. I made peace with that long ago.

GORDON: Do you think you are the Devil?

DANA: Excuse me for laughing but that is a bit insulting Agent, I thought we were on good terms?

GORDON: I mean no disrespect. I'm just trying to understand. Please continue.

DANA: No, I am not the Devil. I am not an angel or demon. I am just as human as you are. I just see things a little differently, as do we all Special Agent. No one sees the world the same. That's why art is such a beautiful thing.

CHRIS: Do you consider what you were doing art?

DANA: No, I do not. I was just giving a thought and example. Would you like me to continue?

CHRIS: Please do.

DANA: The next morning, I found him asleep, hanging there. I jammed his sock in his mouth which woke him and told him to follow my instructions very carefully. "When you have to go to the bathroom, we use the bucket" I tell him. I asked him to nod if he agreed and he did. I asked if he had to go, he nodded yes. I asked to nod which he had to do, one to pee, two for crap and three for both. He gave me three nods. So, I collected the feces and urine in the bucket like this for three days. During this time, I didn't say anymore then asking what he had to do. He wined and whimpered, all the while as I sat and watched him on a rug. I watched from my wakening moment till I fell asleep. Staring constantly into his eyes and he cried under the sock. At the end of the third day, I take his urine and clean him.

CHRIS: Clean him?

DANA: I used wet cloths to keep him exceptionally clean, always getting everything. I decide to tell Elijah a story. Elijah, I say, have you ever heard of the "Mo'ohta Natone'ŏse Emese" it's from the Cheyenne's nation. Its literal meaning is "The Black Stomach Eater", it was a ritual. I tell Elijah that it is an especially important sacrificial right that wasn't used often in the Nation of the Cheyenne. That's what made it so incredibly special. I knew that the ritual would be the light of my dream. I dreamed about the ritual and knew that it was meant to be done for Elijah.

GORDON: Did you dream about this ritual before you kidnapped Mr. Phillips.

DANA: I did, it was the second dream that I had after the fire. I tell Elijah that the ritual was used for the few of the nation's people that just couldn't, let's just say, fall in line. I tell Elijah it's for "Those rabid dogs of Cheyenne society that prayed of the others. You see, I'm going to show you this ritual Elijah because you fit that category, you pray on others. The beauty of the ritual is that we're going to experience it together". I return to work and all is well. I go on to the work data base and make a special order. I tell the boss I will pay for it. He doesn't care because it cost less than five dollars and tells me not to worry about it. My order arrives the next day, one large saguaro cactus needle. I also ensure that the needle that I ordered would not draw attention. I tell the owner of the restaurant; I was working at that certain cactus recipe that used the needles to make a great tea. This needle is four inches in length and dipped into the feces and urine mix with in the bucket. It's left there for three more days to cure in the bile. By now I tell my boss that I have to go away for a while and apologies for the inconvenience. He understands and now I can spend as much time as needed to work on Elijah. Elijah wonders what I'm doing with the needle. So, I tell him that in the morning I'm going to insert it in his belly button.

CHRIS: In his stomach?

DANA: In his stomach. Elijah begins to scream, so I sit down on the rug and watch him scream until I fall asleep. I get up early the next morning and get some antiseptic materials for Elijah and see a piece of paper on the sliding door of the Pharmacy. On that page is a picture of Elijah and a phone number to call because he's missing. Apparently, his wife is a curious woman. I find out through talk that Elijah had cheated on his wife years ago, so she always checks in on him. No one knew where Elijah as, so she filed a missing person's report. She is a very smart woman. It didn't matter anyway. Elijah was mine until I'm done.

GORDON: Could you tell if the town or the Organization was acting any differently by Mr. Phillips missing?

DANA: No, nothing was different. I expected to see police cars patrolling around, I never did see that. I guess everyone thought Elijah took a pretty girl on vacation and didn't take Elijah's wife seriously.

CHRIS: You said he cheated before. Did he at one time take a girl on vacation?

DANA: By luck, coincidence, or heavenly intervention. Elijah did the same thing I did with the texts. So, they didn't really think he was missing. He texted his wife telling her it was a business trip and his work telling them it was a family emergency. Life has a funny way of working out sometimes. And yes, he took his secretary.

GORDON: You went to the store to by antibiotics? Did anyone recognize you?

DANA: I go through the Pharmacy without a problem and get what I needed. I needed the antibiotics to keep Elijah healthy. I return to the Sharp's house and Elijah is still where I left him. By now he is nervous, why not. What I was about to do will hurt more then he can imagine. Elijah is clearly sweating. his eyes are huge and staring at me. I put on surgical gloves and wipe his stomach clean with a disinfectant wipe. I comment to Elijah that I know disinfectant wipes aren't traditional, but it still applies to what was intended. I pick the bucket up and give it one last good stir with the needle. I tell Elijah that this part of the ritual is important. "We have to be clean so I can't have you struggle too much". So, I put the bucket down and take some robe and secure it tightly around his waist. I pull the cactus needle from the filth with the utmost care and inspect it carefully. The needle has changed color, not the white, waxy, almost translucent appendence is gone. What remains is darker, and sinister, the vileness has taken hold of the needle. I secure Elijah tightly, he can breathe but only barley, I can't have him move. I put my hand firmly on Elijah's stomach, line up the needle and with one fast movement;

I push the needle in to the flesh leaving a small nub so I can pull it out later. Elijah is screaming, writhing in a panic but still unable to move, his wailing is pointless because of the walls. I was so glad I thought of sound proofing, I had the privacy I need. I step back and look at my work, I'm pleased. I did the job with a surgeon's skilled hand. All seven inches of the needle, gone into his body, only an inch remains visible. I wonder if Elijah can see sticking out. I then wander if he saw me insert the needle. I'm guessing he had his eyes closed. I wonder to myself if I should have taped his eyes open. I second guess that idea thinking it would have been too had to tape them. I should have just cut his eye lids off altogether. Too late now, I tell myself now as I watch Elijah slip in and out of consciousness. As I watch Elijah, he regains cognizance, I tell Elijah that the needle will remain in his stomach overnight, and in the morning, I'll pull it out. You two are noticeably quiet. I can stop if you want. I can imagine how all of this must sounds.

GORDON: Oh, no, it's ok. We didn't mean to be so quiet. We were just listening and taking all of what you said in.

CHRIS: Now that there is a pause, I have to ask. Where did you learn about this ritual?

DANA: From my father actually. My father loved to read, the den of the house, wall to wall books. Anything you could possibly imagine. I came across a book about obscure Native American rights in rituals. This was around my junior year of high school. I did a report on some the rituals and did quite well. The Mo'ohta Natone'ŏse Emese is the one ritual that stuck out to me. I remembered it because it shocked me. I felt it was perfect repentance for Elijah. The real ironic part of all of this, Elijah from the Bible is a great man and a profit of God. They were two totally different people with two totally different purposes in life. Do you want me to continue?

CHRIS: And what do you consider Mr. Johnsons purpose in life?

DANA: That, Agent Chris, I do not know. I know how he affected my life. What his meaning in life is? I cannot say, Elijah was not my creation. So, I have no plan or purpose in that.

GORDON: So, basically, you're saying, Mr. Johnson is Gods problem.

DANA: That's exactly what I'm saying. He isn't my problem.

GORDON: Please go on.

DANA: The morning comes fast. Elijah actually was asleep the whole night. I was surprised by that.

GORDON: How did you know he slept all night? Isn't he gaged?

DANA: I watched him all night and yes, he's gaged. As the ritual says to do, I carefully pull out the needle. The pain from the needle woke Elijah; his eyes were huge with terror. I told him to relax which I know he can't. I started to clean the area around his stomach and start to explain to Elijah that now I will feed him well from now on. And I do feed him, a very well balanced and good three to five meals a day.

CHRIS: Wait, you're feeding him well? I don't understand.

DANA: I wanted Elijah to stay fit and as well as possible. The ritual requires a strong mind and soul. So, I keep him as well as possible.

CHRIS: I understand, thank you. Please continue.

DANA: No problem. So, Elijah tries to start conversation with me, but I just ignore him. I truly feel no need for interaction on a personal level with Elijah. That time has passed. Every day for the next three days, I clean the wound and feed him well as to plan. I use iodine around the wound itself and rubbing alcohol on the skin surrounding.

GORDON: If I can interrupt for a second?

DANA: Please do.

GORDON: There are a lot of threes in this ritual. This must be the fourth or fifth time a series of three is mentioned. Is this just a coincidence or does it have a purpose?

DANA: It was believed that three was a clean number, it had power. A lot of cultures actually believe it too; three, six, and twelve. It was also believed that the number five was a number of nature. It's amazing how three was an appropriate amount of time for many things.

CHRIS: How long have you had Mr. Johnson by this point?

DANA: It's been almost two weeks since I kidnapped him. I might as well call it what it is. It was kidnapping.

GORDON: Please continue.

DANA: It takes about three days after the use of the needle that things start getting interesting. See, threes again and again. Elijah stars sweating more and sleeping more, I can only assume it's because of an infection. Elijah says that he's feeling cold and uncomfortable. I tell him that it is what it is, and you will get used to it. This is also the point where I don't think a gage is necessary anymore; Elijah is just too weak to scream. It's about three days later when the flies show up and start to buzz around Elijah. I can see it on his face that he is uncomfortable with this.

CHRIS: Uncomfortable with what exactly. I mean aside from the obvious, which I'm guessing you mean.

DANA: He's uncomfortable with seeing all the flies. There were a lot of them. I can see by the seventh day, Elijah's running a fever. I start him on mild antibiotics which I got from the local drug store. The flies become a constant theme now, they are always around. You could hear them all the time. I keep cleaning Elijah's wound and feeding him regularly. I also try and keep the flies away as best I can from Elijah. It was nine days in when Elijah starts talking to himself and less whining then normal. He also has diarrhea and vomiting. According to the ritual, this is what is called "the time of the truth". He will not lie, Elijah can't lie, he's just too delirious. He starts to confess all his sins to me like I was a priest. I didn't start by asking him, Elijah just starts talking. Elijah tells me that he was the one that orchestrated the damage to my car. I already knew but it was nice to confirm it. What I didn't expect to hear was that Elijah was the one who told Litton where I lived. I truly wasn't ready for that. Elijah tells me that Litton shows up at the lodge and Elijah simply gives him my name and my address and points him in the right direction.

GORDON: It was Mr. Johnson; he kept that secret after all these years.

DANA: If it weren't for Elijah, Litton would have died. I genuinely believe that deep down. My dad did what he had to do, but it didn't need to happen.

GORDON: I would agree with you.

DANA: Elijah was a snake, and now you see that for yourself. Anyway, by the eleventh day, I had to up the antibiotics. The infection was becoming too great. The area around the belly button was swollen and hot to the touch. You could see the redness on the skin and bluish vanes were starting to vine there way from the infection. I also start cleaning out the maggots that are resting on his skin and there is now a defiant smell. Elijah's head is extremely hot to the touch, but he is still aware of his surroundings and what's going on. It's been four weeks by now. The sounds at night were the most unusual. When the house settles at night, that's just a normal sound. But at night you can hear a slithering and crawling sound coming from Elijah. I remember it being a wet sound, almost obese in its nature. Either the antibiotics or the slithering sound makes Elijah more aware of what is happening inside him. I could see it on his face. The flies were everywhere. It was a living cloud that hung around Elijah at all times. I clean out more maggots daily and keep the flies away as much as possible. It's the sixteenth day when Elijah

starts another fever, it was a steady 103°. He tells me everything about his life, every small detail. How he met his wife, the affair that he had and was still going. He tells me of countless corruptive acts and even skimming money off the *Organizations* bank accounts. As I clean him, I can start to see movement under the skin now. His skin crawls and moves. You can now hear the sound from across the room, you can tell its chewing. The smell from Elijah is harsh and putrid, which is not surprising in the least. Big fat bloated flies buzz around Elijah, they are so big you can see their purple irradiance. They look like little raisins in the air, buzzing in small circles. Here and there, you can hear a plop, plop sound as maggots falling out of the wound in Elijah's stomach. The hole is easy to see now. It's about the size of a golf ball.

CHRIS: A golf ball, oh my God!

DANA: I can stop if you need me to.

CHRIS: No, it's ok, please go on.

DANA: It's been about nineteen days now. The wound is now exceptionally large, as I said. It grows daily. It has a greenish puckered lip look. By the twenty first day you can smell the wound, it fills the whole room. The chewing is very loud, hard to not hear. Elijah is confused and delirious. He starts to go in and out of consciousness regularly. This is on day twenty-four. By twenty-six days, the smell is rancid, smaller wounds have developed throughout Elijah's body. The little holes are about the size of pea and growing fast. The chewing is very loud and there is a puss coming out of every wound. His skin is crawling everywhere. I expect him to die soon. I ask how he's doing. Elijah starts sobbing and tells me that he can hear the maggots eating him. He tells me that he can feel them inside, eating everything, eating him away. Finally, Elijah losses consciousness, never waking up again, his body holds on for two more days. Maggots have eaten a good portion of his left eye and coming out of his left ear. His body is trembling at this point. His body is dying. I only know this because maggots are coming out of every hole in his body. He dies later that night and the ritual was completed. I felt complete.

GORDON: What did you do with Mr. Johnson's body?

DANA: I used Elijah's cell phone to call his wife and told her the address and said she needed to come and get him.

CHRIS: Did you tell her what happened?

DANA: No. At the time I felt it was right for her to find out. I was wrong for that. Elijah's wife had nothing to do with the house burning and my car. In the end, I punished her most, which wasn't the intent obviously. At the time, I never saw it that way. It took months for me to look at it from that direction. What I did hurt her more than I ever heart Elijah. When she called me a monster in court, I deserved it.

GORDON: Do you think you were wrong for what you did.

DANA: No, I don't. I don't regret what I did. He took everything from me because I tried to do the right thing and get out.

CHRIS: Does that really justify you taken Mr. Johnsons life?

DANA: No, it doesn't, and I admit that. I did wrong, is that what you are trying to get me to say. I admitted then it was wrong, I admitted it in the court room and even pleaded guilty. And to this day, I still say it was wrong, but he deserved punishment and I deserved justice for what he did to me. The broken system wouldn't give me the peace I wanted so I took it.

GORDON: So how were you caught?

DANA: I called the Sheriff after Elijah's wife. I was arrested and probably made every new station throughout the county.

CHRIS: Try the world.

DANA: Really? I didn't expect that.

CHRIS: I was personally in Canada when I hear about it.

DANA: I know the country was shocked that I pleaded guilty to the crimes. I didn't even take a plea bargain. Why would I? I owned what I did. Elijah deserved it.

GORDON: You really believe he deserved to die?

DANA: I do, his sins were awful.

CHRIS: Do you feel you deserve the same as Mr. Johnson?

DANA: Do you mean death?

CHRIS: Yes.

DANA: I deserve death. Washington State doesn't believe in the death penalty. So here I sit, rotting away. I know what I did was wrong. I know that the world portrayed me as a neo-Nazi. That's why I don't do interviews often. I'm not what the world tries to say I am.

GORDON: We appreciated the interview. Is there anything that you would like to add?

DANA: There is, I just hope you keep this in its original form. I'm not a bad guy. I've just done bad things.

GORDON: This is Special Agent Sean Gordon. Its 12:25 P.M. in Washington state penitentiary, Walla Walla, Maximum detention Block, Pod 2, Interview room. We have just finished interviewing Marcus Eric Dana. Case file: 31008539-A, Operation Vanguard or "The Matthews Incident".

This formally concludes the interview with Marcus Eric Dana. No further entries were made on this date or for this part of the interview.

Interview of Former Captain Bryant Justin Tessle

Thursday, October 12th, 2028
United States Disciplinary Barracks (USDB)
Fort Leavenworth, Kansas

GORDON: Its 9:15 A.M. in United States Disciplinary Barracks, Fort Leavenworth Kansas, Maximum Security Wing, Block 5. Seated next to me is Special Agent William Chris. Across from us, at the interview table is Captain Bryant Justin Tessle, Former Administrative clerk, Personal Assistant, and Records Officer to Brigadier General Matthew's: Case file 31008539-A, Operation Vanguard or "The Matthews Incident". Capt. Tessle is 35 years of age, is 5'10", weight is 149 Lbs. He is of slender build, brown hair, has no discernable marks or scars, has blue eyes, and a light completion. He is Caucasian and an American. His fingerprints are on file and classification code 1 for the flowing: several counts of involuntary manslaughter. He is also accused of treason and conspiracy of treason, terrorism and is considered a traitor of the United States of America. He is currently awaiting Court Martial. We have returned to speak with Captain Tessle for a dialog of Brigadier General Matthew's regarding Mr. Dana.

*Key testimony involving the death of Elijah Phillip Johnson. Captain Tessle is at this time currently at liberty to speak about Brigadier General Mathews, Operation Vanguard and Elijah Phillip Johnson by the Supreme Court and is not placed under a gag order. It should also be known that Elijah Phillip Johnson's family has given prior consent for this interview.

GORDON: Good Morning Captain Tessle.

TESSLE: With all due respect Special Agent, I was stripped of my rank and kicked out of the Corp as a traitor. I was finally court marshalled earlier this week. But no worries, the judge says I have access to all the documentation that you will require. One your investigation is up; I no longer have admittance to those files. You can just call me Bryant. I also know how uptight and professional you both will be anyway so, Mr. Tessle is also excitable.

GORDON: Very well, Mr. Tessle it is. We spoke with Mr. Dana a week and a half ago as you suggested. We appreciate the interview suggestion but really didn't understand the relevance to our case.

TESSLE: It's about General Matthews finding the story interesting. You have to understand how Matthews was. He was always learning and adapting. The story of Marcus Dana is a wild one, beyond belief. But that's why General Matthews found so much insight in what was said. Situations like Marcus Dana don't happen every day. A truly wise man can learn a lot from his story. That's why I suggested it. It will help you understand General Matthews.

GORDON: Do you have the information ready on Brigadier General Matthews?

TESSLE: I have it ready. I wouldn't have sent you to speak with Marcus Dana if I didn't already know what information could be useful. Come on Special Agent. What do you take me for, a fool?

GORDON: No, not in the least. I've learned to never estimate anything, nor take guesses.

TESSLE: Wise words Agent Gordon, Wise words. General Matthews would have liked you. You are always thinking. That's a good thing. I'm ready whenever you would like to start.

GORDON: Please continue then.

TESSLE: General Matthews hears about Mr. Dana's actions and tells the Battalion Commanders that there will be a formation the following morning. His next instructions were to me. He told me to mail a letter to Mr. Dana, as I did.

CHRIS: We heard about the letter. Mr. Dana no longer had it.

TESSLE: It wasn't long and drawn out, just simply "good initiative, bad judgment. You, Mr. Dana changed the world, just not how you thought". That is, short and sweet, nothing more to it.

The next morning, there we are, standing tall in formation waiting for General Matthews to speak. He steps out onto the parade deck and looks at us for second then bows his head like he in in a deep thought or prayer. There he stands for a long moment, not moving, a living statue. Finally, without looking, in a small tone he begins to speak.

"My children, my brothers and sisters, my Marines,

What a truly maddening time we live in. What a sorrowful day and age. The fine life of real and unreal is truly blurred at every minute. The world is a ship with no sail or star to guide her by. We are surly adrift, lost.

Matthews raises his head to us, looking at us slowly. His head moving from left to right, scanning the crowed of Marines before him. General Matthews looks sad and very tired. I know for a fact that Matthews hasn't been sleeping well. I personally wonder if he has left base and gone home in the last week. I suspect he has been sleeping in his office.

CHRIS: What has General Matthews been doing all that time?

TESSLE: Reading the newspapers that he has delivered, watching the news. Did you know that General Matthews would

CHRIS: Why?

TESSLE: I asked him once. He said you could tell a lot about an author by reading all their work. He would recognize certain journalist from reading the day-to-day articles of the papers. Matthews said that you can understand an author's beliefs if you just read between the lines of what is written. Matthews also said, "Don't trust what the author says as what they think. Writing news is a job not a pool of opinions. They aren't paid to write what they think but what the reader should think". Anyway, General Matthew's continued on.

"As He died to make men holy, let us die to make men free". No such truer words in this time. We, all of us put our lives on the line for freedom. That especially includes oppression. Let me make this clear, we make them, the civilian free. We protect the right to be equal. Unfortunately, we also protect their right to be stupid. We all see the flag burnings and desecration to our standard. Some of the populous belief that burning the flag is an important statement, but it's not, it does nothing but show ignorance. Because you have the right to do something, doesn't mean you should. I have never use racial slang words, we can all agree on that, but I still have the right to do so if I chose. It's the same. No one of us is greater than the next. But sir, you say. You just said men. I mean mankind; too often do people try to twist words to cause problems. Male, female, all equals. Many will try to sell you the lie that we aren't equal. it's just that, a lie. It's obvious that there are rich and poor because you have money doesn't make your life more valuable.

There more lies then that of course, sexism is just one. The lie that one "race, is better than the next". Race, that a joke too. My body is no different than anyone before me. The idea that because you have a different skin than me means you are somehow superior or inferior is a weak argument. A *darker shade of red on a crap art canvas isn't going to make it a masterpiece, just as a masterpiece is no less valuable because of a different shade of green. This brings me to my point. I read yesterday about a man by the name of Marcus Dana committed a horrible act. If you haven't heard yet, he brutally tortured another man that allegedly tried to kill him. This whole insane thing started with racism, real racism. Not the kind your generation loved to throw around. No, the kind that kills another man does not hurt their feelings because you lost an argument. Your generation feels that racist words can be thrown around as simply as a greeting. The meaning of the terrible word has been lost because of the crybabies of the world. You don't like my shirt because it offends you, I must be a racist. All because I don't like what you do. When in truth, that shirt had nothing to do with "race" at all. Anyone with different beliefs is now a racist! Anyone who disagrees with you is a racist! Anyone that thinks differently...must be a racist!*

Now Mr. Dana, he, and the unnamed individuals, they were true racist. They believed they were better than one group of people. You know what; they KNEW they were better than those people. Are they? Again, no they are not. But you couldn't tell them or Dana that. And when they saw difference, they burned difference's home down and took everything from them! True racism, the kind of racism that Dr. Martin Luther King Jr so long ago. He fought and won agents with the price of his life. The article didn't mention who Marcus Dana associated with. But honestly, it doesn't matter. It's all wrong. And yes, these individuals where white, and yes, they did horrible things. But not all "whites" are like that. But be clear and honest, racism is a two-way street. The myth that only white people can be racist is laughable. Anyone that believes that only whites are racist is the same person that believes that "white privilege" exists. Both are pure ignorance. Frankly, the believers of this unicorn known as "white privilege" are no better than the hood wearers.

I'm sure I've hurt feelings right now, I know, it's terrible to accept responsibility for one's own actions. Terrible me, mean old me. It's easy to blame others. We see racism in what we call justice too. Years ago, reparations were mentioned in this country, which I have no problem with...When it was 1865. It was owed and deserved, and that should never be questioned. That was then, not 200 years later. My father talked about when it was brought to the table by the government. My father was enraged by the idea that the government wanted him to pay for something that he had nothing to do with. I know people are mad right now in my formation for saying that, but my Father was a second generation Italian/ Jew that came here generation after the slave trade and plantations ended. He was told by the government and people that because he looked white, he had to pay. Mind you, that's racist in itself. Thankfully, it never happened. Say thankfully only because it wasn't right that he was being forced to pay because of his color. That's the part miss, my father never minded helping other, and he never minded giving. He minded be told too. That's the face of racism, its ignorance. You probably say to yourself now, Sir, isn't that racist? No! It isn't, grow up and use the word right!

Another word that has no meaning, destroyed by the same generation is "Nazi". Here we are again brothers and sisters. A word that's thrown out because an individual was probably offended. Most likely because of a lost argument or is difference of opinion. Probably called that name and doesn't deserve it. There weak mind can't handle the fact that they aren't always right. Words are not violence, words hurt but not physically. You probably think this is a hate speech, I'm sure you do. Even though it's the truth and should be heard. Because a person has a different view doesn't mean he is goose steeping in an SS uniform. You clearly haven't read a book, done some basic research. The Nazi were vile and to utter their names because of simple disagreement is shameful.

We are better than this, we are more than this. It sickens me to see what people have become. Weak mined and weak backed, Lazy, and truly incompetent.

At this point he dismisses the unit to continue the day. It stops their gentlemen.

GORDON: Wow, General Matthews was fired up.

CHRIS: That was intense!

GORDON: I don't understand the connection for Mr. Dana and General Matthews.

TESSLE: General Matthews took the fact the Marcus Dana reformed and changed. He felt others could change like Dana did.

CHRIS: But was it necessary to have the formation just for that.

TESSLE: Why not. He's in command. Matthews could do as he pleases. Understand that there is no racism in the Marines. Everyone is equal there. It bothered Matthews to see the country argue over such things. Matthews was loud with his opinions and points of views. He didn't mind saying them. I'm not saying he's right or wrong. But he was really getting Marines worked up.

GORDON: Was this the final incident that finally pushed Brigadier General Mathews?

TESSLE: Actually, no it wasn't. It actually happened a month later. Do you remember Robert Barrie? That affected Matthews deeply. He was so outraged.

CHRIS: I do remember.

GORDON: I do too. I remember the court trial on TV. It was a really big deal. It changed a lot of laws in this country. It also changed how the judicial system dealt with people. That's when the Barrie Act was enacted.

CHRIS: The crime rate for most cities went through the roof because of that act.

TESSLE: That's when General Matthews really went off. He felt very strongly about what that act represented.

CHRIS: We will check that out what we can and do some digging.

GORDON: Can you get that recording of Matthews about the Barrie Act for us? Will that be a problem?

TESSLE: I can, it will obviously take time. I don't mind.

GORDON: We will meet again, thank you.

TESSLE: Thank you.

GORDON: This is Special Agent Sean Gordon. Its 11 A.M. in United States Disciplinary Barracks, Fort Leavenworth Kansas, Maximum Security Wing, Block 5. We have just finished interviewing former Captain Bryant Justin Tessle. Case file: 31008539-A, Operation Vanguard or "The Matthews Incident".

This formally concludes the interview with former Captain Bryant Tessle. No further entries were made on this date or for this part of the interview.

Memorandum from Special Agent Sean Gordon

To: Brian Samuels, Director of the Federal Bureau of Investigations

From: Sean Gordon, Special Agent

Good Moring,

As per protocol, I am giving my informal opinion of the investigation of Death of Elijah Johnson Phillips and my person opinion to what I witnessed.

I spoke with a Mr. Marcus Dana at the request of Bryant Tessle. I wasn't exactly sure of the connection when I heard Mr. Danas Story. Mr. Dana pleaded guilty to the torture and involuntary manslaughter of one Elijah Johnson. The story the Mr. Dana told was very graphic and of a shocking nature. The violence of Mr. Johnson death made headlines across both the nation and the world. The connection was just that, national headlines. According to Mr. Dana, General Matthews reached out to Mr. Dana via a letter that Mr. Dana no longer possessed. It was confirmed later by Mr. Tessle that a letter was sent. The Letter basically said that Mr. Dana "changed things, just not how he wanted".

After Speaking with Mr. Tessle, we find that Matthews felt strongly about what Mr. Dana had done. According to Mr. Tessle, Matthews was also looking very worn out, spending much of his time at work and on base. Base records were checked, and the fact was confirmed by the Provost Marshals Office (MP's) that General Matthews left the base very rarely at this particular time. After hearing General Matthews speak about what Mr. Dana had done, it was obvious that General Matthews did not approve in racism in any for or degree. He spoke of strict opposition to anyone with segregated belief. This was in fact one of General Matthews most energetic speeches. I brought the question up to Mr. Tessle weather or not this was the point that General Matthews had decided on Operation Vanguard. Mr. Tessle said this was not the point. I believe it is a key point in Matthews's life where he is starting tip over the edge, and eventually something had to happen.

General Matthews at this point was a rubber band stretched too far. I believe his was pushing himself mentally, physically, and spiritually to the brink. I say spiritually one because of the incredible amount of time he has been working. Something had to give and when it did, the result was Operation Vanguard.

The next investigation brings us to Robert Barrie and the Barrie law. Matthews's journal notes stop at this incident. Also, it was conferment by Mr. Tessle that this is the next step in General Matthews's evaluation.

Sincerely,
S.A. Sean Gordon.

Eyewitness accounts of Operation Vanguard

"I was there when it started. I saw the vehicles show up. You could hear shots inside the White House. See the flashes in the windows. I couldn't understand what was happening.

-Isaac Steelier (Morning News 14, Barbra)

"There was this cop just sitting on the curb with his hands resting next to him. He was about twenty-five yards away from where we were hiding. He just sat there breathing hard and staring off. I then saw blood running out of his left sleeve of his shirt cuff, he has blood pulling around him. It took a moment when I saw a small hole in his chest. As I looked into his face, I realized that he died like that; just sitting there. To this day I wonder what was going through his mind. It was so awful to watch."

-Amy Diluent (Good Morning New York, Gaullist)

"I actually saw that Matthews guy as being led out of the area by the police. He stood out; you couldn't miss him. There were all these soldiers escorting into the White House. It was like a circle around that Matthews. There must have been fifteen or twenty of them all around, there weapons pointing outward. So how did he stick out? He wasn't wearing camouflage like all the other soldiers. He had a pressed green uniform on. He also walked like all the craziness wasn't going on around him. He walked like he was in total control."

-Sam Wallace (Washington26.com, Mallard)

ROBERT CHARLES BARRIE AND THE BARRIE ACT

Interview of Robert Charles Barrie

Friday, November 3rd, 2028
Allen County Jail
Lima, Ohio

WANTED
BY F.B.I.
Statue: Captured

F.B.I. No. 198214
WANTED FOR: MANSLAUGHTER

Robert Charles Barrie
ALIAS: IV (4)

Description

AGE:	18	SCARS OR MARKS:	NONE
HEIGHT:	5'10"	EYES:	BROWN
WEIGHT:	140LBS	COMPLEXION:	MEDIUM
BUILD:	MEDIUM	RACE:	CAUCASAIN
HAIR:	BARK BROWN	NATIONALITY:	AMERICAN
OCCUPATION:	STUDENT	FINGERPRINTS:	ON FILE
		CLASSIFICATION:	FELONY LEVEL 3

CAUTION

Current status is captured and beheld by
the Department of Correction.

IF YOU HAVE ANY INFORMATION CONCERNING THIS PERSON
PLEASE CONTACT YOUR LOCAL F.B.I. OFFICE IMMEDIATELY

This recorded session is called to order by the head of the
Federal Bureau of Investigations, Special Investigations Unit.

GORDON: Its 2:45 P.M.in Allen County Jail, Lima, Ohio and currently
seated in the Interview Office. Seated next to me is Special
Agent William Chris. Seated next to me is Special Agent
William Chris. Across from us, at the interview table is
Robert Charles Barrie. Case file: 31008539-A, Operation

Vanguard or "The Matthews Incident". Robert Barrie is 18 years of age, is 5'11", weight is 179 Lbs. He is of medium build, dark brown hair, has no discernable marks or scars, has brown eyes, and a medium completion. He is Caucasian and an American. His fingerprints are on file and classification code 3 for the flowing: Manslaughter. Mr. Barrie pled guilty for manslaughter and serving a five to ten year sentences. Mr. Barrie has currently served three of his ten years and due for parole in two years for good behavior.

Key testimony involving the deaths of Tiffany Defoe, Shawn Manos, Joshua Cartwright and Kathy cartwright and the months leading up to the incident. It should also n=be known that the families of Tiffany Defoe, Shawn Manos, Joshua Cartwright, and Kathy Cartwright have given prior consent to this interview. Mr. Barrie is at this time at liberty to speak about Brigadier General Matthews and Operation Vanguard by the Supreme Court and is under no Gag order.

GORDON: Good Afternoon Mr. Barrie.

BARRIE: Good Afternoon.

CHRIS: We appreciate you taking this time to talk to us.

BARRIE: All I have is time. Makes no difference to me, I just agreed because I've never met an F.B.I. agent.

GORDON: we still appreciate it, whatever the reason.

BARRIE: So, what's this interview all about, there not trying to put me back in trial, are they?

GORDON: No, why would you think that?

BARRIE: A lot of protesters and the families of the individuals involved think I didn't get nearly enough time for the things I did. I was never tried for a lot of other stuff; I'm wondering if that had all caught up with me.

GORDON: It's nothing like that at all. We are currently investigation evolving Brigadier General Matthews and Operation Vanguard.

BARRIE: Okay? I have no idea why you would be here for that?

CHRIS: You know nothing about Operation Vanguard or General Matthews?

BARRIE: I have no idea what you're even talking about.

GORDON: The Operation Vanguard. According to our records, your case and incident was probably the most researched by Brigadier General Matthews. He was very actively trying to reverse the Barrie act. Going to the lengths of contacting several congressmen and senators personally

BARRIE: You mean the thing that happened in Washington a few years ago? Is that what you are talking about?

CHRIS: That's the very incident.

BARRIE: I'm confused. I had nothing to do with that. I don't sell weapons and don't know any army guys.

GORDON: We know that, we just want to ask some questions about your incident and what basically lead up to you becoming incarcerated. We know that brigadier General Matthews found your case interesting. Speaking with you will hopefully help us understand General Matthews's motives for Vanguard. Are you willing to tell your story answer some questions?

BARRIE: I guess, I mean I plead guilty, so I see no reason not talk about what I did. I have a ten year sentence which I just served three years in ODRC.

GORDON: ODRC?

BARRIE: The Ohio Department of Rehabilitations and Correction. I was committed when I was fifteen. I am now eighteen years. I'm in big boy jail now. Where do we start other than that?

CHRIS: Well, how about the letter?

BARRIE: What letter? I get mail all the time. You the crazies that send me mail or the fan mail?

GORDON: The letter he sent you?

BARRIE: He who?

CHRIS: Brigadier General Matthews.

BARRIE: I've never met the guy, let alone ever gotten a letter from him.

CHRIS: You didn't get a letter from General Matthews? Are you sure?

BARRIE: Yeah, I'm positive. I don't get a lot of mail, real mail at least. My mom mostly sends the letters, and my dad here and there. My mom has never mentioned a General Matthews.

GORDON: How about any phone calls from General Matthews?

BARRIE: No, no phone call! I've gotten nothing! How many times do I have to say that! Was he supposed to contact me or something because he didn't!

CHRIS: Sorry, were not trying to upset you.

BARRIE: Well, you did. You're asking the same question over and over again. Are you trying to catch me in a lie or something because I'm not lying.

CHRIS: We're not trying to do that.

GORDON: General Matthews has reached out to everyone he took interest in. Until this point, everyone he talked about has been contacted. Brigadier General Matthews not contacting you is very inconsistent and unusual for him. It's frankly different and strange.

CHRIS: Do you think we should continue the interview, Gordon?

GORDON: I don't see why we shouldn't. There may be a clue or reason Mr. Barrie's wasn't contacted. Mr. Barrie's story may explain the difference in General Matthews's actions.

BARRIE: Do you guys still want to talk to me?

GORDON: We will see what we can learn. What we currently know is that General Matthews spoke to his Marines about this. If we don't talk to you, the case recording of Brigadier General Matthews won't make sense. We will continue if that's oaky with you.

BARRIE: I'm fine with it, I have nothing but time. So, what's the next question then since the first was a bomb.

GORDON: The next is easy, just talk. Talk about your childhood, your parents, what happened to get you to this point. Just talk.

BARRIE: I've never interviewed like this before.

CHRIS: Just tell your story. It's just that simple.

BARRIE: Okay. I'm from Lima, Ohio. It's just your average town. I lived there my whole live. My parents didn't grow up Lima. My Parents are from other parts of Ohio. We lived in the good section of the city. My parents come from money, so life for me wasn't hard. Lima is a good sized town, lots of people. I enjoyed it and not a bad place.

GORDON: What was your childhood like?

BARRIE: You mean the childhood before here?

GORDON: Yes, I forgot how young you are and how long you have been here.

BARRIE: Well, I was a lonely child that honestly got pretty much whatever I wanted and enjoyed it. If my parents could afford it, it was mine. I found life to be very boring most of the time. School was no better. I had friends, as many as I wanted. I didn't have to care about any. I was never alone. As I said, I didn't find school interesting until I took Chemistry that was something that I took interest in and figured out. I understood all the theories and principles. It was like a road map to anything you wanted. You want an acid to melt stuff, I can make that. You want to burn something down; I can do that too. How about blow something up, oh, yeah right here. It was all laid out before me like a blueprint. I just had to figure out the missing pieces to the puzzles. I loved it.

CHRIS: That's impressive that you took to chemistry so well. It's a hard thing for a lot of people to wrap their minds around.

BARRIE: Not for me, it was a second natural language.

GORDON: Tell me about your parents?

BARRIE: My father, Justin Gordon works for the county of Allen as an Auditor. He goes around to the county government facilities and make sure money was spent appropriately and their books balanced. He loves his job. He works a lot of overtime by choice and is happy in his work. I'm socially, a lot like him. He kept a lot of friends and found numbers rewarding. He had no real hobbies that I can remember. My dad was the kind that doesn't have a work bench in his garage, never messed with the cars. He always had friends for that kind of work or has others do it. I never saw him show any interest in sports or movies. He is just a quiet guy that never broke a sweat.

CHRIS: How about your mom.

BARRIE: She kept to herself. She was more outgoing than my dad though. She's the head registered Nurse in Allen County Hospital, and active in the PTA. She is part of a book club, outside of that. There's not much more than that.

GORDON: So how about the big question.

BARRIE: Okay?

GORDON: How did you end up in here? How did all of this start?

BARRIE: I had a problem in school one day after school. Some jerks given me a hard time, that kind of thing. It's nothing new but that one particular day, I felt disrespected. Then I just had this idea. I felt that I wanted respect and some quick cash.

CHRIS: You mean you were board.

BARRIE: Yeah, that's the real bottom line. I thought about me, and how I could get some money. I really didn't want a job and didn't feel the need to get one. I was sitting at the dinner table when the idea hit me. As soon as I was done eating, I created an account on deleted. I thought my idea was perfect.

GORDON: What was the idea?

BARRIE: I thought that I would hide my face for the camera and threaten the local community with random acts of violence. It's kind of like holding the town hostage.

CHRIS: It is.

BARRIE: Well, yeah, but different.

CHRIS: How is any different than other terrorist groups do?

BARRIE: I wasn't a terrorist! I had a reason for what I did.

GORDON: Anyway, please continue.

BARRIE: Well, if the county or property didn't pay up, I break or burn something important it had to be something really special, or one of a kind if I can, nothing that no one would care less about. It was a perfect plan. I linked my page to the town's page so I could watch them if they said anything or posted about my threats. The link was made so that county will get whatever I send out, threats or pictures, whatever it is. Best part is everyone that's liked to the county page will see everything I post too. That way everyone knows of the coercions I make. That night I send out my first invitation of terror.

CHRIS: Invitation of terror?

BARRIE: That's what I was calling my movement. The "Invitation of terror", sounds good, right?

GORDON: Why did you call it a movement?

BARRIE: I was hopping others would fallow my example. You know, jump on board or at the very least copy what I was doing. In the end, it didn't actually happen. Anyway, I go to my room ready. I hung a black sheet behind me and made the room real dark. I started recording my first message. It took me several tries to get it right. But when I finally got it right and edited it, it was perfect.

CHRIS: What did your invitation of terror say?

GORDON: Chris, really?

CHRIS: What was the message Mr. Barrie?

BARRIE: I basically said that if the town of Lima doesn't pay me five thousand dollars, I would violate one of the major parks. I gave them fourth-eight hours to respond.

GORDON: And did they respond?

BARRIE: No, they didn't. Not even a comment. I gave them another 24 hours in case they didn't get the first one.

CHRIS: Anything then?

BARRIE: Still no response. So, I started to look for a place to do my first act of violence. I decided on the James Cocker Park on Freedmen Street. It's big enough that people should notice if I do something. So, after the 24 hour mark passes, I send out the message that the time has passed, and I was ignored. I also said that ignoring me was a foolish thing to do and they would pay for their transgressions.

CHRIS: And you are not a terrorist group?

BARRIE: No.

GORDON: Please continue.

BARRIE: I went to business. I expected there to be police there watching the parks, surprisingly there wasn't. I took rocks and broke out all the streetlamps to cover what I was doing. I stood in the largest part of the field and thought to myself "what am I going to write" I thought something simple, so I wrote "hate" in eight foot letters in gas. When I was done pouring the gas, I realized that I hadn't spray pated on anything. I thought the fire might not get to much attention, so I left if for the time. I spray painted on pavilion the same as the grass. I also painted on the basketball court too. I was happy with the work and hoped the gas would still light when I went back to it. It did. Huge letters, bright and gleaming, I was proud. I went home and took a shower in case anyone saw me. I then till the next morning to see what happened. I hear the fire trucks going towards the Park, which was expected. I finally fell asleep around three in the morning. The next morning, I check the papers. I was angry!

GORDON: It wasn't mentioned?

BARRIE: It was mentioned, on the fifth page, under small town news. They were going to pay for that, I was beyond angry. There wasn't even a picture. So, I did the same as last time, making a statement that in forty-eight hours another act of violence would happen. I sent the new video waited two days as I said I would.

CHRIS: Did the township respond this time?

BARRIE: The Township didn't but others did. People commented with all kinds of mean and terrible things about me, like they even know who I am. Worst off, they called me a copycat. They obviously didn't realize that I was the one doing this in the first place. It made me so angry. So, I chose two new parks, Hatfield Park on Ocean drive and Grey Park on Oliver Street. So, I did the same as before going out and painting the Parks and writing my message on the grass. This time I painted "Know" at the first Park and "Time" at the second. I was hoping they got the message. I ran home as before and waited. I checked the paper in the morning, this time I made the front page. I read the article and realized one mistake I made.

GORDON: What's that?

BERRIE: I never gave myself a name. It's not a big mistake, well not really a mistake at all. But it's important. The reporter that writes the article calls me "IV" or "4" because of the number of letters I used in the grass.

CHRIS: How did that name make you feel?

BARRIE: It really got to me, I hated it. They didn't realize that I can only carry so much. That's why the four letters. It wasn't even a cool name, it was lame. But there it was. The article said I was a child trying to make a statement.

That wasn't true, I just wanted money. The guy that wrote the article clearly hadn't spoken to anyone about the incident. I waited a few days this time, about a week maybe. Then I sent the next invitation of terror. This time I wanted ten thousand dollars. I was wondering if they would take me seriously now. I finally got a response, a stupid response. I was told that acting like this "4 Guy" could get me in trouble. I was so angry that I wrote them saying it was me. They only responded back by making more fun of me.

GORDON: Who is "they"?

BARRIE: It was the township, I'm not sure who writes for them, but they represented the town hall.

GORDON: Did you continue with your plan?

BARRIE: I did. At the end of the 48 hours, I collected my stuff and headed out of the house. There were cops patrolling the parks this time. That wasn't my objective. I told the township I had a surprise. The surprise was I didn't say it would be a Park. I went to the Newtown Cemetery. I brought gas and a sledgehammer. For the next few hours, I broke as many headstones as I possibly could. It had to be forty maybe even fifty stones. I broke into the thirteen mausoleums there too. I took all the plaques off the seals. I smashed up the war memorial.

CHRIS: Why the war memorial?

BARRIE: Why not, what have they done for me? They don't deserve the monuments. They ask to sign up, no one makes them.

CHRIS: What about Viet Nam?

BARRIE: I've never heard of that?

GORDON: Agent Chris. Please continue Mr. Barrie:

BARRIE: I wrote in the grass again. This time I wrote "Done" and "left". The next morning, front page again! They mentioned that they received the comments that I left and the person that responded to me was being questioned. There were pictures this time. I thought they would take me seriously now.

CHRIS: Did they finally?

BARRIE: Nope, not at all. So, I knew I had to show them. I made my next announcement, I said it would be a theater and I wanted twenty thousand dollars. I gave them the forty eight hours and waited. It made the news that I made the theater statement. People were listening now. However, they didn't try to contact me. I found out that five theaters were closing that night to keep problems from happening. The forty eight hour mark hit, so off I went. I stopped at the name deleted theater on twenty-first and Oak. It's a good sized theater, real nice one. They were obviously not taking my threat seriously. I went in, bought a ticket for Name Deleted, it was new at the time and everyone wanted to see it. The place was packed. I waited for about thirty minutes into the movie. I reached into my pocket and pulled out a lighter and some fireworks. I lit the fireworks and threw them towards the back wall. I stood up and yelled "fire!" real loud as the fireworks started to go off and got the hell out of there. It took the people a few seconds to react. I guess me running got them to move. I went home and showered; I didn't have to wait. The fire was all over the news. The news said that the fireworks set a girl's dress on fire.

CHRIS: Were name was Kathy Cartwright.

BARRIE: Yeah, that's it. Her brother tried to help her put the fire out. They both caught on fire and died.

CHRIS: Joshua Cartwright.

BARRIE: That's them. I guess two others were also killed. I guess they were trampled to death or something.

CHRIS: That was Tiffany Defoe and Shawn Manos.

GORDON: How did that make you feel knowing you were responsible for the deaths of four people?

BARRIE: That wasn't my fault. That was Lima cities fault. They didn't pay the money. They knew what they were doing. All they had to do was pay. The problem would have been solved.

GORDON: So, you take no responsibility at all. Do you feel bad at least?

BARRIE: No, I don't. I warned them.

GORDON: How did you do that?

BARRIE: They shouldn't have gone to the movies that night. It's that simple. They didn't have to go. My threat was all over the news, they all knew.

CHRIS: So how did you finally get caught?

BARRIE: Well, I set up another Invitation of Terror. This time a gas station would be my target, this time it would be twenty-five thousand dollars.

GORDON: Did they respond this time?

BARRIE: They did, within an hour. They said they would pay. So, I told them to drop the money off in a trash can on fourth street and vine at midnight. I also told them to drop the money off three nights from when we spoke. I went by the Garbage can at two in the morning to pull the bag and got jumped by the cops. I tried to say it wasn't me, but I guess all the firecrackers didn't go off and they had my fingerprints on them. They had me. I was tried and sentenced to ten years. The governor of Ohio took this whole thing way out of control.

GORDON: You mean the Barrie Act.

BARRIE: Not only does this guy try to make a law about what I did, and then he throws my name on it.

CHRIS: They did make it a law after you. It should be named after you.

BARRIE: Whatever, you get my point. So now this law allowed a judge to treat anyone of the age of seven or older as an adult. Depending on the nature of the crime, you fight in school, assault, and battery. If you shoplift, three years in jail without question. If you have a weapon on you, you will get weapons felony charges. It was totally insane. Then they go as far as saying that words are now violence. So, if I threaten someone, it's like saying I physically hit the guy. I just said I would do it, and now charged like I did it. Oh, and get this. If I say something that offends someone, I could be charged like I was harassing them. It is out of control. Social media was affected too. You can't say your opinions anymore without someone fining you one thousand dollars for hurting their feelings. Did you know that in California, it was illegal to curse in public because of the Barrie Act? Or how about this, I say something on the east coast that's okay, but on the west coast there offended, I'd still go to jail. It's just Outrageous. I really don't have any more to say. My story is pretty cut and dry. Here I am.

GORDON: Well, we appreciate the time you took. Thank you.

GORDON: This is Special Agent Sean Gordon. Its 3:52 P.M. in Allen County Jail, Lima, Ohio. We have just finished interviewing Robert Charles Barrie. Case file: 31008539-A, Operation Vanguard or "The Matthews Incident".

This formally concludes the interview with Robert Charles Barrie. No further entries were made on this date or for this part of the interview.

Interview of Former Captain Bryant Justin Tessle

Wednesday, November 22nd, 2028
United States Disciplinary Barracks (USDB)
Fort Leavenworth, Kansas

GORDON: Its 11:30 A.M. in United States Disciplinary Barracks, Fort Leavenworth Kansas, Maximum Security Wing, Block 5. Seated next to me is Special Agent William Chris. Across from us, at the interview table is Former Captain Bryant Justin Tessle, Former Administrative clerk, Personal Assistant, and Records Officer to Brigadier General Matthew's: Case file: 31008539-A, Operation Vanguard or "The Matthews Incident". Former Capt. Tessle is 35 years of age, is 5'10", weight is 149 Lbs. He is of slender build, brown hair, has no discernable marks or scars, has blue eyes, and a light completion. He is Caucasian and an American. His fingerprints are on file and classification code 1 for the flowing: several counts of involuntary manslaughter. He is also convicted of treason and conspiracy of treason, terrorism. We have returned to speak with Captain Tessle for a dialog of Brigadier General Matthew's regarding Mr. Barrie.

Key testimony involving incident of Robert Charles Barrie and the months leading up to the incident. It also concerns the Barrie act. Former Captain Tessle is at liberty to speak about Brigadier General Mathews, Operation Vanguard by the Supreme Court and is not placed under a gag order. It should also be known that the families involved have given prior consent for this interview.

GORDON: Good Morning Mr. Tessle.

TESSLE: Good Morning gentlemen. So, this will most likely be our last interview together.

CHRIS: I guess it is. This was the last recorded speech by Brigadier General Matthews.

TESSLE: It is. After this talk, he no longer has his formations. General Matthews also starts his planning of Operation Vanguard.

GORDON: Are you ready to start?

TESSLE: I am, here we are. That Morning General Matthews call for a formation at the end of the workday, that's at 4:30 P.M. He passed the word that the formation is mandatory that everyone is to be there. Not like any of his formations already weren't. It was in fact the first time he pressed for everyone to be there. We were standing, ready for Matthews when he marched out to stand before us. He looked tired, just worn. The talk in the unit was that he hadn't been home in weeks. General Matthews straightens up and begins.

"Sons, daughters, my children,

"Mine eyes have seen" oh they have seen. This day has finally come. Our country has fallen into such depravity that we are no longer free. Our most basic of right is now being violated by the same government that makes us free. Your right to say as you feel is in the direst of jeopardy because of the Barrie Act. In fact, for me to speaking ill of the poor decision of the government makes me a criminal.

(Laughter heard in background)

Sadly, I'm being honest. The first amendment had been flitted away because there are those in this county that cannot tolerate dealing with others. Our rights are being voted on and chipped away piece by piece. Those that we appointed to hold, and our liberty together are the ones that are chaining us. The vote on the Barrie act was unanimous. Out congress and senate are no longer using their power for the people, but for themselves.

We are the ones that are responsible. We have voted these criminals into their offices. We gave them the power to take our most basic fundamental blocks of democracy. Those that sit in Capitol Hill have gone too far. Changes need to happen, the broken must be mended. The people of this great nation should not be afraid of their government. You have the right to be whoever you want and express yourself anyway that you feel you need. Only if it does infringe on other rights to be free. That is Democracy, the right to choose and be free. Now it has been voted away.

It has gone as far as saying that if you offend someone, you could be fined or jailed. In parts of the county, they are making certain words illegal. You are being told how to think and act. And somehow the people of this nation agreed to it. How does this happen? We are walking away from a democracy and marching to a totalitarian society. It's hard to imagine that if you have a different point of view then someone else that you are committing a crime. I guess the next thing to be taken is our rights to religion or the press. I guess the press went with the Barrie act, reports can't report unpopular things now. Is that really news? Is that freedom?

Something needs to change; something needs to happen. The idol of lies in our country needs to be taken down. It needs fixed! The government has too much power! When will enough be enough? When will we as a people decide that it has gone too far and needs to stop? The Lies, the corruption, all of it needs to

(Distant voice) *"Then do something!"*

What was that Captain Tessle?

(Distant voice) *I said, "Then do something Sir."*

GORDON: Are you okay Mr. Tessle?

TESSLE: It's all my fault.

GORDON: It's all my fault, all the death, it's my entire fault. Why did I do this? I am a killer.

GORDON: I don't understand Mr. Tessle. It was just a comment.

TESSLE: "Then do something"

GORDON: This is Special Agent Sean Gordon. Its 12:00 P.M. in United States Disciplinary Barracks, Fort Leavenworth Kansas, Maximum Security Wing, Block 5. We have just finished interviewing former Captain Bryant Justin Tessle. Case file: 31008539-A, Operation Vanguard or "The Matthews Incident".

*This formally concludes the interview with Former Captain Bryant Tessle. No further entries were made on this date or for this part of the interview.

Memorandum from Special Agent Sean Gordon

To: Brian Samuels, Director of the Federal Bureau of Investigations

From: Sean Gordon, Special Agent

Good Moring,

As per protocol, I am giving my informal opinion of the investigation of Robert Charles Barrie and the Barrie act. This is my person opinion to what I witnessed.

The pieces are not put together in this puzzle. After interviewing, I realize that Robert Barrie was a small piece of the puzzle, an exceedingly small piece. My first observance was that General Matthews broke his pattern. Robert Barrie was not contacted. My understanding is that General Matthews slowly was moving to the decision of Operation Vanguard. At first the interview with Mr. Barrie was confusing. At the time of the interview, I didn't understand the significance of what Robert Barrie actually did. In fact, it wasn't him at all, in reality it was congress and the way they reacted to Mr. Barrie. The Barrie Act was so earmarked by congress that was a far cry from the original intent for the law. Its intent was to punish juveniles as adults but was mutated to basically but a strong grasp on the first amendment. It allowed the government to be more aggressive agent's people's right to speak out. That's really what drove General Matthews. Yes Mr. Barrie was a small cog in the machine that would later be Vanguard. But it was that small part of the Act that put it all together.

I truly feel for Mr. Tessle. What I saw during the last interview was a man that has never realized the true scope of his action. With three small words, thousands would be dead in a few years and the country and world would be changed. I wonder if somehow, he was drawn to tell us to speak with Mr. Barrie. Was it Mr. Tessle subconscious telling him to face what he had done? What I saw was a broken man. The once smug, almost carless arrogance was replaced by a sobbing shell of his former self. I was told the day after the interview that Mr. Tessle was taking to the psych wing of the facility. I was told by doctors that

Mr. Tessle had a full breakdown. It's been weeks since the interview, I spoke with the doctors again. They report that Mr. Tessle just sits in a chair staring at the wall. He has been on fluid IV's since admittance. He is officially reported as catatonic. The Medical Staff are not sure if Mr. Tessle will ever recover.

I also wonder if General Matthews would have come to the same conclusion on his own. That being said, he had the power to maybe change how he saw the government as broken. Little is known about what Matthews was thinking after the last speech. His war journals are incomplete or just missing.

If we had those books, it may shed light onto whether General Matthews was of sound mind and body. I see no reason to call General Matthews sane. I think General Matthews was perfectly in the right state of mind. This is not me saying that what he did was right, far from it. I can understand why General Matthews started planning. Operation Vanguard was the use of power that no other person had at their disposal and General Matthews knew that. He felt that no one else could hold the government's feet to the fire except him. I think that he took great pride in his Marines and I find it hard to believe that so many service men and woman would have obeyed a madman. They knew General Matthews wasn't crazy, they admired him. They loved him and most of all respected him. I realized that an argument can contradict this point, that being Nazi Germany. Yes, the army of Germany followed a madman. The circumstances were vastly different with a different planed outcome.

It's in my professional opinion that Matthews was on his way to planning Vanguard weather or not he knew it. All the Barry act did was potentially pushing his motives along faster. If General Matthews hadn't been so upset about the Barry act, something else would have taken its place and he would have still reacted. I don't necessarily believe that General Matthews was predictable, quite to the contrary. I just think Matthews was a train on a track. Vanguard was going to happen, either then or sometime after. It was inevitable.

Sincerely,
S.A. Sean Gordon.

Eyewitness accounts of Operation Vanguard

"I was there when the Marines surrendered. I watched as the one the called Captain Tessle came out of the White House. He was giving orders to continue as planned, and that Misfit one was down. Where I was hiding, there was a radio that one of the Marines was caring at one time. I never asked the cop how he got it. I really didn't want to know. I remember the radio saying "This is Tango 1 actual, Misfit is down, repeat Misfit is down. Continue with Vanguard as order, mission complete." As soon as I heard that, I saw Captain Tessle lay face down on the lawn. There were Marines coming out of the White House behind him and doing the same. That's when all the Marines came out of their vehicle and did the same thing. Laying down weapons and laying on the ground."

-Sam Kessler (Morning News 14, Barbra)

"The gun fire just stopped, I had no idea why, but I was grateful. We all waited at least ten minutes before we came out of the building because we heard more sirens. We could see the Washing Police arresting several of the military people. We were told to go back into the house and wait. We stayed there another two hours until the police showed up and said we could leave."

-Nathan James (The weekly Journal, Anson, 2026, p. 1)

"We were overwhelmed, I had no idea how we could detain all these Marines. It took every law enforcement agency with seven states to help process them all."

-Lieutenant Brian Suttner D.C. Police Department
(Washington 26 News.com, Nettleton)

"HIS TRUTH IS MARCHING ON" OPERATION VANGUARD

Note

['van. gärd]

NOUN

1. An assembly of people moving towards different or new ideas.

    • At the very begging of new change.

2. The beginning or forefront of an advancing army meant for invasion or to conquer.

The document presented is a compiling of all the interviews that were directly involved in Operation Vanguard. These are eyewitness accounts or personal accounts of what took place that day. The interviews are not in chronological order of the time they were interviewed, but in order of events. This gives a proper layout of the events that took place on Thursday, September 11th, 2025.

Nothing was changed from its original content; all interviews are intact. Specific details may be hard for some readers to understand and the graphic nature may be disturbing.

THE INVASION OF THE WHITE HOUSE

Interview of Katie Putler

Wednesday, March 8th, 2028
Hartford, Connecticut

GORDON: Its 8:30 A.M. in Hartford, Connecticut, we are currently at the home of Katie Putler. Currently seated in the living room is Special Agent William Chris and across from us Mrs. Putler. Case file: 31008539-A, Operation Vanguard or "The Matthews Incident". Mrs. Putler is 27 years of age, is 5'5", weight is 119 LBS., she is of slender build, brown hair, is currently employed as a case worker, has no discernable marks or scars, has green eyes, and a tan completion. She is Caucasian and an American. Has no fingerprints on file and she has no classification code.

GORDON: Good Morning Mrs. Putler.

PUTLER: Good morning to you both. How can I help you today?

GORDON: We are here to get an interview about what you saw or experienced with Operation Vanguard. Would you mind telling us what you saw?

PUTLER: I don't mind, I've been interviewed a lot. What would you like to know exactly? There was a lot happening that day.

CHRIS: We would like to know about the invasion of the White House. How about that?

PUTLER: Sure, where would you like me to start from?

CHRIS: Wherever you feel that it should.

PUTLER: It was late when we got to D.C. the night before. We were all really excited to be there.

CHRIS: Who is "we"? Who were you with?

PUTLER: It was me. My two kids, name deleted, and name deleted, and my husband name deleted.

GORDON: Thank you, please continue.

PUTLER: We had planned the trip for a while, about the better part of the previous year. My kids had always wanted to see Washington D.C. The paperwork we needed to get into the White House was unbelievable. It took two months to get the clearance we needed to go in. My husband and I had finally gotten it all together finally and we were ready to go. We left the hotel that morning and got breakfast. All we had to do to go into the White House Gift Shop Center, which is about a block away from the White House and they would have the tickets waiting. We were group five that day and would be going in sometime around ten that morning. After getting the tickets we walked up to the main gate and eventually were let onto the property. Everything that morning seemed normal and fine. The only thing different was it was September eleventh.

GORDON   So noting struck you as unusual that day?

PUTLER: No, just an average day. It was nice out. We had the whole day planed out. There was a lot going on in D.C. that day, it being 9-11 and all. So, we walked up to the front door and were greeted by the agents at the front door of the White House. They were so nice and polite. They asked for our Identification and checked a computer in front of them tow double check who were. I could see that they were comparing photos that we submitted previously to our drivers' licenses that we just gave them. They said that we were clear and then the agents took a look through our bags. There was quite a line and the process took a while, but we understood why. It's the home of the President of the United States. Security is going to be high and tough to get through. We knew that and that's why we came early.

GORDON: How many people were in a group?

PUTLER: It was twenty-five to a group, unless you had a baby. They didn't count in that number.

CHRIS: Was there any group ahead of you?

PUTLER: There were four already and one ahead of us.

CHRIS: Anything unusual about that group?

PUTLER: There was nothing out of the norm about them.

GORDON: What did you see? What exactly did you see around you and going on at that time?

PUTLER: The front doors to the White House were standing open. They were these two giant wooden doors that looked reinforced. There were also tow secret service men stand on each side of those doors. I could just barely see into the doorway. It was a small room that led into a much bigger room the interior of the White House itself. As I got a better look, I could see a smaller area to the right of the first small room as you walked in.

CHRIS: Like a small control room?

PUTLER: What's that?

CHRIS: It's like an attached room with a glass window and commuters. It's usually where people are monitoring movement or watching cameras.

PUTLER: It was just like that. There were two or three people in that small control room. They had two metal detectors set up for people and two for property. Each had two individuals operating the machines. There were cameras everywhere. I could new see a little better because the line was moving along. There was what appeared to be a greeter at the door, this tall gentleman that was checking everyone's tickets.

GORDON: About how long did you wait at the front entrance?

PUTLER: We were told to be a half hour early. I think we were there almost an hour early. The groups in front of us just slowly went in. I could see that everyone was actious to go in. It was about twenty minutes into our wait when the group in front of us was starting to go in and the first group was coming out. As we were moving up, I could see that there more of the metal detectors.

CHRIS: How many more?

PUTLER: Two more to be exact. They were having the groups go through the detectors in while letting groups out through the other side and through those metal detectors. I watched as the first three people go in the group in front of us. The other side starts to let the other group out. The third individual coming out of the detectors suddenly turned on the scanner worker and the others in that group start to grab workers too. As the workers were being grabbing the group ahead of us rushed in through the detectors. They moved fast and low to the ground, they made me think that something in the movies. I hear 1 sharp bang and then three more, my husband says to get down. The guards at the door were struggling with two of these people from the group. Two more bangs, I realize its gunfire. I see these knifes that the people ahead of us start pulling out. They didn't look metal.

CHRIS: What did they look like?

PUTLER: They looked very flat, and not shiny like metal. I now know that they were made from carbon fiber and hard to catch in metal detectors.

CHRIS: What about the gun fire. Who was shooting?

PUTLER: It was the people in the groups in front of us. They were caring these little boxes that acted like guns but didn't look like guns.

GORDON: What did they look like?

PUTLER: They were small and sleek but not shiny. They looked like cigarette boxes; they were that shape. The guns looked like they were made from the same material as the knives. They were just being thrown away after one use. As soon as a guard was taken to the ground, they took their guns and started using them on the other guards.

CHRIS: Who was doing the shooting?

PUTLER: Both groups, I could also hear shooting inside the building too.

GORDON: So, the people coming out of the White House were using those black guns?

PUTLER: Yes, they had them.

GORDON: What did the individual's in the group in front of you look like? Can you describe them for me?

PUTLER: They were about eighteen to twenty years old. They were all really clean cut. There were both men and woman, I didn't notice at the time, but the men's haircuts were noticeably short on the sides. The women all had either short shoulder hair or pulled back in buns. They took the guards over very quickly. There was a lot of blood.

CHRIS: What about the guard in the little room, the control room?

PUTLER: I saw that his glass was broken. The guys in the room were all slumped over the controls. It all happened so fast. You could hear shooting inside the White House. I'm not sure if I already said that.

GORDON: You did. Did the shooting last awfully long?

PUTLER: No, not long at all. You would hear a little here and there after a while. But it was as constant in the beginning.

CHRIS: About how long was the main shooting going on for?

PUTLER: Maybe ten minutes, it's hard to say. Through all of the commotion, time seemed to slow and speed up. Ten minutes is my best guess, but I really can't be certain.

CHRIS: I understand. What was happening after the shooting started to slow?

PUTLER: People were running and screaming. One of those young guys from the group in front of us turns and yells at our group, "Run! Get! Go! Get the deleted out of here!" My husband grabbed my arm and spun me around and we started running for the gate. Now you could hear shooting from the outside the White House.

GORDON: Where outside?

PUTLER: From everywhere. It was in every direction. I started seeing these large green and tan vehicles... I guess they were tanks. They started to bust through the fence off to our left. I saw the secret serve agents coming from everywhere and they were just being shot down. I saw fifteen more military vehicles coming from our right.

CHRIS: What did those vehicles look like?

PUTLER: The looked like tractor trailers with a camouflage tarp over the back.

GORDON: Where did you go after you got to the gate?

PUTLER: A secret service agent directed us to a cop across the street. We saw the cop, by his car and ran to him. The cop told us to get in and so we did. We all squeezed into the back of his car. The cop then turns around to tell us that we were going to be okay. Just as he finished saying that saying that...I'm sorry, give me a second.

CHRIS: It's okay, take your time.

PUTLER: As he says that we will be okay, half of his head just blows off. It was just horrible, the worst thing I've ever seen. We were all screaming when we saw him die. His head just rocked back, and he fell to the ground. We were stuck in that car for about two hours until another cop snuck us out. The shooting just continued for what seemed like forever until the lawn of the white house was covered in military people and their vehicle.

GORDON: Who was the military fighting?

PUTLER: everyone. They were fighting the local cops, fighting the secret service members. It wasn't going good for them either.

CHRIS: Them who, the military on the lawn or the local officials?

PUTLER: The local cops were not doing well. It seemed like every time one of them would move, at least three of the military people would shoot them.

GORDON: Can you guess how many Marines you saw?

PUTLER: I can't, there were just too many.

CHRIS: Can you give a good guess?

PUTLER: It was thousands. It was like a football stadium just let out. There was so many of them, hundreds of vehicles too. It looked like one hundred military to every one police officer there.

GORDON: How many police did you see?

PUTLER: At first only a few, you could hear the sirens as we got into the car. We tried not to watch. But I saw a lot of police officers dead. The streets were full. Thirty maybe forty empty cop cars, all just sitting there with lights flashing with cops either lying around the cars or in. There were several cars with cops still behind the wheel, just slumped over. The police couldn't stop them.

GORDON: Did you see any of the fighting?

PUTLER: Unfortunately, I did. I would see a cop car show up and it was just hit with so many bullets. It was like that for a long while.

CHRIS: It changed?

PUTLER: It did. After a while, the shooting slowed down, and the military was taking more permanent places on the law. One and a while we would see some movement on top of the White House and then you would hear a crack and see a flash from the white house roof.

GORDON: There were snipers on the roof of the White House then?

PUTLER: I guess, I'm not sure. That's really all I saw that day; I don't remember too much more. Eventually an officer got to our car and let us out. We were rushed away by the police; we were told to stay low and quiet. As we were leaving, I could see the bodies of the secret service agents in front steps of the White House. We were taken to a local restaurant and stayed there until it was all over.

CHRIS: Do you remember the restaurant's name?

PUTLER: It was something like Jamie's place or Susie's place, I can't remember, I'm sorry.

CHRIS: It's okay, that's fine.

GORDON: How far was the restraint from the White House?

PUTLER: It was about five or six blocks. It was far enough from the fighting but not far enough that we couldn't hear shooting.

CHRIS: So, you still heard shooting. Was it constant or intermittent?

PUTLER: At one point, it got bad. You could tell that the fighting started again.

GORDON: How long did that shooting last.

PUTLER: It wasn't long. No more than a half hour at most.

GORDON: Where was the shooting at?

PUTLER: It was far away; we couldn't see it. It might have been the White House. That's all I got. We didn't see anyone for hours until the shooting stopped, and we were all escorted out of the city.

GORDON: We thank you for your time.

GORDON: This is Special Agent Sean Gordon. Its 9:48 A.M. in Hartford, Connecticut. We have just finished interviewing Katie Putler. Case file: 31008539-A, Operation Vanguard or "The Matthews Incident".

This formally concludes the interview with Katie Putler. No further entries were made on this date or for this part of the interview.

Interview of Alex Mast

Tuesday, October 17ᵗʰ, 2028
Trent woods, North Carolina

*This recorded session is called to order by the head of the Federal Bureau of Investigations, Special Investigations Unit.

GORDON: Its 9:00 A.M. in Trent Woods, North Carolina, we are currently at the home of Alex Mast. Currently seated in the living room is Special Agent William Chris and across from us Mr. Mast. Case file: 31008539-A, Operation Vanguard or "The Matthews Incident". Mr. Mast is 34 years of age, is 6'1", weight is 171 LBS., he is of medium build, brown hair, is currently employed as a hotel clerk, has no discernable marks or scars, has brown eyes, and a tan completion. He is African American and an American, has no fingerprints on file and he has no classification code.

GORDON: Good Morning Mr. Mast

MAST: Good Morning.

GORDON: Mr. Mast, we are here to ask about details about the morning of Operation Vanguard. We understand that you had seen quite a lot that morning. Is that true?

MAST: That is absolutely true. I saw more than most people did.

GORDON: Do you have a problem going through the series of events that morning.

MAST: I can do that for you.

CHRIS: At any time, if you need a break, please say so. We do understand. We can only imagine how overwhelming the memories can be.

MAST: I understand. I've been to therapy and have talked openly about that day. I've come to terms with what I've seen.

CHRIS: That's a good thing. Bottling things up isn't healthy.

MAST: So how much do you want to hear?

GORDON: We want to have you walk through the morning's events, the whole thing. As much as you can remember or are comfortable talking about.

MAST: I can do that. Do you just want me to start then?

GORDON: Go head, we're listening?

MAST: Um, Well, I started driving that morning before the incident about 3 A.M. I wanted to get to DC before the heavy traffic and to get a good parking space near the Smithsonian.

GORDON: Where were you driving from, that seems awfully early?

MAST: I was stay just outside of D.C. I wanted to be early, get some breakfast. My plan was to get to D.C. early and just walk around until things opened. Then I would visit as much as I could that day and stay the night. The next morning, I would go and walk around the White House. I got onto interstate 95 and was heading north. I was driving for a while when I saw a long… I guess you would call it a convoy of military vehicles. They had things I've never seen before in flat beds. It was impressive. I figured they were heading to a base or something. My hope was they were having a parade the following day, the next day being 9-11.

CHRIS: How long was the Convoy you saw?

MAST: It stretched for miles, at least 10 miles. I've never seen anything like it before.

CHRIS: Did you recognize any of the Vehicles on the flatbeds?

MAST: I saw the Humvee things you see in the movies and TV.

CHRIS: How many of those do you think you saw?

MAST: I couldn't say. It was a lot.

GORDON: Can you take an educated guess? We're just asking for a ballpark number, not an exact number.

MAST: If I were to guess, eighty maybe two maybe three hundred of them.

GORDON: That many!?!

MAST: At the least. It was defiantly a lot. It looked like a large car dealership of military vehicles just up and moved.

CHRIS: Was it just Humvee's or were there other vehicles too?

MAST: No, there were a lot of different things. I saw these big trucks; I could see military men in the back with guns. They had tanks being pulled on flatbeds too.

CHRIS: About how many tanks?

MAST: There had to be about eighty of them of them. Then there were these large guns, like things that were being pulled by trucks. They were really long guns. I mean like ten or fifteen feet in length.

GORDON: Those were probably howitzers. That's what they sound like.

CHRIS: You mentioned the troop trucks. About how many of there were there?

MAST: Hundreds! There where hundreds of those trucks. I've never seen so many military vehicles in my life. I mean, you see them occasionally traveling on the main roads from time to time. But not like this. It was just so many. I could count how many of those, trucks there were.

GORDON: Was it one big convoy or was it broken into several small ones making the big one? I can't remember if you said.

MAST: It was just one. One really long snake of military stuff being hauled.

GORDON: So, you saw them going north. Did you see the convoy on the road again or another?

MAST: No just that one time and only that one.

GORDON: So, after you saw the vehicles, what happened with the rest of the trip?

MAST: I got to D.C. without a problem and checked into my hotel.

CHRIS: Do you remember the hotels name and location?

MAST: It was called "Washington's finniest" and was about a thirty minute walk from the Lincoln Monument. From there, I went to the Smithsonian. I spent the majority of the day there. When I Left the Smithsonian, I started to drive back to the hotel. I saw Military Vehicles again, this time parked all around the streets of D.C. On the sides of the vehicles, there was a sign that said Parade Vehicles. I just assumed there would be a parade the next day.

GORDON: Are you sure they were the same vehicles?

MAST: I can only guess that they were from the convoy. There just so many. As I said, they were everywhere.

CHRIS: Did you see any Marines with the vehicles?

MAST: I did see them around the vehicles.

CHRIS: Did they seem hostile at all?

MAST: No, they just stood around the vehicles, looking around, or were sitting on them. The looked relaxed.

CHRIS: Did they have weapons on them?

MAST: Yeah, they had weapons on them.

GORDON: So, you were heading back to the hotel when you saw them?

MAST: Correct. I had an early day and was walking all day. I was pretty tired, so I went back to the hotel. My intention was to get up the next morning and start walking around early again.

GORDON: Is that what you did?

MAST: I did. I got up about 6 A.M. and headed out after an early breakfast. I had some good sneakers on and was ready to see D.C. and all the monuments.

GORDON: Were you driving or walking the city?

MAST: I was walking the city.

GORDON: That's a lot of walking.

MAST: I didn't mind, I like walking.

CHRIS: Where did you go to first?

MAST: I walked my way to Pennsylvania Avenue. That's about 30 minutes form my hotel. I was heading towards the White House. That was one of the baggiest attractions that I wanted to see. I found out at the hotel that it is quite a process to get tickets, I figured at best I could see it and visit the center later.

CHRIS: About what time was this?

MAST: I walked up to the fence about 8:50.

CHRIS: Did you see the military vehicles again?

MAST: I did, but nowhere around the White house area.

GORDON: How close exactly.

MAST: The vehicles were about two blocks away from Pennsylvania Avenue.

CHRIS: Everything was quiet?

MAST   No, everything thing seemed fine, Birds flying around, that kind of thing. It was a nice day. I did see a cop pulling up to the light. That was the only thing other than normal people and traffic. As I'm thinking about it, there was this generator sound, like a hum in the air. I guess that was strange. I didn't think about that until now.

GORDON: Generator sound?

MAST: Yeah, like the rumble of a generator running. It sounded just like that.

CHRIS: Where was the sound coming from?

MAST: I don't know exactly; it was just all around.

CHRIS: So, you have no idea what was making the noise then?

MAST: No, no idea. It just could be heard from everywhere.

GORDON: Nothing else unusual?

MAST: Not at the moment, nothing unusual.

GORDON: Please continue on.

MAST: I start to take some pictures with my phone. All seemed normal. My watch beeped that it was 9 A.M. and the rumble I heard became a roar.

CHRIS: The rumble, became a roar? It was that loud?

MAST: It was. It was unbelievably loud.

GORDON: Could you tell then what it was or where it was coming from?

MAST: I couldn't tell where it was coming from at first. I realized it was all the military vehicles that were around the area.

CHRIS: So, they were in the same positions as the night before?

MAST: They were. There were more solders all around them, a lot more. But again, that was a few blocks away and almost an hour before.

CHRIS: what were the soldiers doing? Just standing around or in files around the vehicles, formations?

MAST: Formations?

GORDON: Yes formations, like a square or rectangle. All organized.

MAST: Yes, just like that. They were organized in squares.

GORDON: Other than the Generator, was there anything else?

MAST: There was, that's why I remember the time so well. As soon as my watch chimed, I could hear the sound of popcorn from the White House.

CHRIS: The popping behind you, in was the White House?

MAST: Yeah, like popcorn. I could see these flashes of lights from the front door and the windows. The cop I mentioned, the one at the intersection, he pulls his vehicle over and gets out of the car yelling on his radio "Shots fired at the White House, Shots Fired!" He yells at me to get away and get down. That's when the Military vehicles started to show up with the Solders, they were all heading towards the White House. It was happening in every direction.

GORDON: When you say every direction, I assume you mean all the surrounding streets?

MAST: That's exactly what I mean. They started to roll towards the White House. The solders started to shoot at the agents at the front gate and police in the area as they were moving. I see down the nearest street that the same thing was happing everywhere, military shooting at police.

GORDON: So, every road was filling with Solders and vehicles?

MAST: All of the streets. It looked like bees coming out of a beehive.

GORDON: Did you see anything else?

MAST: The cop jumped back into his car and headed towards the main gate of the White House. He runs the vehicle up to the curb, gets out and starts yelling to this family to get into his car. I saw the officer get shot, I'm not sure where he was shot, and I just saw him hit the ground. The military vehicles were braking through the fences of the White House and heading though the lawn. The Solders were following the vehicles through the gates filing and spreading out on the lawn while still moving towards the White House. I could see a firefight between the Military and the secret service agents of The White House. I saw agents get shot and fall but I don't remember the Military losing anyone.

CHRIS: Where were you when all this happened?

MAST: I ducked behind a car to keep from being shot. I saw that the soldiers were rushing into building that surrounded the White House. I thought it was unusual.

GORDON: What was unusual aside from them entering the buildings?

MAST: Well, the soldiers went in, but I heard no shooting. I saw people coming out of those buildings. The only shooting was coming from the White House or towards it.

GORDON: How long did this go on for?

MAST: The start only took like 5 minutes. It was a few minutes later that the police started to show up. By that point, the military had control of the White House.

CHRIS: Why do you believe that?

MAST: No more shooting from the White House.

GORDON: You said the police started to respond, about how many?

MAST: It was an unbelievable amount, at least twenty or thirty cars. The shooting started up again as they arrived. The police were doing their best. Things really started to get ugly by that point. I saw a flash from one of the higher windows of the White House, and then another. Following each flash was this distinct Boom. I saw a cop get shot through the car and heard that boom again.

CHRIS: You mean he was in the car when he was shot?

MAST: No, he was behind the car.

CHRIS: Behind the car?

MAST: Yes, behind it, next to the wheel. I saw him just go to pieces and I heard that boom again. They were shooting through the cars. I'm not sure what the military was shooting with, but it was going through cop cars with no problem. And what it did to those poor cops was just awful. It just…tore them apart. I saw a cop's arm get ripped off at the shoulder, and then heard that boom again. I started hearing shooting now from the building behind me. I could see a flash and a huge boom from the building.

GORDON: Just one shot at a time.

MAST: Just one at a time. The shooting went on for about forty minutes and then died down with a shot here or there. This huge square vehicle pulls up, and this large antenna comes out from the top. That antenna was probably thirty feet tall. I thought it was strange. It just sat there, in the White House lawn. I don't know what it did. I could hear some of the police radios from the cars and some on the officers that were still alive. They were trying to contact the National Guar. But when that square vehicle showed up, all the radios made this whining sound. It all then just went quiet. Well, except the White House, the shooting continued for a while. It wasn't nearly as heavy. So, I just sat there, and waited for someone to help me.

GORDON: How long did you sit there behind that vehicle.

MAST: It was about two hours.

GORDON: Nothing happened within those two hours.

MAST: There were police and medics trying to pull people out quietly. I saw a few officers leading people away from where we were or getting people out of their vehicles and trying to get those people to safety.

CHRIS: Why didn't you go? I don't understand why you would just stay where you were.

MAST: I was too far for them to come and get me and I wasn't about to move. Either the soldiers didn't see me or thought I wasn't a threat. Either way, I thought I was ok where I was.

GORDON: Was anything else happening at the White House?

MAST: By that time, the shooting had stopped completely. It was about an hour after that, I saw that the military people were pulling bodies out of the While House and laying them on the lawn. One of those Humvee things drove up and they were loading the injured and dead into it.

GORDON: Where were they taking them?

MAST: The soldiers drove the people to the largest opening in the fence, right in front. I could see people bandaged up. After several trips, the Humvee pulled away. I could hear a speaker crackled and then a voice saying, "come get your dead and wounded, if you try anything. Snipers will shoot you". They repeated this a few times. An ambulance pulled up and started loading hurt people in it, and then a few more medical vehicles showed up to help. They got all the injured away from the scene. I was about to run when I saw an officer stand up behind a vehicle to my left. I had no idea he was even there. Within seconds, he was shot and killed.

GORDON: About how much time has passed since this all started?

MAST: It was just after noon, so three hours. A few hours after that, I'd say 2 P.M., I could hear more shooting from a distance. It was heavy too, that stopped after a few hours. It was about six, when the last thing I saw happened. This Humvee comes through the big hole in the fence. It wasn't like the other. This one was moving slowly and had a huge escort. It pulls up to the White House. This tall man emerges from it, not in camouflage, but a green suit. He moved slowly, without care. He walked with his hands clasped behind his back and moved with slow purpose. This guy walks up to the White House with this escort of like thirty solders. It chilled me to my core. That guy was so calm and collected. I now know that was General Matthews walking in. A few minutes after seeing General Matthews, I was lead from behind the car by a swat team. That when the shooting started again. The police were trying to fight in the buildings that the soldiers had taken earlier. I didn't see anything after that. I was loaded into a police vehicle and transported out of the city.

GORDON: We appreciate the interview and thank you for your time.

MAST: It's not a problem. I just hope I could help.

CHRIS: If you don't mind, how have been since all this.

MAST: I don't sleep much to be honest; I see that cop getting shot through the car every night. It was horrible. I wish I could forget it.

GORDON: This is Special Agent Sean Gordon. Its 10:48 A.M. in Trent Woods, North Carolina. We have just finished interviewing Alex Mast. Case file: 31008539-A, Operation Vanguard or "The Matthews Incident".

            This formally concludes the interview with Alex Mast. No further entries were made on this date or for this part of the interview.

Interview of Agent Matthew Arnold Aries

Tuesday, July 18th, 2028
US Secret Service Headquarters
Washington, D.C.

GORDON: Its 1:00 P.M. in Washington D.C. We are currently at the Secret Service Headquarters. We are currently seated in the Briefing room on the fourth floor. Sitting next to me is Special Agent William Chris and across from us Agent Matthew Arnold Aries. Case file: 31008539-A, Operation Vanguard or "The Matthews Incident". Agent Aries is 28 years of age, is 6'0", weight is 165 LBS., he is of Slim build, no hair, is currently employed as a Secret Service Agent, has a long scar going across his cheek horizontally and walks with a cane, has brown eyes, and a tan completion. He is Caucasian and an American; has fingerprints on file and he has no classification code.

GORDON: Good afternoon Agent Aries.

ARIES: Good afternoon agents. So, I'm told you want to talk about the Matthews Incident?

GORDON: We do, we wanted to know if you could share your story. The breakdown of what happened in the White House. Would that be okay with you?

ARIES: That's perfectly fine. Where would you want me to start?

GORDON: The beginning of that day would be fine.

ARIES: I don't want to go into too much detail on things that probably shouldn't be said to the public, but I'll do my best to lay it all out. I will obviously not tell anything that could be damaging to the secret service or national security. I know you already understand that I just thought I'd say it anyway. Just so we are all clear, of course.

GORDON: Of course, we do understand that. We are clear on it. Thank you for the heads up.

ARIES:	I start my day at five and get to the security station in the White House around seven. You will have to forgive that I can't give detail, that's just say it's strict. My post is on the third floor of the White House, East Wing. I don't mind the post, its quiet. That morning was no different. The only difference to the day was during the morning briefing. It was asked by one of the agents if our alert status was elevated because of the day. That morning was 9-11, and the fact that we have two members of the Joint Chief's that will be on sight. We were told it was not changing. Which was pretty mind blowing, but it's not my business. It's my job to act not think.
CHRIS:	Did you know about the vehicles all around the city?
ARIES:	We did, that was also a topic that was brought up in the brief. Want to guess what or director said?
CHRIS:	What did the director say when asked?
ARIES:	He says, "The vehicles in the city say parade for a reason, stop asking stupid questions", yeah, how did that work out. By the way, he is no longer our director. Isn't that something? Anyway, so we had a few tours that were going through the White House that day. The tours start somewhere between eight and nine depending on the day's schedule. The groups were going through pretty quick that morning. It was twenty-five to a group that particular morning. I thought I must be an academy or university going through. I reported it and was told, nothing was unusual.
CHRIS:	Why did you think that?
ARIES:	The looked like word deleted Marines! They all had high and tight haircuts, clean shaven. They had button up polos and they were tucked into their nice paints. They were clean. Way to clean for normal, everyday population.

People just don't dress like that anymore. Honestly, people look like slobs on an average day. Seeing them was just strange.

CHRIS: So why did you think they were Marines? Why not Army?

ARIES: I was right, wasn't I?

GORDON: You were right. But how did you identify them so fast and correctly?

ARIES: I was a navy Corpsman for six years. I spent a lot of time with the Devil Dogs. They have this air about them. When you meet an active duty Jarhead, you don't forget it. The retired ones are just resting, make one angry. You learn a lesson; they are still Marines and still dangerous. You see the thing is Marines love to fight. Only second to fighting is a strong will to win. And when that's over, they brag. The other branches talk deleted about them. But it's always behind the Marines backs. A Marine will look you in the eye and ask you what you said when you talk trash to them. Few men and women are like that, the men and woman walking through that morning were like that. They look like they own the place, no offence. But in forty-five minutes they did own the White House. That's how I knew. It probably saved my life. You ever seen a Fighting Marine Agent Chris? How about you Special Agent?

CHRIS: No, I haven't.

GORDON: I have, in Ramadi in 2004. I was with a contract crew sent out to aid the army for Intelligence. We were looking for tips on finding wanted terrorist. Those individuals were seen in the area a week before. So, I was sent to investigate. I was really new in the Bureau and this was a Non-Combat mission. A year tops, no longer. We took contact and got stuck in building. Marines came to out distress call that the Army sent out over the radio for anyone nearby to help us. The solders we were with got a raw deal with us, six agents and none of us were armed. I understood why the Captain called for backup. I could see this one individual shoot at the marines from across the street. All the Marines shot back, not one but all. Then they went hunting for they guy that shot at them. They all shoot back and then hunt you down. It was scary. They act like a wolf pack.

CHRIS: I didn't know that.

GORDON: We all have our little things. Enough about me, Lets continue, morning tours.

ARIES: So, I get told to stand down and just watch my post. My post is the billiards room and sleeping areas for visitors. I can't complain, it's a good post. It was nine exactly when I started to hear shooting. I could tell it was a mix of 9mm and .45 ACP. We don't carry .45 ACP which really concerned me. I could hear it from down the hall. Agent Deleted was down on the North end of the third floor. That's where the shooting was coming from. I drew my service weapon and started forward to the north wing.

exact details of the layout of the White House were changed after this interview for security reason.

CHRIS: Why the north wing, where would that take you?

ARIES: The north wing has the stairway. Plus, I knew I could meet up with other agents there. My radio was going crazy with agents reporting contacts everywhere throughout the building. No one had time on the radio calls to say what the contacts looked like. No reports at all, just that agents were having contact. I headed down the hall to the end where the flight of stairs would be and took the right turn. I take the corner real slow, and don't see anything at first. I look down as this young plain clothed female starts to come up the steps. Our eyes meet as I'm telling her to get down. She suddenly grabs at her waist and draws this long grayish black block. It looked like a pack of cigarettes, but I start to draw my weapon on her. I see a flash from the little box and pain shoots through my mouth. That's how I got this pretty scar.

Agent Aries points to the side of his face

I was dazed just long enough for her to reach the top of the stars. I get her in my sights and get one shot off and I missed. My eyesight was blurry because of my mouth, my eyes were watering. This young woman is only a few paces from me, she lunges and disarmed me. It was fast, took the gun right from my hands.

CHRIS: She actually got the gun from you?

ARIES: She did. We have been trained to avoid this from happening. Her training was clearly to keep me from avoid her attack. She was well trained.

GORDON: Please continue.

ARIES: The next few seconds went fast and to be honest. I had time to knock the weapon from her hands. She takes a step back into a real boxer pose. She stares at me with the dark gray eyes. She tells me to put my hands up. No sooner did she say that she was all over me. She was giving me the beating of my life. I think within a few strikes, she broke a rib on my left side, then hit me with a side kick and broke a rib or two on my right side. I got one good hit on her right in the face, it was pure desperation. She falls back to the ground in this limp, like a rag doll. She just crumbled to the floor. A second goes by and she looks up at me with this innocent look and said to me "you hit me". My first reflex was to relax and say I'm sorry and start to reach for her.

CHRIS: You were going to help her? She just tried to shoot you in the face.

ARIES: I don't know what I was thinking. She just caught me off guard and I reacted.

CHRIS: You could have paid for that with your life. It was a bad mistake.

ARIES: Yes, it was, I misjudged her, and I admit that. It almost cost me my life. She shoots up like a rattle snake and uncoils at me. In one quick move, she drives her head into my nose, breaking it instantly. My eyes full of tears. She grabs my wrist and drags me into an armbar position. She locks her legs around my head and starts to apply the move. She was going to break my deleted arm! I start to try and resist her onslaught. She starts to strike at me, hitting me in the face.

CHRIS: Why was she doing that? It has nothing to do with an armbar.

ARIES: She was trying to loosen me up for the technique. I realized this had to end fast and now. I know for a fact that my shoulder and arm were going to be separated in a very few seconds. I roll us over and get to my feet, struggling against her weight and mine. I stagger to the stairs and throw our weight over the railing of the stairs. We tumble, she lands on her back and rolls down the stairs. I land on my left side, lying at the middle of the stairs. She immediately starts to roll over and get to her feet. She starts to come up the stairs as I roll onto my back and kick her as hard as I could in the chest. She falls back with a hard thump and a gasp. I think to myself "this deleted won't die"! As fast I can, I scramble to my knees and make my way up the steps and look for a weapon. I hope I can fine my personal weapon. I see it and grab it. I rack the weapon for good measure to make sure it's loaded. I look up and hope she doesn't come back. I hear a noise on the stairs, she is climbing the stairs. I couldn't believe it. I take carful aim and as soon as I see her. I put three clean shots in her chest. We both drop. Me from exhaustion and her, well, you get the point.

GORDON: That is intense! She fought hard!

ARIES: She was a warrior, no doubt. I wish I knew her name. She earned my respect. I put on my earpiece in hopes to find someone else. My radio is just giving a loud whelp. I figured as much.

CHRIS: Why do you say that?

ARIES: It just makes sense. You should always make sure the enemy can't talk. If they communicate, it causes chaos. That is an easy way to get over the enemy. I was betting they were using an MRAP and I was right.

CHRIS: An MRAP?

GORDON: Mine-Resistant Ambush Protective. It's a vehicle the Marines use to keep from being hit by rockets or running over mines. I can also jam cell phones, and radio waves. Even worse, intercept those transitions.

CHRIS: Really? I knew about the mines but not the radios.

ARIES: They do, and I was betting that they were using it.

GORDON: You are correct, they were using an MRAP.

ARIES: I thought so. So, my radio at this point isn't worth a Deleted. I still need to head down to the first floor, the flight I'm on only goes down one flight. The second floor will take me straight to the west wing hall then to the rear stairs. The rear stairs on the west wing hall will then take me directly to the first level.

CHRIS: It seems like a lot of zig-zagging.

ARIES: It is, the only straight path at this point would be the main stairs and that would be suicide. The building is designed to confuse. If you don't know the layout, it could take a while to traverse. I know where I am and how to get where I want. For me it will take no time. I just had to avoid contact at all possible.

CHRIS: That makes sense, it's a maze.

ARIES: Exactly. I get myself together, checking to see how many rounds I have. I'm good so I start to go down the flight of steps that just moments before I killed that woman. As I approach the stairs, see three more Marines at the bottom. They are checking over their comrade that I just killed, they start to come up the stairs I need to go down. I'm basically trapped. I try to go back the way I came; I'll take a bullet in the back. If I stay, I'm out gunned. It's a real rock and a hard place kind of situation that has faced me. I decide to stand my ground and hope for the best. I hug the wall, making me catty-corner to the stairs.

GORDON: Basically, on a forty-five degree angle to you?

ARIES: Correct, I will see their backs as the come up the stairs. I see them before they see me. I took the only position I could that would give me a chance and some sort of advantage. I take a knee and watch the steps as I hear them approach. As soon as I see the top of the first one's head, I take my time and squeeze the trigger. It's a good shot but I have to be fast. I run to the ledge and start to shoot. I hit the second in the upper arm and chest. The third individual takes cover dives down the steps and takes cover, out of my view. I'm at an advantage. They can't use radios so they can't call for help. That's provided that the shots don't attract attention.

GORDON: So, you think their radios were jammed as well?

ARIES: They were obviously moving in small squads and she was not able to warn the three. They must not be able to talk. Those three didn't come looking for a fight, they were patrolling.

GORDON: That makes sense. Please continue.

ARIES: I'm not sure if I killed or just wounded the second. I know the first is dead and the third isn't hurt at all. As I'm debating oh how to handle the situation, I hear a click and see a small cylinder fly up the stairs at me. I can tell it's a flashbang. He made a bad throw, and it goes past me down the hall. I know it will be loud, but I won't be blind. I crouch down next to a table on the corner and take steady aim and wait for it to go off. Bang, it goes off and I yell "my eyes", I see the Marines face emerges from the stairwell. Our eyes meet and he knows he made a mistake. Slow steady squeeze.

CHRIS: That was smart.

ARIES: That was luck. If he threw better, I'd be dead. I rush the stairs and see the second Marine dead next to the female Marine. I head down the stairs and move to the west wing stairway at the far end. I'll be honest, I was running blindly. I should have been more careful. But I was lucky so far. I clear the area at the end of the hall, there's no one at the stairs. I start to go down. At the bottom of the first floor landing, I see two of them. The two Marines are talking. One gives directions to the other and the other walks away, down the nearest corridor, the north corridor. This Marine's back is to me. I slink down quietly and hit him as hard as I could on the head with my weapon. I check if he's still breathing. "He is I think to myself", then I ask myself why I am not patting these guys down. I cursed myself feeling the stupidity of my mistake.

GORDON: Because they might have weapons?

ARIES: Yeah, it didn't occur to me at the moment. I could have had more ammo or something better than just a handgun. I search the downed Marine and find this knife, not a standard military knife. This thing was Carbon Fiber.

GORDON: That's interesting.

ARIES: It is.

GORDON: Well, not for what you think. We have heard the use of carbon fiber knifes in passed interviews. I can only guess that the small box guns were carbon fiber as well.

ARIES: They were.

GORDON: I figured as much. Please go on.

ARIES: I hurry down the hall, the north hall. The Marine went down earlier. I see that he's slinking and clearing as he goes. So, I realize they haven't been here before, that's good news. "Sorry for your luck my man", I tell myself.

CHRIS: Why kill him and not the other?

ARIES: The other was armed with a handgun. I felt I could take him down. The other had a sub machine gun.

CHRIS: I never realized this question until know.

ARIES: What's that?

CHRIS: Where exactly are you heading?

ARIES: To the President, where else.

GORDON: It just never came to mind to ask. I just thought the
            same thing. It makes sense when we think about it now.
            It's your job to protect him, so obviously you have to
            get to him.

ARIES: I guess I could have made that clearer.

GORDON: Its fine, please go on.

ARIES: So, I creep up behind the Marine in the northern
            corridor. I'm so close that I can smell him. In one fast
            action, I reach around him with one arm and push the
            knife in the back of his neck. Aiming just at the bulge of
            the spine, he crumbles to the floor silently. I pick up the
            name deleted; it was fully loaded. I'm lucky that I trained
            with this type of sub machine gun before. It's only a few
            more doors to go until the oval office. I'm almost there.
            I move quietly and as smooth as possible. I hear gunfire
            ahead of me. The sound increases, gunfire from the end
            of the hall. I see huddled masses in the middle of the hall
            ahead of me. I keep going until I get to the door. The two
            agents that guard the door are dead and two Marines as
            well, they obviously killed each other in a close quarters
            combat. I move past the agents and use my key card and
            the door opens. I hurry inside the door and shut it. Inside
            the Oval Office are the President, Johnathan Howl and
            The Joint Chief for the Army, General Shawn Kiplyn.
            I ask if they are alright. They both said they were. The
            President asked what was happening and I briefed him
            quickly on what I knew. I told him we need to get to the
            bunker. I tell them to keep their heads down and move
            fast, there is a firefight in the hall in front of us. I can
            hear the fighting is dying, I can't tell who is winning so

I feel we have to move fast. I open the door quietly and clear the hall. We take a right down the same passage I took to get there. We move fast but only fast enough that I can clear as we go, checking every corridor intersection. We pass the last Marine I took down with the knife. We get to the second intersection. This was the intersection that leads to the safe bunker. I start to clear the area and notice four Marines guarding the entrance to the bunker. I try to duck back behind the wall, it's too late, they spotted me. we start to exchange gunfire. The president yells that they are behind us now. I look over my shoulder and am struck in the right thigh. I hit the ground hard. I felt the slug hit bone and I know it's bad. I try to stand up when I see a Marine over me. I'm hit in the face, I lost consciousness.

GORDON: Where did you wake up?

ARIES: I woke a few minutes later as I was being dragged down the same hallway. I saw the Marines had the President and General at gun point and were leading them down a hallway. I lost my barring's so had no idea where I was at first.

CHRIS: The brought you with them?

ARIES: They did.

CHRIS: Why?

GORDON: Because Marines will never deny anyone medical treatment, even an enemy.

ARIES: That's exactly it. They were going to treat my leg, that's why I was going. They wouldn't leave me to bleed out.

CHRIS: Where did they end up taking you?

ARIES: Ironically, they took us to the Oval Office. The Marines separated us. They took the President and General

Kiplyn to the seats in the center of the Office and I was taken to the side. The Marines started to work on my leg. There were two of them dressing my wound. I went out again and woke up on the lawn of the white house, being placed in an ambulance. That was the last I saw of the President and the General.

CHRIS: You said the Marines dressed the wound?

ARIES: I did, and they did.

CHRIS: You said they shot you? That still makes no sense.

ARIES: That's how they are. They treat everyone the same when injured. All are equal, friend or foe. The country could learn a lot from the Jarheads. Besides, we're all Americans, they know that. There is a reason they were doing what they were doing. What that is, I don't know. But they always have a reason for what they do. Is there anything else I can help you with? That really all I know.

GORDON: No that's all we needed, and we appreciate you helping us.

GORDON: This is Special Agent Sean Gordon. Its 2:39 P.M. in Washington D.C. We are currently at the Secret Service Headquarters, fourth floor Briefing room. We have just finished interviewing Agent Matthew Arnold Aries. Case file: 31008539-A, Operation Vanguard or "The Matthews Incident".

This formally concludes the interview with Agent Matthew Arnold Aries. No further entries were made on this date or for this part of the interview.

Interview of Shawn Daniel Kiplyn (Army General Retired)

Thursday, June 13th, 2028
Granbury, Texas

This recorded session is called to order by the head of the Federal Bureau of Investigations, Special Investigations Unit.

GORDON: Its 9:45 A.M. in Granbury, Texas. We are currently at the home of Retired General Shawn Kiplyn. We are currently seated in the living room. Sitting next to me is Special Agent William Chris and across from us, General Kiplyn: case file 31008539-A, Operation Vanguard or "The Matthews Incident". General Kiplyn is 61 years of age, is 5'9", weight is 143 LBS. He is of medium build, grey hair. He is currently retired, has no discernable marks or scars, has blue eyes, and a light completion. He is Caucasian and an American. Has fingerprints on file and he has no classification code.

GORDON: Good Morning General Kiplyn.

KIPLYN: Good Morning to you both. Welcome to Granbury, Texas.

GORDON: Thank you. We appreciate you having us and taking the time to talk to us.

KIPLYN: So, my understanding is you want to talk about the Invasion of the White House. I'm also assuming you want to talk about General Matthews as well.

GORDON: That is correct General. We wanted to know what you experienced. What you saw that day, specifically the first twelve hours. Would you have a problem with that?

KIPLYN: I can do that, not a problem. It would be my pleasure to share that with you.

GORDON: Thank again General, it will be helpful. You can start with a simple why you were at the White House the morning of Operation Vanguard. Just start from the beginning, sound good?

KIPLYN: Not a problem. Well, to start, I was assigned as a Joint Chief Member when President Howl took office. Operation Vanguard happened about a year after President Howl was elected. I was due to meet with the President Howl that morning and another General in a discussion piece on basic military reform, budget, and the spending for the Marine Corp.

GORDON: Were these kinds of meetings unusual?

KIPLYN: No, this is pretty standard. The only difference was it was the first time for the Marine Corp from Second Marine Division. I had already spoken with a commander of the Navy the prior month about the pacific fleet. I was to meet an Air Force commander the following month regarding European Bases. I was speaking with individual commanders of bases and then later that year, meeting with their respective top generals. There was no specific order, due to scheduling conflicts.

GORDON: And to whom where you meeting with?

KIPLYN: We were to meet with Brigadier General Matthews, that morning. He's the commanding officer of Second Marine Division.

GORDON: Who called asked for this meeting?

KIPLYN: General Matthews did, he specifically requested. The date was set up by him as well.

CHRIS: So, nothing struck you as out of the norm, I realize that question has been asked already. It's just conformation.

KIPLYN: The meeting, no. As I said, it was pretty standard. The only thing that was unusual was the parade that was expected that day. No one seemed to know anything about it, yet everyone was calm about it.

CHRIS: That is strange.

KIPLYN: It was. So, I arrived at the White House around six that morning. I went through the normal security measures and went up to see the President around a quarter after seven. I was early, which is also normal for me. The President never minded people being early. We just talked for a few minutes and the conversation eventually wondered to the military vehicles around the city. He supposed that it was already a planned thing. Other presidents have done it in the past, so President Howl just assumed it was already scheduled. So, he thought nothing of it. We were served coffee around eight and were waiting for the meeting to start at nine.

GORDON: You were early.

KIPLYN: It just makes things easier in the end. No rushing around. I actually expected General Matthews to be early as well. So, the President and I just talk about little things to kill the time. It was actually nice to have this much personal time with him. At exactly nine, we started to hear shots in the hallway outside the office. The doors were already closed and there were secret service members outside the door for our security. It was startling to say, the White House has a very tight security team. If someone is attacking that building, they have to be highly organized. We started to hear gun shots outside of the building as well. Through the window in the office, I could see Abrams tanks breach the fence line. With each tank that came through the fence, each had easily two hundred Marines in tow. I thought at first that it was a training exercise. I saw the President pick up that phone and call out. I could tell from the conversation that it was a call to the security staff. The President hangs up the receiver and tells me that no one was answering the phones at the security officer. It was obvious by this point that their problem. I happen to look out the window to see an MRAP pull up and its antenna started to extent, I realized now after seeing that it was defiantly no exercise, and we are in trouble.

CHRIS: So, the tanks didn't worry you, but this MRAP did?

KIPLYN: Yes, exactly. You use an MRAP to really cause chaos on a battlefield. We could call out of the White House and now no one could call in either. The President tells me that the phone just went dead, which didn't surprise me. We tried out cell phones anyway knowing it was pointless. And it was the same thing, no signal. We went to the center of the room and waited for more of the secret service to come in.

GORDON: Did anymore arrive?

KIPLYN: No, none arrived. That just further concerned us. That means that their hands were full with the gunfire outside and in the building. There first priority is to get in this room. It didn't happen.

CHRIS: What about the two agents in the room with you?

KIPLYN: They exited the room and secured the door behind them. They were going to keep external security. A short time after they left the room, we heard gun fire, no one tried to enter the room.

CHRIS: So, you both just stayed in the Oval Office then?

KIPLYN: We both felt that we shouldn't open the door and we should just wait it out. There was nothing we could do as long as that MRAP was functioning. Minutes passed until one agent came in to finally help us. His name was Agent Aries and he looked like hell. He tells us to keep our heads down and we are going to try and make it to the bunker. The Agent opens the door and leads us out into the hall. I can hear gunfire from other parts of the White House. As we move through the halls on our way to the safe room, we get caught in crossfire, and Aries goes down. He takes a pretty bad shot through the thigh. I was concerned that he would die. There was a lot of blood and he was bleeding extremely fast. He did a brave thing, and really did his best but he was outnumbered easily nine to one. We are told to put our hands on heads by plain clothed Marines and walked backed through the halls to the Oval Office. One of the Marines picks up Aries and brings him with us. Once there, we were placed on our knees and told to be quiet. They laid Aries out on the floor and dressed his wound. The last I saw of him; he was being carried out of the room. I was glad when I was told later that he survived.

GORDON: How long did you sit in the office.

KIPLYN: It was for a long while. I couldn't tell how much time had passed. I had a watch but wouldn't dare to put my hands down or move them unless I was told to do so. I was also smart enough not to look around. I just stared at the floor and tried to remain clam. At One point we were allowed to use the bathroom in the office. With the bathroom door open and at gun point of course.

CHRIS: How did the Marines treat you, General?

KIPLYN: Like I was a prisoner of war, but respectfully. Marines are very polite but stern fighters. The called me General or sir, but that was as far as niceties went. They are all business. Don't misunderstand them. They are not machines or as people love to say, brain washed. It's the farthest from the truth. Marines are not stupid and can function just as well as a team or independently. They are all trained to be leaders. That goes all the way through the chain-of-command. Every one of them is always ready to fill the leader's boots if called upon. And if that moment arises, they will act accordingly, as a leader should. You don't just cut the head off that snake, it doesn't work. They can and will make decisions on the fly if necessary. I know better than to misjudge them. To misjudge a Marine is a death wish.

CHRIS: How about food and water? Did they provide that?

KIPLYN: As I said, they treated us like POW's, and treated us with respect. They fed us and had water for us.

CHRIS: That's interesting.

KIPLYN: That's just how they are. Anyway, it wasn't till about six in the evening, I'm guessing. Like I said I couldn't really tell. That's about when something finally happened. I could hear talking form outside the door of the Oval Office, all the Marines got real tense. The door opens and a file of fully combat armored Marines files into the room. Half of them go left and the others right, clearing the room as they enter. They moved along the walls until we were surrounded. When they finished moving, one of them yelled "clear" then yelled "attention on deck", all of the Marines went to perfect attention. The two plain clothed Marines Pull us to our feet and then go to attention as well. This tall Officer in utilities walks into the officer. I can tell by the rank on his uniform that he is a Captain. One of the plain clothed Marines goes out of attention and marches to the Captain then gives a formal report about all is secure and then the Captain dismisses them to go and help with the dead and wounded. He then also tells them to change in to camies. Two other Marines that were flanking the captain walk over behind us pointing their weapons at our backs and forcing us to our knees again. The President asks the Captain politely but sternly why he is doing this. The Captain says to the President "your Honorable Mr. President, I am not in charge here, I apologies if you think that. I follow order just as my other Marines." The Captain looks at me and says "Sir, you can at least understand that". I decide to keep my composure and say nothing. I feel it's in my best interest to just not speak. The Captain looks down at me and smirks, "I would remain quiet too" he says. The President speaks up, "Well then, who is…". A voice from behind the Captain says, "I am, good sir". The Captain steps aside and yells "Attention on deck!" we are both dragged to our feet again. A tall man steps through the doorway, you can hear the Marines gasp in a breath as he enters. The room is deadly silent, and the air is heavy. It really feels like the air has fell and left the room. The man that enters is wearing a military green uniform known as Alphas by the marines. On the jacket lapels is a single gold star, shining as if it was new. The Officer addresses us both, "I am Brigadier General Matthews. I'm in charge now, so at ease." I am pushed to the ground again, this time hard and fast. The President is left standing in front of Matthews.

CHRIS: What was he like? I mean General Matthews.

KIPLYN: The first thing I notice was how tall he was. He was maybe 6'4 or 6'5, exceptionally clean and well kept, the Marines were very observant of him.

GORDON: What do you mean?

KIPLYN: They just moved differently when in Matthews's presence. They let you know he was in charge by their obedience and mannerisms. Like dogs wanting to please the master. He looked stern, cold, and didn't seem like a man that had much time for humor. His face had no laugh lines. He had these piercing blue eyes, dark and hallow. Those eyes made you feel naked when he looked at you. It was like they looked into you, or through you. He had the manor of someone you don't screw with.

GORDON: He sounded intense.

KIPLYN: He was. I had been in the Army for a better part of three decades. I haven't felt that uncomfortable in front of someone since boot camp. He walked into the office slowly with his hands calmly clasped behind his back. He looked down at me and his head cocked to one side and pauses. He studies me for a second and his head cocked back ever so slightly as to look down at me. He says, "General Kiplyn, so nice to finally meet you". General Matthews simply glances at one of the Marines and I'm forced to my feet. General Matthews makes an open handed gesture for me to sit at the couch. I stand my ground and don't move. He drops his hand, closes his eyes, placing the hand once again behind his back. I see his head slightly tilt to one side, and then slowly straiten his head as he takes in a deep breath. I get the impression that he's thinking or calculating what to either say or do or trying to keep his patience. I really couldn't tell. Matthews's eyes open suddenly, looking straight at me, no movement, and right into mine. He says, "move him, if he refuses, kill him".

CHRIS: Those Marines wouldn't really kill you. You're an Army General?

KIPLYN: Yes, yes, they would Agent Chris. He is their leader, they will obey. The will not hastate to follow his order. I'm as good as dead if General Matthews wishes. Like I said before, don't misjudge the Marines. My rank means nothing when it comes from an order from a commanding General.

CHRIS: But you're a commanding General as well.

GORDON: That's not how things work, Agent Chris. Yes, he's a
             General and under different circumstances, the Marne's
             would obey and respect General Kiplyn authority. This
             is not one of those times, to them, this is combat, there
             job. They will obey their commands of their officers, its
             law, and their duty.

KIPLYN: That is correct Special Agent Gordon.

GORDON: Please continue.

KIPLYN: I decide to just move to the couch and sit. I honestly felt
             it was in my best interest to just listen.

CHRIS: Why?

KIPLYN: If Matthews wanted me dead, I would be. Clearly, he
             doesn't wish me dead.

CHRIS: Far enough.

KIPLYN: Matthews's eyes dart to the left without the head moving
             in the slightest. Just one quick motion to look dead into
             the Presidents eyes. "You're Honorable Mr. President, so
             nice to meet you as well. We have business to discuss,
             but not for now. Consider yourself properly relieved.
             Keeping your title of President of course, just without
             the power that goes with it, you won't need that. In case
             you are wondering, no, I don't want it. It is all yours and
             when my mission is complete, provided you cooperate,
             you will have this county back under your supervision.
             As I said, consider yourself properly relieved, at least for
             the time being. Also, consider this a verbal contract,
             as I said. When we are done, provided you do as I ask,
             you will not be harmed." The President looks straight
             at General Matthew's and spits back, "I will not betray
             this country or its people!" Matthews smirks, he says to

the President," I have misinformed you, Sir. I will not compromise your integrity."

GORDON: That's so puzzling.

KIPLYN: It was. I thought the same thing and so did President Howl.

GORDON: Did the President respond to that?

KIPLYN: He did. He asked General Matthews very plainly, "Then why are we doing this"?

GORDON: How Did General Matthews take that question?

KIPLYN: He Looks the President and says very calmly, "I guess we will find out, wont we. You will know soon enough. It will all be clear soon".

CHRIS: Did the president say anything else?

KIPLYN: No, he just stood there, looking very uneasy and slightly scared. I could tell that President Howl didn't want to push the issue any further. Without moving his head or breaking eye contact with the President, General Matthews speaks sharply. I could see the President jump slightly when Matthews barked, "Captain Tessle". The tall Captain responds with a crisp, "Yes sir!" "Is the Capital Building still on lock-down?" Matthews ask the Captain without looking at him and still staring at the President. The Captain tells General Matthews that the Capital building is still on lockdown. General Matthews closes his eyes for a second and turns his to look over his left shoulder at the Captain. "Very well", Matthews says "Break it, as we discussed". The Captain turns quickly to right and goes down the hall. Several Marines that were out of my sight, clearly guarding the door walk past and follow the Captain out of sight.

CHRIS: What did General Matthews mean when he said, "break it"?

KIPLYN: I had no idea. I knew that it probably wouldn't be good. "Corporal Witlit!" Matthews yells, never breaking eye contact with the president. This green eyed Marine appeasers in the doorway, "Yes Sir" he snaps. "Follow Captain Tessle don't leave his side", Matthews says. The Marine yells a crisp "Yes, Sir", turns and leaves the doorway. The President speaks up "You don't have to do this General; this is treason!" "Treason", Matthews grins, "that's just the beginning". "Sit him down, I don't want a stray bullet killing him, understand", the two Marines in unison say ", Yes Sir". The President was forced to sit across from me in the other couch. "You may relax, you may talk, and we will feed you. But I don't need you dying before I am done with you" Matthews tells us. The shooting outside starts again, I can tell it catches Matthew's attention. He walks over to the window and looks out. A slightly older Marine enters the doorway, "yes Sergeant" he says without looking.

CHRIS: He didn't look over to see who it was?

KIPLYN: No, he didn't. It scared me, to be honest. He undoubtedly knew his Marines well; I honestly only knew my Cabinet Officers and my Sergeant Majors. He clearly knew them all. It also seemed that he knew them almost personally, by name. He knew how they moved, walked even how they talked.

GORDON: What did the Sargent say?

KIPLYN: She starts to report that a resistance is starting in the streets and the Marines are taking fire, she requested permission to return to ROE and engage.

CHRIS: ROE?

GORDON: It means "Rules of Engagement". They are simply rules of combat, when to shoot and when not too.

CHRIS: I get it, please go on.

KIPLYN: He tells her that ROE stands, and they may return fire and she's dismissed. She disappears out the doorway. I can hear the shooting outside get more intense. It easily triples very quickly and continues for the better part of an hour. General Matthews checks his watch and walks over to us. "Gentleman", he says "I'm leaving for now, I will return shortly". The President snaps at Matthews, "You never told my why, Traitor. I have a right to know". Matthews laughs. "I'm the traitor...? I've never sold missiles to the enemy. I've never let the veterans of this countries war, which you help start by the way, starve, and freeze to death on the streets. But I'm the traitor? That's laughable. You spend and spend the money of the people, raising their taxes, lower the income until milk cost nearly $9.00 a gallon. But I'm the traitor! You sit in this building and those leaches in the fat gloated Capital building workings less than two months a year, but I'm the traitor. I've given you thirty-eight years of my life, almost as long as most of the worthless congressmen that are nearly 90 years old. They take and take, but I'm the traitor. It seems to me that you don't understand who the traitor is. What you don't understand is simple, its time." Time for what the President says. Matthews looks down at him under those deep set eyebrows and says, "I am the reaper and it's time to harvest". Matthews turns and a Marine yells "Attention on Deck", we are forced to stand as Matthews exits. We are forced to sit and listen to the gun fire. I don't see General Matthew's again until he returns much latter.

GORDON: That seems very precis, you remember everything he said?

KIPLYN: I do. Time under those stresses seems to elongate and move slow. I remember his ribbons, the smell of the office. The whole incident is burned into my memory.

GORDON: I can respect that. I don't understand it. But respect it. General, were going to end this portion of the interview formally end. I will start the recorder again shortly, so we can hear the second half. Is that ok?

KIPLYN: That's perfectly fine.

GORDON: This is Special Agent Sean Gordon. Its 11:30 A.M. in Granbury, Texas. We are currently at the home of Retired General Shawn Kiplyn. We have just finished interviewing Retired General Shawn Kiplyn. Case file: 31008539-A, Operation Vanguard or "The Matthews Incident".

This formally concludes the interview with Retired General Shawn Kiplyn. No further entries were made on this date or for this part of the interview.

Interview of Marry Bridling

Tuesday, February 22nd, 2028
Washington, D.C.

GORDON: Its 11:45 A.M. Washington, D.C. We are currently at the home of Marry Bridling. We are currently seated in the living room. Sitting next to me is Special Agent William Chris and across from us, Ms. Bridling: case file 31008539-A, Operation Vanguard or "The Matthews Incident". Ms. Bridling is 27 years of age, is 5'5", weight is 119 LBS., she is of thin build, Red hair, is a florist, has no discernable marks or scars, has green eyes, and a light completion. She is Caucasian and an American; has no fingerprints on file and he has no classification code.

GORDON: Good Morning Ms. Bridling.

BRIDLING: Good Morning guys, how are you today?

CHRIS: We are good, thank you for asking

GORDON: Ms. Bridling, we are here to ask that you tell what you saw and experienced the day of the Matthews Incident. Would you mind talking about that with us?

BRIDLING: I don't mind at all. What how far back you want me to go.

GORDON: Just that morning is fine, unless you can think of something the day before that would be helpful.

BRIDLING: I can start that morning. I hadn't noticed anything unusual before that morning.

GORDON: That's fine, you can start whenever you ready.

BRIDLING: I work right down the street from Pennsylvania Avenue. The shop I work at is far enough that you can't see The White House. I work in a floral shop called Name Deleted, and we opened at nine in the morning. As we started to open, I hear the shooting, I recognized it right away and told everyone in the shop to get down and stay away from the windows. I told them, if possible, hide behind something solid.

GORDON: How did you know it was gunfire?

BRIDLING: At one point, I was attending Name Deleted academy to become a Police officer. The week before graduation, I realized that I'm just not right for the job. We always heard about the last minute dropouts. We hear about it from the instructors. Anyway, because of my training, I recognized the shooting. As I said, I told everyone to get down and stay away from the windows. I later saw troops march by with military vehicles. I was about to go out and ask for help when I saw the police and military start shooting at each other. I decided that it was in my best interest to stay hidden until I understood more of what was going on. We tried to call for help, our phones weren't working. The phones had no dial tone or ring tone, they were dead. We hid in that shop until someone finally came for us.

CHRIS: What did you see during that time you were waiting there?

BRIDLING: We saw police vehicles drive by and ambulances, even a few firetrucks. No one came for us or in fact was looking for anyone. The shooting finally died down around noon. We could hear an intercom say to come get the wounded and dead. We all decided that now was the time to leave the shop and head south. We though that staying as far as possible from The White House was the best plan. We ran into a police officer who told us to keep going the way we were going, which was south, I think. We found a small grocery story that was abandoned, and all went in there to hold out. We found that I cell phones were working again. I tried 9-1-1 with no luck. I all I heard was just this beeping noise. I got ahold of my boyfriend who was in Boston at the time on a work trip. We were freaking out, just like most of the people's families were. We took turns using the phone to call loved ones. We would try 9-1-1 in between call with no luck. It was about two in the afternoon when we saw more military vehicles pull through the streets. The uniforms were different with these soldiers. These solders were looking for wounded and checking buildings. One of the soldiers found us and said they were National Guard, and someone would come for us or we could head south for more safety. He said anywhere but near the White House. We all voted and thought to take our chances, so we were going south. As we started out and down the street, the shooting starting again to our right. We could see down the street that the two military were shooting at each other. The ones that took the White House were shooting the National Guard to pieces. We just froze as we watched the Nation Guard get cut down. We all scattered in different directions; I went back to the grocery store with two others. We just waited it out.

CHRIS: Did help eventually come?

BRIDLING: It did, just not the way we expected. It was a group of police and regular citizens. They formed; well, I guess you would say a militia. It was big too. As I spoke to the one of the police officers, I could others from the militia taking cover in the street and small groups going from building to building searching for enemy or survivors.

BRIDLING: What did the Officer say to you?

BRIDLING: She asked if any of us know how to shoot. I said that I did and the two others I was with did not. She asked if we wanted to help, I spoke up and said yes, one of the two I was with said they wanted to help too. The officer was pleased that we were on board to fight. She yelled for someone and they ran over and talked to talk with her for a few moments. When they were done talking, that guy runs off and he returns with two others with him. They give me a weapon, a rifle and the girl that was with me got a backpack full of ammo, a med kit, and some supplies. The girl that was with me was told to stay with me and do as I needed, which she was already doing anyway.

GORDON: What about the third person in your group, the one that couldn't shoot?

BRIDLING: She was led away. I could see others being led away as well. They were being taking south, away from all of the shooting.

CHRIS: What was this militias plan?

BRIDLING: The police and anyone with trading were going through the buildings trying to root out the enemy soldiers that were in there. The officers suspected that there many f then in the buildings they hadn't seen any yet.

GORDON: How did they know about that?

BRIDLING: The medics in the ambulances had reported to the police when they were pulling away. That they could see weapons and movement in the windows. They also said they didn't look civilian.

CHRIS: Who was actually going in the houses?

BRIDLING: The police or anyone with that kind of experience.

CHRIS: What about the civilians, what were they doing while the police were going from house to house?

BRIDLING: We were providing cover fire for the police. We would just watch their backs as they entered, well, we would be. There wasn't a lot of shooting yet, but the officer said that we are right at the threshold of the fight and I had to be ready. After my little briefing, we walked out into the street, I got a real view of how ragtag militia was, and that was surprising. It was a mix of every kind of law enforcement, civil population, and even gang members! It was shocking. Twenty-four hours ago, they could have been fighting and now they are working together.

GORDON: What do you think really brought them together?

BRIDLING: The city had a feeling about it, not a good one either. It's like everyone knew something had to be done. The officer told me that most of the recent shooting that we were hearing was the National Guard trying to fight, but the reports that she heard weren't good. Eventually we were ordered to start down the streets. It was a slow movement forward.

CHRIS: Where were you heading?

BRIDLING: Towards the White House.

GORDON: You said the Movement was slow paced?

BRIDLING: Very. Every time a door came up to us, the police went in. A few minutes later, they came out telling us it was clear, sometimes with people like me. Some handed weapons, others bags, and the rest sent back. We approached one of the National Guard vehicles. It was some kind of truck and it was on its side. The medics were called and the people with bags started to help the injured in the vehicles. I saw a few police enter a door across the street, gun fire started, and the air was alive with shooting again. We took cover and tried to shoot back.

CHRIS: Was it an ambush?

BRIDLING: If anything, we ambushed them. They had no idea we were coming. The fighting seemed to go on and on. But we moved forward. A few officers dragged the military enemy out of the building. They were calling for medics to help the enemy. Someone yelled back, "Why help them!" The officer yelled back that they were Americans too. People started to help them. We fought all the way back to my shop and then beyond until we turned the corner. They were waiting for us. Everyone took positions behind anything that could stop a bullet and just started to shoot back. I just stared at the patch-work army fighting back agent the guys that took The White House. I just couldn't believe it; local cops, gang members, average citizens... side by side, working together. I just couldn't believe it, I still can't. You had regular people taking care of the wounded and hurt. Criminals helping the police! It was the most inspiring and horrible sight I will ever see again. As the fighting raged on, I saw a military vehicle in front of the White House load up with this guy wearing all green. The vehicle he got in was surrounded with nasty looking military vehicles; he got in his vehicle and the drove away from the White House. Whoever he was, he was well protected.

GORDON: What direction were those vehicles heading?

BRIDLING: The vehicles were heading direction towards the Capital Building.

CHRIS: You said that the military was shooting at you and the others?

BRIDLING: The enemy fire increased and we had to pull back. We fought but it was no good. We didn't have the resources to continue to fight. We just kept losing ground until the shooting stopped. But we owned a few buildings that were now maned by our people. We didn't win the war, but we took some ground.

CHRIS: Who did they keep in those buildings?

BRIDLING: I saw S.W.A.T. team members go up there and some local police. It was a handful of civilians too. From my understanding, they were told to keep from shooting unless it was necessary.

CHRIS: Why was that?

BRIDLING: We were just that low on ammunition. We stayed there for the next day and a half. There was no more fighting. It felt like a quiet stalemate, until it was all over, and the enemy military surrendered. That's about it really. The weapons were collected up and I was asked where I lived. The police were taking statements and some of us were asked if we could help the police with gathering weapons. I agreed and did as much as I could to help. Most of it was caring for the wounded. There were a lot of wounded.

CHRIS: About how many?

BRIDLING: I couldn't say. There were a lot. And there were many more dead then wounded. I ended up later helping with the dead too. We tried to do what we could to help. I was asked if I lived far enough away from the White House if it was safe. It was far enough that I was taken home, after the local doctors checked me out.

GORDON: We appreciate the information and the time you took for us, thank you.

BRIDLING: It was my pleasure, thank you.

GORDON: We thank you for your time.

GORDON: This is Special Agent Sean Gordon. Its 1:10 P.M. Washington, D.C., We are currently at the home of Marry Bridling. We have just finished interviewing Marry Bridling. Case file: 31008539-A, Operation Vanguard or "The Matthews Incident".

This formally concludes the interview with Mary Bridling. No further entries were made on this date or for this part of the interview.

Memorandum from Special Agent Sean Gordon

To: Brian Samuels, Director of the Federal Bureau of Investigations

From: Sean Gordon, Special Agent

Good Moring,

As per protocol, I am giving my informal opinion of the investigation of the invasion of the White House and my person opinion to what I witnessed.

After many interviews, I realize that the attack on the White House happened fast and without notice. It was clearly well planned and well-orchestrated. General Matthews had thought of everything. Small Carbon fiver knives and guns, both having no metal so to not alert the secret service.

The eyewitness reports also confirm that the vehicles and troops main objective was the White House. Photo evidence showed that the white house was encircled by the Marines. The invasion in its entirety only took approximately thirty minutes. This was mostly due the capability of jamming radio and phone reception. General Matthews kept the law enforcement community in a constant state of confusion and chaos.

I also admired the fact the civilian population tried to fight back. It's inspiring to hear things like that. I was truly appreciative of the time that I had with the interviewees.

Sincerely,
S.A. Sean Gordon.

THE SIEGE OF THE
CAPITOL BUILDING

Interview of Congressmen
William A. Pruitt (R-Mo. Second District)

Monday, April 17th, 2028
Congressional Office Building
Washington, D.C.

This recorded session is called to order by the head of the Federal Bureau of Investigations, Special Investigations Unit.

GORDON: Its 11:45 A.M. Congressional Office Building, Washington, D.C. We are currently in the office of Congressmen William Pruitt. Sitting next to me is Special Agent William Chris and across from us, Congressmen Pruitt: case file 31008539-A, Operation Vanguard or "The Matthews Incident". Congressmen Pruitt is 47 years of age, is 5'11", weight is 170 LBS., he is of medium build, brown hair, is a Congressmen for Missouri, Second District, has no discernable marks or scars, has brown eyes, and a tan completion. He is Caucasian and an American; has fingerprints on file and he has no classification code.

GORDON: Good Morning Congressmen Pruitt.

PRUITT: Good Morning to you Special Agent. My secretary tells me that you wanted an interview to talk about the Matthews incident, correct?

GORDON: That is correct, Sir. We understand that you had the best vantage point to everything that transpired in the House Chambers. Is that right?

PRUITT: That is correct; I'm one of the few that pretty much face-to-face with General Matthews when he was in the House Chamber.

GORDON: Would you mind walking us through what happened that day?

PRUITT: My secretary said that you recommended bringing notes with me, so I did.

GORDON: That great. That will help us out a great deal. You can begin whenever you are ready.

PRUITT: We had just started session at eight that morning. We
             had a few bills on the docket for the day's discussion.
             Most of the day was going to be discussion pieces on
             the explanation of the bills. It wasn't hopeful that we
             would actually be voting, let alone that week. We were
             on Congressional Bill No. 1345, which was going to be
             the biggest one for the day and probably would take us
             through till the next day. We were being optimistic to
             get to the three others bills. The Bill was concerning
             appropriating funding for the Farming industry and
             the possible Tax increase for those funds, just standard
             work. It was just after nine when word came from one
             of the Police that Guard the Capital. The White House
             had been attacked and there was shooting outside out
             building and maybe inside. Several Congressmen asked
             what we should do. The Speaker convened us and told
             us to just stay put. The police locked the three entrances
             to the capital Building, and we waited. We were tired
             and hungry, and nothing was happening. Boredom sets
             in so a few of us were allowed to talk and stand in the
             Rotunda.

CHRIS: Could you see how the police sealed the door?

PRUITT: It's a metal slide door that comes from the ground and
             it's reinforced.

CHRIS: How many officers were in the building?

PRUITT: There are about twenty inside, outside is more. I'm not
             sure of exact numbers.

GORDON: Could you see anything happening outside?

PRUITT: No, we were told to stay away from any windows. But
             I could hear the shooting. One of the Officers told me
             that military vehicles were surrounding the building. I
             was confused because he looked concerned when he told

me this. I asked his "isn't that a good thing?" He tells me "yeah, if they weren't the ones killing the other officers outside!" I immediately thought that we were being invaded by another country, I was later reassured that wasn't the case. I was told it might be a military Coup. I admitted that things seemed worse every time I heard something new. It was about this time, maybe two or three that the police told us to stand by and head back to the House Chambers. We all went back and took our seats nervously. Nothing happened for a long while. I asked one of the officers' what's going on. He said the last thing he was told is that a large military vehicle pulled up in front of the building. I asked him what it is doing and simply said that the radios are all down. I told him that I never knew the radios could stop working, he simply said as he walked away, "they can't". More time elapsed. it was a pure waiting game.

CHRIS: You didn't notice anything out of the ordinary, any sounds?

PRUITT: No, it all seemed normal. Other than out phones not working, everything was calm.

GORDON: How long did you wait till?

PRUITT: Till about seven that evening.

CHRIS: What Happened at seven?

PRUITT: I got the deleted scared out of me, that's what happened. Its wall went downhill quick. We were allowed to move around again, so I was at the Rotunda again. We hear this whine from outside the main door, one of the other Congressmen runs up and says they hear a vehicle pull up to the Congressional doors.

CHRIS: To the doors? That means they drove up the steps, correct?

PRUITT: Correct. I could hear the door creak as if something were pushing at the wooden doors. I found out later that two military vehicles were used as barricades on the congressional entrance and the Senate as well. The officers start to yell for us to get back and run toward the Chambers. It was too late. The wall that was holding the door blows in by the power of this M1 Tank. They used it like a giant battering ram! Two officers were crushed by the vehicle. The officers were standing in front of the doors when the vehicle came through. The tank pulls into the Rotunda and all these solders swarm into the building and start shooting the remaining officers. I run to the chambers just in time for the doors to be shut by other congressmen. The shooting doesn't last long.

CHRIS: Approximately how long?

PRUITT: Five maybe six minutes, then all went silent. We could make out the humming of the tank engine and hear slight voices coming from the other side of the door. The Speaker of the house tells us to remain calm and to take our seats. He says we will deal with this as it happens, just don't panic. The lights flicker for a moment and the shooting stops as fast as it starts. Moments pass like hours. Then without warning, at the door is a knock.

GORDON: Like you knock on someone's house?

PRUITT: Yes, just like that. It was so quiet of a knock that it silenced the room. Everyone went quiet, hardly breathing. We heard the knock again and someone behind me says "should we answer it?" I heard someone else say, "hell no!" There was a third knock, again a pause, and then we hear from the other side of the door "breach it". A Congressman that was in the military yells for us to not look at the door, close our eyes. Most of us did as he said, turning our heads or facing away. The ones that didn't were temporarily blinded and deaf from the door being blown it. The solders swarm in a file like veins from an artery. Every one of the soldiers stands behind a congressman and points a rifle into our backs. We were then forced to our knees and told to be quiet. Two of the soldiers went to the speaker of the house's podium and told him to come down to the floor. They stood there like statues, weapons on us. A few minutes pass when we hear "Attention on Deck", we are forced to our feet and turned to turn towards the blowout doors. A man in a Marine uniform walks through the door. He's much older than the other Marines behind us, and he has general stars on his uniform. He says, "at ease, take them to their seats" and we are all forced to our respected seats. I thought to myself, this really is a coup, we are so screwed. The older Marine walks to the front and to where the speaker of the house was kneeling and points to a chair as the marine takes the podium. Without an uttered word, the other Marines take the speaker of the House and place him the chair that was pointed out.

CHRIS: He just had the speaker moved?

PRUITT: He did, and without command.

GORDON: Who was the speaker at the time?

PRUITT: I know for a fact that he doesn't want his name used in the official record.

CHRIS: Why not?

PRUITT: He told me it would ruin his reputation if people knew how easily he gave up his seat.

CHRIS: He doesn't think that he should have fought for it, does he? He was at gun point. It's just a chair.

PRUITT: That's politics for you. It's his reasons, not mine. I'm just saying what he said. I thought it would be easier on everyone if I didn't name him after our conversation. Also, this is the point that I'll be using my notes, the microphones were on so I we caught the exact words of what the older Marine said, which was obviously, Matthews, but I didn't know that at the time. I thought my notes would help for posterity sake.

GORDON: We appreciate that, thank you. Please continue.

PRUITT: The General takes the speakers position but not sitting now, he chooses to stand. He begins to speak to us.

"Ladies and gentlemen of Congress,

I am Brigadier General Joshua Matthews and I have something important to say". Matthews was interrupted by Congresswoman Myra Clash as he spoke *"We will not be intimidated, and we are not afraid!"* Matthews took a long look at her, *"You should be Ma'am, I'm the people and the people are done with the snake tonic you feed us. You and they rest of this Capital have gone too far! You have failed this nation and its people, failed!"* Congresswoman Clash says *"You have no power here! We refuse to comply with whatever madness you think will happen, General."* Matthews pauses and takes a deep breath, *"Ladies and Gentlemen, tonight you are no longer Democrats or Republicans, tonight you are Americans working towards a better future. A world with…"* This time Congressman Joseph Patterson interrupts General Matthews. *"You forgot the Independent Party".* Matthews's closes his eyes and speaks slowly," *there, that right there is the problem. Everyone here had failed to realize the situation of this county. It's now so bad that you fail to realize the situation you are currently in. Marines, the next person that interrupts me, shoot them!"* The Marines respond in unison, "Ah-Ah Sir!" Matthews steady's himself and begins again. *"You will be working for a better future tonight. You will be fixing you past botches. Think of this as a start over, it's you chance to prove to this nation that you care, and you are not as petty and selfish as it seems to us. You get to be the hero in this story. I have saved you the trouble of being the villain. Fix what's broken. Give back to those that give to you. You have a duty and a responsibility. This is the chance to own that responsibility. I have several bills that you will discuss and then vote on when you are done. I will go to the Senate and we will fix this country even further. I will not interfere with the discussion and I will let you vote on these bills without interruption. If you truly don't believe in the bills, then don't vote for them. You will not be punished for disagreeing with them. I want you vote agents them if you think they violate civil rights or just won't work. You are the professionals and I expect you to do your professional duty. Today the Democracy will thrive, and the Republic will be better for it. Now to address the Socialist amongst you, today that lie will be shown clear. You might as well drop that silly idea. You are millionaires that talk about distribution of wealth, you own several houses and spend endless amounts of money on things you don't need but merely want. You want me to buy that fairytale, sell your extra homes and give away all but what you need. We all know that won't happen so let's just move on then. You will be saving this nation and its people that should have always been the concern from the start. Just look at me as simply focusing you. My men are handing out the first of several Bills to be looked at, read them, and make an educated opinion. Do what you are paid to do. Look out for the benefit of this county. Am I being clear enough?"*

Congresswoman Clash speaks up again, General Matthews does not look happy about her outburst. *"You can't make me, or anyone vote on your insane and crazy ideas".* Matthews looks down at her, *"Haven't you ever been told, calling a crazy person crazy usually doesn't end well. Thankfully, I'm not crazy. I am driven." I refuse to comply",* Congresswoman Clash says. Matthews goes silent, he yells at her *"All I'm asking you to do if you job, nothing more! One series of votes and you go home to whatever life you have. That's what I'm asking and that is my order. You give me a day's work and we leave, that simple. It's an order and a promise".* It's the first time I see the General loose his cool," *"Are you really that pathetic and petty that you would gamble over your own life because of your laziness?" "I don't care what you have to say"* she says. Matthews yells again, *"Then you are not willing to work for the people, therefor you are against the people. That makes you a true Treasonist! Corporal Witlit, front and center."* I see a young Marine run down the aisle to the Speaks area and reports to General Matthews. The young Marine is told by General Matthews to post behind the Congresswomen. And so, he does. The young Marine pulls a pistol from its holster and points it at the back of her head. Matthews asks calmly *"will you comply?"* She says *"no"*, and the room is filled with a bang. From my seat, I can see the red spray and see her slump forward in her seat. Her head makes a hollow thud as it hits the oak desk. *"Anyone else"* Matthews's askes, *"I'm not playing..."* Matthews is interrupted again by Congressmen Patterson who stood up and starts to yell *"You have..."* The thunder rings out again as he falls into his seat. *The Marine behind him pushes* Congressmen Patterson forward, again that wet thud. *"As I was going to say, I'm not playing around, and I mean what I say. Are there any questions"* the room goes, silent as the Marines hand out the first Bill.

GORDON: What was the Bill?

PRUITT: I can't actually say at this time. I hope you understand. I'm not sure if that was cleared to be discussed because of the incident.

GORDON: I understand, please, go on.

PRUITT: For the next eight hours, around four in the morning we were finished.

GORDON: About how many Bills did you vote and discuss?

C. Pruitt: It was seven total.

GORDON: Did you pass all seven?

PRUITT: No, only five. We were concerned when the second was voted down. Matthews was good to his word. He never said anything.

CHRIS: Did anything change in that eight hours?

PRUITT: Actually yes. When we started to work, he orders his Marines to the outer walls. A Captain did most of the paper running. He even let the speaker do his job. General Matthews just watched us and let us work. As he said he would.

CHRIS: What Happened when you were done?

PRUITT: The Captain collected the paperwork he needed. Matthews sent a Marine out of the Chamber who came back an hour later. We hear a motor start outside our chambers door and the door opened. General Matthews told the speaker to convene everyone and told us to simply leave. So, we did.

GORDON: Any problems?

PRUITT: No, we were escorted to our vehicle and aloud to leave. It was very bazar. That was all that happened for me. I don't have any more to add to this, unfortunately.

GORDON: You have been a tremendous help, thank you for the recorded notes. It really helped understand what was said and how it all happened.

CHRIS: One last question.

PRUITT: Sure.

CHRIS: What happened to Congresswoman Clash and Congressmen Patterson? I mean their bodies.

PRUITT: They were taken out immediately after we started to work. The Marines placed them in body bags and took them away. My understanding is that Matthews allowed an ambulance to come through the siege line. The Marines cleaned the blood up. And nothing more was said.

CHRIS: Thank you.

GORDON: What about the Police, those that were hurt or dead inside when it all started.

PRUITT: The wounded was treated and sent out and the ambulance took them with the dead. I understand that they were very respectful.

GORDON: This is Special Agent Sean Gordon. Its 1:07 P.M.in the Congressional Office Building, Washington, D.C. We have just finished interviewing Congressmen William Pruitt. Case file: 31008539-A, Operation Vanguard or "The Matthews Incident".

This formally concludes the interview with Congressmen William Pruitt. No further entries were made on this date or for this part of the interview.

Interview of Senator Oliver Payne (D-CO)

Thursday, May 18th, 2028
Hart Senate Office Building
Washington, D.C.

GORDON: Its 9:45 A.M., the Hart Senate Office Building, Washington, D.C. We are currently in the office of Senator Oliver Payne. Sitting next to me is Special Agent William Chris and across from us, Senator Payne: case file 31008539-A, Operation Vanguard or "The Matthews Incident". Senator Payne is 51 years of age, is 6'1", weight is 185 LBS., he is of medium build, grey hair, is a Senator for Colorado, has no discernable marks or scars, has brown eyes, and a tan completion. He is African American and an American; has fingerprints on file and he has no classification code.

GORDON: Good Morning Mr. Senator.

PAYNE: Good Morning to you both as well? How is your day so far?

GORDON: We are both well, Sir. Thank you for asking. I assume you remember why we asked to have this interview, Senator?

PAYNE: I do, you wanted to speak to me about the Matthews Incident and what I saw. I brought the notes you asked for.

GORDON: We deeply appreciate that; we realize it must have been some work to get those recorded noted.

PAYNE: It wasn't too bad, that why I had to postpone several times on you. I didn't have them yet. Sorry for the inconvenience.

GORDON: It's truly not a problem and we appreciate the troubles you went through. So, let's begin, we already understand what happened on the first day. We also understand about the Tank coming through the building. We are interested in the details after that.

PAYNE: I heard that congress was allowed to walk around the building most of the time all the craziness was happening. Vice President Tyler did not feel the same way. He would not let us leave, except for bathroom breaks and it was buddy system the entire time. When the take came through, we just sat and waited. It wasn't till about eight that the next morning before anything really happened for us. At one point the day before we heard a vehicle pull up to our door. Vice President Tayler said the troops outside were sealing us in. At about a quarter to nine, we here a polite knock at the chamber door, the vice president told one of the Senators to open the door. To her reluctance, she did. The door opened and a tall Captain, I recognized the rank on the lapel. He walked in with a swarm of others military behind him, Army sort of guys. They line the walls and wait as General Matthews walks through the doors. The captain brings us all to attention and Matthews tells us to have a seat. We all tried to do as we were told.

GORDON: You all seem very compliant, why?

PAYNE: The Vice President said to be respectful and polite and we might get through all of this. So, we listened. General Matthews walks down the aisle and curtly addresses the Vice President then turns to address us.

CHRIS: I have a question? You mean the Vice president was in DC while the President was? I thought they couldn't be in the same state.

PAYNE: That is a movie myth. They are and can be.

CHRIS: Got it, please go on.

PAYNE: I have the notes on what Matthews said and what happened.

Matthews starts, *Ladies and Gentlemen of the senate, today marks a new day of change. A rebirth of sorts, a change for the better, a clean nation. No, I'm not committing a coup, so please get that out of your mind. I'm simply fixing a broken machine, namely you. For far too long, you have played games with the people because of political agenda or simply stupid disagreements with others that have nothing to do with your responsibilities as a senator. I won't vote on this Bill because a Democrat wrote it, regardless of if it is a good idea. I won't vote on it because a republican endorses it. That ends now and is part of the dead past. You will own the oath that you took. You are the people voting for the betterment of the people. Show the nation that you know what you are doing. I have several Bills that you will vote on. I promise you that I will not get in your way, I will not influence you. I will let you work. These Bills have gone through congress and were voted on. Just like congress, when you are done, I will let you go. Unfortunately, You Mr. Vice President will have to stay behind. If you all do your job, nothing will happen.* A Senator speaks up from the back, "*Sir, are we able to vote down a Bill. That wouldn't be democracy, would it not? I just realized that I never introduced myself. I apologize, I am Brigadier General Matthews. To answer that question, yes, you can vote it down. If you do not agree with what I suggest, disagree, and push it down. As I said before, I want you to work, to simply do your jobs. Do we understand?*" Senator Patrick Sharpe speaks up and only refuses to comply saying that it isn't democracy and how do we know that Matthews didn't for congress. "*I will not get into your business, it's not my place. I assure you I will take no actions to push you* says Matthews. "Look at all that you have done, it wouldn't surprise me that you are lying to us now" Sharpe says. Several Senators agree with Sharpe and start to verbalize their dislike for this. Matthews says to the group, "*I was hoping we wouldn't have to go through this again, I killed two congressmen and I'll kill another two senators to get freedom to ring.*" "He's lying" Sharpe says. *One of the other Senators that was siding with Sharp says, "How do you know he's lying?"* Sharpe starts to say that things like this don't happen. He's trying to scare us. Matthews says to the Vice President, "*control your people Sir or I will. I don't want that. This is my last and final warning. I made a promise. I'm good to my word, Sir.*" Vice President

Tayler slams his gavel to get control and it works. However, Sharpe does not it. "Last warning Mr. Senator, I'm not bluffing." "Deleted you and deleted your word, I'm not doing deleted. So, you can delete yourself" Sharpe says. A Marine walk up behind Sharpe, commanded by just a look from Matthews. *"So be it, Corporal Witlit."* says Matthews. Suddenly there is a loud bang! I can see parts of the Senators face blown away. He just crumples to the floor. I see two of the Marines come and take the dead senator away. You probably want to as where they took him. I have no idea, but I never see him again. The air got thick and quiet. The vice President asked Matthews if that was necessary? Matthews's replies with one word *"unfortunately"* and looks at us. *"I admire the tenacity your partner had; I admire his drive. Just not his mouth and manors. I'm here to set the book straight and clean the clock of its dust. I understand if you can't see that. Just see that your job needs to be done. I will not harm those who work with me. You fight me, you will die. It's just that simple.* Matthews orders a Captain to hand out copies of the first Bill and we are set to work. Matthews took a seat and watched us as we worked until we were done.

GORDON: How long were you there?

PAYNE: We were there for ten hours and voted to pass all of Matthews's resolutions. He did not force us, we voted fairly on them. Matthews just sat there, watching us. It was surprising how well we worked together. I wish it were just that easy sometimes. Matthew's Captain collected all the paperwork, and we were let out Chamber door. As I was leaving, I could see the Vice President and Matthews enter a military vehicle and drive away with a huge escort. That was the last time I saw Matthews. I wish there were more, but our experience was very brief.

GORDON: No, its fine. We do understand. Beside we knew most of what had already happened the first fourteen hours anyway. We do appreciate your time and the interview.

GORDON: This is Special Agent Sean Gordon. Its 10:20 A.M., the Hart Senate Office Building, Washington, D.C. We have just finished interviewing Senator Oliver Payne. Case file: 31008539-A, Operation Vanguard or "The Matthews Incident".

This formally concludes the interview with Senator Oliver Payne. No further entries were made on this date or for this part of the interview.

Memorandum from Special Agent Sean Gordon

To: Brian Samuels, Director of the Federal Bureau of Investigations

From: Sean Gordon, Special Agent

Good Moring,

As per protocol, I am giving my informal opinion of the investigation of Siege of the Capital Building and my person opinion to what I witnessed.

I want to acknowledge the loss of life from what we were told by the witnesses. The spilling of blood is a tough thing to really wrap the mind around. Not in the sense of wither its confusion but of the idea that "was it necessary"? I look at the death of the congressmen and the senator and hope that they were standing for freedom and not some petty ideology of "I'm in charge here". I want to believe that they were heroes that stood up to General Matthews.

By examining the point of them being heroes, we hope that General Matthews could have stood down agents them and no more blood would have been shed. I reviewed the voting records of the individuals and found that most of them have a questionable past. For those that aren't familiar with the term earmark, it refers to the act of giving something to win a vote. That specific something is usually funding for a specific place or object, that money is drawn from whatever Bill is being discussed. For example: you give me X amount of money for the great northern owl of Montana and you have my vote. The bill in question will most likely have nothing to do with animal conservation. This act of earmarking is constitutionally legal but the ethics in practice are the bigger concern.

With that point standing, I wonder then of the congressmen and senators that stood up did it for their pockets. If we look at it from a point that isn't heroic, what is left? They did if for their rights. I find it unlikely. This is not a statement saying that they or the others are corrupt. I'm also not saying that General Matthews was right in what he had ordered and did. It does make one wonder if the corruption really did exist and to what level in fact if it was there. Were they simply standing to just protect themselves from their own lifestyle or lies? I guess no one can really answer that question.

General Matthews clearly felt very strongly about what the constitution meant. He clearly insisted that the senators and congressmen do their jobs appropriately, without his influence or interference. It was also said that General Matthews's ordered his men to stand down as others worked. It was never mentioned if anyone influenced their vote, I could only assume no. I feel that it would have been brought up within our conversations.

Sincerely,
S.A. Sean Gordon.

The Power of the Pen

Interview of Shawn Daniel Kiplyn (Army General Retired)

Interview B
Thursday, June 13th, 2028
Granbury, Texas

GORDON: Its 11:30 A.M. in Granbury, Texas. We are currently at the home of Retired General Shawn Kiplyn. We are currently seated in the living room. Sitting next to me is Special Agent William Chris and across from us, General Kiplyn: case file 31008539-A, Operation Vanguard or "The Matthews Incident". General Kiplyn is 61 years of age, is 5'9", weight is 143 LBS. He is of medium build, grey hair. He is currently retired, has no discernable marks or scars, has blue eyes, and a light completion. He is Caucasian and an American. Has fingerprints on file and he has no classification code.

*Continuance

GORDON: Please continue where you left off. That would be after General Matthews left the Oval Office and the White House.

KIPLYN: So, we just sat there. At first in silence, but we asked if we could talk and one of the Marne's said that you could do as you wish, just as long as we didn't try and get up. The Marine also said, if we needed anything to still ask. He gave a few examples like food water paper, things like that. So, we just sat and talked, eventually eating, and having coffee. Apparently, the Marines captured the cook and asked them to make meals for everyone, including us.

CHRIS: Were there any other hostages?

KIPLYN: I couldn't say that we were hostages, they weren't making demands.

CHRIS: I can respect that.

KIPLYN: That's the point right there. We were respected. In no way where we harmed as long as we followed their rules, which the Marines were noticeably clear and concise and truly clear with. As long as we worked within those rules, we could do as we wanted. We were just captured and held until further notice. It had been nearly twenty-four hours until General Matthews returned. We were sitting and talking when we heard the familiar "attention on deck", this time we didn't need to be dragged to our feet. Genera Matthews entered the Oval Office, and slowly surveys the room. "I hope you are both well" Matthews says to us. Behind him, the Vice President was brought in. Immediately the President says in shock, "Tom! Are you ok?" To which the Vice President responds with a quiet "yes". Surprisingly, General Matthews allowed this small conversation, and was patient until its conclusion. General Matthews then asked the Vice President and us to have a seat to which we did. "Don't Worry Mr. President he's fine" Matthews says. "It's time we have our talk now Mr. President. Please have a seat at your desk." The President complies but looks concerned. He walks over to his desk and has a seat, waiting for what General Matthews wants next. General Matthews looks over his shoulder and calls for Captain Tessle. The tall captain appears at the door with a crisp, "Yes sir". Matthews Ask for his briefcase, the captain gives another crisp response of "Aye Sir" and disappears through the doorway. A few moments Late, Captain Tessle returns with the black suitcase. The suitcase is handed to General Matthews. Matthews walks the case over to the President's desk, places on the edge and opens it. From the case General Matthews pulls out a folder, walks around the desk to stand next to the seated President and places the fold in front of him.

GORDON: Do you know what was in the folder?

KIPLYN: No, Not at the time.

GORDON: and how large was the folder.

KIPLYN: It was pretty big, at least a few hundred pages.

CHRIS: You said that you later found out what the folder contained. What was it?

KIPLYN: It was Matthews Bills and the voting records of each bill.

GORDON: What was the President's reaction to the folder?

KIPLYN: President Howl looks at the folder for a second and asks what it is. Matthews says "it's "the sum of hard work and real dedication to this country. Is a physical piece of what people can do when they decide to put differences aside and work together as a unit instead of one's self. This is how things should work, this is the proof that it does work. I hope you find it in yourself to do the same. Congress and the Senate finally seen eye to eye for a change and did as they should." "I'm sure by gun point" the President says to General Matthews. Matthews Smirks for a second and thinks "that's a fare stamen, I never told you what my intention was and how I was to do it. If I were in your shoes, I would suspect the same. The answer is no. they were not at gun point. The president looked hesitant and not convinced. Matthews noticing this simply said to ask the Vice President. President Howl looks at Vice President Taylor who confirms that the Capital Building was treated with respect to this point. The Vice President continues by saying that General Matthews has also been good to his word. General Matthews looks at President Howl and says" You do what your job requires, and you simply go home." The President replies to General Matthews with a questioning look. "And what about you General?

What happens to you?" "What about me Mr. President" Matthews says, "I turn myself in and send my Marines back to base, which is my deal. The plain and simple and will be followed. No one else needs to get hurt. Simply look at the folder read and review it." The President takes a moment then picks up the folder and looks at Matthews, "what is on this folder?" Matthews moves away from the President's side and starts to pace the room as he talks, "Mr. President, what is on that folder is what remains of the last three people that didn't do as I asked. It would be an awful shame to have your Vice President do as I ask when they drag your body out." General Matthews looks at the Vice President and says to him, "that is why you are here. You are a witness to what will happen. If President Howl signs or vetoes the papers, you go home. If he resists, you will take his place. The President took a long hard look at the folder and opens it, they are Bills" he says, surprisingly. Matthews agrees that they are and tell Howl that he should consider them and only sign them is he agrees. The President looks at Matthews, "what if I don't sign them?' Well, if you refuse to sign them, the consequences will be dire. If you don't agree with them after reading them nothing happens to you, just as I said before, Veto them. I will send you send you home. It's all the simple". Matthews keeps pacing and says to me, "General Kiplyn do you know your part in all of this?" "No, I replay. I have no idea." "You are also my witness that I never made the president sign, that's your job. When he is done, you may leave as well". Matthews continues to pace while President Howl opens the folder. From where I'm seated, I can now see a smear of blood on the front of the folder as Howl opens it. President Howl begins to go pap by page as he starts to read the Bills. General Matthews speaks up and says,

"I also provided the voting records of each bill and included two Bills that we not passed, in case you wanted to see them as well." We sat there for two hours waiting as Matthews walks the room. "I don't Understand" says the President. "What's to understand" as Matthews circles the room then goes to stands behind to the left the President. "It's all very simple…" Suddenly Matthews Jerks forward, his uniform is ripped open and he crumbles to the floor. He twists for a few moments as the Marines run to him, but the shot was a good one. Right through the heart, General Matthews was dead before he hit the floor. I was in total shock and very confused. I just kept looking at the broken window behind the President's desk.

GORDON: What about the President?

KIPLYN: As he saw Matthews get hit, he dove out of his chair and took cover agents the wall.

GORDON: Who Shot General Matthews?

KIPLYN: I was told that there were S.W.A.T. snipers in one building about 1,000 yards out. He saw the chance and took it. It was a perfect shot.

CHRIS: What did the Marines do after General Matthews was killed?

KIPLYN: Captain Tessle said to the Marines, "we have our orders, Misfit-1 Actual is down, lay down your weapons, bring Misfit-1 Actual outside."

CHRIS: Misfit-1 Actual?

KIPLYN: That must have General Matthews's call sign.

CHRIS: I understand, please go in.

KIPLYN: The Captain walked to the window, took out a flashlight and flashed it twice. The Captain simply turned to us and said, "Have a good day Gentleman" and went out of the Oval Office following his Marines. We were stunned. We all went to the window and Seen the Captain on the radio. All the Marines were lying down around their vehicles, laying on the lawn or coming out of buildings and laying on the street. The cell phones came back on and we contacted 9-1-1 and the head of security. I could see secret service going to General Matthew's body, they were searched for weapons, none were found. All they found was a thumb drive.

GORDON: I wish we had that Thumb Drive.

KIPLYN: Here, I knew someone would ask for it. we have a copy. It has been declassified, so don't worry about that.

GORDON: Why did you keep it?

KIPLYN: I was told too.

GORDON: By whom?

KIPLYN: Ok, here is the truth. When General Matthews died, and we were waiting for the police to come in. I saw the president sit at the desk and stare at his pen. He opens the folder and starts signing the Bills and then shuts the folder. He tells me "if anyone askes, he made me". I told him I can't make promises. He threw the thumb drive to me, then do was right, my eyes have seen to mush today. I'm giving it to you for the truth to finally be told. I do you will do the right thing.

GORDON: This is Special Agent Sean Gordon. Its 12:15 P.M. in Granbury, Texas. We are currently at the home of Retired General Shawn Kiplyn. We have just finished interviewing Retired General Shawn Kiplyn. Case file: 31008539-A, Operation Vanguard or "The Matthews Incident".

This formally concludes the interview with Retired General Shawn Kiplyn. No further entries were made on this date or for this part of the interview.

"I CAN READ HIS RIGHTEOUS SENTENCE."

MANIFESTO OF BRIGADIER GENERAL MATTHEWS

To whomever is reading this,

I am Brigadier General Joshua Matthews of the 2nd Marine Division and I am its base Commandant and the leader of Operation Vanguard. If you are reading this, it's obvious to assume that I'm dead and most likely considered to be a madman or at the very least a Treasonist and certainly not a hero. Let me say that being a madman is far from the truth. I am free from any mental derangement or deficiencies. I am of a sound and healthy of mind showing reason, sound judgment, and rational thought. I have not acted out of malice or hate, but dedication and honor. I have no ill will towards those that have been harmed to achieve my goal. I also feel no regret for what I had to do. I'm currently writing this as I sit in front of the White House. It has been twenty-four hours since I started this. I'm currently heading to meet with the President for the last time. I'm not sure that I will walk out of the White House. That is not for me to decide but the Lord almighty. I hope that no more blood needs to be shed today, but I'm certain mine will have to be. If that is how it has to be, then I accept that.

This is my declaration of intent or my manifesto for the word to see and understand me. I'm sure that my intentions will be misconstrued, and I will forever go down in history as someone widely regarded being similar to Hitler or Mussolini. I am neither of those people and have no intention of being labeled as such. The question will undoubtedly be, "Why did I do it?" I have seen things in my life that just made me sick and I could no longer tolerate it and I had the power to do something about it. We all have the power to do something for our world, it just seemed like no one was going to act, so I did. All of this could have been avoided, all of it. We as people in this world need to learn to take some personal responsibility. We ignore the cries for help on a daily basis and move on through the day ignoring the needs of others. I decided that I was no longer going to watch the country implode. I was going to reset the government and its people. The government was doing nothing to better its people or itself but get fat on its greed and gluttony. I realize that the force I used was extreme and the lives lost were a great number, it had to be done this way. I had no other alternative. Many will say that I did. I challenge them to show how their ideas will have the effect that mine did.

I forced no one to act on my behalf, my Marines were following my orders because they saw what I was trying to accomplish. We did this for the greater good. I did not force Congress or the Senate to act. I simply made the machine do its work and do it for the better of its people. I simply guided the government to do the right thing. That's really what this was all about, if those few people did what they should have, looking out for one and another and caring. This would have been avoided. I meet chaos with chaos to fix it.

The obvious question still remains, "Why?" It is remarkably simple. I did if for my family. Years ago, a drunk driver took my wife and child. This is not an excuse for my actions just a motive. No one except me really cared about the death of them. It didn't even make the local papers. The local papers were worried about a scandal between two movie stars. There was no balance, the driver that killed my family walked away from his trial because he was not read his rights properly. I pushed the local authorities for justice, but they weren't interested in pursuing it, my family was just ignored. So, to find my own peace, I pushed my Marines to be better to hopefully fix the world we live in. I worked them hard to build them physically, mentally, and morally. Then one day, a PFC by the name of Eckhart took his life. All his brothers and in arms couldn't tell me why they didn't see his suicide coming. The Marines just said, "He seemed okay". Clearly, he wasn't. It burned my soul, and pushed me to action, something had to be done. I started to watch the news from all over the country. I tried to help those I could. I tried to fix the broken. I worked hard to reach out to as many as I could. I went as far as reaching out to those who have done wrong as well.

My mission had two operational points. First was to get control of the government so that I could force it to work properly. This would be the hardest part. Taking control of the White house and the Capital building would be a large task. I used every available asset I had including jammers and tanks. We would secure a perimeter and hold it until the second phase was completed.

Phase two was the introduction of seven bills that I felt would better the nation. These are the following bills.

Effects of the Bill if passed:

Bill No.1 (Passed)

All bills from will voted on without prior knowledge of its author or affiliated party. No Bill that is introduced will have specific project funding not associated with bills intention. This is referred to as earmarking and would now be unconstitutional. Anyone found doing such actions or trying to enact these actions will immediately dismissal and is no longer a member of the Congress, Senate, or Presidency. A vote by the House, Senate or President will never be a political move. Votes will be unbiased and fair. All Bills will be treated with the same respect regardless of party affiliation.

Bill No.2 (Passed)

The Barrie Act is from this point forward, expunged. A child will learn from their actions from responsible figures. Simply throwing a child in jail will not produce civil children, it stunts them. A juvenile offender will be allowed to continue their normal education routs and activates depending on the crime. Capital crimes will still be in effect, minor crimes will base upon the Judges discursion; as it has always been.

A) Every juvenile that commits a crime will be held accountable for their actions. This may result in fines if over seventeen. That the parents will not have to pay the fines of their child. If the child is unable to pay, he will be court ordered public service. If that juvenile does not attend of finish the public service in the allotted time. No good time is given, and the new adult will be held to the max limits the law calls for.

B) From seven to seventeen, the juvenile will have public service. If public service is not meet by allotted time, they will be tried at the age eighteen as an adult for the max of that crime. No good time will be given.

C) Section A and B will be at the deaccession of the judge of jury proceeding over the individual. These are guidelines and not mandatory. This is meant to teach accountability and responsibility for their actions.

D) Juveniles that fail to attend school will not be allowed to quit the education system until eighteen. Failure to comply will result in sections A through C.

E) A Juveniles will no longer be pushed through the Education System. If necessary, the individual will continue to repeat a grade until minimal standards are meet or individual turns eighteen.

Bill No. 3 (Passed)
AMENDMENT XXII (original)

No person shall be elected to the office of the President more than twice, and no person who has held the office of President, or acted as President, for more than two years of a term to which some other person was elected President shall be elected to the office of the President more than once. But this Article shall not apply to any person holding the office of President, when this Article was proposed by the Congress, and shall not prevent any person who may be holding the office of President, or acting as President, during the term within which this Article becomes operative from holding the office of President or acting as President during the remainder of such term.

*Amended
AMENDMENT XXII

No person shall be elected to the office of the President, Congress or Senate more than twice, and no person who has held the office of President, congress, or Senate, or acted as President, congressmen, or Senator, for more than two years of a term to which some other person was elected President, Congress or Senate shall be elected to the office of the President Congress or Senate more than once. But this Article shall not apply to any person holding the office of President Congress or Senate, when this Article was proposed by the Congress, and shall not prevent any person who may be holding the office of President Congress or Senate, or acting as President, Congress or Senate, during the term within which this Article becomes operative from holding the office of President, Congress or Senate or acting as President, Congress or Senate during the remainder of such term.

Bill No. 4 (Passed)

Holding an individual accountable for actions done verbally will no longer be tolerated. The defamation of one's character after two decades is extreme and unreadable and will no longer have effect on that person's place or work or personal life. Should that person's character be in question on past events that took place, it should be noted that individuals change, and their beliefs change.

A) Litigations upon a person will no longer be tolerated because the other party was "offended" by the first party's opinion or verbalization. An individual's feelings do not dictate law, finding something "offence" is purely subjective and not considered facts.

B) Words will no longer be considered violence since the definition of violence does not work in these circumstances; Words do not do physical harm and should be treat as just words. Fines will no longer be issued by States or local government in these instances and are cover under the First Amendment.

C) Those that do harm to others because of political differences will be held accountable for their actions. The definition of "protest" still stands with the base line of peaceful actions. Non-peaceful actions will be held as an act of rioting and individuals will be held legally accountable.

D) Protests of large numbers that interfere with daily traffic on roadways will be considered in violation of the law and will be prosecuted if they do not have the proper licenses and prior notifications required by local law. Mass groups of people standing in traffic will be held accountable for any damage done to the vehicles and will be prosecuted, drivers will not be accountable. This applies to only Major interstates. If an emergency vehicle is being stopped by an illegal protest, protester will be charged with manslaughter or involuntary manslaughter if individual needed medical treatment succumbs to injury or lack of medical attention die to individuals in streets.

E) Individuals found to be instinctually inciting a protest to a riot or throwing objects while in riot or protest will be prosecuted under the grounds of assault with a deadly weapon.

Bill No. 5 (Passed)

The original unalienable rights, First and Second Amendments will be brought back to their original state as writing in the original constitution. They will no longer be able to be altered or misread to fit political agendas. Our right to speech, press, peaceful assembly, and the right to bear arms will never be altered or infringed upon and make no new laws to change them. They are intact.

Bill No. 6 (Vetoed)

Within the accordance of the United States, mandatory service in the armed forces in enforced. This Act will enable the military to maintain a significant number of assigned troops. The service will be mandatory for no more than two years. When the two years of active service is complete, individuals are properly discharged. The enrolment of individuals in the military will be the age of eighteen or after completion of schooling.

Enrolment training (boot camp) will not count as the mandatory two years. The discharge process will begin after the two years is completed honorably. The individual will have an option of military branch unless a dire need is call upon for recruitment in one particular branch.

Bill No. 7(Vetoed)

The current voting and driving age is eighteen with some states allowing driving at sixteen. This corresponds with adult hood. By current law and standards, individuals are not permitted to consume alcoholic beverages or buy firearms till the age of twenty-one. Thus, the right of voting and the privilege of driving will be held until the age of twenty-one. These prior laws are enacted for the benefit of the individual, ensure prober adult designs.

These seven Bills I have written, were set to bring the country back under control and to allow the people to be free and respectful of others freedom. You may not agree with them, but they are here for the betterment of this country. I do not know obviously what happened to me after my actions in the White House. All that I ask is that you treat my Marines with dignity. They fallowed my orders, because we felt the country was broken and needed a new start. A start without lies, a start without political agenda and a start with dignity in one's self.

I am sure I was labeled a madman. I was of sound mind and body when I committed my actions. I did this for us. With my death, my asset I leave to those that died in the line of duty to stop me. The money was given to me when my family was taken by a drunk driver, he walked, and my family was buried. He never once apologized for what he did. He is just an example of the people we have in this culture today. The Good die and the Evil inherit, I guess.

I formally end this now saying I willfully played the Devil in my actions and am willing to be called that. I'm willing to take the blame and I'm willing to have my years of service destroyed or even forgotten for my deeds. I apologies for the lives I ruined, I apologies for those I've hurt. Sometimes that kind of sacrifice is needed for the betterment of humanity. Imagine how all this would have been if people were just a bit more responsible and kinder. May God forgive me for what I have done.

J. Matthews Brigadier General, USMC
September 12th, 2025

Memorandum from Special Agent Sean Gordon

To: **Brian Samuels, Director of the Federal Bureau of Investigations**

From: **Sean Gordon, Special Agent**

Good Moring,

    I have formally submitted my report on Brigadier General Matthews and Operation Vanguard. As per protocol, I am giving my informal opinion of the investigation and my person opinion to what I witnessed.

    I would like to say first that what happened was tragedy, not only for the victims of Operation Vanguard but all those that Matthews took an interest in. There was a lot of pain, unnecessary pain. Before I was given this assignment, I was unaware of the people that Matthews kept in contact with. I knew before these interviews how the public had seen General Matthews, the public sees monster. But I see now what General Matthews intended and I know the differences he made. Every day, so many people are affected by tragedy and horrors that they feel that they cannot endure, yet the move on. That's the part that I noticed the most. People just moved on when they knew they could have helped other; they turn a blind eye to the suffering.

    Those that I interviewed, some of them were rather pleasant to talk to and others I personally had no liking towards. But they all moved forward. I see the pain they have endured or the pain they caused molded each of them in a different way, some became stronger, some wiser and some just felt endless guilt. To the other, revenge, hate, and bloodshed were the only alternative they saw fit to throw in the world. They became destroyers and plowed their way through innocent lives. Some felt remorse, and some could care less, all affected the world.

    General Matthews understood one principle that most people miss, that is decision making. When confronted at an intersection there are three options. You can turn left or right or not move at all. The latter is the part people miss. By you not making a decision is in fact making a decision. You simply being causes change. You leaving your home or not leaving changes everything. We are all a cog in the machine that is life. Our rolls change from day to day. Some cogs are bigger than others, but it doesn't mean you don't play a vital part. The problem is people do want to recognize that they influence others. That person you disrespected in the street may take their own life because of what you may have said. You go about the day, no wiser for what you have caused and done. Life is cause and effect; too many people are lost to that fact. General Matthews recognized that and knew it.

I understand that simply a dictation of those people cannot convey certain parts of who they are by how emotionless a recording is. I was grateful to have had the opportunity to talk to that I Interviewed. I enjoyed the accents in their speech and colors of their expressing. I talked to Mothers and killers alike and found both interesting. They were always open to talk about what happened to them or even what they have done. Some were more shameful than others.

You can't hear the tears in this document that is the biggest shame of the knowledge we gained. We gained so much information but sometimes the feelings were lost. I wish you could have heard Sergeant Hillard cry about Private First Class Eckhart and how chocked up he was. Or how sarcastic some others were, like Mrs. McCarter or Corporal Witlit. Real emotions lost in the words that are written, that's the truest tragedy sometimes. I could see it in their faces and hear the love or hate in their voices, sometimes even the regret. It seems the smarter we are the more disconnected we become.

I learned a lot about things that I already though I had known. I never realized how deep General Matthews actually was. I thought he was crazy, this guy that had me trapped in my office in Washington DC for thirty hours. He was deeper than that, they all were. I see the terrible things that he did and acknowledge them openly. I also see the world he crated. Crime in the U.S. is down by 40%. Families have more respect for themselves. Politicians aren't looked at as liars anymore but people to admire. They talk more than argue now. They don't say such extreme things anymore and you see them in the local towns now, all the time. Those same politicians know names of the people that vote for them or don't. Voting was at an all-time high, even though President Howl was voted out of office. No one really complained when he lost. That's a step that our founding fathers couldn't workout. You see more kids playing in yards now too, surprisingly with their parents. People really appreciate all that they have now, I guess what Matthews did was to bring this us and this county together.

Sincerely,
S.A. Sawn Gordon

FROM THE AUTHOR

I never actually thought I could write a book. It was one of those things that I always wanted to do and try. It felt like a mountain too big to climb. This book means a lot to me. The years in which this book was written I lost just about everything except the book. I lost friends and family that year to suicide and death. I lost family pets and then finally at the end of that second year. I lost my house to a fire that took everything but what I and my family were wearing.

The loss of that house was not a total tragedy, however. My family got out and it made us stronger than we could ever believe. At the time, "Mine Eyes" was set aside for while my family and healed. To understand the tragedy, we went through was to know that the house was destroyed by someone who we didn't know. They drove by the house flicking a cigarette out the window of their window on a windy November day. Carelessness casted us our home... cause and effect. That knowledge can trouble a person and a marriage. The family and I picked the broken pieces of our lives up and kept moving forward. The book was in an ugly unedited state collecting dust as we sifted through the broken life that we had left. Then on my Birthday, my wife gave me a gift that reminded me why I wrote this book and now I want to share that with you. It all restarted with a pen and a metal plaque.

This book was about following a dream and taking hold of it. It's not about money or fame. I'm honestly not expecting that will happen, and that's okay. My honest goal is to sell one book to someone I never meet and hope that person liked it. It's about the art of sharing something personal. It's about showing whoever is reading this something that no one else until this point has seen. And what that one this is reading what I'm thinking inside, the inner me. Reading a person's words is an intimate thing. You see me for who I really am. You hear my inner voice and read how I see the world in story form. This is something pure and awesome.

The book started out as a few small stories that I made up over time and one day thought I would just put notes down about the stories. As I did that, I realized they were all connected. The book is full of symbolism and hidden meaning, all things about me and who I am. The book seems simple, but it is deep with heavy meaning. I had a hard time figuring out how I would tell these stories. I had the idea of a different form of storytelling. Letting the reading be told a story and letting their imagination fill in the small details. I don't want to tell you the car a person drives, so I leave out names like that. I want the person imagination to tell that part of the story. It makes every person experience different with each reader.

So now the story was told in the format that you read, words omitted for your own imagination and hopefully the book made you feel something. I hope you liked some characters and hated others. I personally did not like Witlit. All the Characters in my books are fictional and names were made up. However, I was going for a sense of realism while you were reading. I hoped at some point you wondered if any this was real. If you did, I feel great knowing that I made you look at the world just a little differently for a little while. If you, the reader didn't like my book, I can respect that and am sorry you didn't. I hope you can at least see the hard work I put into this. And that I did this for all the right reasons.

Just before I go, I wanted to thank a few people. First my wife, she has always stood by me, through the good times and the hard. She has never waived and always put a smile on my face. She knows the person I am inside and that's something that most people never understand. She has always inspired me and drives me to do better.

Second is Mike. He was like a father to me. When my father wasn't around, it was Mike that raised me. He showed me life lesions that I still use today. More importantly, how to me myself and to think for myself, things you can't put a price too. I respect him for all he did for me and could never thank them enough.

Lastly are Sue and Larry. I had some hard times, they seen me through them. I was taken under their wings and treated like one of their children. I can't thank them enough for all they have done for me. I couldn't have asked for better people in my life.

I almost forgot, thank you for taking the time to read my first book. I appreciate you and couldn't have done it without you.

- *A. M. Moulton* September 20th, 2028